# MISS MORGAN'S BOOK BRIGADE

## ALSO BY JANET SKESLIEN CHARLES

*The Paris Library: A Novel*
*Moonlight in Odessa: A Novel*

# MISS MORGAN'S BOOK BRIGADE

*A NOVEL*

## JANET SKESLIEN CHARLES

**ATRIA** BOOKS

NEW YORK   LONDON   TORONTO   SYDNEY   NEW DELHI

**ATRIA**
BOOKS

An Imprint of Simon & Schuster, LLC
1230 Avenue of the Americas
New York, NY 10020

Please see page 319 for Illustration Credits.

First Atria Books hardcover edition April 2024

**ATRIA** BOOKS and colophon are trademarks of Simon & Schuster, LLC

Simon & Schuster: Celebrating 100 Years of Publishing in 2024

For information about special discounts for bulk purchases,
please contact Simon & Schuster Special Sales at 1-866-506-1949 or
business@simonandschuster.com.

The Simon & Schuster Speakers Bureau can bring authors to your live event.
For more information or to book an event, contact the Simon & Schuster Speakers
Bureau at 1-866-248-3049 or visit our website at www.simonspeakers.com.

*Interior design by Lexy East*

Manufactured in the United States of America

1   3   5   7   9   10   8   6   4   2

Library of Congress Cataloging-in-Publication Data has been applied for.

ISBN 978-1-6680-0898-0
ISBN 978-1-6680-0900-0 (ebook)

*To my husband, Eddy Charles*

Never can I get the picture of those villages out of my mind.
The bravery of the people and the courage with which
they come back to begin in the middle of their ruins. . . .
Did you know that the Countess d'Evry lives in a cart
in her stable yard so that she can help the soldiers
work to clear the gardens of her people,
so that they may come back to their land?
Meanwhile, her château is in ruins on the hill.
The need is now.

—A letter from Anne Morgan to her mother

# MISS MORGAN'S BOOK BRIGADE

# PROLOGUE

**Y**ou can learn a lot about a life by looking in someone's closet. I stand before mine, pondering which outfit to wear tonight, and thumb through fitted cardigans and slacks, remnants of a long career. Cramped to the side are relics of a past life: the witch's hat and smock that pupils begged me to wear each Halloween; a wedding gown that didn't quite make it to the altar; and the uniform of the American Committee for Devastated France—horizon blue, the same color that the French army wore. I can't help but touch the hem of the skirt. Seventy years old, and the wool blend, warm and light, still embodies the quality that Paris is famous for. The stories this cloth could tell . . . the fabric of life during the Great War. It had seen love and hate, sacrifice and stinginess, longing and hope, despair and courage. Always courage.

My fingers continue along the sleeve, to the rust-colored stain on the cuff. No matter how we washed it—dabbed with seltzer water, soaked in iodine, scrubbed with Marseille soap—his blood wouldn't come out. No matter. The material is nearly dark enough to conceal it, and the discoloration can be attributed to a splatter of ratatouille.

To free the uniform, I seize the shoulders and pull, allowing myself to cradle the jacket as if it were a woman I could embrace. Something digs into my chest. On the lapel, a medal hangs from a blue-and-white striped ribbon. The silver has tarnished, but I can make out the griffin, the symbol of the Cards. On the reverse is engraved DO RIGHT AND FEAR NO MAN.

If I don the uniform, would it fit? Only one way to find out. Yes, the jacket is elegant over my blouse. Encouraged, I shimmy out of my slacks, only to find that the skirt bites at the waist. Still, it feels right, as if the uniform wants to be worn. The final touch is the handkerchief, its cloth worn thin by time. I slide it into my pocket.

I glance at my watch. Nearly 7:00 p.m. The decision of what to wear has been made—if I don't leave now, I'll be late.

I rush from the apartment, up Fifth Avenue, to the New York Public Library. Shoulders squared, I march up the steps like I have thousands of times before. Upon my arrival in Manhattan, this was my school, my social life, my home.

In the hall, my fingertips trace scuff marks along the walls. Some may see imperfections, but I remember crates being delivered, a runaway book cart crashing down the staircase, and apprentices like me accidentally smudging the white paint with blotter ink that clung to our skin like perfume.

The past presses on me, memories fill the air. I clutch the handkerchief and know that now, finally, it's time.

# CHAPTER 1

JESSIE CARSON
THE NORTH OF FRANCE, JANUARY 1918
*FORTY MILES FROM THE FRONT*

The narrow dirt road was pockmarked from shelling. Lewis, the chauffeur, advanced through shrapnel and around gaping potholes. In the passenger seat, I held tight to the door. The Ford hit a rut, and my head snapped back. I winced, not merely from the pain, but from the sight of fields stitched with barbed wire.

Destruction stretched to the horizon. There was not a single soul, nor a blade of grass, and the countryside blended with the gray clouds to form a colorless, hopeless terrain. Inhabitants had fled or been taken prisoner. The German army had obliterated homes and schools, churches and hospitals, libraries and lives. On farms, they bombed the rows of wheat that stood up to them. In orchards, they took axes to innocent apple trees. Branches lay on the ground, their dried-up leaves whispering in the wind.

At the checkpoint that would allow us to enter the war zone, we slowed to a stop behind five military trucks. Lewis cut the engine and lit a cigarette, which meant that we'd be here for a while. I pulled the collar of my woolen coat closer as the damp cold closed in. While Lewis sifted through the documents—passports, working papers, and authorizations stamped with blue ink, I squinted at the flakes of frost that clung to the corner of the windshield and discovered a kaleidoscope of designs. Silvery butterfly wings. A child's mitten. Yes, my father had been right: even in the grimmest places, beauty abounded, if only you knew how to look.

"What a stiffrump!" Lewis gestured to a French military policeman who seemed to scrutinize each syllable of a truck driver's paperwork. "At this rate, we'll never get through."

As we waited, scenes of my journey flitted through my mind, flapping like pages of a book caught in the wind. The ocean passage, in which my cabin-mate, a Red Cross volunteer, wore her life jacket the entire three weeks. Though afraid our ship would be torpedoed like the *Lusitania,* she sailed anyway. What courage! On our arrival in Bordeaux, my shipmates and I tasted real French wine and glimpsed angels and gargoyles in the architecture. Motoring to Paris, our Peugeot putted past lines of poplars that shaded the road. In the capital, Lewis helped me obtain authorizations to enter the war zone. We queued for hours at the police station to receive a stamped paper before dashing across the cobblestones to the Ministry of War, only to stand in line again. A three-day, herky-jerky, foreign-language obstacle course. I'd been in France for ten days, long enough to marvel at two elements—the awe-inspiring architecture and the mind-numbing administration.

Finally, the truck in front of us, which transported crates of cabbage alongside kegs of gunpowder, advanced. It was our turn. As he examined the papers, the MP frowned.

Seeing me tug nervously at my handkerchief, Lewis said, "You needn't fret."

The MP pointed to a line at the bottom of a document. Lewis flipped the page and pointed to the prefect's scrawl. "We've done our bit. Now do yours and let us through."

He gestured to me. "But it says that she's a li—"

"We're with the Morgan Brigade," Lewis informed him in crisp, I'm-nearing-the-end-of-my-patience French.

The MP went slack-jawed. "Merci." He waved us through.

I asked why he'd thanked us. Lewis responded that Anne Morgan's efforts were known in these parts. And not just here. Miss Morgan was the reason I'd come. She'd commissioned a photographer and a filmmaker to record the effects of war. Back home, in a cinema around the corner from the New York Public Library, the audience had gaped at the images of a wan, white-haired farm couple dressed head to toe in black. Their craggy faces conveyed that they'd toiled under an unforgiving sun their entire lives. The Germans had slaughtered their goat and gelding, set their seeds on fire, and reduced their farmhouse to rubble. Arms limp at their sides, the couple lingered in front of their bombed-out barn, ghosts left with nothing to haunt. After the viewing, I couldn't just sit home and pray.

Lewis and I were to drive straight from Paris to CARD Headquarters in the village of Blérancourt, where I'd report for duty as the newest recruit of the American Committee for Devastated France, *Le Comité américain pour les régions dévastées* (CARD). We passed through what used to be a village—cottages blown open, their shutters charred. On the outskirts, a roadside grave—at the head, a helmet on a cross, and standing upright at the base, a rusty bayonet. We inched by so slowly that I had time to read "Unknown soldier, August 1914."

The scene, so forlorn, called out to me.

"Lewis," I said, "please pull over."

In CARD, we called each other by our surnames. When I'd first heard that someone named Lewis was going to be my chauffeur, I pictured a bald man with a monocle, not a sunny brunette Vassar girl. She and I were both in uniform, a horizon-blue jacket and skirt.

Lewis turned the wide steering wheel and maneuvered past debris to a clear patch on the side of the road. At the makeshift grave, we bowed our heads. In New York, street hawkers shouted until they were hoarse; horses nickered as they clopped down Fifth Avenue, milk wagons groaned under the weight of the cream; plump pigeons cooed the conditional language of love; from time to time, a lonely crow cawed. Here there was only an eerie silence.

Stiff from hours in the Ford, Lewis and I ambled toward rows of homes that had been reduced to mounds of stones that barely reached my waist. In the garden, there were ruins of rabbit hutches, the wood torn and twisted. Hand grenades and unexploded shells lay in the soil. Inside, where a dining room used to be, we could make out splintered table and chairs, a bassinet whose lace had been torn and dotted with dirt.

I could hardly believe I was finally here, in the midst of this mute, desolate madness. I remembered my boss's riposte upon learning that I'd enlisted: "What the hell is a librarian going to do in the middle of a war zone?"

"Whatever I can to help."

"How will you get to Europe?" she'd demanded with a smirk.

We both knew the ocean crossing cost more than I earned in a year.

I recalled the sheer satisfaction at disclosing that Miss Morgan had paid for my passage. Well, Miss Morgan's brigade. For once, my boss, Winnifred Smythe—the brightest, oldest star in the constellation of the NYPL's children section—had been speechless.

Never had I enjoyed a silence more.

"How does she know you?" she finally demanded. "You're a nobody."

It was unlikely that a librarian and the heiress to the largest U.S. banking fortune would cross paths. I replied that Miss Morgan might have heard of my efforts for the National League for Woman's Service, which was founded so that we could contribute to the war effort. Naturally, Miss Morgan was treasurer. One of 250,000 volunteers, I headed the business unit. According to the secretary of the NYPL director, Miss Morgan had requested me by name.

"Why would she want you?" my boss muttered. "Why you and not me?"

My mother maintained that the "seek and ye shall find" passage of Matthew 7:7 referred to reading, that most answers could be found in books. I recalled the League's 1917 manifesto: *Resolved, that this National League for Woman's Service shall be the consecration of Woman's Power; that it shall be kept free from self-seeking and from politics . . .*

No self-seeking or politics. That was why.

Lewis and I wandered along the cobblestone street. In front of a well, she paused to pick up a sooty rag doll. "I've made this trip ten times now." She wiped its face clean. "But I never become inured to these remnants of families driven from their homes."

We passed vestiges of what had been. In what used to be a cottage, a smashed curio cabinet, a sodden divan. In what used to be a backyard, Lewis positioned the doll on a chair whose legs had been hacked away. On the outskirts, I moseyed over the soft soil of farmland. No rebel wildflowers were tempted to put down roots here. No field mice scurried at the sound of my footsteps. No sparrows greeted us with wary chirps. Would the birds ever return?

The landscape reminded me of Willa Cather's depiction of the Great Plains. Suddenly, I left this parcel for the library of my mind. It was two stories high, with a rolling ladder to access tomes on the top shelves. With its plump pillows and downy quilt, the window seat beckoned, and I often curled up with a book and gazed out at the secret garden, lush with roses and lavender. Now, I quickly crossed the creaking parquet to fetch *My Ántonia*. *I wanted to walk straight on through the red grass and over the edge of the world, which could not be very far away.*

"Carson!" I heard Lewis shout.

I returned from my cozy library to the present, where I'd managed to maroon myself in the middle of a muddy field.

"It's full of land mines," she said. "Find your exact footprints and walk back to me. Slowly."

I turned my head. The grayish brown path stretched before me, an eternity to Lewis. I looked for my tracks—What was a rut? Where was the curve of my heel? My whole body shook, in part because of the cold, but mostly because I'd never been so frightened. On my first day in the war zone, I'd done what my boss had foretold—gotten myself in trouble. Actually, she'd predicted that I'd get myself killed. She lamented that I lived in my head, not in the real world. She was against my coming here. She was against me, period. I would prove her wrong.

I peered at the lumpy mud—had that puddle been there, or was that where I'd stepped? My heart thumped loud and hard. I was freezing, yet sweat dripped from my forehead. I wiped my brow with my father's handkerchief and took my first step. I didn't want to die. I didn't want my boss to be right. Right, left. Right, left.

At the car, my whole body pulsed with panic, and I could barely catch my breath. I expected Lewis to lay into me, but all she said was "What a curfuggle!" The word meant "mess," but was she referring to the situation or to me?

I sank into the passenger seat. Instead of slamming the door as I deserved, Lewis closed it gently and said, "Poor dear, you're pale as snow." The blanket of her concern warmed me, and the fear finally passed.

As she maneuvered onto the road, Lewis explained that we'd arrived in the Red Zone, where German soldiers had sown explosives the same way they used to plant potatoes. I recalled the description from the CARD report: *Completely devastated. Damage to properties: 100%. Damage to Agriculture: 100%. Impossible to clean. Human life impossible.*

Thus far, she had chatted away, glancing at me as much as at the road. Last Thursday, she'd turned twenty-five, which made her fifteen years younger than me. I remembered the constant inquiries that came with this delicate age. *Do you have a beau? What does he do for a living? Has he proposed? How many children does he want?* It was a relief that the questions had mostly stopped, though Mother occasionally whispered a wistful *There's still time.*

"The girls managed to find some champagne," Lewis had recounted. "My birthday party was a corking time! We Cards work like nailers, but know how to have fun, too. You'll see." She'd been here six months and was in charge of maintaining vehicles. Back home, she'd had her own car and chauffeur—now she repaired punctured tires, fixed engines, and scraped muck from the undercarriages.

"In the motor service," she said, "we call ourselves *les chauffeuses*."

Lewis loved to watch Frenchmen as she passed in the Ford. "They've never seen a woman drive—they don't think it's natural. Eyes bulging! Jaws dropped! It's too killing!" she said, and we laughed. "Between the greasy spark plugs and the lack of hot water, my fingernails are black. Dear Mama—Philadelphia's premier hostess—would be appalled!"

Lewis held up her hands, encased in expensive kidskin gloves. Instinctively, I covered a worn spot on my woolen ones. Most Cards were like Lewis, wealthy volunteers who paid their own expenses, whereas I drew a salary and had my costs, such as lessons to brush up my French and the ocean passage, covered. A uniform couldn't erase the difference between us.

I told her that because I was a children's librarian, my hands were either pink from paper cuts or blue from the ink blotter used to stamp books.

"How thrilling to share your knowledge with little ones," she replied. I feared she was mocking me until she added, "Growing up, I had French and Latin tutors. After college, my father refused to permit me to seek employment."

Suddenly, I felt sorry for an heiress. "What about translation work?" I asked. It could be done at home.

"Father said my knowledge is for my future husband. He expected me to select one of his employees—fine young stockbrokers—to marry."

"My mother did the same. At Mass, there was a steady parade of suitors in our pew."

"It's enough to make a girl an atheist!"

I chuckled. "I never blamed God. And I never found out how Mother managed to unearth so many bachelors."

The truth was, I wanted to support myself and was content in my career. However, I was ready for a challenge and longed to see new faces. And there were things I was ready to leave behind. Lewis and I had different upbringings, but here we were on the same scarred road, a pair of Cards with the goal of helping French villagers.

The sorrow of the land seeped into us. The rest of the journey felt like a funeral; we remained silent in order to pay our respects to the dead. She kept her eyes on the ruts as we drove through an hour of nothingness.

When it began to rain, Lewis said, "I trust you brought galoshes. This drizzle has been a near constant, and mud has taken over."

As she stepped on the clutch to gear down, I ogled her suede button boots, which fit like a second skin, clearly crafted especially for her.

I wore boxy work boots—the only kind I could afford. Was I exchanging a difficult boss for spoiled socialites?

"Are the other Cards easy to get along with?" I asked.

"For the most part, the girls are kind and hard workers. Miss Morgan and Dr. M.D.—that's what we call CARD president Dr. Anne Murray Dike—run a tight unit. When a debutante hurkle-durkled in bed until 10:00 a.m., Dr. M.D. shipped her back to Boston."

Unease gripped me at the thought of being discarded like a defective lamp. My boss would cackle, *I told you so.*

"Then there's the girl who couldn't cope," Lewis continued. "After two weeks, she fled to Le Ritz."

I wondered why she'd given up. Was she not entirely fluent in French? Or had homesickness overwhelmed her? I'd signed a contract—two years without seeing my sister and mother. What had I been thinking? I'd so looked forward to being in France that I hadn't considered that the job meant leaving behind family.

"Here we are," Lewis said.

We entered the war-torn village of Blérancourt at dusk. The fading light did not cloak the ruins of a stone cottage. Under what was left of the roof, a pug-nosed teen with pigtails perched on a pile of rubble, hunched over a book. She was so taken by the story that the beams of our headlamps did not register.

"That's Marcelle Moreau," Lewis said. "In what's left of her house. Now they live in a quarry. Her father died on the battlefield. While her mother works as a laundress and seamstress, Marcelle looks after three rambunctious brothers. Madame Moreau doesn't give her a moment of peace."

"Books can be that moment." Helping children like her was why I'd come. I needed to put aside my fears over being inadequate. "Will you introduce us?"

"I can try." Lewis slowed the car. "She usually runs off."

I dug into my purse and pulled out *Anne of Green Gables*, a comfort read that I was attempting in French. Anne *always remembered the silvery, peaceful beauty and fragrant calm of that night. It was the last night before sorrow touched her life; and no life is ever quite the same again when once that cold, sanctifying touch has been laid upon it.* I had a feeling that the girl would understand. From the window of the Ford, I proffered the novel, not unlike a carrot for Black Beauty. She snatched it.

"Would you like a few more?" I asked in French.

"Ma told me not to talk to devil-women!"

*Diablesses.* I suppressed a laugh. I was flattered—no one had ever considered me a bad influence. "I love reading, just like you. I'm the new librarian."

She cocked her head. "Liar! Everyone knows that librarians are men."

"Times are changing," I told her.

"Not here." Marcelle sized up Lewis. "Ma says that only harlots smoke or bob their hair."

"Yet it's acceptable for men to smoke and frequent the barber?" I asked.

Contemplating my words, Marcelle gnawed on the tip of her pigtail.

"You reflect on that double standard," I added.

"Come find me when you realize it's unfair," Lewis said. "I'll teach you to 'chauff.'"

Books and driving—who could resist the tantalizing offer? Marcelle stepped toward us.

"I sent you to the well to fill our pails," we heard a woman holler. "How many times have I told you not to pester *les dames?*"

Eyes wide, the teen scampered off.

"Shouldn't we go after her?" I asked Lewis.

"Nothing doing. Even I'm intimidated by Marcelle's mom."

As the Ford bounced over the cobblestones, Lewis pointed out the town hall, a two-story building that housed the municipal library. Miraculously, all four walls were intact. Instinctively, I patted my satchel, where I kept my blueprint for the children's library. I couldn't wait to share it with Miss Morgan. First impressions were lasting impressions, my father had believed. I'd prove that she'd made the right choice in employing me.

Our Headquarters—a demolished castle—came into view. Only a section of it remained intact. The golden glow from its ground-floor windows beckoned. We crossed over the stone bridge and dried-up moat, past a copse of spindly spruces. I was never so happy to see trees. As Willa Cather wrote, *Trees were so rare in that country, and they had to make such a hard fight to grow, that we used to feel anxious about them, and visit them as if they were persons.* We continued through the arch of the grand sandstone gate to a hamlet of prefabricated wooden barracks topped with tin roofs. Lewis pointed out the garage, the mercantile where villagers purchased items at reduced prices, and a clinic. Six of the barracks were bedrooms; the seventh, called le club-house, was a community center where meals were served. She parked in front of the sliver of château still standing. In the moonlight, the tall sandstone castle resembled a satin wedding dress; the ruins of rubble stretched beside it brought to mind a lace train.

When we alighted from the Ford, a terrier swirled around my skirt. "Hello, boy," I said.

Lewis explained that during bombardments, pets had become separated from their owners and now roamed the *rues* in search of food and affection.

"We all have dogs, and we all have fleas," she added cheerfully.

As we stroked his head, Lewis stiffened like a soldier waiting to be told, *At ease.*

"It's the two Annes," she whispered.

I watched the duo exiting the imposing oak door of the château and recognized Anne Morgan from newspaper photos. With her wealth, one might have expected to read about her in the society pages—where she wintered and which duke asked for her hand in marriage. Instead, front-page profile pieces described her advocacy for working women—pushing for better salaries, safer conditions in factories, and paid vacation. She and her high-society friends picketed the streets of Manhattan with impoverished garment workers, knowing that where the well-heeled went, newspapermen with cameras would follow.

These days, articles underscored her efforts in France. When war broke out in 1914, Anne Morgan opened her villa in Versailles to con-valescing soldiers. By 1916, she served as the treasurer of the American Fund for the French Wounded. In 1917, she and nine other women were given permission by Général Pétain to settle in Blérancourt in order to help civilians.

Tonight, Miss Morgan's graying curls escaped from underneath her CARD hat, which tilted to the side. She wore a starched white shirt and a black tie with her uniform. Her eyes were fiercely intelligent, and her chin was slightly raised, as though she was accustomed to doing battle. At her side was Dr. Anne Murray Dike.

According to Lewis, the Scot was a force of nature, too. After study-ing medicine in Canada, Dr. M.D. had wed a Boston professor. They later parted ways; some blamed the divorce on Miss Morgan. The two Annes were inseparable.

Where Miss Morgan was robust, Dr. M.D. was tall and svelte. Waves of strawberry blond hair framed her oval face. She fixed me with a pensive regard.

"Welcome, Carson." Miss Morgan's voice was low and authorita-tive. "We kept one eye on our work, the other on the window. We wanted to be the first to greet you. How was the trip?"

I looked askance at Lewis, fully expecting her to recount my mis-step in the field.

"Uneventful," she replied airily.

"How are you holding up?" Miss Morgan asked me. "I remember the first time we drove through the devastation. It quite does some-thing to you."

This was where I should have said something. *Those miles were a heart-rending sight? Nice to meet you? I'd love to show you my blueprints?* Unable to decide, I realized I'd created a clumsy silence only when Miss Morgan said, "I propose a restorative drink."

Unsure if the invitation was a form of politeness, I turned to Lewis, who grinned. "Let's!"

The terrier and I followed the Cards into the château, eager for the next chapter to begin.

# CHAPTER 2

JESSIE CARSON
BLÉRANCOURT, JANUARY 1918

A castle in ruins. A glowing hearth. A gilded French desk. *When I used to read fairy tales, I fancied that kind of thing never happened, and now here I am in the middle of one!* I felt like Alice in Wonderland, albeit with a gray terrier instead of a white rabbit. Gauging the Turkish rug and antique furniture, I worried the delicate legs of the chairs would make excellent chew toys. "Shall I take the dog outside?"

"Whatever for?" Miss Morgan replied.

Lewis and I moved to the velvet divan, and the terrier settled at my feet. Dr. Murray Dike sat primly on the Louis XIV chair, near Miss Morgan, who perched on her desk. A serving girl poured ratafia, and Dr. M.D. raised her glass. "To Carson's safe arrival."

The others partook, but I froze, my arm still raised. I gawked at Miss Morgan, a woman who not only defied polite society but reshaped it.

Surely accustomed to people being in awe of her, she whispered, "Take a taste," and I sipped the sweet wine. She then tendered her mother-of-pearl cigarette case. I declined, but Lewis lit up and inhaled deeply. Miss Morgan puffed on her cigarette as if it were a pipe. After hours in the car, I sighed and reveled in the soft, immobile cushions. Lewis debriefed the two Annes on a meeting at the CARD depot in Paris, where Cards tracked down the seeds that farmers requested, as well as chalk and slates for pupils.

Lewis stubbed out her cigarette. "I've got to make sure Bessie's in fine form for tomorrow's treks."

"Bessie?" I asked.

"The Ford." Lewis bid me goodbye with a reassuring squeeze to my shoulder.

"I'm sure you've kept au courant about the war," Miss Morgan told me, "however, because this region was behind enemy lines, the newspapers weren't able to convey what happened."

She explained that in the autumn of 1914, fields and towns in northeastern France became battlefields. During the retreat of Allied forces, inhabitants—mainly women and children, since Frenchmen served in the army—either fled or stood their ground. A brutal occupation by German soldiers began. Some Frenchwomen were arrested and sent to the Fatherland, where they were brutalized as prisoners of war. Those who remained were forced to do backbreaking work. With no livestock or tractors, women replaced the oxen that helped sow the wheat. Children as young as four harvested potatoes for twelve hours each day, and now suffered from malnutrition, skin diseases, and curvature of the spine. One boy witnessed his mother killed before his eyes by a bomb dropped from an enemy plane.

"There are wee ones we've never seen smile," Dr. M.D. added. "With everything they've been through, I'm not sure they know how."

"Oh." The desolate sound escaped my lips. Words were my life, but now I had none. My heart ached for the families and all they'd endured. I didn't realize that I'd balled up my father's handkerchief in my fist until the terrier's nose brushed my knuckles. Dogs always seemed to know when solace was needed.

After three years of warfare, the Allies had regained this territory; however, the retreating German army destroyed buildings and booby-trapped fields in their wake. The church, schoolhouse, and homes were in ruins. No one had a complete roof over their heads. Every sort of paper—plain, tarred, oiled—was used to fill in holes made by machine guns. Rebuilding houses and clearing agricultural land remained CARD's priorities. If families couldn't make a living, they wouldn't return.

Even as enemy bombs continued to fall forty miles away, the land was being cleared of barbed wire and unexploded shells, trenches filled in, carcasses of animals removed, the remains of fallen soldiers and civilians transferred to burial grounds. Villagers resided in quarries, stables, sod houses, or in the debris of their own homes. I couldn't imagine having to unearth bodies, couldn't imagine facing the danger of being blown up in order to plant the fields, couldn't imagine losing my home, though I knew what it felt like to start over again.

I swigged the ratafia as I absorbed the harsh realities that the French faced. What did this mean for the library I was hired to create?

"Forgive us, Carson," Dr. M.D. said apologetically. "We do tend to go on."

"There is good news," Miss Morgan said. "Last autumn, CARD hired teachers. After three endless years of the occupation, children are back in school."

I nodded, reassured that children had returned to their routine.

"School and reading are important," Dr. M.D. said, "however, the library work might have to wait."

"What?" I asked.

A Card rushed in and came to a stop in front of Miss Morgan. A long strand of pearls brushed against the lapels of her uniform. "Where is she? Lewis said she's here."

"Yes, Breckie, Carson has finally arrived." Miss Morgan beamed.

"You're just in time—our bookshelves are positively bare," Breckie told me. Silvery strands from her bob brushed her plump cheeks. She was my age, yet had the same spritely energy as Lewis. "Tell me you've brought the latest novels!"

"As many as I could fit into my trunk." Her request made me like her immediately. I always had friends in fellow readers.

"I'm one of the nurses. My name is Mary Breckinridge, but Anne"—she gestured to Miss Morgan—"says my surname is a mouthful for the French, so everyone calls me Breckie."

"Our new arrival is looking peaked," Dr. M.D. said to her. "Why don't you help her settle in?"

"But what did you mean about postponing library work?" I asked.

"We'll discuss it later," Miss Morgan assured as she ushered me out.

The terrier and I trailed Breckie to a barrack where I was to have one of the four rooms. Inside, I found a single bed; a dressing table with a pitcher of water and a basin, since there was no running water; and a bouquet of dried flowers in the copper shell of a bomb. Noting my surprise, Breckie said, "Nothing goes to waste here."

"Well, if you can transform deadly weapons into floral arrangements, I feel I'm in good hands."

"You are."

As we spoke, the terrier swiveled his head between Breckie and me, following the conversation.

"It appears this discerning dog has adopted you," she said. "What will you name him?"

I contemplated his wise eyes and bushy whiskers. "Max," I said, and he waggled his tail.

Just then, Lewis dragged in my battered trunk. "What do you have in here? Rocks?"

"Books," I replied.

"Same thing," she said with a playful wink.

"We'll let you rest," Breckie said. "Cookie rings the dinner bell at seven."

———

MAX WATCHED AS I TUCKED MY FLANNEL NIGHTGOWNS IN THE DRAWER and hung my dresses in the wardrobe. *Armoire*, in French. French. Good Lord in heaven, *le bon Dieu au paradis*, I was in France. *En France*.

"Can you believe it?" I asked him.

He licked my fingers in response.

I set *My Ántonia*, *The Count of Monte Cristo*, and *Anne of Avonlea* on the nightstand. I kept my favorite people close—impossible to sleep without them.

Restless, I picked up a pen, intending to write to my sister. With the time change, I imagined Mabel on her lunch break, away from her desk and the beady eyes of her boss. I pictured her in the house with Mother, heating the stew on the stove, hiding the carrots and leeks in the thick broth so that Mother would eat them. On the porch, in the early morning, a week before my departure, I'd fretted to Mabel. My fingers entwined like guilt and love, like fear and hope, like Mabel and me. *You think of everyone but yourself,* she insisted. *You said this is your calling. You must go.* How I missed her.

I dipped my pen in the inkwell. *Dear Mabel, I'm here! Unpacking makes it official. For the next two years, I'll be the librarian of No Man's Land . . .*

I lost track of time, startling when the dinner bell clanged. In le club-house, a fire beckoned in the hearth. Cards gathered at four round tables, each with five place settings of earthenware. Several were youthful like Lewis, one studied her reflection in the back of her spoon, another applied a coat of lipstick. Others were closer to my age. Were they all wealthy, or did a few draw a salary like me? I waited for an opening, but deep in conversation, no one noticed me. I felt like an outsider, like I was peering over an oversize book that separated me from them.

Breckie, the nurse, waved me over and patted the empty chair next to her. As I waded through the sea of horizon blue to join her, Lewis, and the two Annes, I heard a Card grumble, "Why does *she* get to sit at the head table?"

Even in war, in a relief organization, one could not escape life's hierarchy. Manhattan's social scene was chock-full of heiresses and millionaires' wives. A librarian would never be invited.

In the din, Dr. M.D. clapped thrice like a headmistress calling pupils to attention. The chatter stopped. She asked me to introduce myself, and twenty Cards regarded me expectantly. My mouth went dry, as did my brain. What could I say? That I spoke of characters in books as if they were friends? That though my boss refused to allow *The Wonderful Wizard of Oz* on the library shelf, the setting I longed to explore was Emerald City? That my favorite writer was Willa Cather, because like her, I understood the beauty of the plains, the beauty of the plain?

"I'm a graduate of the Carnegie Library School. I worked in Pittsburgh for seven years; in Tacoma, Washington, as the director of the children's department for seven more; then in New York." I wasn't ready to talk about that tenure just yet.

"Gollywhoppers!" Lewis said. "You've worked on both coasts. Until I came here, my parents barely let me go anywhere. You're very brave."

"No braver than you all," I said.

"An explorer!" Breckie said. "Like the frontiersman Kit Carson, hero of my favorite dime novels."

"Shall we call you Kit?" Lewis asked.

I'd never had a nickname, and Kit sounded friendlier than Carson. Feeling shy about being the center of attention, I could only nod my assent.

Miss Morgan drew a silver brooch from her pocket. I now noticed that the others wore the same. "It's a griffin," she said, "our emblem."

The mythical beast—half lion, half eagle; a symbol of wisdom and courage—suited the group. As Miss Morgan pinned it to my lapel, I straightened. Of all the library candidates, she'd chosen me. Somehow, I would find a way to make a difference. *Books are bridges,* my father had said to me when I was a child. *They show how we're connected.* I clutched his handkerchief in my pocket, tracing the stitching of his initials. *SC* for Samuel Carson.

"To our Library Card!" Miss Morgan said.

Everyone raised their glasses.

"To Kit!" Lewis said.

"You're one of us," Breckie added.

I knew I was blushing. Aside from story hour, when children's eyes were upon me, I was used to being invisible.

Squeaking hinges heralded dinner. Since she held silver platters in both hands, the cook opened the swinging door with her derriere. Her apron was fastened loosely around her wasp waist. How odd to receive a first impression from a person's backside. (The only other such occasion for me had been a late arrival to the symphony, where the conductor was in full swing.) She pivoted and gestured for two apprentices to set platters of deviled eggs, cauliflower baked in béchamel sauce, and wilted greens on each table. The creamy aroma made my mouth water.

The cook regarded me. "A new girl?"

"Jessie Carson, an NYPL librarian on loan," I responded.

"On loan like a book?"

"Yes, though for two years rather than two weeks."

"I'm a fellow New Yorker. Marie Jones. Everyone calls me Cookie. Welcome," she said before moving to the next table.

As Miss Morgan heaped cauliflower onto her plate, she recounted her last trip to Manhattan, where she'd lured Cookie away from the household of her dearest enemy.

"The coup is one of your greatest accomplishments," Breckie said.

"Join us, Cookie," Miss Morgan entreated. "I hired you to oversee the kitchen, not wash every blasted pan yourself."

The cook wiped the sweat from her forehead with the back of her hand, leaving a smear of flour. "Too much to do," she declared. The apprentices followed her to the kitchen, trailing like ladies-in-waiting.

So someone *could* say no to the formidable Miss Morgan.

I helped myself to the cauliflower. The buttery spoonful melted in my mouth. Heaven.

"You'll accompany a few of the Cards through a day's work to get a better understanding of the place and of our role here," Dr. M.D. said. "A home visit with Breckie and the mercantile with Lewis."

"What sorts of things do you sell?" I asked.

"Everything from beets to eggs to garden rakes to artificial limbs," Lewis replied.

There was an uneasy lull. One moment, Cards chin-wagged like we were back home, and the next, we retreated into silence. In the distance, I could hear the din of shelling. I gulped. Glancing around, I wondered if the others were scared, or at least nervous, but they kept eating.

"Currently," Miss Morgan said, "we're 'chickenizing' this region. Ordering enough hens so that people have eggs and settling disputes as villagers argue about pecking order. A mayoress and a countess nearly came to blows over a rooster."

Miss Morgan was masterful—with the trials and tribulations of "chickenizing," we were back to chuckling.

"*Madame, madame!*" The teenage girl from earlier, Marcelle Moreau, burst into the room, clutching a lantern in her hand, and wound between tables until she found Breckie. "*Mon petit frère!*"

"*La fièvre?*" Breckie put her palm to her forehead to indicate checking for fever.

"*Oui,*" Marcelle panted. She must have run the entire way.

"*Tenez.*" I offered the girl a glass of water, which she guzzled.

"It must be serious if Madame Moreau is asking for help," Miss Morgan said.

Clearly used to being on call, Breckie tugged a black satchel from beneath her chair. She explained that there were no other medical personnel nearby and asked if I'd assist. I was scared, not just of falling bombs. I was scared I wouldn't be any help.

"You can stick your toe in the lake and shiver, saying you're not ready," Breckie said, "or you can jump in. Folks here need a hand and we've got to give it."

I touched my brooch. The griffin was a symbol of rapid action. *There are some things you learn best in calm, and some in storm.* I'd come to the North to help, and that's exactly what I meant to do.

———

BRECKIE AND I DONNED OUR COATS AND FOLLOWED MARCELLE OUT into the night, leaving the cobblestone streets of the village and continuing along a path. The dim flames of our lanterns weren't all that lit our way. Shells whistled and soared, lighting up the sky, then burst with terrifying booms. Flames rose, and a charred smell lacerated the air. It felt like at any moment we could be hit. To put fear from my mind, I focused on not tripping as we ran the entire fifteen-minute trip to a man-made cliff. Marcelle climbed down jagged wooden steps, then raised her lantern to light the way as we descended into a sandstone pit strewn with rocks, to a tin door affixed to the tall earthen wall. From inside, I could hear a child wailing. We entered a damp, pitch-black cavern. Marcelle had needed the lantern to find the way, which meant leaving her mother and three little brothers without light.

Breckie and I greeted Madame Moreau, who cradled her fidgety son. Like Marcelle, she had dark hair and wore mourning.

"It came on sudden." She looked like she was about to cry. I understood French, but as she recited her son's symptoms, I could barely keep up. "Hot . . . too hot . . . vomit . . . cries . . . no sleep."

Breckie patted the boy's spindly arm. He looked to be three years old.

My eyes adjusted to the dim space. Beyond the wood-burning stove was a kitchen table piled with dishes, as well as pallets on the floor. There were two children's books on one of the pillows. The thick earthen roof muffled the sound of the bombing, and I moved from fearing for my life to fearing for this family. I knew firsthand how quickly fevers carried away loved ones. My father had been fine on Sunday. By Friday, he was gone. Pneumonia.

Breckie examined the boy. Was he red from fever or from wailing? I prayed that he would have many adventures ahead. *Treasure Island. Around the World in Eighty Days.*

"If Maurice cries, it's good," Breckie explained. "It means there's life force. If he's listless and cries no more—that's when we worry."

She gestured to a cast-iron tub, and I poured cool water from the pail into it. We wet Maurice's limbs before immersing his body. Breckie moved deftly, as if she'd done this a thousand times in a dank quarry. Maurice cried even louder. Marcelle's two other brothers buried themselves in the folds of her skirt, and she put her arms around them. Madame Moreau clasped her hands so hard that the skin turned white.

"Sing to him," Breckie urged. "Hearing your voice will help."

Madame warbled "*Frère Jacques*," and Marcelle and her brothers joined in. Maurice kicked, angrily at first, then slowly until he calmed and cooed at us. It felt as if hours had gone by. The cold of the quarry bled through my coat into my bones.

I glanced at Breckie, hoping for a positive prognosis.

She felt his forehead. "Better," she declared.

We dried Maurice and swaddled him in a soft blanket. "Get some sleep," she told Madame Moreau. "You need your rest."

"Merci," she replied, then glared at her daughter. "I told Marcelle not to bother you ladies. She never listens!"

"It was no bother," Breckie said.

"I'm teaching my children to be self-sufficient."

Madame Moreau reminded me of my own mother—never be a bother, don't burden anyone, that's not ladylike, it's best to be seen and not heard. Marcelle was watching us intently. What would she take from tonight?

"When to go it alone or when to ask for help is one of the most important lessons that children can learn." I regarded Madame, but my words were for Marcelle.

"You learn that lesson from raising kids?" Madame replied.

Beside me, I felt Breckie flinch. She concentrated on putting instruments in her satchel, so I replied to Madame's barb. "I know that from being young once myself."

Curious, I peered around the quarry but didn't see the book I'd loaned Marcelle. Perhaps she felt the need to hide things.

"Thank you for coming, ladies," Madame said. "Though it wasn't necessary."

"It was most necessary," I replied. "Your well-being is important."

Again, I felt Marcelle observing us, the way I used to observe my mother.

Mercifully, the bombing had stopped. Breckie and I returned to Headquarters. "Would you believe that little Maurice is nearly six years old?" she asked.

"Nearly six? I thought he was only three."

"We have a time keeping any weight on him. Madame Moreau is scrawny herself—the case of most mothers in the region. The Germans nearly starved them to death. Of course, the dampness of the quarry doesn't help, but with no other housing available . . ."

In her fundraising efforts in New York, Miss Morgan had circulated photographs to underscore civilians' suffering, but it was quite another thing to witness it firsthand. I couldn't speak. Words weren't enough.

If words weren't enough, what was I doing here? These people needed more than library books. They needed more than I could give.

# CHAPTER 3

WENDY PETERSON

NEW YORK, JANUARY 1987

Imagine being surrounded by more books than anyone could read in a lifetime. Imagine the limitless possibilities of stories and truths and adventures. Imagine protecting these tomes for future generations, as a member of the Remembrance crew. That's me.

Eight a.m., Monday through Friday, I climb the subway steps onto Fifth Avenue, wending between businessmen in pin-striped suits; tourists clutching Canons as they photograph drag queens on their way home from a night out; sleepy students rushing to class, backpacks slung over one shoulder; and potbellied retirees kvetching en route to the corner deli. Even after living in New York for six years, I still sense the energy that comes from millions of people, passions, and tales. And thanks to my job, I have unlimited access to reading material and no late fees.

This morning's wind, icier than usual, is like a heavy shield that I battle to get to work. Luckily, the library has heat, unlike my sixth-floor walk-up. The furnace in my building clanks and grunts, but is no match for winter.

When I arrive, I greet Patience and Fortitude, the mud-smeared marble lions who guard the New York Public Library. Ralph Waldo Emerson wrote, *Patience and fortitude conquer all things,* and since I began at the NYPL two years ago, it's been my motto. Not so much for the job, but for my writing career.

I walk the hallowed halls that other writers have walked before me—Audre Lorde, Ann Beattie, and Tama Janowitz. Knowing that they have wrangled words under the same green lamps of the reading room makes me feel that I could become like them—an author.

Today, as I enter the staff room, I nod to coworkers. The children's librarian wears beige no-nonsense shoes for running after rambunctious toddlers; the latest program manager has a shaved head and a penchant for tie-dyed flak jackets. "Gnarly program tonight," she says. "You should both come."

When I explain that my writing workshop is this evening, she registers no surprise; in New York, there are more wannabe writers than waiters.

"After eight hours of telling kids to quit picking their noses, I want to get home, put my feet up, and down a berry wine cooler," the children's librarian grumbles as she sets her Tupperware lunch box in her locker.

"I get it," the program manager replies. "At evening events, I long for patrons to ask about the book, but the main question is 'Where's the john?'"

Granted, dealing with the public is trickier than guarding documents. In the Remembrance Department—that's what we call the basement microfiche center, where we pay tribute to the dearly (and not-so-dearly) departed—my job is to photograph collections, from Zora Neale Hurston's correspondence to Beatrix Potter's letters with illustrations of Peter Rabbit, in order to conserve them.

As I thaw enough to shed my purple puffer, Roberto enters, sporting his signature bomber jacket and aviator scarf, a stack of classics tucked under his arm. In our employee vote, which is run as seriously as a presidential election, he has thrice won the title of hottest librarian. Exit polls cite his "soulful brown eyes" and "scrumptious ass."

According to the gossip, he'd been working his way up the library ladder, destined for a plum top-shelf role, when he offended a bigwig. The incident involved children's scissors, a trustee's fur coat, and a Diet Coke. The big boss deemed Roberto an anarchist and barred the bodacious librarian from working with the public. Relegated to Remembrance, he reigns over shelves of archival boxes. He remains cheerful, giving it his all and working long hours, except when the big boss pops in to threaten us with budget cuts. Rankled, Roberto mutters about "dis-membrance."

Despite the demotion, he loves the library and believes in the mission of Remembrance, to ensure the past is saved for posterity. But occasionally, confused patrons wash up on these basement shores and ask for directions to the reading room. Roberto always escorts them upstairs. A regretful smile lights his face, and I see his sadness at what he has lost.

In the fluorescent bunker, twelve of us twenty-somethings come and go. When actors land parts, it's the end of their roles at the NYPL. During finals week, the place is dead. Roberto is the only constant. Each of us has a desk with a mounted camera next to an archive box. We pull out a document, photograph it, then place it upside down. Repeat as needed. When we finish, we move on to the next subject. Some are more interesting than others.

Upon learning that I'm fascinated by "herstory," Roberto orchestrated a shell game in which he swaps out archive boxes featuring bearded grumps in bowler hats (and the accompanying financial reports) to make sure I get first pick of the suffragettes, the flappers, and the Barbizon. For this, I love him.

If Roberto were a book, blurbs on his leather jacket would proclaim, "Clever!," "Quirky," "Hot!" For better or worse, I'm his favorite. Maybe because I'm a steady ship in his sea of interchangeable boats. Maybe because I play his game. This morning, he hangs his jacket next to mine. Our sleeves brush, and I find myself wishing my fingers could graze his. I sneak a peek at him and wonder if he likes me, too. I am working up the nerve to invite him on a date. Sometimes, I think he wants to ask me out, too. According to the Archivist, the staff remains scarred from the Great Breakup of 1984, when two librarians dated, eloped, and divorced, then demanded that coworkers take sides. Factions were created, war ensued.

"Category, children's literary," Roberto says in the guise of hello. The way he looks at me makes me feel like we're the only people in the library. "For one hundred points: 'I can't say that I enjoyed your last visit. It was obvious that you had too much on your mind to pay any attention to what I was trying to say.'"

Trying to best Roberto is the best part of my day. I flip through the Filofax of my mind to find the bookish reference. "*From the Mixed-Up Files of Mrs. Basil E. Frankweiler*?"

"Correct," he replies as we make our way to Remembrance. "Two hundred points, same category: 'Pa, where are you going with that ax?'"

"*Charlotte's Web*. But it's actually 'Where's Papa going with that ax?'"

"No back talk from the contestants."

"Since when does the host pick the category?" I demand.

"Shhh!" He points to the children's room as we pass by. "This is a library."

On any given workday, I have no idea which version of Roberto I'll find. Today is *Jeopardy!* Roberto. Yesterday was Linguistics Roberto. Language revelations mainly come to him while he's taking a shower, he'd told me. "I was lathering up with a sliver of Irish Spring when I wondered: Why call someone who is sexy 'foxy'? Why not say they're 'minky'?" I still can't get the image of him naked, beads of hot water flowing down his chest, out of my mind.

Radio host Roberto has him delving into his guests' favorite novels on a weekly basis. When he invited me on his "show" (a.k.a. lunch in the staff room), we argued about every book but *Slaughterhouse-Five*. Our favorite line is *And I asked myself about the present: how wide it was, how deep it was, how much was mine to keep.*

Now, in Remembrance, we're greeted by mumbled hellos. I take my seat beside Ted-the-off-Broadway-actor. He has luscious lips and to-die-for Bon Jovi hair, but he'll never be a leading man—he's got the charisma of an aardvark. Ted is efficient, though. He plops a document down. Snaps the photo. Slides the paper to the right and takes another. Plop. Snap. Slide. Plop. Snap. Slide. It's like he doesn't see the possibilities before him. *Young legend Joe DiMaggio . . . the next Yankee icon . . . his majestic, infallible swing . . . brought the Bronx Bombers back to dynastic status.* I want to continue reading, but Ted slides the story away and starts on the next.

"Aren't you even a little curious?"

"Nope," he replies.

With a devilish grin, Roberto places a large cardboard box with a fitted lid before me.

"What's this?" I ask, but he's already back at his desk, immortalizing NYPL newsletters from the 1970s.

I lay a yellowing document under the camera. Like Ted, I try not to care, but of its own volition, my eye focuses on the masthead, an American and a French flag undulating side by side. Beneath it, the title "*Under Two Flags,* a weekly bulletin of the work in France and in America, from the American Committee for Devastated France." And in small letters: *Recognized and approved by the French government.*

Published in New York in 1918, the first article is titled AT BLÉRAN-COURT.

The Town Crier was out last night. Down the crooked street of Blérancourt one could hear his hobnailed shoes click on the cobblestones before his clanging bell brought the curious to the glassless windows and the frameless doors.

The Crier recounts the news. When the Germans refused to sign the peace terms the Crier made the news public; when a neighbor loses her wallet (by carelessly forgetting to put it in her stocking) the Crier calls upon the people of the town to find it. Last night the Crier announced the distribution of clothing.

Three articles per woman are allowed, of which she may choose between shoes, an apron, a flannel petticoat, and an undershirt. The petticoats are colorful like barber poles. The young girls are

as particular over their choice of red-striped or
blue as our more pampered sisters are concerning
the lace and ribbons of their lingerie.

What is this Committee? Who are these pampered sisters? The article is like nothing I've read before. The box is a treasure chest. I stare at Roberto until he feels my gaze.

"Thank you," I mouth.

He nods in acknowledgment, and I resume.

Committee members make the rounds through more
than one hundred villages to help French refugees who have nothing. The villagers who return
to their land now lodge in dugouts and ruins.
They cook and sleep and live on what they can
find in the debris. To them we give something to
start life again—a quilt, some sheets, a shawl,
some stockings (Oh! How they are needed), and
a pot or a pan. To them, it is not so much the
gift as it is the consciousness that someone
sees their plight and extends an expression of
sympathy.

We are "standing by" while refugees struggle
to their feet. We lend a helping hand to lighten
the burden of destruction which has come onto the
people of the North through virtue of their in-
domitable resistance, while for four years they
stood as the bulwark to all civilization.

A group of women volunteered during the Great War? Intrigued, I reread the article. *The bulwark to all civilization.* Was the writer stating that in the war, the French were a defensive wall that the whole world counted on?

Anxious to learn more, I read the *Under Two Flags* bulletin from cover to cover. Apparently, less than forty miles from the front, a group of 350 women from the United States, Canada, and Great Britain worked to rebuild northern France from 1917 to 1924. While the war was raging, they replanted 7,300 fruit trees. They distributed goats, chickens, rabbits, clothing, linens, furniture, oil-burning lamps, and stoves. They sowed 7,500 acres of land with seeds.

I can't help but turn to the next edition.

### OUR FARMERETTES

Anne Murray Dike, our president in France, writes in relation to the accomplishments of our agricultural unit, which has received the commendation of the American Army Garden Service in France.

"Our volunteers are on the same footing as men. Although we are not able to be at the front in the trenches, we have a great deal to do in fighting in the rear.

"We must be careful to have the highest possible grade of women. The probationary period will allow us to eliminate undesirables."

It's rad that soldiers and volunteers worked together to grow gardens to feed people, but the way the president writes about eliminating "undesirables" makes me cringe.

Sensing someone watching me, I glance up. Sure enough, Roberto is giving me the stink eye. "Don't forget to document," he mouths. With his index finger, he makes a clicking gesture.

"You're not the boss of me," I tell him.

"I have seniority."

I snort. "You got to Remembrance two weeks before I did."

"Every second counts. I remember the day you arrived like it was yesterday."

"I doubt it."

He doesn't insist. Again, I think he likes me as much as I like him, though sometimes I fear it's wistful thinking. In any case, to appease Roberto, I photograph a page before I read it. At 2:00 p.m., I realize that I'm so into the bulletins that I forgot to eat lunch. In the staff room, I hork down my peanut butter sandwich and hurry back to my desk to the next article.

### LIBRARIAN ARRIVES IN BLÉRANCOURT

The New York Public Library lends more than books! In a great boon for CARD, Jessie Carson is on loan from the NYPL in order to create France's first ever children's libraries. Anne Morgan, CARD vice president, states, "Carson was a rising star in the National League for Woman's Service and is an excellent advocate for children."

CARD president Anne Murray Dike says, "We are still rebuilding, and while education is a priority, we may have to delay library work."

Winnifred Smythe, superintendent of the NYPL children's section, declares, "I'm sure our little Jessie will do an adequate job."

Chills. I get chills. An NYPL employee—like me—in France during the Great War? I couldn't be prouder if Jessie Carson were a blood relative. Did she build libraries out of the rubble? What happened to her?

At 6:00 p.m., I still haven't finished going through the articles, and haven't found more information about Jessie Carson. I don't want to put the women back in the box, where they've been for nearly seventy years. When Roberto isn't looking, I slip a few bulletins under my sweater. Sadly, no one will notice they are missing.

———

I RUSH TO MY EVENING CLASS AT THE NEW SCHOOL. OUT OF BREATH, I slide into a front-row seat and nod at Professor Hill, dapper in his designer blazer; its suede elbow patches distinguish him from mere businessmen. From his lectern, he doesn't acknowledge me. He begins speaking, and a dozen writers—more disciples than students—lean forward. He recounts how his agent took him to the Russian Tea Room, a restaurant so iconic that we'd heard of it back home in Saskatchewan. He ordered the most expensive caviar. "It. Tasted. Like. Victory. The restaurant reeks of success. Promise me you will go there when you sell your first book."

We promise. I chose to attend university in New York in order to be closer to the publishing realm—F. Scott Fitzgerald, James Baldwin, Tama Janowitz, and soon, Wendy Peterson. My dad wasn't keen, but with the scholarships I received, he couldn't say no. He did say, *Why don't you major in accounting instead? You don't need to study English. You already speak English.* My mom would have understood. After she died, he and I spent my high school years on the opposite shores of arguments, shouting at each other. Mom had been our bridge. And without that connection, my dad and I ceased understanding each other. Since I left for college, he hasn't phoned—his excuse is that he never knows if I'm home or not. Mom would have told him that's why I have an answering machine and encouraged him to reach out. For my part, I call home for the holiday hat trick—Thanksgiving, Christmas, and his birthday.

Being in contact with a real author like Professor Hill makes me feel like one day I'll be published, too. Each week, we students come prepared with short stories still warm from our word processors, hoping that Professor Hill will choose ours.

Tonight, he points at me. Trying not to preen, I hand him the story of an outsider in New York who grapples with the loss of her mother by riding the subway for hours. At least in this way, she figures, both are underground.

"'It began freshman year,'" Professor Hill reads crisply. My sentences sound good in his mouth. Classmates sigh in the right spots, which reassures me. He reads all seven pages aloud, and when he finishes, the workshop awaits his verdict. I grip my pencil, though it is a buoy unlikely to save me. I took to heart Hill's advice to write what you know, but now feel exposed in front of my classmates and his condescending stare. Finally, he states: "This is just notes. There's no story here."

He throws the pages onto the lectern. A few fall to the floor. He leaves them there.

As flattered as I was when he chose me, I'm dejected now. Spring semester of my first year of grad school, and so far, I haven't made any progress.

The bell rings. Hill leaves without a goodbye. The other students file out; I crouch to gather my pages from the floor. My long black hair cloaks my expression. I contemplate the linoleum, relieved that no one can see me tearing up.

As usual, the others grab a beer and a bite at the Dive Next Door. As usual, I can't afford an evening out. On my way home, I pass bar after bar packed with stockbrokers downing shots that cost the same as a hardcover. At the Strand Book Store, I press my nose against the glass. I want in, want my novel on their shelf. I want my words in a book, for all the times I couldn't talk, couldn't say what I felt.

From across the street, the intoxicating scent of pepperoni pizza floats out, but I'm unable to eat. *This is just notes, there's no story here.* I forge on and find myself on the steps between Patience and Fortitude. At the NYPL, there are always other loners, some as blue as me.

Under the light of the streetlamp, I inhale the CARD bulletins, hunting for Jessie Carson.

# CHAPTER 4

JESSIE "KIT" CARSON
BLÉRANCOURT, JANUARY 1918

Throughout the first night of my arrival, a relentless offensive continued. Shells shrieked and exploded, seeming to land closer and closer—thunderous, deadly. The blasts nearly shook Max and me from the bed. He whimpered under the quilt, and my hand trembled as I petted him. Was this echoing bombardment normal? Surely we should seek cover. In an air raid, the Moreaus' quarry would be the safest place. I listened for the creak of the floorboards. Since Breckie and Lewis stayed put, so did I.

At daybreak, the pounding of machine guns ceased, but my nerves were stretched tight and my head ached from lack of sleep. Timid sunlight peeked through the lace curtains. Sounds wafted in: snippets of conversations in French and English; the *tap-tick-trick* of a typewriter; a Ford chugging, impatient to be off. The air was so frosty that I almost didn't want to leave the downy duvet. I donned my uniform and braided my hair into a crown before splashing my face with water from the pitcher.

In le club-house, I joined Breckie for oatmeal and war coffee. She was alone.

"Will the two Annes join us?" I asked.

"They get an early start, with tea and toast at their desks." With her spoon, she gestured in the direction of the château.

I realized that I was the last one up. Breckie had kindly stayed for me.

"Chicory just isn't the same," she sighed as she poured me a cup. "How can I be a morning person without coffee?"

I had a feeling that she was lovely at any time of the day.

"How is the Moreau family?" I asked.

"Better," she said. "I just checked on little Maurice."

"After such a scare, I'm not sure Madame Moreau slept a wink. It must be difficult to raise four children alone."

"Marcelle is a big help. How that girl remains cheerful despite her mother's henpecking, I'll never know."

"I'm sure Madame Moreau does her best." I thought of my own mother before adding, "Sometimes the people who want the best for us are the worst for us." Refusing to dwell on the negative, I changed the subject. "Any words of wisdom for my first week?"

"You know, I've learned from folks here. How to be a better listener. You came to give, but you'll receive."

I nodded. "At library school, I saw myself as giving the gift of literacy, but I was the one who received from children—their sense of wonder, their imagination, their optimism."

She explained that she conducted home visits on Tuesdays. "Do come! I'm looking forward to showing you the ropes."

"I'd love to," I said.

"Splendid."

*Some librarian you are,* Miss Smythe's voice echoed in my head. *I'd have inspected the library before I even unpacked.*

"Actually, I'd best see about the library," I said. Though she was a continent away, I'd chosen my former boss over getting to know the other Cards and learning about the region. When would I quit caring about her opinion?

"Kit, about the library . . . there's damage," Breckie warned.

*How bad can it be?* I wondered. *The walls were still standing.*

Breckie looked at me and hesitated, then said, "You'll see."

As I rose to leave, she asked what my favorite children's book was.

"It changes, depending on my mood. Today, it's *The Secret Garden* because I, too, feel as if I'm discovering a new realm."

"I bought that one to read to my daughter," she said wistfully.

"Your daughter?"

"Never mind. I don't want to keep you." Breckie's face, thus far friendly and open, shut like a diary with a lock.

———

I WAS STILL THINKING ABOUT THE SURPRISING TURN IN OUR CONVERSA-tion as I walked along the cobbled path toward the town hall, which housed the library, where *mamans* and *enfants* would come to *la biblio-thèque* to check out *livres*.

Outside the mercantile, villagers waited in line for their daily bread. Marcelle Moreau exited with a loaf in one hand and *Anne of Green Ga-bles* in the other. When she saw me, she grinned and held up the book in a jaunty wave.

Fast on her heels, her mother advised, "Pay with exact change. Otherwise, we'll end up with a pillowcase full of centimes."

I moved to say hello, but like actors on the stage, each was intent on her role, a beleaguered daughter and put-upon mother. The dynamic reminded me of how my mother always had to get in her two cents, whether it was about the books I'd read, the classes I attended, the suit-ors I didn't entertain, or the way I moved out West to work in Tacoma.

"And don't grin at the *dame américaine*," Madame Moreau contin-ued. "It gives the impression that you're feebleminded."

"She smiled first!" Marcelle protested.

"If you don't listen—"

"I listen, I just don't obey." Jaw thrust out, Marcelle picked up the pace, but her mother kept lecturing. Peck. Peck. Peck.

Beside me, a woman stopped. Dull brown eyes matched the hair she'd scraped into a bun. Though tired lines stretched over her fore-head, she appeared to be about thirty. She was slender, and like most villagers, she, too, wore mourning. No, she was mourning itself. She observed Marcelle, and I wondered if she saw what I did—a spirited teen who remained cheerful despite a barrage of criticism.

I smiled at the woman in a commiserating way. "Did your mother chastise you like that?"

"Madame Moreau is correct. Smiling for no reason denotes feeble-mindedness."

Before I could respond, she strode into the mercantile, pointed to a roll, and flung the exact change onto the counter. I couldn't help but think of Marilla in *Anne of Green Gables. Here sat Marilla Cuthbert, when she sat at all, always slightly distrustful of sunshine, which seemed to her too dancing and irresponsible a thing for a world which was meant to be taken seriously.*

Still, my hand moved to my chest, as if the woman's jab had left a bruise there.

Miss Morgan sidled up to me. She was much taller than I was. Even here, in the midst of ruins, her blouse was a pristine white. Her black eyes shone with empathy as she whispered, "That's Sidonie Devereux, the village recluse. Don't take her words to heart. After she received word of her husband's death, she . . . shattered."

"How much heartache can one village hold?" I wondered.

"More than I ever thought possible," Miss Morgan responded as she continued on her way.

At the town hall, Max sniffed at the door as I pried it open. I envisioned a darkened foyer with no electricity; instead, light filled the space. My heart sang along to the French nursery rhyme "Alouette," and I imagined a future of bustling story hours complete with games and cakes. My gaze followed a sunbeam to the welcome desk, but the scene brought a tightness to my throat. Instead of a bespeckled clerk sifting through files, I found a charred cadaver of a desk. Scattered on the floor were singed papers and smashed slate shingles.

Sunlight made its way through jagged holes in the ceiling. Clearly, bombs had blown through. Last night, in the shadowy dusk, I'd perceived the silhouette of the town hall, but not the damage.

Breckie had tried to warn me. *About the library* . . . How foolish of me to assume that it was intact. I waded through the debris to discover what was left. The collection of two hundred tomes, strewn on the floor and soaked by rain, was now clumped with mildew. The bloated shelves, emptied of books, were good only for kindling. I don't know how long I stared at this graveyard of books, an ache in my soul, as I absorbed the loss.

Though stories were eternal, books were as fragile as people. Gingerly, I picked up the French translation of Jack London's *White Fang*. The mummified *Croc Blanc* crumbled in my hand. I picked up another book, and another. Many appeared to be ripped in half. German soldiers had destroyed the collection, waging a war on words, ideas, and our need for communication. Books, newspapers, and journals contained our past, the way we saw things, and the way we wished things would be. They carried our longings, our dreams for children, an hour of escape, and an education.

I'd expected to inventory books, but instead cataloged damage: the roof needed to be repaired, walls replastered, warped shelving and parquet replaced, and books repaired or new ones purchased. I would not simply be carving out a children's section, I would be restoring an entire building. It would be months before I could hold story hour. That is, if CARD could acquire the raw materials. Most were reserved for the army.

Max moved to my side. He regarded me with what seemed to be a pained expression. Crouching beside him, I buried my face in his fur and let myself mourn. When a child was having a down day, whether from a scraped knee or a bruised heart, I told them, *It's all right to feel wretched. Take the time that you need.* And now this is what I told myself.

*We don't pay you to mope,* Miss Smythe scolded, before adding her favorite admonishment to overtired children: *You get what you get, so don't throw a fit!*

The door creaked. Peering up, I almost expected to see my former boss wag a bony finger at me. Instead, it was Marcelle.

I quickly righted myself. "Bonjour."

"Thank you for helping my family last night. And for loaning me *Anne of Green Gables. J'adore!*"

What a pleasure to read something new! she said. Each evening, she recited the same books—the only two they owned—to her brothers. The fables soothed them. And with the war, they needed soothing. Sometimes at night, they heard their mother weep. Marcelle and her brothers used to worry about their father at the front, and Marcelle thought that fear was the worst emotion they could feel . . . until they learned that he'd been killed. In war, stories were the siblings' only escape.

"Anne was an orphan," Marcelle continued. "Yet she remained cheerful in dark times. She says, 'My future seemed to stretch out before me like a straight road. I thought I could see along it for many a milestone. Now there is a bend in it. I don't know what lies around the bend, but I'm going to believe that the best does.'" Marcelle's gray eyes gazed at me hopefully. "I know you understand me, because you love books, too."

"I do." I supposed that at home, Madame Moreau did the talking. Now, Marcelle's words flowed like water, and I would be the vase to capture them. Children deserved to be heard.

"I want to help."

Marcelle impressed and inspired me. After all her family had endured, here she was, ready to lend a hand.

I pointed toward the window. "Over there, we'll put the history section. Near the entry, we'll create a nook for children."

I imagined the bookshelves as a body—planks of pine the skeleton, books the flesh and blood, and on top, a globe, its round face contemplating readers.

"Kids in the library?" Marcelle uttered in the same incredulous tone one might say, *Bear cubs in church?* I imagined other unlikely things—a yak in the kitchen, a walrus in the chestnut tree, an owl in the abbey. I could illustrate a children's book with amusing scenes. Then I imagined Miss Smythe scowling. *Children don't need fanciful. They need moral guidance.*

"Mademoiselle?" I heard Marcelle say.

"Excuse me. I was daydreaming. Yes, kids in the library. And you can call me Kit."

Marcelle and I swept up jagged shards of wood and moldy chunks of plaster. We then carried pile after pile to bins outside. Gusts of wind blew the gray clouds away. I raised my face to the sun. Despite this wasteland of smashed windows and shattered shingles, with Marcelle at my side, I felt optimistic. We would rebuild.

In the alcove, I scooped up books from the floor. Those on the top had been waterlogged and were now moldy. The ones underneath weren't as damaged. *L'Histoire de la Picardie, The History of Picardie* by Gaston Devereux, had been torn in half, but seemed to have been sheltered from the rain. Pages were detached from the binding, the corners blackened, but it was not a complete loss.

Devereux. I asked if the author was related to the village recluse, Sidonie. Marcelle confirmed Gaston was her husband. He'd been proud of his adopted region's history, his book a labor of love, with Sundays spent poring over documents (though Ma insisted it was an excuse to skip Mass). Unfortunately, there was but one copy. He'd intended to find a publisher, but the war had made it impossible.

I had an idea.

"Have you ever noticed that books are shaped like doors?" I asked.

"And windows."

"Both are entries."

"That open to new realms," Marcelle said. "And to new friends."

"This book could start a conversation. Bookbinding isn't my forte, but I'll do my best to repair it."

"Then Sidonie Devereux will have to talk to you!" Marcelle nodded approvingly.

"The most important thing is that she'll recover her husband's work."

*Concentrate on what you can fix, not on what you can't,* I told myself, banishing Miss Smythe's voice from my mind.

In my barrack, I opened my trunk to get the typewriter. When Marcelle saw the stacks of books in French, she said, "Oh là là. A treasure chest! May I look at them?"

"You may."

Gingerly, she scrutinized each, from the font of *The Adventures of*

*Maya the Bee* to the illustrations of *Treasure Island*. She traced the gold lettering of *Anne d'Avonlea* with her finger. "Her story continues?"

I nodded and explained that filling out a library card would enable her and the other children to check out a book for two weeks.

Marcelle cocked her head. "You're telling me that I can take these home? And all I have to do is sign my name?"

"Yes."

"Me, not my mother?"

"Exactly."

Her eyes narrowed as though she sensed I was hoodwinking her, but she couldn't quite picture how. "What if the book gets dropped through the hole of the outhouse? Or left out in the rain?"

"I trust you. And your brothers, too."

"Trusting them is like counting on a storm cloud to keep your umbrella dry," she noted wryly.

"Would you like to check some out?"

"*Mais oui!*" She signed her name.

Now to the restoration work at hand. We laid *The History of Picardie* on my desk as if it was a body. Examining it like coroners, we noted the leather cover was completely ruined. The flyleaf and first three pages had turned to pulp, their words barely legible. Mold had set in on the corners, but it was dried now. The pages were rippled with water damage but otherwise intact. Since Gaston Devereux had typed the manuscript, his widow would likely prefer his handiwork to new pages. Thus, I made the decision to replace only the truly damaged ones.

I set the typewriter on the desk, so we could replace those passages.

"Would you like to be a book doctor?" I asked Marcelle. "You can either clean pages or type new ones."

She gnawed on her pigtail as she pondered the question. "Both! Teach me everything."

I put my handkerchief over my nose and mouth, and advised Marcelle to do the same. "We resemble bandits!" she proclaimed gleefully. While she pecked at the keys to replace the text, I used my chewed-up toothbrush to gently scrape-scrape-scrape spores of mold from the prologue. Happy with my handiwork, I took a break and watched Marcelle as she squinted at the paper.

"Now that I think about it, shouldn't you be in class?" I asked.

She explained that she'd earned her *certificat d'étude,* and to continue her education, she'd have to go off to boarding school, something her family could no longer afford.

"Maybe you could teach me to librarian," she suggested.

*To librarian.* It's true the job was action, and therefore a verb.

"That's a fine idea."

Side by side, as we took turns typing and scraping, I peppered her with questions. "What's your favorite book?"

She regarded me as if I'd asked an absurd question. "All books, any books." Then she added, "*The Last Lesson* by Alphonse Daudet. He wrote about Alsace-Lorraine falling into the hands of the Prussians in 1870. A schoolmaster was permitted to give one last French lesson before classes would be taught in German. 'Monsieur Hamel informed us that French was the most beautiful language in the world . . . we must always protect it, because even if people become enslaved, as long as they retain their language, it's like holding the key to the prison.'"

Language was a key.

"What a beautiful sentiment." I was astounded by her lucidity, her poise in recognizing the parallel to what happened to this region in 1914, and how she found succor in literature and language.

She shrugged. "Ma says that memorizing pretty passages won't put food on the table."

Not wanting to contradict her mother, I merely said, "They do put joy in our hearts," and moved on to ask how many children lived in the village.

"Before, two hundred. Now there aren't even a dozen. I wish my friends would come back."

"Will you draw me a map of the surrounding area?"

Gnawing on the tip of her pigtail, she created a solar system of towns, with Headquarters in Blérancourt as the sun. By each star, she added a name—Soissons, Ham, Vic—in penmanship that rivaled a calligrapher's. An hour later, I was surprised to see over one hundred towns.

"I drew the ones in the Red Zone, even though they don't exist anymore."

The enemy had blown entire towns off the map. The way she spoke about destruction so matter-of-factly broke my heart.

"Did they warn you about the Zone?" Marcelle asked.

I recalled the phrase *human life impossible* from the CARD briefing.

"It's full of dangers," she continued. "Only I know two sisters who still . . ."

"Yes?"

"I went to school with sisters from there."

She was holding something back. I couldn't blame her. We didn't know each other well. Yet.

"Have you ever attended a story hour?" I asked.

"What's story hour?"

"Do families here possess many books?"

"Most have the Bible, and maybe a prayer book. Before the war, Sidonie Devereux had a whole wall of books. I spied it from her window. You should have seen the colors—burgundy and forest green and a sumptuous gold. The spines shone like stained glass."

By the time we finished cleaning the pages, I'd learned a lot. And I suspected that it wouldn't be long before Marcelle confided about those two girls.

To bind the book, we used one of the ledgers I'd brought to note the date that reading material went on loan. With a penknife, I removed the empty pages from the plain brown casing. As I glued the spine and inserted the manuscript pages, I wished I'd splurged for a beautiful blue leather. With my best calligraphy, I wrote *L'Histoire de la Picardie* by Gaston Devereux on the front.

"Good as new," I proclaimed.

Marcelle snorted. "Not even close."

A part of me thought, *What a little stinker!* while the rest was glad-dened that the war hadn't dampened her spirit.

"Still," Marcelle continued, "she'll treasure it. I can't wait to see her expression when we give her the book."

"Do you know Madame Devereux's address? We could take it to her."

"Her cottage in Blérancourt was destroyed. Now she lives in the country, near the Red Zone. It's pretty scary." Marcelle eyed me, per-haps wondering if I would change my mind.

"I should go alone. I don't want you in harm's way."

"This is a war zone," she said softly. "We're all in danger."

She was right, but I didn't want to put her at greater risk. A bit regretfully, I played the safety card and told her I'd go another time.

Unsurprisingly, Marcelle possessed the trump card. "Who'll show you the way?"

On hearing the note of triumph in her voice, I realized I'd played into her hand.

We left the cobbled streets of the village and hurried down the pockmarked road. The stench from the ditch accompanied us, and I tried not to look too closely at the debris that the war had left behind— abandoned canteens and mess kits, helmets and boots, gas cans and flat tires, animal and maybe even human bones. It was nearly a mile to the interim lodging of Sidonie Devereux, a knoll that German soldiers had used as a dugout. The two windows had been blown out and were covered with wood planks. Tufts of grass grew on the "roof," where a chimney pipe puffed smoke from the wood-burning stove. It reminded me of pioneer houses in the American West, something from history books—except for the shards of glass that glinted in the dirt, and the sinister backdrop of the forest of burned trees. Some trunks lay on the ground, others stood straight and cast long shadows.

I knew about the dangers in the shadows. Once, at the NYPL, I'd worked late, on my own. Or so I thought. The lights were already off, and I hurried along the row of stacks toward the exit. A man jumped out and accosted me. He tried to cover my mouth, but I was able to shout; fortunately, the superintendent's wife came running from their apartment, butcher knife in hand. The man ran for it. Afterward, I understood the danger of the dark. I felt that same menace now.

I rapped on Sidonie's door. "Bonjour, Madame?"

We could hear movement, but Sidonie Devereux didn't respond.

"I'm Kit, the librarian," I continued. "We have something for you." No answer.

"Hello, Madame Devereux," Marcelle said. "Please open up." Silence.

There was nothing more to do. Marcelle propped *The History of Picardie* against the door. We'd expected to see Sidonie Devereux's expression when she saw her husband's book. Now, I just hoped that she'd give the gift the once-over before pitching it.

Marcelle and I hastened through the garden of glass to the road. *You're useless,* my boss snickered. *What book could possibly make a difference in this woman's suffering?*

"Why so forlorn?" Marcelle asked. "We did a good thing."

"Thank you for that reminder." I tugged gently on her braid.

"Will Lewis really teach me how to drive?"

On to the next possibility. This was one of the joys of working with children—no dwelling on the past. Each day promised an exciting tomorrow. I suspected that life as a Card was the same—you bounded from bed never knowing what could happen.

"If she doesn't have time, I will," I promised.

---

That evening, I joined the two Annes for a digestif before a cozy fire in the château. They settled on the settee, I sat off to the side on a Louis XIV chair. I asked about the books torn in two. Miss Morgan explained that while some devastation had been wrought by bombs ordered by faraway generals, most damage had been inflicted by the German soldiers who'd occupied the region. When the Allies launched an offensive, forcing the German army to withdraw, *Soldaten* were given orders to annihilate—the fields that had fed them, the homes where they'd found shelter—as they retreated. The soldiers burned family Bibles and bassinets. They smashed porcelain plates and mirrors. They ripped the stuffing from settees and beds. They took pliers to lockets and photo albums. They tore up books.

"And speaking of books," Dr. M.D. said to Miss Morgan. "We may have been premature in bringing in a librarian."

"Nonsense," she responded.

"I require a secretary. Carson can write articles for the bulletin and help with bookkeeping."

Bookkeeping? I didn't travel to France to tally numbers. If I'd wanted to remain an assistant, I'd have stayed at the NYPL.

"Things aren't going to plan," Dr. M.D. continued. "Back home, everyone is expecting us to fail."

"Not everyone."

"My ex-husband—"

"What about him?" Miss Morgan demanded.

"He snickered when I recounted our plans. Called us the 'Heiress Brigade.'"

"Why were you confiding in him?"

"I can picture him and his MIT cronies at the University Club," Dr. M.D. said. "Swilling their cognac, mocking us from the comfort of their wingback chairs."

"He constantly underestimates you."

"It's not just him. Even our supporters predict that we'll fail."

"We won't," Miss Morgan said.

"You can't know that! What about our budget?" Dr. M.D.'s voice rose an octave. "We're accountable to our donors. Every penny counts, and we're paying a librarian who can't do her job."

"If I may?" Like a pupil, I raised my hand to speak.

They turned to me, and I could see they'd forgotten I was in the room.

"Go ahead, Carson," Miss Morgan replied.

"Children have had no respite from the daily hardships. They're parched for books, for the spark of imagination that stories bring. The way a novel transforms into a flying chariot that takes us far from sorrow, the time of a chapter. They deserve the thrill of turning the pages to learn what happens next. Reading must be a priority."

"We'll take your opinion under advisement," said Dr. Murray Dike, her lips curdling in displeasure at my outburst.

Our uniforms were modeled on the military, as was the unspoken CARD hierarchy. The two Annes regarded me, I understood an order had been given: *Dismissed!*

They could not understand what books meant to me. Unbidden, a memory rose to meet me on the road to my barrack. On my twelfth birthday, my father promised a surprise that took the two of us out of town. The train swayed gently, and from the window of our compartment, we watched fir trees flit by. I had a case of the sniffles; Father handed me his handkerchief. Instead of blowing my nose, I breathed in the woody tobacco scent that imbued the starched cotton. Not wishing to soil it, I used my sleeve and tucked his handkerchief in my pocket. I liked to keep pieces of people.

"Times are changing," my father said as we pulled into the station. "Women will work outside the home. I don't want you to depend on a husband for happiness or money."

That future seemed far off. We alighted onto the platform. All of New York seemed to teem in the station. Newsboys shouted, women hawked packets of sunflower seeds, men in three-piece suits like my father elbowed us out of the way. Outside, horse-drawn wagons clop-clop-clopped along. On the sidewalk, Father and I weaved between people.

"When will we get there?" I asked.

"You'll know."

We arrived at an immense Beaux Arts building whose entrance was guarded by gleaming marble lions. In the hallowed halls, I let my fingers glide along the pristine wall. It felt good to touch the library. At tables lit with lamps, grownups bowed over documents. The reading room was a quiet, majestic cathedral. No, it was heaven. I hadn't known where I belonged, until now.

"This could be your realm," my father told me. "You could make a living with books."

And now, my life's work was sharing a love of reading, so that children here would have a lifetime of stories and adventures.

Before, I might have apologized to the two Annes for my outburst. But Marcelle had reminded me that books were a lifeline. In the devastated zone, I vowed to make sure every child had the much-needed pleasure, spark of imagination, and escape that books brought. I would lead story hour and create a library. The only question was how.

# CHAPTER 5

In le club-house, over oatmeal drizzled with honey, Breckie, Lewis, and I decided that the day's house calls would be the perfect occasion to teach Marcelle to drive. Lewis asked a younger Card to babysit the Moreau brothers. After breakfast, I followed Breckie to the larder, where she filled an empty cigar box with scones to share with villagers. She explained that when the Cards first conducted house calls, Northerners proffered the stew from their stoves, their last crumbs of cake. It was impossible for folks to invite us in and not feed us; yet Cards couldn't accept, knowing that it might be all they had. Of course, food was not the only nourishment we could offer. I filled my satchel with books.

Outside, Marcelle finished loading medical supplies while Lewis cranked, cranked, cranked the Ford.

"Marcelle, meet Bessie, Bessie, meet Marcelle." Lewis nudged her into the driver's seat.

"Truly?" Marcelle asked. "You don't think I'm too young?"

"We wouldn't offer if we didn't think you were ready," I replied.

With Marcelle at the helm, it was a bouncy ride.

"You're supposed to avoid the ruts," Lewis teased.

"This road is one big pothole," Marcelle replied.

She picked up speed, and we clipped along at a breakneck twenty miles per hour. Lewis complimented her on the way she worked the pedals.

"Driving isn't as hard as I thought," Marcelle said. "It's like dancing."

Lewis explained that the real challenge of "chauffing" lay in engine repairs, fixing punctured tires, and general upkeep. Marcelle would also have to pass the French drivers' exam.

"Does your mother really not want you to apprentice with us?" Breckie asked.

"She'd hate it," Marcelle replied.

Taken aback by her bluntness, I asked why.

"She believes driving is unladylike."

"Do you agree?"

"Oh, yes," Marcelle said with a mischievous smile. "It's marvelous." Her mien turned solemn. "Though I don't like it when Ma frets. She says training with you will ruin my chance at a proper marriage."

"What do you think?" Lewis asked.

"This war ruined my chances—the boys I liked were sent to the front, and now they're dead."

I envisioned a tidy row of tombstones for Marcelle's suitors, tombstones for the children she might have had, tombstones for all the people who'd given their lives. And for what?

A series of bombs exploded, the detonation so loud that I turned to see if they'd gone off behind us. I asked if we should be worried.

Lewis shrugged. "You get used to it."

Our first stop was to the Hugo family, who now lived in a shed in the shadow of their demolished cottage, its roof blown off, its bright blue shutters askew. As Marcelle pulled to a stop, they—parents and an infant in a pram as well as a six-year-old boy—formed a line as if receiving royalty. "*Oh là là, les dames arrivent,*" Madame said worriedly. She straightened her collar; Monsieur patted his cowlick. Though he'd been discharged from the army due to grave injuries, he wore his uniform. Like everything else he'd owned, his civilian clothes had been destroyed.

To put them at ease, Breckie spoke the universal language: weather. "Can you believe the rain these last weeks?"

"I'm worried it will flood my garden," Madame replied.

The couple's nervousness dissipated like the morning fog. Breckie proffered scones and Madame served dandelion tea. The yard served as a dining room; hay bales replaced tables and chairs. To make it homey, Madame laid a singed tablecloth over the straw.

"Sorry we can't offer better," she murmured. "I'm sure you fine ladies are used to a different standard."

"Breckie told me that the hostesses in Picardie are the best," I replied. "She's never felt so welcome."

Madame glowed with pleasure.

When I introduced myself as the librarian, Madame Hugo explained that before the war, they could afford books, but now what little money they had went toward food and replacing destroyed items—furniture, linens, clothing. She used to read to her son at bedtime, but their books had burned along with the parquet and piano.

"Oh, Madame," I said. There was so much that I wanted to say but could not find words strong enough—in French or in English. "I'm sorry."

She gazed at her husband. "We have each other. That's more than most folks."

Like her, I believed that loving relationships were more important than material things. However, it would be terrible to lose one's house and livelihood. I could only admire Madame's stoicism and courage.

When we finished eating, she wiped the crumbs from the tablecloth onto the ground. "One of the perks of no longer having a parquet," she said dryly.

Monsieur hauled the scale from the bed of the truck and set it on a bale of hay. It was clear from the tense set of his shoulders that his war injuries pained him.

Breckie weighed the infant. "He's gained two hundred grams. Wonderful news!"

"*Dieu merci*." Madame made a sign of the cross. "When Benoit was little, we had plenty of food, but now . . . I was sure Sebastien was losing weight."

"It's normal to worry," Breckie assured her. "That's why we weigh and measure—facts reassure. Nonetheless, we'll double the family's milk rations."

Breckie asked about Monsieur's wounds. In the doorjamb of the shed, he unbuttoned his shirt. His shoulder was riddled with fierce red shrapnel scars. To give them privacy, I watched Lewis, who'd begun to teach Marcelle how to change a tire. Marcelle wielded the jack like a jump rope, light and easy. She positioned it under the frame and raised the Ford. Afterward, she wiped the sweat from her forehead and cheeks, leaving smears of grease. It could not camouflage her joy, perhaps at learning something new, perhaps at being taken seriously.

I set a few children's books and novels on a bale. Monsieur and Madame Hugo gawked at them like they were rare jewels, too beautiful to touch.

"Go ahead," I encouraged.

"I want the children to dive into books so they learn our history." Monsieur thumbed the collection of *Fables*. "I want them to learn how to read and write, and how to reason."

"I want that, too," I said. "CARD is planning to construct a library."

"Wonderful news!" Madame clapped her hands together.

"Villagers have needed to rebuild houses," Monsieur added, "so we haven't given the town hall the attention it deserves. But once our home is restored, we'll do anything we can to help."

I was heartened by the response. Books were necessities. Villagers wanted this library.

"In the meantime, there are novels in le club-house for you to borrow."

The infant began to fuss, and Madame went into the shed to change his diaper. Little Benoit held out *The Lion and the Mouse*. The fable took me back to my own childhood. When Mother had first recited it, Mabel and I settled onto her lap and fell under the spell of the talking animals. In discussing the moral, each of us had our own idea: Mabel was imbued with the importance of generosity; I the pleasure of unlikely friendships;

while Mother insisted no matter your size or station in life, you could contribute. Now, I wondered what this new generation would see in the fable. Benoit gestured for me to join him on the bale.

"Once upon a time . . ." As I turned the pages, he burrowed into my side. In all the world, is there a better feeling?

―――――

OVER TEN HOUSE CALLS, WE DISTRIBUTED POMADE FOR FLEABITES AND mustard plasters for coughs, measured children for back braces, and listened to villagers' stories. Since Marcelle had gotten the hang of driving, we dropped Lewis off at the mercantile so she could prepare tomorrow's deliveries.

After lunch, we three continued our house calls. I found myself in awe of the villagers—the way they were able to begin again and look to the positive, how they coped with heavy losses. I felt a pang of homesickness and longed to share everything I was experiencing with Mabel. In the library of my mind, I dipped my pen into the well: *Picture this village with stone manors in ruins; the glory of the old château; the Frenchwomen who manage to make a shed feel homey, with a feminine, even artistic touch of embroidery. They comment on the discomfort for your sake—there are few complaints about their own.*

We passed the pockmarked road that bordered the Red Zone, the one that led to Sidonie Devereux's knoll. Not everyone was faring well. Not everyone had family.

"Stop," I told Marcelle.

She slammed on the brakes.

A mourning period was normal, but the way Sidonie Devereux had isolated herself was not. After my father's death, my sister and I watched our mother withdraw from the church and from us. Through patience and the songs of the choir, Mabel and I had coaxed Mother back to us and to the bosom of her congregation. For Sidonie Devereux, I suspected that books might be a solace. Characters could keep her company, and when she was ready, the right book might spark conversation. But perhaps she didn't desire company. Perhaps insisting made me a busybody.

I recalled a man in our community who'd lost his wife to leukemia. He stopped his daily walk in the park, stopped reading the newspaper, stopped his visits to the barber. The wisdom was to let him be. That he would come around. Then he took his own life.

"We have one last house call," I told Marcelle.

On the way, she recounted that first Christmas of the war. Sidonie Devereux had been eight months pregnant when she learned her husband's submarine had been torpedoed, leaving no survivors. She gave birth to a healthy baby in subzero winter, but the girl got chilblains. Though Sidonie Devereux begged the priest for firewood, he refused, insisting that the lumber was for caskets. When her daughter died of pneumonia, she lay her little girl in a pine coffin and nailed it shut herself.

Marcelle pulled to a stop in front of the knoll. "Though that priest is long gone, Madame Devereux hasn't returned to Mass."

"Who can blame her?" I found myself furious on Sidonie's behalf and pounded on her rusty tin door.

Though we could hear her puttering around inside, she did not respond.

"Did you receive your husband's book?" Marcelle shouted through the door.

Sidonie Devereux opened it a crack. "Ah, the calling Cards," she said with a sneer. "Ladies of bounty come to bestow baked goods upon me."

Marcelle hid the offending foodstuff behind her back, and I felt myself flush. Sidonie Devereux had experienced a lifetime of sorrow that no amount of literature could make up for. Maybe we shouldn't be here. I looked to Breckie. *Should we leave her in peace?* She responded with a shake of the head.

"I've heard about you," Sidonie Devereux said. "And I suppose you've heard about me." She glared at Marcelle. "People are parrots— they love to repeat."

"It comes from a place of concern," I said.

She didn't open the door any wider.

"Did you receive your husband's book?" Marcelle asked again. "We repaired it as best we could."

Sidonie Devereux gestured for us to join her at her table. The cellar-like room smelled of apples. The air was damp. I could see why she pulled a gray shawl tight around her shoulders. She lit a lantern, which made me realize she'd remained in the dark gloom of the earthen dugout. On the wall, a metal crucifix hung at an angle. I wondered if she didn't have a nail to restore it, or if the crooked cross symbolized her view of religion. Beside the table was a bed, on the nightstand, only one book: her husband's. At seeing it, I felt a jolt of satisfaction. I then wondered if she had time to read, or if she was too busy with chores.

She took the pan of cider from the wood-burning stove and poured four teacups.

She sat erectly, tense, her spine two inches from the backrest. She was wan, as if she hadn't spent much time outside. When was the last time she'd eaten? I set *O Pioneers!* by Willa Cather before her, but she did not acknowledge it.

A boom from a cannon shook the cups in their saucers. Breckie, Marcelle, and I flinched; Sidonie Devereux merely took a sip.

"Aren't you scared?" I asked her.

"*Mais non,*" she replied. "Cannons only kill people who have something to live for."

Most mornings, I sprang from bed, eager to see what the day would bring, but Sidonie Devereux had lost any desire for a future. To be in the presence of such despair was frightening.

"*Mais vous avez, vous êtes . . .*" But you have, you are—this inadequate conjugation of verbs was as far as I got. And really, what could I say? Most of my knowledge of heartache came from books.

"What about those pastries?" Sidonie Devereux demanded. "We might as well eat."

Marcelle set the box of scones before her.

Sidonie Devereux took a bite. "Not bad," she said begrudgingly.

I tried to find common ground. Perhaps talk about the death of my father, but how could my loss compare to hers? Instead, I said, "You're not alone. Many of us are acquainted with tragedy. Confiding might make you feel better."

"How can you people understand what I've been through?" she demanded.

Beside me, I felt Breckie start. Even Marcelle, who always seemed to have a pithy retort, was at a loss for words. I rose to leave, but Breckie pulled me back.

Her lips twisted in a bitter smile. "I married young," she said in her velvety lilt. "Henry and I met at my debutante ball. While we waltzed, he kept stepping on the hem of my dress. That endeared him to me." She adjusted her skirt, as if she were dancing in his arms. "We wed and became true friends. We talked about everything—he was open-minded, for a man. More than anything, we yearned for a family. Years went by. When . . . it didn't happen, I felt like a failure, like something was wrong with me. After all, I was only twenty-four. I traveled from our home in Ohio to a clinic in New York. Henry was to finish a work project and join me a week later." She stared into her cider. "On the train, he was struck with appendicitis and died. I tell myself, 'If only I hadn't had trouble conceiving. If only we'd stayed home. He might still be alive.'"

"You can't blame yourself," I said.

She lifted her head, her face drawn. "Oh, but I do."

Sidonie Devereux leaned closer. "What did you do?"

"After a year of sipping tepid tea on my mother's settee, I discarded my black crepe veil and enrolled in a nursing program. In New York, I worked nights at Saint Luke's nursery ward. I tended newborns, with the eternal heartache that I did not have one of my own. But the job gave me purpose. Twenty babies to feed and change, and never enough diapers! I sneaked into the surgical supply closet to purloin cotton and gauze. At 5:00 p.m., when the head nurse went home, she switched off the radiator. The east wind, from over the river, penetrated cracks in the windows. We nurses used our sweaters to swathe the shivering newborns. At times, we worked thirty hours straight. I ordered coffee two cups at a time, drinking both to keep warm and to stay alert.

"We nurses visited tenements. Families of ten lived in two tiny rooms. I remember one mother who didn't have diapers or baby clothes. She'd wrapped her daughter in her dirty shawl. So many families suffered. I could never do enough."

Breckie's eyes met mine. That's how we felt now.

"After three years, my mother called me home." Her tone turned wooden. "She disapproved of me working, didn't think college education was good for girls. It might give 'em ideas. She introduced me to a suitor. I married Richard and got pregnant right away. We had a baby girl."

"Weren't you happy?" Sidonie Devereux asked.

"I'm afraid she died after only a few hours."

"Oh, Breckie." I took her hand in mine. She'd seemed so serene, with a voice that brimmed with light. One would never suspect that she'd been through such heartache. I felt a stirring of admiration and even love. What strength, and what generosity of spirit, to share such a painful part of her past.

"You know what it is to lose a child," Sidonie Devereux said.

"I do. It never leaves you."

"But you have your husband," she argued.

"*Oui et non*. While I grieved, he turned to other women. He and I . . . separated."

"Divorce," Marcelle gasped. In the village, it was a graver transgression than treason.

"Richard didn't love me enough to remain faithful. It was a singular kind of misery."

"At least my Gaston did not choose to leave," Sidonie Devereux murmured to herself.

"I'm here to help children," Breckie said. "After two weddings, I took a new vow, a vow to be of use. You must do the same. You have strength. You have a mind. Through our experience, we're in a position to help others."

Sidonie saw that we Cards were not saints, swooping down with novels and scones in our fleet of Fords. We were women like her, with something to give and something to lose.

"Thank you for not giving up," she told me. "And for restoring my Gaston's book."

"We could read it together."

She didn't reply. Perhaps it was one thing to recoup a keepsake, and another to examine it closely.

"Perhaps we can begin with this book about pioneers," she finally said. "Will you call on me again?"

"With pleasure."

At Headquarters, Marcelle said, "Sidonie Devereux was shut tight like a jar of jam that Lewis sells in the mercantile." She turned to Breckie. "You were the butter knife that slid under her lid to break the seal." She tucked her arm through mine. "And you were the twist."

"We managed to create an opening," I admitted, knowing full well that Sidonie Devereux could close back up, tighter than before.

————

At dinner, Cookie's roasted greens in buttery béchamel melted in our mouths. At the head table, while most of us chatted about our day, Dr. M.D. read through a list of statistics. She tapped her pencil against the side of her face, inadvertently creating a constellation of gray freckles. "In 1917, CARD distributed 1,269,000 vegetable plants and two hundred pounds of seeds," she announced.

Breckie told her that was all well and good, but she needed to stop working and eat in order to keep up her strength.

With a pink eraser, Miss Morgan tenderly removed the pencil marks. "You're my report Card."

Dr. M.D. often frowned, bogged down by statistics and all there was yet to accomplish.

Miss Morgan got her to unwind by recounting amusing tidbits that we could never quite verify.

"Did you know that our idiom 'A bad workman blames his tools' has a unique equivalent in Russian? 'A bad dancer blames his testicles.'"

We chuckled. Breckie, who spoke a smattering of Russian, had a glint in her eye, but would neither confirm nor deny. Miss Morgan's wit kept us in stitches. When the clock struck ten, she tucked Dr. M.D.'s pencil in her pocket and advised us to get some rest.

———

AT MY DESK, I STARED AT MARCELLE'S MAP, WONDERING HOW TO GET books to all those towns. I was about to turn in when Breckie entered my room. Self-conscious, I couldn't help but compare my dowdy flannel nightgown to her frilly peignoir.

"You're smarter than I." She lifted the satin lapel. "You brought the right gear. I should've been more practical."

"You're glamorous."

"Sweet girl, you know how to make me feel better. The truth is, I'm freezing my bloomers off."

I covered her shoulders with a shawl.

"Much better. Now, how about a beauty nightcap?" She brandished a jar of cold cream. "We deserve some pampering."

I rubbed a dollop into the cracked skin of my fingers and sighed at the silky feel. "Thank you for this luxury."

Like girls at a slumber party, we climbed on the bed and leaned against the headboard to settle in for a chat, our faces covered in cold cream.

"We resemble ghosts," she said, pointing to our reflection in the mirror.

Ghosts. I wondered if Breckie heard from ghosts, too. I could hear my former boss say, *Ghosts! This foolishness is what comes of reading fanciful books. You're a failure, a librarian without a library.*

I shooed away the voice like it was a wasp that could sting me.

"My, you're fidgety," Breckie remarked.

"Sometimes, in my head . . ." I didn't know if I should tell, if she could understand.

"In your head?"

"Do you ever hear voices? I mean of people who aren't here?"

Breckie tapped her temple. "I've got a whole chorus. Mama, Daddy, my brothers, even an old beau or two."

"Maybe I'm lucky. I have more of a soloist situation."

"Or maybe it's harder to drown one person out. After a while, my people start bickering with each other and leave me out of it."

I laughed.

"Who's your soloist?" Breckie asked.

"My former boss, Winnifred Smythe, an admirable woman. She created a children's section in every NYPL branch. She was the first to allow children to check out books—before, parents signed for them. She never talks down to kids."

"Meaning she has no qualms about talking down to adults."

Breckie could read between my lines—yes, Miss Smythe could be condescending. However, she'd made the profession what it is today. Criticizing her felt disloyal.

My former boss loved children. Yet when it came to books and grown-ups, either she liked or she loathed. With her, within the 375,000 square feet of the NYPL, there was no room for discussion. Her way was the only way.

In Washington State, I spoke at conferences on story hour and how to select books for children. Newspapers proclaimed, "Miss Carson is recognized as the leading children's librarian of the entire Northwest," then "Miss Carson is considered the most capable children's librarian on the Pacific Coast." After seven years, I longed to be closer to family, and ever since my father had taken me to the NYPL, I had viewed it as an ideal, as book heaven. I still recalled how protected and loved I'd felt as we visited it the way others might a museum. Working there would honor his wishes for me; it was a way to stay close to him. The step down from director of the children's section in Tacoma to assistant director seemed worth it—after all, I would be at the pinnacle of the New York book world, the home of publishers, writers, and illustrators.

Winnifred Smythe viewed me as the assistant *to* the director, assigning me tasks such as scheduling her appointments and fetching her coffee. She denied me the pleasures of the children's room, from leading story hour to creating book displays. I recalled her withering tone at the last committee meeting. *Speak up, Miss Carson. No one can hear what you're saying.* Five minutes later: *Pipe down, Miss Carson. You're so loud that construction workers on Staten Island can hear you.*

The situation never improved. I doggedly did my best, because that was who my parents raised me to be: someone who refused to give up. I began to retreat to the library of my mind.

After taking in my account, Breckie looped her arm through mine. "Sounds to me like you must figure out why you still care what that harridan thinks."

More than anything, I wanted my former boss, *the* reference in children's libraries, to acknowledge that I did good work.

"I'm on your side," Breckie said.

*I'm on your side.* How wonderful those words sounded.

As she rose to leave, she added, "A wise woman once told me that some folks who say they want the best for us are the worst for us."

# CHAPTER 6

At dawn, I awoke to something rough and sharp jabbing my ribs. In a panic, I looked around my bedroom, but I was alone. Lifting the covers, I spied Max on his side, whimpering, yet sound asleep. His paws dug into me, as if he were scared and running. I petted him softly. "Max, it's just a nightmare." Then not sure he understood English, I added, "*C'est juste un cauchemar.*" As I dressed, I reflected that every living thing here was traumatized—inhabitants, animals, trees riddled with bullet holes. They required solace and escape and tenderness.

As if afraid to let me out of his sight, Max accompanied me to the château, where the two Annes pored over documents at their desk. I announced that I would not be a secretary. The library wasn't ready, but the children were. Parents didn't have money to purchase food, let alone books. Children needed stories. Though we did not yet have a building, we had a community.

"And how can you host story hour without a library?" Dr. M.D. asked archly.

"We'll hold it in le club-house. The sooner the better."

I held my breath as the two Annes conversed in their own way. Miss Morgan raised a brow; Dr. M.D. shook her head. Miss Morgan gestured to the window. Outside, Marcelle's brothers knelt before a puddle and formed mud pies. Though village children possessed few material things, they had imaginations that needed to be nourished. Dr. M.D. capitulated with a nod.

"Well, Carson, we're convinced," Miss Morgan said.

My mind raced through the stacks. Which book? What age group?

Miss Morgan typed ten invitations in French: *Friday at two p.m. join us at HQ for story hour led by Mademoiselle Jessie Carson.* Lewis drove from home to home, hand-delivering them. Meanwhile, in my room, I practiced reciting Mark Twain in French. Beside me on the bed, Max listened to me trill the r's. He was too polite to admit that it sounded as if I was expelling phlegm.

I spent the rest of the morning before the bookshelves in le clubhouse, cataloging dozens of books brought from New York as well as those I'd selected in Paris. For now, the bilingual library would be housed here. At lunchtime, a dozen younger Cards squealed when they saw the novels. They checked out the ones in English, depleting the shelves, while the French tomes waited stoically for story hour.

Cookie approached. A bandanna covered her hair, and smears of flour dotted her cheeks. She wielded her ladle like a cudgel, striking my ledger. "Enough. Time to eat."

"But I haven't finished."

She led me to my chair.

"You signed up for two years," Miss Morgan said. "No need to accomplish everything in the first month."

As Cookie served the rutabaga soup, I asked, "What if no one attends story hour?"

"They will," she replied. "Picardie isn't like New York, with hundreds of distractions. Children will love story hour, but mothers will get more out of it."

"Really?"

"Most are on their own. Their husbands are fighting at the front or dead," Miss Morgan said. "The handful who've returned are wounded, so their wives take care of them, too. Women don't have a moment for themselves."

That I could believe.

"We'll offer them tea and cake," Cookie said. "They'll rest their feet and chat with each other, something they only do after Mass, but even then, they hurry home to fix Sunday lunch."

"Life's made of small pleasures," Breckie said. "A cup of tea, a heart-to-heart with a friend, listening to a favorite song under the light of the moon. Pleasures that folks here don't have time for. What you're doing will benefit the whole family."

The Cards had reassured me. Strange to feel fortunate in the midst of war. But in such company, I did. As Anne Shirley would say, "*Kindred spirits are not so scarce as I used to think. It's splendid to find out there are so many of them in the world.*"

After we finished our crêpes slathered with apricot jam, Max and I accompanied Lewis on home visits. She'd loaded Bessie with crates of cabbages and carrots, condensed milk and oats, as well as linens and utensils. If Lewis were the heroine of a children's book, I would have described her as a twinkling in the night sky, a star you wished to follow. Now, that light was muted.

"What is it?" I asked.

"At the mercantile, customers and I make easy small talk. Children giggle and make me feel optimistic. Deliveries are harder. They're mainly to infirm folks who can't make it to the store. You see mementos—a photo, a valentine, a locket—of loved ones who died or disappeared."

She explained that our first visit was to Madame Petit, who had two daughters, Jeanne and Suzanne. In 1915, when the enemy bombardment began, the twins were on the train, on their way home from boarding school in order to surprise their mother. Midtrip, enemy soldiers boarded the train and arrested the passengers.

Madame Petit didn't know of the girls' plan. Assuming they were safe at lycée, she evacuated to Brittany. When she learned of their fate, Madame returned immediately and found her farmhouse had been bombed, then pillaged by German soldiers. Undaunted, she petitioned the German general to free her daughters. She learned the twins had been separated.

As a prisoner of war, Jeanne was forced into two years of hard labor. When released, she refused to speak of her sentence—the conditions of the POW camp, or how her foot had been cut off. The doctoress who measured the prosthesis said that the bone had been severed, as if by saber. CARD had fitted her for a prosthetic leg, but the young woman left her home only for Mass. She rarely spoke. No one knew what had happened to her sister, Suzanne.

All they had left of her was a pink ribbon that still smelled of her jasmine perfume. Though the situations were different, I knew what it was like to have only one piece of a loved one left. I stroked my father's handkerchief in my pocket.

"One thing I've learned is that people have got to talk." Lewis swallowed. "They've been through such loss, so much that if they hold it inside, it will destroy them. They need us to listen. You probably think that's silly."

"Not at all. It's why we read—to know that others feel the same, that we're not alone. That's why I'm here. I have plans, and books and story hour are just the beginning."

At the farmhouse, a pile of rubble, really, Madame met us at the gate. Her white bun stood in stark contrast to her black dress. "It's one of Jeanne's good days," she whispered before welcoming us into her kitchen, the only room still standing.

Lewis and I joined Jeanne, seated at the butcher's block. The two were nearly the same age, but the resemblance stopped there. Jeanne's shoulders were stooped, her moss-green eyes dead.

"We sleep in here now." Madame pointed to the cots near the wood-burning stove. "It's warmer than the bedroom ever was. Should have put the beds here years ago." She poured a spot of tea and set the chipped teacups before us. "I'm just relieved we're back," she continued, stroking Max's head. Her gaze skittered to Jeanne, so frail and thin.

I drew five novels from my satchel and fanned them out before Jeanne. For half a second, I thought I saw a spark in her eyes. She touched the cover of each lightly.

"Go ahead," I encouraged.

She reached for one after the other, thumbing through each. She moved like a woman with rheumatism.

"Borrow the ones that you like," I offered. "We can bring more."

"May I borrow this novel?" Jeanne pointed to *Alice in Wonderland, Alice au pays des merveilles* in French.

"If you enjoy it, I have the sequel."

Clasping the book in her lap, Jeanne said *merci*.

Lewis brought in crates of food and asked what we could deliver next time.

"We only have two spoons," Madame said. "*Le bon Dieu* only knows what the *Boches* did with the rest. We need another, for when Suzanne returns."

At the mention of her twin's name, Jeanne gnawed on her lip.

"What is she like?" I asked.

"She had the best laugh. When you heard her, you wanted to laugh. She has the highest marks in our school. She dressed head to toe in pink. To dye her clothes, she dipped them—socks, frocks, bloomers— in beet juice." Jeanne took a hair ribbon from her pocket. "This was hers. Maman and I take it everywhere."

I showed her my handkerchief. "I do the same thing. It makes me feel as if my father and I are still connected."

"You understand."

"Little things keep great love alive," I said.

Madame Petit saw us out. "All around the village, I hear good things about you girls, and now you've made my Jeanne happy. I try my best to take her mind from what happened. I worry about her and never let her out of my sight. I'm afraid to."

She glanced at Jeanne, still taken with the books.

"Your parents must be proud," Madame continued. "I wonder if I'd have let my Jeanne travel to a war zone halfway across the world. Why on earth did you come here?" Her tone was tinged with bewilderment, as if she couldn't decide if we were courageous or crazy.

Lewis's sunny expression was now covered with clouds. "The boys I knew started enlisting in the spring of 1915. The U.S. hadn't officially entered the war, so they joined the Lafayette Flying Corps and flew in the French Air Force."

"Brave lads," Madame said.

"That was a strange time, like being at a sumptuous ball, waltzing with my favorite beaux, until one by one, they disappeared. I was left alone on the dance floor. Those men were my friends, and it didn't seem right that they were risking their lives, and I was home doing nothing. I wanted to be brave, too. My parents had forbidden me to work—my role was to marry well. I wanted that, too. But in the meantime, I had other plans."

"You should obey your parents," Madame said.

"What if they're wrong?" Lewis sputtered. "I have as much to offer as the men! I drive. I speak French. I know first aid. My parents could stop me from getting a job at home, but not here."

"Disobedient girl," said Madame with warmth in her gaze.

"I intend to do my part."

I'd viewed Lewis as always cheerful and quick with a joke. Now I saw her determination, and wondered what her decision to volunteer had cost.

"What you said about your parents . . . ," I ventured to Lewis as we motored to the next home.

Shakily, she pulled a cigarette from her case. "My father was pro-war. As the president of the Philadelphia Stock exchange, he had a recruitment table built on the floor to encourage young traders to enlist." She took a drag on her Gitane. "He never would have let me come, and would have hated me spending time with you 'new women.' But he died last year."

"I'm sorry." I clutched her hand. "I know what it is to lose a parent."

"I miss him terribly." She exhaled the smoke in a forceful stream. "Yet it's strange to realize that if he were alive, I wouldn't be here."

Death changed life. I knew that, too.

"Volunteering has been a solace," Lewis continued. "It's the most important thing I've ever done. Now I see things differently. I had a great life—family, boys, parties, girlfriends who loved fashion as much as I did. But I never had to make an effort, like a mannequin being fitted for a dress. Modistes basted the hem, pinned the bodice, exclaimed how fetching I'd be. Before, I never helped anyone, any more than buttoning a friend's dress. Some of it was my family's fault, keeping me cloistered, but most of it was my own. We have problems in Philadelphia, too. The poor, the hungry. I used to look away from such people. When I get home, I won't look away."

# CHAPTER 7

JESSIE "KIT" CARSON
BLÉRANCOURT, JANUARY 1918

oday was our first story hour. After lunch, Breckie and I pushed the tables to the side and grouped chairs for mothers accompanying their little ones. I expected the two Annes to return to the château, but they remained in le club-house. At 2:00 p.m. on the dot, the Hugo family were the first to arrive, Monsieur pushing the baby buggy, Madame holding Benoit's hand.

"Welcome, *bienvenue*," said Cookie as she served gingerbread.

We tried to get Benoit to venture to the shelf laden with illustrated books—*Heidi, Around the World in Eighty Days, The Jungle Book,* and *Black Beauty,* but he remained enveloped in his mother's skirt.

Marcelle poked her pug nose inside and was pushed through the doorjamb by her brothers. At five, eight, and twelve, the boys resembled freckle-faced nesting dolls. They elbowed their way to the book display. *I'm the biggest, I'm the littlest, Ma always lets me go first.*

"Is your mother coming?" I asked.

Marcelle snorted. "Friday is washday."

"Why didn't we think?" Miss Morgan asked with an exasperated sigh. "We should have chosen any other day."

She explained that the women were at the *lavoir,* an open-air washhouse near the stream, where they knelt to scrub their laundry before wringing it, rinsing it, wringing it again, then pinning it to the line to dry.

"It's for the best," Marcelle said. "If Ma finds out we're here . . ."

"Better read quickly," Lewis told me, only half-jokingly.

I invited the Moreau children to check out books.

Marcelle turned to her brothers. "No proof. We can't take them home. Ma'll be furious when she finds out I brought you."

The youngest pulled his thumb from his mouth. "But you got to check out a book."

"But nothing," Marcelle replied. "I'm sneaky. You can't pick your nose without Ma finding out."

"Don't matter what we do, Ma's always mad," the eldest brother said.

From across the room, I felt Dr. M.D.'s disdainful regard. *Instead of listening to children bicker, we could be finishing paperwork.*

The Moreau quartet continued their whispery summit meeting. I assumed that Marcelle was a dictator, but when three grubby hands went up, and she was outvoted, it was clear that the siblings formed a democracy. As the boys selected books and signed their names, it seemed to me that they stood a little straighter.

Twenty empty chairs. It was 2:15. Only two families in attendance. I was a letdown, a soon-to-be bookkeeper stuck in a stuffy office, balancing the CARD budget, a failure at that, too.

*Dismal,* my former boss said.

*Focus on the kids,* I told myself. *The ones who are supposed to be here are here.*

All eyes were on me. Hold out for more attendees, or begin?

"Story hour is novel." Lewis regarded me, but her words were for Dr. Murray Dike. "Give families time."

"There was short notice," Breckie added. "Folks can't drop everything."

Soon, seats were filled with Cards rooting for me.

Since there were no small chairs for children, I spread a blanket before the hearth. Sitting cross-legged, I gestured for them to join me. Marcelle and her brothers took their seats. Agog at my unladylike conduct, Benoit looked to his father, who nudged him forward. I held up *Les Aventures de Tom Sawyer* so they could see the cover. He traced his finger along *Le Mississippi.* I said the name of the river aloud, and the children giggled.

"Do you like adventure?" I asked in French. "We'll follow Tom. Are you ready? Shut your eyes."

Back home, kids closed their eyes for all of three seconds before opening them and demanding I tell the tale. But these children had lived without whimsy. They'd learned to follow orders to the letter. Under bombardments, wasted seconds could cost a life. Observing their solemn faces, eyes scrunched shut, I grasped how difficult their lives were.

"Open your eyes, children."

Humbled, I read aloud quietly. French words bumped against each other in my mouth, but the children didn't seem to mind. It gave me the confidence to read louder. Were they getting into the story? I had my answer when we arrived at the passage where Tom convinces his friend to paint the fence. Marcelle's littlest brother covered his mouth, unable to believe a boy could be so cheeky.

When I finished, the kids and Cards applauded. I set the book in my lap, my heart full. I'd succeeded in making children happy. This was what I'd wanted, why I'd come.

When the applause subsided, Benoit asked, "Why did Tom live with his aunt?"

In my years as a librarian, no one had ever raised the question.

"Maybe his house was bombed," Marcelle said matter-of-factly. "His parents probably died in the war."

———

ON SATURDAY, THE CARD CAROUSEL SLOWED. THE MERCANTILE AND clinic opened at 10:00 a.m. instead of 8:30. Breckie, Lewis, and I enjoyed a leisurely breakfast with languid refills of chicory au lait and toasted war bread slathered with honey.

Marcelle's mother entered. Her lips were a narrow line that led nowhere. Her shoulders were stooped, her hands a chapped, raw red from her work as a laundress. In the crook of her elbow were the picture books her sons had checked out.

"You!" She shook them in my face. "How dare you loan these to my children?"

Was she concerned about the stories' message? Did she consider them too fanciful?

"How can you hand out such treasures?" Madame continued.

On one thing, we could agree: Books were priceless. I noted that she didn't bring *Anne of Green Gables*. Marcelle must have hidden it well.

"And when my sons destroy them? We don't have the funds to reimburse you. What were you thinking, woman?"

"Your children enjoyed them?" I asked.

"That's neither here nor there!"

"But did they?"

"It was the first time my boys behaved themselves for more than ten minutes," Madame admitted, expression mulish.

"Is that not good?"

"I don't want my kids loafing around and daydreaming about rivers they'll never float."

"But—"

"Don't think I haven't noticed Marcelle's interest in you lot. She should be babysitting her brothers, not socializing! Life is hardship and loneliness and death. It's getting up at six in the morning, even on Sunday; calluses on your hands and hate in your heart. I don't want you teaching her that life is giggly sleepovers and short skirts. She must learn that heartache awaits. The better she's prepared, the less disappointed she'll be."

"She knows, Madame," I said gently. "More than anyone, your Marcelle knows."

I patted the chair beside me. She ignored the invitation.

"You're right," I continued. "Books are treasures; their value only rises with use. They should be cherished until their bindings break and their pages fall out, until smudges and tearstains obscure the words."

"Marcelle has her head in the clouds. It takes all my effort to keep her feet on the ground. Then you lot come along, grinning ear to ear, teaching her to drive, making her dream of the impossible. You and your big plans and impossible fairy tales. Stop feeding her fantasy. She won't have a happy ending."

"But, Madame, Marcelle is an intelligent girl. I know that compulsory education ends at fourteen, but she could go much, much further. With a few years of schooling, she could become a teacher."

"With what money? Who's going to pay for this grand scheme? What if she doesn't succeed? Who'll mend her heart?" Madame set the books on the table and stalked out.

I understood her concerns, yet I suspected that she had left something unsaid. But what?

I'd find out. For now, I had two years with bright, ambitious, hardworking Marcelle. Then and there, I swore she'd have the best possible life. I would make certain of it. But how?

———

Over lunch, Breckie and Lewis chatted with Miss Morgan about couture (Schiaparelli? Spaghetti? Confetti?), gossip gleaned from a champagne brunch at the residence of the American ambassador (I didn't know the name of the current one), taking the water at a spa in Switzerland (when I heard the cost of just one week, tea spurted from my nose). This opulence was more foreign to me than French. Feeling left out, I assembled the empty plates to return to the kitchen.

"A serving girl can do that," Breckie protested.

"I'm stretching my legs."

Pushing through the swinging door, I recognized the sound of an egg cracked against a bowl. This was my language, the language of work. I donned an apron and joined Cookie at the counter.

"What are we making?"

"Scones."

As I sifted flour, she said, "You're not like the other Cards."

My dander went up. Wasn't I good enough? "What's that supposed to mean?"

"You don't natter about thoroughbreds or couture dresses."

"Because I don't own them. But the girls don't mean anything by their reminiscing."

"I know they'd never brag," she replied. "To them, wealth is normal. It doesn't cross their minds that not everyone attends debutante balls."

"Not that they're insensitive!"

"Not at all. Sometimes they forget that not everyone has visited the Alps."

"And that the only reason some of us were able to travel to France is because of the war."

She poured the flour, baking powder, and sugar in a large bowl. I added the butter. Side by side, we rubbed the mixture with our fingertips until it resembled bread crumbs. I was grateful to contribute to the task, yes, but also to the conversation.

I scanned the scone recipe, which was for eighty servings. "So many for twenty-five Cards?"

As she rolled out the dough, Cookie explained that most Sunday afternoons, a party was held at Headquarters—two weeks ago, the doctoresses from the Scottish Women's Hospital; tomorrow, men from the 7th Infantry.

"A party with soldiers?" I picked at dried bits under my nails. I never knew what to say in social situations. Maybe that's why I read, wielding a book like a shield, a partition that protected me from my mother's matchmaking. *When are you going to get married? Howard's a good provider. Quit being so picky. You'll end up an old maid.* (*God willing*, I wanted to retort.) Still fed up from the meddling, even after all these years, I slashed through the dough with a dull knife.

"I said 'triangle,'" Cookie said. "That's a cattywampus rhombus!" As skittish as she was in the dining room of le club-house, she was a queen in her kingdom of the kitchen.

We learned that we'd once lived two blocks from each other and frequented the same food market. She'd moved into a maid's room in the mansion where she worked, but wished she had kept her independent lodging.

"A handsy boss?" I asked.

"How'd you guess?"

"You tie your apron loosely to hide your figure."

"Self-preservation. You?"

"In Pittsburgh, fresh from library school. My first boss, Philemon White III, hired young ladies. Patrons assumed the director was progressive. In truth, he desired pert underlings to grope. I glued my backside to the stacks so he couldn't pinch my bottom. When I filed a complaint, the board transferred me to a far-flung branch."

"I covered my hair with netting, not that the master of the house noticed—he slobbered at the sight of my bosom."

"They can't hurt us now."

"There are thousands like them. The only defense is savings."

Money. Money equaled freedom.

"My wages here will let me take or leave any position when I return to New York," she continued.

My brows shot up. "You're like me, drawing a salary?"

"Yes. I thought I was the only one."

We sliced through the dough with knowing smiles, knowing we were kindred spirits.

———

ON THE WAY TO SUNDAY MASS, THE COLD QUICKENED OUR STEP. CHATting in groups of three or four, twenty-five Cards scurried along the muddy road, leaping between puddles. It appeared as if we were chasing our frosty breath.

"Cacklefarts, it's freezing!" Lewis tugged her silk scarf higher onto her neck.

I shoved my hands into my pockets, wishing my wool gloves were as warm as her fur muff.

Like the town hall, the church had walls; however, most of the roof was missing. The stained-glass windows had shattered, the shards swept to the side with the broken slate shingles. Inside was colder than out.

Peering at the cloudy sky, I couldn't help but wonder when the next bombs would fall.

"We're blessed in Blérancourt," Madame Petit told me. "We have a church. Many were completely destroyed. Of course, the damn Boches burned our pews and stole the bell."

She glanced about. Her daughter stood off to the side, near the pile of rubble.

"Thank you for bringing books to Jeanne," Madame whispered. "She's limping less and less. Healing physically, but emotionally . . ."

The balding pastor bellowed, "Welcome, welcome," to signal the beginning of Mass. He'd brought in a handful of rattan chairs for frail folk. Since there weren't enough for everyone, no one sat, not even the Countess d'Evry, who was eighty if she was a day and wore two mink coats to keep warm. Casting anxious glances in her direction, the pastor rapidly recited the gospel and a brief homily. As he preached, I escaped to the library of my mind. Perched on the window seat, I reflected on my first weeks in the war zone. Already I was changed. In my career, my approach had been a cautious wait and see. But here, each shrill shell that soared then exploded made me realize that life is now or never. Instead of observing and writing reports, I'd clashed with the two Annes about the importance of the library. I was proud of myself for fighting for the villagers' right to read, but there was still much work to be done. Instinctively, I'd always felt that reading was a lifeline, but now, in this region without books, I saw anew the importance of connecting through the written word. I just needed to figure out how to reach nearby towns with story hour and books for all.

Released from Mass, many parishioners streamed outside. The smell of smoky incense brought me back. Still inside the church, Jeanne tugged on my sleeve.

"Would you have more books for me?" she asked.

I asked what she was in the mood for.

"Nothing morose. Something romantic?" She nibbled on her lip, taking the time to compose her thoughts. "Even though I'm home, I feel cut off from friends like I did as a prisoner in Germany. When I was little, I used to find pleasure, and escape, in stories."

I squeezed her hand. "Books can bring solace."

She glanced around. "I shouldn't have said anything. Maman says we're not to complain."

"Sometimes confiding is the best thing you can do."

"I want to think happy thoughts, and to be happy. I'm not sure how. If I start reading, perhaps that pleasure will return."

"I'll bring you more books."

A brawny young man approached. His hair stood straight up, reminding me of a hedgehog. His empty sleeve was sewn shut at the cuff. A soldier discharged due to injuries.

"You're the Library Card?" he asked me. "My name is Henri, I was—"

When he noticed Jeanne, he stopped short and gaped at her. She smiled shyly, bathing in the light of his tender attention.

"Apologies, Mademoiselle," he said. "I didn't mean to interrupt."

"Jeanne? Jeanne! Where are you?" Panic rose in Madame Petit's voice.

"She barely lets me out of her sight." Jeanne turned to her mother. "I'm here, *maman*. A scant meter away."

"Let's go home, where it's safe." Madame pulled her toward the door.

Jeanne glanced back. Mooning at the young man, she said, "See you next week at church."

Clearly, I wasn't the only one who'd realized that life was now or never, that saying what was on your mind was better than hiding thoughts in your heart.

"What an angel," Henri told me. "Does she enjoy reading, too?"

––––––––

THE AFTERNOON SUN TORE THROUGH THE CLOUDS. AT HEADQUARters, we soaked in the rare rays. The younger Cards passed around Lewis's last tube of lipstick. At the sight of their brick-red mouths,

Breckie and I exchanged glances. "It reminds me of my debutante days," she said with a wink. As the American army truck sped over the moat, the girls squealed and checked their reflections in the window of le club-house one last time.

Two young soldiers in khaki jumped from the cab. One cradled a gramophone to his chest. A gramophone! I couldn't have been more surprised if he carried a kangaroo. The large horn obscured his head. Lewis giggled at the sight—all we could see were his bowlegs.

"I've brought your favorite songs," the soldier told her.

"Thanks, Jimmy. We'll have a ripping time!"

A dozen soldiers climbed from the truck bed. To make room for dancing, they shoved the chairs against the wall and carried all but one of the tables into the chilly courtyard. The remaining one was soon laden with scones and a pitcher of water tinged with grenadine syrup. Lewis cranked up the gramophone, and Jimmy jokingly admonished, "Careful! It's not a Ford, it's fragile." And before you could say bonjour, the dancing had begun. Breckie and Cookie remained on the perimeter, indulgent chaperones. Not knowing what to do with myself, I served punch to the soldiers. With their wispy mustaches and pink cheeks, it seemed like they should have been attending a school dance instead of fighting this war.

"We're thrilled to have a taste of home," one told Miss Morgan, who was standing next to me. When he finished his scone, he added, "In the trenches, the grub has the tang of mud."

"Like the coffee, I suppose," she replied. "Enjoy the food, son. Cookie made it for you."

I tapped my boot to the music and eavesdropped as Lewis caught up with a trio of privates from Philadelphia. Endeavoring to be gentlemanly, they nibbled on their scones; Lewis shoved chunks into her mouth.

Jimmy held out his hand to her.

"Thought you'd never ask!" Lewis said.

They shouted over the jazz as they danced alongside other couples. The floor bore the lively steps with an occasional groan. It was like they were at a ball. The war had never happened. The only reminder was our uniforms.

As usual, I was on the periphery of the fun, though I had changed countries and continents. A gush of loneliness hit me so hard that I took a step back. I stumbled and almost dropped the pitcher. Righting myself, I sheepishly looked around to ensure no one saw me lose my composure. Outside the window, I glimpsed Marcelle. Oh, how I understood her expression of longing. I gestured for her to enter.

Upon seeing her, Cookie glided over. Lewis left the dance floor, whipped a lipstick from her jacket pocket, and traced the contour of Marcelle's mouth.

"I don't know how to dance," she admitted.

"Let's teach this girl the fox-trot," I said. The pitcher in my hand was my partner. One-two-three. One-two-three. Soon, Marcelle and Cookie moved to the dance floor to practice. Marcelle shot me an I'm-really-doing-this! grin. I continued along, in sync with my pitcher, until I heard a husky voice say, "Hello."

I turned to face the soldier. He appeared to be about my age, with dark hair that was graying at the temples. Given the number of stripes and bars on his jacket, he must have been a captain. I couldn't be certain, but I thought there was a book peeking out of his breast pocket. Perhaps it was a notepad.

"Good afternoon," I replied.

"Normally, I'd offer to fetch you some punch, but you're holding the pitcher."

His hazel eyes sparkled with wry humor. He took it from me and poured two glasses.

"To serendipitous meetings," he toasted, and we let the rims of our glasses touch.

"Wouldn't it be lovely to have a whole week of Sundays?" I asked.

"Even better, a whole month of laughing, eating sweets, reading books, and talking to a pretty girl."

"Well, I talk to pretty girls every day." I gestured to the Cards.

"Lucky you!"

He told me his name was Tom. I introduced myself as Kit.

He regarded me quizzically. "As in a first-aid kit?"

"I do bandage books."

"Books?"

"I'm a librarian."

"Reading's my favorite pastime," he said.

"What's your favorite book?"

"These days, anything I can get my hands on. In the hangar, we've only got three, and I've read them a dozen times." He drew *The Road* by Jack London from his pocket.

"I'd be happy to loan you some."

His face lit up. "Really?"

"Of course. I have a whole shelf."

He frowned. "Maybe it's not a good idea. I'm not sure if . . . when . . . I could return them."

Though we did our best not to think about it, we were surrounded by carnage. War was everywhere—on my desk, where a small brass shell held my fountain pen; at the hearth, where we used a rusty bayonet as a poker.

"I'd be proud to *give* you some books."

"*A* book. I wouldn't want to overstep."

"How to choose just one?"

"I don't envy you your task," he teased.

In my room, I perused my personal stash and fell upon the perfect choice. On the way out, I paused in front of the mirror. My eyes shone like Lewis's. For once, I was enjoying a party. I found it easy to talk to Tom. Perhaps because I was a librarian just doing her job, perhaps because he was a good listener. Back in le club-house, I held out *The Count of Monte Cristo* and surprised myself telling Tom, "I hope that you'll think of me when you read it."

"I'll think of you even when I'm not reading it. Would you care to dance?"

"Oh." I felt myself flush.

"Oh?" He seemed to hold his breath.

"Yes."

We joined the others on the dance floor. His hand felt lovely on my waist. I forgot everyone else in the room. I forgot myself. Waltzing with him was like floating in the clouds.

Though the silence between us felt good to me, I knew silence made some people uncomfortable. I racked my brain. "Lovely music" was the best I could come up with.

"Lovelier still when you have someone to share it with." He gazed at me.

It had been ages since a man admired me. The heat in his eyes was too much. "What were you . . . before?" I prevaricated.

"A mechanic. Growing up on the farm, machinery was always breaking down, so I learned to fix it. Pa didn't have the patience to tinker. If something didn't work, he'd take a hammer to it."

"No!"

Tom laughed. "He's one impatient cuss. Now, I overhaul planes. An engine's an engine, I've learned."

We swayed until the songs blended together, we swayed even when the music stopped while Lewis cranked the handle of the gramophone, we swayed to the next record and the next.

"I hate to cut in," Jimmy said, "but it's time to go. The general will be hopping mad if we're late."

"May I call on you again?" Tom asked me. "I'd like to finish our dance."

I nodded, and he gave me a soft peck on the cheek.

Wishing his lips could linger, I told him, "In France, it's two."

"*Vive la France!*"

He kissed my cheek slowly, his skin caressing mine as he moved from one to the other. We stood inches apart. I looked at his chest, his Adam's apple, his lips. There was so much I longed to say. *It would be wonderful to see you again. Soon.*

Tom patted *The Count* in his breast pocket. "I'll share my book review with you."

We Cards escorted the men to the army truck. The two Annes

bid the officers farewell. A gaunt colonel shook Miss Morgan's hand. "Thank you for your hospitality, ma'am. It makes all the difference to my men."

"What can you tell us about the situation?" she asked, not releasing his hand until she got her briefing.

"This past week, the Germans have used the cover of fog to move men and armaments. It might mean nothing—"

"Or it might mean another offensive," Miss Morgan finished.

Were the soldiers in danger? Were we? I noticed wisps of dark smoke in the sky. A faint buzzing sound grew louder, until I began to shake. Shouldn't we be seeking shelter? I looked to Lewis and Breckie to see if they felt the same fear I did.

"A plane," Breckie said. "There was just a dogfight."

She explained that an Allied pilot and a German pilot had taken to the sky to fight to the death. The sound we heard was the plane of the victor returning to base. We were too far away to see the colors, to know which side had won.

"Jimmy's a pilot," Lewis said. "I hate to think of him up there. I hate to think of any of them up there."

"At least he's safe," I replied.

"For now." She took a drag on her cigarette. "We're safe for now. But who knows what tomorrow will bring?"

# CHAPTER 8

WENDY PETERSON
NEW YORK, JANUARY 1987

When my alarm clock goes off, I smack the buzzer like a seasoned *Jeopardy!* champ and jump out of bed. Roberto is the main reason I've become a morning person, even when I read long into the night. The Cards are better than any book. *Under Two Flags* brings history to life. It was sheer decadence to read the bulletins as I lolled in bed. I shower and slip on a pair of jeans and a T-shirt, then tuck the yellowed pages into my backpack. I shouldn't have sneaked them out of the NYPL.

**WHAT IS TO BECOME OF FRENCH CIVILIANS?**

With the retreat of the Germans, under whose do-
minion these French people have suffered since
1914, they are free but destitute. Their factories
have been demolished. They cannot make clothes,
for they cannot manufacture their material. Every
ounce of metal has been carried off, and they have
no implements of trade, nor of agriculture.

Schools have been wrecked and books destroyed,
so children can have no education. There are
thousands of women and children, but only a few
men. The Committee is trying to save these people
from disease (for pneumonia, typhoid, and dysentery are rampant) and from starvation, for food
is difficult to get.

> Will dehydrating kitchens send some of their
> vegetables? Will groups buy rice or grain? Will
> individuals send blankets? Don't dawdle, winter
> is coming.

Now, in the murky cavern of the subway, amidst the unnatural quiet of commuters, doubt about my future creeps in. I ruminate on last night's class with Professor Hill and can't help but wonder when my literary career will take off. If I can't pen a decent short story, how can I complete a whole manuscript? And if I can't publish a book, what am I even doing with my life? I moved to New York to make it, but I barely make rent. On any given day in the fluorescent bunker of Remembrance, I'm surrounded by coworkers—dancers, actors, musicians—who eventually progress to gigs in their fields. When will I move on? I'm working on this master's degree in creative writing, but maybe Dad's right, I should move back to Saskatchewan and become a vet tech. I love animals, but the thought depresses me. In my small town, no one believes I can become an author. In that world of welders and waitresses, of bankers and teachers, it's impossible to understand something intangible like writing. The consensus: *Not for people like us.* I've stopped talking about my dreams, except with Roberto.

On the hard plastic seat, I clutch the backpack. "Almost there," I whisper to the women of CARD tucked inside. "I bet most of you have never taken the subway."

The rich—even long dead—leave behind traces of their lives. Portraits of their forefathers hang in museums. Photographers document marriages and other mergers. In newspapers and magazines, articles about these prominent citizens abound. Bulletins about good deeds and derring-do. Historical societies and libraries preserve diaries, memoirs, and letters of the wealthy and powerful. In the New York Public Library, clues about their inner lives are laid to rest in tidy, acid-free boxes, and are measured in linear feet. The Milton family have fifty, the Hawthornes twenty.

The poor fade into obscurity without a trace. I am no Rockefeller, no Vanderbilt. When I die, no future biographer will care what years I lived in New York. I'll be gone forever. That said, I'm grateful for CARD vestiges.

When I arrive at work, coworkers are bent over viewfinders, so it's the perfect occasion to sneak the "borrowed" bulletins into the archive box. I reach into my backpack, but just then, Walkman on, Roberto bobs into Remembrance on a Bowie high. His eyes skim over the rows of coworkers until they land on mine. I love that he seeks me out. Sometimes I sense that he likes me back. But maybe it's yet another thing I've got wrong.

At his desk, he pours us each a cup of café au lait from his thermos. The first time he shared with me, he joked it was "café olé," raising his arm above his head and snapping his fingers. Now, at my workstation, he regards me with concern. I could get lost in his eyes. He's so close, I can smell the bergamot and citrus of his soap. I want to rest my head on his chest. To distract myself from the doubts about my future, I take a sip.

"What is it?" he asks.

"Thoughts."

"Dark thoughts?"

He'll pester me until I tell. Might as well save us an hour. "My writing. Well, my workshop."

Roberto calls my class "the installment plan," since I've recounted every episode from the first week, when students—chosen ones, we believed, since we'd had to submit writing samples to be granted one of twelve coveted spots—postured about where we'd publish our stories. We quickly learned that our instructor was at once the five-star general of our writing battalion and an enemy who launched grenades in our direction.

"Professor Hill hated my story," I admit.

"His job is to help you improve your writing. It shouldn't matter if he liked it or not."

"It matters."

"Does he like anyone's stories?"

Now that I think about it . . . "Not really."

"I bet that shriveled crouton has a curated list of digs that he trots out each term. The students change but his criticism stay the same: 'Contrived,' 'The main character is never in any peril,' 'This is just notes.'"

*This is just notes.* I cock my head. How does he know what Hill said?

"Could he be so obsessed with his own experience that he isn't able to help his students?" Roberto continues.

"Doubtful. Everyone says he is brilliant."

"You can't care too much about one person's opinion. There are millions of readers."

"You weren't there."

"I didn't have to be. I know you. You're talented. Tenacious."

The heat of his gaze warms me. I want to believe him. I want him.

"Why not write about Jessie Carson?" he continues. "There's a story there. I can tell that you're into it."

"I don't know enough about her. I'm not sure I can even find her." I trace the block lettering on the side of the CARD archive box.

He snatches the box. "Maybe I should give this to Ted."

I hug it to my chest. "The Aardvark doesn't deserve it."

"That's the spirit!" He returns to his desk.

As usual, five minutes with Roberto has buoyed me. Is he encouraging me because he's nice, or because he believes in me?

I dig into the box and put a fresh bulletin on my desk. Noting the headline CARD RECEIVES FRENCH HONORS, I can't help but read on.

France recognizes Committee volunteers for their work in the war zone. The Académie d'Agriculture honored CARD for their successful efforts in raising wheat, thus helping farmers to become self-supporting. Miss Anne Morgan and Dr. Anne Murray Dike received the cross of the Légion d'honneur. Eighteen Cards were decorated with the

Croix de Guerre, the War Cross medal, for services rendered under fire. The Silver Medal was
awarded to Mrs. Mary Breckinridge and Miss Jessie
Carson, the former treated patients, the latter
treated children to books in 160 villages via
monthly bookmobile visits.

There she is again, my NYPL librarian. At noon in the staffroom, I poll a dozen coworkers to ascertain if they've heard of CARD or Jessie Carson. None have, not even the Archivist. I feel like a reporter with a scoop. Roberto is right, I must follow this lead. Surely, Jessie Carson is in the NYPL archives. Perhaps a staff photo or candid of her leading story hour?

After lunch, I follow the Archivist up the marble staircase to the institutional records, where she and I browse through dog-eared catalogs with key words such as Jessie Carson and Librarian for the years 1914–1917. An hour later, we haven't even found her personnel file.

"What does it mean?" I ask. "She was employed here before the war, and probably after."

"Are you sure she came back?"

It didn't occur to me that Jessie Carson didn't make it. *Pneumonia, typhoid, and dysentery are rampant.* Maybe that's why no one's heard of her. "I'm not sure of anything. She worked in the war zone."

The Archivist nods. "It didn't have to be a bullet that killed her. She could have died from Spanish flu."

"The flu?"

I must have sounded skeptical, because she replies, "Believe it or not, the symptoms of the Spanish flu were as bewildering as AIDS is now."

I return to Remembrance empty-handed.

"You're late," Roberto scolds. "Where were you?"

"Between the pages." That's what we call the reading room and archives. "I bet you just got back from lunch, too." I allow myself the luxury of touching a tuft of his black hair. It's still chilled, which means he just walked in. His hair is surprisingly silky, and I want to run my fingers through it, to bring his face closer to mine.

I'm aware of the Aardvark staring at us. My hand drops to my side.

"Get a room," Ted jokes mirthlessly.

"Get a life," I respond.

"Get to work," Ted says. "I'm tired of picking up your slack."

Roberto ushers me into the hall, out of the Aardvark's earshot. "Why didn't you ask me for help? I'm a cross between a librarian and a bloodhound, between Sherlock Holmes and Paul Newman. I'll help find your elusive librarian."

"You will?"

"Of course."

The truth is, he knows the NYPL like no one else.

"Once the stars align, and Venus is in Aries. It's the best time. The only time."

I give him a playful shove. "Will you be serious?"

"Fine. Are there other names associated with Jessie Carson?"

He explains that a person can be located through family members, classmates, or coworkers. I don't know the names of her NYPL colleagues, or if she married or had kids.

"Pay attention to names next to hers. They're clues."

I give a snappy salute and a sir-yes-sir, and return to my desk with a grin and his suggestion to parse the deck of Cards. As I document, I note a recurring name: Anne Morgan. Sometimes CARD is referred to as "Miss Morgan's Brigade." Could she be the daughter or wayward niece of the financier J. P. Morgan? I work late, until the closing bell rings, until Remembrance empties out so I can sneak the bulletins into the archive box. Though I didn't find a mention of Jessie Carson in the pile, I like to think that the Cards were delighted to take leave of the NYPL and revisit Manhattan. Still, I shouldn't have taken the risk. The documents are priceless, and I know it. I look around. The coast is clear, so I lean down and grab them.

"What are you doing, skulking about?" I hear Roberto ask from the doorjamb.

He probably returned for his Walkman.

"I-I—" I freeze with the bulletins halfway out of my backpack.

"It's a rhetorical question." His voice is hard. "The NYPL deals with theft constantly. How could you steal documents?"

"I'm putting them back," I protest.

"You're lucky I'm not the boss. I'd fire you."

I've never seen this side of him, never seen him angry. I expect him to break into a grin, to say he's just teasing, that he trusts me. He crosses his arms.

"Oh come on," I cajole. "You know me."

"I thought I did."

"You know I'd never do anything to hurt the library."

"What about the women of CARD? Those bulletins might be all we—'we' as in society—have left to document the work they accomplished. Forty. Miles. From. The. Front. You taking them out of the NYPL is not just stealing from future generations, but also risking that their story is lost forever."

I can't believe how stodgy he is all of a sudden. "Since when do you care about the rules?"

"I care about this library and its priceless collection. Your backpack could have been stolen in the subway. The pipes could have burst in your apartment, flooding your belongings."

"Those things wouldn't have happened."

He shakes his head as if he can't believe what an idiot I am. He looks at me like I'm a stranger. A traitor. We've gone from flirty banter to testy silence. And it's my fault.

"Look, can we talk about this?" I ask.

"I've said all I want to say." He grabs his Walkman from his desk and stalks down the hall.

He's right. Too ashamed to try to stop him, I linger until he's long gone.

On the avenue, I can't focus and bump into people left and right. I barely notice the dog walker and the Doberman until it bares its teeth. The walker yanks the leash, and they continue on. What was I thinking? I've ruined everything between Roberto and me. He's right—the documents could have been lost forever. Already, I worry that this is Jessie Carson's fate.

*Are you sure she came back?* the Archivist asked.

She worked in a war zone. I'm not sure of anything.

*How could you?* Roberto asked.

Disappointed in myself, I wander aimlessly, until my stomach growls, until the streets clear of tourists, until I find myself before a pair of stone lionesses. They guard a building whose walls appear impenetrable. The glistening street lights make the gray marble glow like the moon. The Morgan Library & Museum. Morgan. Could there be information about Anne Morgan here? Could she be the key to finding Jessie Carson?

# CHAPTER 9

**D**ear Mabel and Mother,
  *I pray that you're both well. Thank you for your letters. I miss you so. I do wish you wouldn't fret. The situation in the war zone remains stable. In fact, we held our first story hour, and each session, more children attend. Now I believe I've found a way to take stories on the road.*

*Cards work ten-hour days, yet it feels like we're not doing enough. I'm anticipating a visit from the region's most in-demand VIP—the master carpenter. (Since many men have been killed or are still at the front, retired craftsmen lend a hand.) I ordered building supplies, but don't know when—or if—they'll arrive. Every town in the North needs, well, everything.*

*Yes, I've heard from my former boss. I shove her letters in the bottom drawer. No response will satisfy her, so I don't reply. Any day now, I expect a telegram demanding why I haven't deigned to respond.*

*Love,*
*Kit*

*Dear Jessie,*
*We are very proud of you here in Allegheny. As I tell my prayer group, you arrived at the same place as the finest society matrons, only these ladies paid their way, while you're paid for your expertise.*

*I am gratified to hear that CARD hosts soldiers on Sunday. This is the good, Christian thing to do. Plus, the right man may be stationed nearby. Remember that having a career doesn't mean you can't have a husband. It's never too late.*

*I pray that you're getting enough sleep. Be sensible and don't read all night like you do at home. And don't skimp on breakfast. Keep up your strength. After story hour, drink tea with honey to soothe your throat.*

*Your loving mother*


DEAR KIT,

*I carry your letter and the memory of our conversation. I inhaled* The Count of Monte Cristo *in three nights. In the light of the lantern, I pretended I was camping, and read a few lines, then contemplated the stars. As much as I loved the novel, I want to return it to have the chance to see you again.*

*Yesterday, Jimmy—remember him, the fellow from Philly?—went up in a plane. I'm never so nervous as when watching one of our pilots take off. Recon can always turn into a dogfight. He flew low at first, then rose in altitude. Out of nowhere came a German Albatros, the same model that the Red Baron flies, guns blazing. Jimmy's plane went tail up. Five of us mechanics watched him fall to earth in what seemed like slow motion, yet it went by in an instant.*

*We jumped in a rig to get closer to him, and closer to the enemy territory than any of us wished to be. Fortunately, he was able to land in a field. Thank God for his hours of experience. When we hauled him out of the cockpit, he was trembling, but all bravado, half joking that he begged Millie, the Patron Saint of Extra Chances, for more time. But he was serious, too. We do pray—for time with loved ones, for mercy, for guidance, for courage, for the war to end. Thinking of you gets me through.*

*I wonder how you are, which books you're reading, what you're doing with the little spare time you have.*

*Warmly,*
*Tom*


~~MY DEAR TOM,~~
DEAR TOM,

*I think of you often and pray that you're safe. With last week's bombardments, I feel afraid. The screech of shells still rings in my ears. We Cards*

*huddled in the Moreaus' makeshift home—a quarry—to sweat it out. How*
*to write reassuring letters home? What to say, what to leave out? In her lat-*
*est missive, my mother chastised me for staying up to read. If she only knew.*

*Do you think about home, or does the present absorb your thoughts?*
*I worry for you, and crave our next conversation. Until then, I'm sending*
*along* Thirty-Nine Steps, *featuring spies, a faked suicide, and an impostor.*
*Lewis and her friends—the* Wild Cards—*call it a "shocker." My former*
*boss wouldn't approve, but it distracts from homesickness, mud, rain, and*
*the pounding of gunfire. I hope you'll enjoy it.*

*In haste, because I'm about to propose a "novel" idea to Miss Morgan*
*and Dr. M.D. Wish me luck!*

~~*Your friend,*~~
*Yours,*
*Kit*

UPON ENTERING THE CHÂTEAU, I STEELED MYSELF—SHOULDERS
straight, chin raised—and greeted the two Annes, who were seated at
Miss Morgan's desk. I touted the idea of a rolling story hour to nearby
villages.

"How will this . . . roving story hour work?" Miss Morgan asked.

I proposed that we'd create a weekly schedule so mothers knew
what time and where to bring the children. The town crier would get
the word out about story hour. Lewis or Marcelle would not only drive
me from village to village but also fetch children from farms.

Dr. M.D. tilted her head. In her calculating eyes, I could see her
gauging the cost—from the price of petrol to the hours Lewis would
be away from the mercantile. "I suppose we could try it on a temporary
basis," she declared.

Victory swelled in my chest.

She waved me over, and the three of us peered at a military dia-
gram, the only map of the area to be had. As we waged our literacy
campaign, I tried not to dwell on the zigzag of Allied and German
trenches.

The following day, Marcelle crank-crank-cranked Bessie, and she,

Lewis, and I bounced our way to the first stop, in a nearby village. Upon our arrival, a dozen mothers and children greeted us at the one-room schoolhouse, whose windows had been blown out.

"The children will get plenty of fresh air," I said. "Plus, it's sunny. If we stay bundled up, we'll be warm enough."

"You're learning to look on the bright side," Lewis replied.

"You talk funny," a boy told us.

"Mathieu!" his mother said. "That's not kind." She turned to me. "Please forgive him. In these parts, we don't get many foreign ladies."

None of us acknowledged the fact that the German soldiers had occupied the territory. She wore mourning. I wanted to tell her that I was sorry for her loss, but before I could, she said, "We're glad you're here."

"I sound different because I come from another country," I explained to him.

"From Paris?" he asked.

"Farther away," I replied. "Across the ocean."

His mouth formed a little O.

Inside, Marcelle spread a worn quilt on the floor before the window. What could beat the combination of sunbeams and imagination? Not only that, a picturesque stream flowed past. Gathering the children, I began *Tom Sawyer,* and was just getting to the good part when I glanced outside and saw something shiny bobbing in the stream. A metal plate from a mess kit? No, it was a helmet—with a floating head attached. I froze momentarily, and wondered what to do. At the back of the room, Lewis sensed my distress.

She and I shifted to the window to block the view. "It's only a dead Boche," she whispered in English. She was used to seeing death up close. This was my first time, and I felt unsettled.

"Read!" she ordered between clenched teeth.

The villagers were counting on me, so I returned to Tom and Becky.

When I finished, the children clapped. Marcelle proffered a tin of cookies and little hands reached in.

The elderly mayor approached. "Apologies," he whispered. "We do tend to see more body parts than one would like. Makeshift graves are shallow. When flooding occurs, the rain washes away the soil and, alas, the cadavers."

I glanced at the children, who were enjoying a bite with Marcelle. "Luckily, no harm done," I replied.

In the Ford on the way to our next story hour, Lewis proclaimed, "What a popjoying time!"

"Lesson learned," Marcelle added. "Don't seat kids by the window."

Honestly, that girl never missed a trick.

———

IN THE STATES, MY FOCUS HAD ALWAYS BEEN IN THE CHILDREN'S SEC-tion, but here in France, I found pleasure in recommending books for adults. Now, I was adamant about finding the perfect novel for Sidonie Devereux. I selected *Howards End,* in which a stolen inheritance is re-turned to its rightful owner. How reassuring to believe that everything works out, in fiction if not in real life. In the library of my mind, the novel was on my "keeper" shelf. E. M. Forster had written, "Only con-nect!," which was why Max and I braved the encroaching Red Zone to rap on a rusty door.

Sidonie Devereux took her time in answering.

"Do you think she changed her mind?" I asked Max.

He responded with a friendly yip. "I'll take that as a no."

When the door swung open, Max licked her hand in greeting.

"I wasn't sure you'd come," she said. "Wasn't sure I wanted you to. No offense."

"None taken," I lied. "How about a short stroll?"

"I think better when I walk," she admitted.

We set off, Max bounding at our feet.

"He's happy we're not stuck inside," she commented.

On the dirt road, I spoke of books. *J'aime* Emma. Of New York. *C'est magnifique.* Of Blérancourt. *C'est petit.* With the Cards, I often found myself observing conversations, but with Sidonie, I was a par-ticipant.

"Your French is quite good," she said.

I felt myself blush. I was surrounded by heiresses who had private tutors and who flitted to France for couture fittings. I'd done my best in school, and it seemed that effort had paid off.

"You simply lack confidence," she added.

"Confidence is the most difficult element to master."

"Indeed. But as we say in French—attitude is everything."

We circled back to her sod house. I was about to bid her farewell when she said, "The other day, you didn't say much. I'm sure you have your own story of loss."

"Talking helps some people, but I find comfort in listening."

She nodded. "A woman after my own heart, one who understands that silence can express more than words."

"Marcelle mentioned that you and your husband once had a whole wall of books."

Sidonie pointed to her temple. "Luckily, the stories remain."

I took *Howards End* from my satchel and handed it to her. "'One may as well begin with Helen's letter to her sister,'" she read aloud. "Why did you choose it for me?"

"The book is a promise that life works out in the end."

"Thank you." She held the book to her breast. "In your uniforms, you all look the same. Still, I'm embarrassed to admit that I don't remember your name."

"Kit." I loved my CARD nickname.

"No Madame or Mademoiselle? No surname?"

"Just Kit."

"Are Americans an informal people?" she asked.

"We Cards are."

"Since we'll see each other often, you might as well call me Sidonie."

———

In the early morning, the crash of bombs continued. Spooked, Max nudged my hand with his nose as if asking for reassurance. *With the damn Boches, who needs an alarm clock?* I grumbled to myself. The girls were right—the sound of shelling had become as commonplace as the chugging of Lewis's Ford. To prepare for the day's deliveries, Marcelle, Breckie, and I loaded supplies—medications, condensed milk, sacks of flour, a secondhand table, rewired chicken coops—into the bed of the truck. The unpaved road was full of ruts, and Marcelle frowned in concentration. A pile of books bounced on my lap. We'd sneaked in story time during home visits, so parents could witness first-hand the children's pleasure. Now, I was pleased to see families attend our rolling story hour.

As we three motored along to the town of Ham, folks stopped what they were doing—old men clearing explosives from fields, women scrubbing laundry at the *lavoir*—to gape.

"The people of Picardie like us, I think," Breckie said, "but oh, how we do puzzle them! Whenever we whiz past, I'm sure they think, What are those Wild Cards up to now?"

In the new CARD community barrack, we set up Breckie's scale so she could weigh children and advise mothers. Near the hearth, Marcelle lay a cozy blanket on the floor.

"Why don't you lead story hour today?" I handed her *Around the World in Eighty Days*.

For once, she was speechless.

"You think I'm ready?"

I took such pleasure in seeing her grin. "I know you are."

She swung me around. "Merciiiii, Kit!"

As she acted out Phileas Fogg, the children leaned forward—mouths forming little O's. To rival the roar of the bombs, she read louder and louder. When she closed the book, the children cried, "Encore! More!"

She looked to me, and I nodded. She continued.

In four more villages, folks surrounded our Ford as soon as we arrived. They greeted Breckie by name, and I could see firsthand the way these visits created trust and community ties. Marcelle led story hour. I loved getting to know people and hearing their stories. In Vic, our last stop, Henri, the former soldier, approached me, his brow furrowed in concern.

"Do you have any news of Jeanne, er, Mademoiselle Petit? I attempted to speak with her after Mass, but her mother whisked her away."

I nodded in sympathy. "Madame Petit is very protective."

"Could you tell Mademoiselle that I asked after her?"

"Of course."

"Do you think she likes poetry? Would it be too much to ask you to deliver this collection of sonnets?"

"My pleasure." I pretended not to see the valentine sticking out of the pages.

With a nod of thanks, he turned on his heel and whistled a chipper French tune. With the delivery, I decided to include *A Room with a View*. Jeanne would surely relate. Like Lucy, its main character, she had a strict chaperone. And I had a feeling that Jeanne, like Lucy, would find love.

I hoped that literature could bring Jeanne and Henri closer, that it could bring Sidonie out of her knoll, that it could be a haven for the children at rolling story hour, that it could give poise and confidence to Marcelle. After all they'd suffered, they deserved happiness and heady stories of their own—in books and in life.

On the journey to HQ, Marcelle kept one hand on the wheel, the other on her throat. "This has been the best day of my life," she rasped, her voice but a whisper. "At night when I read to my brothers, I put them to sleep, but here . . . I felt like an opera singer belting out beauty."

"You were a natural," I told her.

"I prepared kvass to soothe that tired throat of yours," Breckie told Marcelle.

"Kvass?" I repeated.

"A delightful drink. I learned to make it when my family lived in Russia, some twenty years ago now, when Daddy was a diplomat."

Marcelle and I exchanged astonished glances. "Good Lord, Breckie!" I said.

"Sake's alive," she replied. "It's not like I said *I* was the ambassador."

In the kitchen, Breckie poured us each a glass. "Tell me what you think."

The cloudy beverage tasted like day-old bread.

"It's, er, refreshing," Marcelle squeaked out.

To be polite, I downed the rest. "Very . . . interesting."

"It was served to the children who attended the coronation of Czar Nicholas II. My, that was a blustery day."

With Breckie, one never knew where a conversation might go—from theories on helping lactating mothers produce more milk to her teen years at a Swiss boarding school to a celebration with the Romanovs. A reminder that these women of means could be anywhere—Martha's Vineyard, Lake Como, Nice—yet they chose to be here in the war zone.

"How's the library renovation coming along?" Breckie asked.

I explained that Monsieur Hugo worked long days on his farm, then helped at the library. Each week, the shadows under his eyes seemed to take over more of his face. There were times I had to tell him to go home.

"Let's see if he's there now," Breckie said.

"I don't wish to impose," I said.

"How is an interest an imposition?" Marcelle rasped.

"We'll take him some kvass," Breckie said.

"Lucky him!" I winked at Marcelle.

We crossed over the moat and continued to the town hall. Monsieur Hugo and another man—surely the master carpenter!—perched on rickety ladders, examining the roof. I prayed repairs would be possible but feared the wood frame that supported the slate shingles would have to be replaced.

Clearly, his injured shoulder and leg hadn't slowed Monsieur down. He'd wedged a clipboard between his forearm and chest, possibly taking notes on supplies that needed to be ordered as the carpenter pointed to a gable.

"Bonjour," Breckie chirped.

The pair were so engrossed in their task that they didn't hear.

"Monsieur, it makes me nervous to see you up there," I shouted.

He grinned. "Then don't look!"

I supposed that after facing enemy fire at the front, carpentry felt relatively safe.

The men climbed down. "What's the verdict?" I asked.

Monsieur Hugo's regard held such concern. My fingers held tight to my handkerchief.

"The roof must be replaced." He spoke gravely, as if announcing the death of a loved one.

I'd held out hope that the damage could be repaired, using the word "renovation" as if a coat of paint would suffice. This was construction. It would be ages before we could open. I was a librarian without a library.

I reminded myself that a building is not a community. It is a body, not a soul. These past weeks, we'd conducted story hours and taken books along on home visits, sneaking in stories the way Mother dripped castor oil into milkshakes. I'd begun the rolling library to take books on the road. We would rebuild, and in the meantime, I would teach everything I could to Marcelle and find other ways to create community around books.

In the distance, bombs exploded, and the ground beneath our feet shuddered. I wondered if our efforts were for naught. I asked Breckie if it was foolish to rebuild before the end of the war.

"Ah, Kit," she replied, "we must live in the now. We don't know what tomorrow holds. What if we delayed until everything was perfect and right? Who would ever plan a trip or have children? Who would ever take a chance?"

Breckie was right. We must live in the now.

———

THAT EVENING, MARCELLE SQUEEZED NEXT TO ME AT THE HEAD TABLE. The two Annes had invited the village pastor, who said grace over steaming bowls of pumpkin soup and war bread made of cornstalks. Cookie served canned prunes for dessert. Dr. M.D. sighed and told the pastor that she craved a sweet, tart orange.

"You said *un orange,* but you meant *une orange,*" Marcelle said matter-of-factly. "The former refers to the color, the latter to the fruit."

Dr. M.D.'s head shot back as if Marcelle had called her an ignoramus. Awkward silence filled the room. I had been here less than two months, and even I knew never to correct our *présidente.* When she liked you, you could do no wrong. If she didn't like you, nothing you did was ever right. She and my former boss were similar in that way.

Hastily changing the subject, Lewis bragged, "Marcelle can repair a punctured tire, squeeze beneath the Ford to scrape the mud from the undercarriage, and has even mastered automotive vocabulary. Positively smashing!"

"Spark plug," Marcelle said in English to prove Lewis's point. "I cleaned them myself."

"Bravo!" I said.

"Well done," Miss Morgan seconded.

At the praise, Marcelle grinned bashfully.

"It's hardly brain surgery," Dr. M.D. muttered.

"Now, now." Miss Morgan frowned. "She's a young girl, not a med student."

"She's uppity."

"Without uppity women, nothing would get done," Miss Morgan replied.

Dr. M.D. glowered at Marcelle, who gobbled her prunes, completely unfazed by the death stare. That seemed to vex Dr. M.D. even more. I suppressed a chuckle. Marcelle had surely become inured to scowls from everyone from the schoolmaster to her mother.

"Don't tell me you're in a huff because Marcelle corrected you?" Miss Morgan asked.

"How galling that a girl should correct her elders!"

"Indeed, it is Gaul-ing." Miss Morgan said with a sly smile before spelling out the name for France during Roman times.

Dr. M.D. slapped her arm playfully. "You know how to put things in perspective."

After we finished dessert, I discreetly asked Miss Morgan if Marcelle could become a Card.

"She already spends her spare time with us," she replied. "I'll order her uniform in Paris."

Madame Moreau entered, brandishing a broom fashioned from branches. I dreaded another confrontation. She came to a stop before Marcelle. "There you are!"

"Sorry, Ma. I lost track of time."

"I could hear you chin-wagging from the other side of the moat. Loafing when there's tidying to be done! You're too young to be out at night."

Marcelle's chin jutted out. "It's only eight."

Madame shook the broom at her daughter. "Don't think I haven't heard about you gadding about in that Ford. You shouldn't be driving. Perhaps when you're older—"

"You said yourself that the war has aged us ten years," Marcelle said pertly. "Which makes me twenty-five."

I needn't have worried. Marcelle handled herself well.

"Your daughter is clever," I told Madame Moreau. "You must be so proud."

"I suppose."

"Driving is an important skill," Lewis said.

"How reassuring that if one of your sons got injured, she could drive him to the hospital," Miss Morgan said. "And the knowledge she learns can be shared."

"That may be so," Madame replied, "but with the torn-up roads, motoring is dangerous." She turned to me. "Marcelle listens to you more than she listens to her own mother. All I hear is, 'According to Kit this,' and 'Kit believes that.'"

"Can I stay for another hour?" Marcelle pleaded.

"Fine!"

I escorted Madame to the door. "I won't let anything happen to your daughter."

"Don't you see? It's already happening. At some point, you ladies will leave. And I'll have to pick up the shards of her shattered heart."

This time, I understood. Marcelle had suffered the loss of her father and home. Madame Moreau hoped to spare her more sorrow.

We lingered in the doorjamb.

"No matter when the Cards return to the States, I'll remain in touch with Marcelle. Can you trust me?" I knew I was asking a lot, and wished she understood how committed we were.

"I suppose."

"What would you say to Marcelle becoming a Card?" I whispered.

As Madame observed Marcelle, her gaze softened. "Do you want to join this lot?" she called out to her daughter.

Marcelle's eyes shimmered. "Truly?"

"Truly."

"Merci, Ma!" She jumped up and down. "Merci, Kit."

"You work as hard as we do," I said. "Might as well make it official."

"I don't want her smoking like some of you girls." Madame glared at Lewis. "We know what that leads to!"

"To good times," Lewis said under her breath.

"We'll keep her on the straight and narrow." Miss Morgan discreetly swept her cigarette case from the table.

"And no lipstick." Madame added. "Or—"

"You've got a deal!" I held out my hand before Madame could add more interdictions to the list.

We shook on it.

———

THE NEXT MORNING, I INTENDED TO DELIVER HENRI'S GIFT TO JEANNE, but found myself taking a detour to Sidonie's. Had she finished or even begun *Howards End*? I found her in the yard, an expanse of dirt where valiant blades of grass gathered in clumps. She was throwing shards of glass in the bin.

"I should have tidied when I moved in," she admitted. "I didn't see the utility of taking care of this bald patch, or even of myself."

"It's never too late to 'cultivate our gardens,'" I said, quoting *Candide*.

"I never much liked Voltaire, a bit glib for my taste. E. M. Forster, on the other hand . . . the headstrong Schlegel sisters were excellent company. I put his novel on my keeper shelf."

Success! Joy swirled in my chest, the way air filled the lungs; however, I was careful not to show it. Sidonie reminded me of a calico cat I'd loved. He ran off at any show of interest, but when I stood still, he ventured to my side. I asked Sidonie if she'd like to accompany me.

"On a stroll?" she asked.

"One with special deliveries."

She regarded me suspiciously. "You're a wily Card with something up her sleeve."

Flattered, I suppressed my smile.

"I sense you have plans for me," she continued. "I'll go at my own pace. Not yours."

We set off. The wind whipped at her long black skirt as she told me she admired Margaret Schlegel but found her sister, Helen, too impetuous.

"The world needs more impetuousness," I argued. My impromptu choice to join CARD was the best decision I'd ever made.

"Perhaps you're right," Sidonie said.

In the north of France, she explained, one mustn't approach a stranger, one must find a common acquaintance to make the introduction. "In Lille, when my husband—who I'd never seen before in my life!—noticed me at the *librairie,* he begged the bookseller to introduce us. Thankfully, he was impulsive."

The corner of her mouth turned up. Pleased to see her revel in the memory, I didn't want to break the spell. We continued to Madame Petit's farmhouse in silence.

Upon seeing Sidonie, Madame clasped my elbow and whispered, "You're a miracle worker."

Jeanne hobbled to the stove to put on the kettle. Seeing her struggle, Sidonie tensed.

When the chamomile tea was poured, I pushed *Avec vue sur l'Arno* (*With a View on the Arno* as *A Room with a View* was called in French) across the butcher block to Jeanne.

"I shall read and return it," she said solemnly.

"And this is a gift from Henri." I placed the collection of sonnets atop the novel.

Jeanne opened the cover and spied the valentine. A smile started at her lips and spread to her eyes.

"What's this?" Madame Petit demanded. "I'm not sure that it's appropriate."

Jeanne closed the collection and looked to me, then to Sidonie, who'd blanched. I reached for her hand. It was clammy. Something was wrong, but what?

"What could be more appropriate than a literary exchange?" I asked, one eye on Jeanne, the other on Sidonie.

"I don't want my Jeanne hurt."

Beads of sweat dotted Sidonie's forehead. "Madame Petit, as a widow, I can tell you that the greatest hurt would have been never getting to know my husband. Please allow Jeanne to see where this innocent pleasure leads."

On the way to the knoll, I felt Sidonie exhale, long and slow. "I see what you're doing."

"Delivering books?"

"A bit more than that." There was an edge to her voice.

"I could use your help with the rolling story hour," I said as nonchalantly as I could. "And later, at the library. We have four counties to serve. Children would love you."

"I'm not ready. Seeing Jeanne's pain, her hope, her belief in a future when I believe in none . . . it hurts too much. I can't help out. I wish I could. But I can't."

---

Over the next week, I longed to check on Sidonie, yet knew it was best to let her be. She'd inform me when she was ready. Meanwhile, Marcelle and I continued rolling story hour, with Lewis quizzing her in preparation for her driver's exam.

When she and Lewis returned from the city, I asked how it went. Marcelle said the written test had lasted an hour and was harder than expected.

"At least the examiner didn't think to ask how old she is," Lewis said. The minimum age was eighteen.

When Marcelle received her license, we threw a CARD party, which was attended by her mother and brothers, whose hair was slicked down and parted in the middle for the occasion; the buck-toothed mayor; Madame Petit and her daughter, Jeanne, who appeared to have a notebook in her purse; book lovers Monsieur and Madame Hugo with their sons Benoit and Sebastien; the aged Countess d'Evry, who lodged in a shed on the grounds of her château and helped her people rebuild. She was a sight as she maneuvered a rusty wheelbarrow loaded with bottles of champagne.

While Madame Petit was chatting with Madame Hugo, Jeanne approached me. "Can you tell Henri that I adored the poems and his valentine?"

I knew how she felt. I loved receiving Tom's letters.

She glanced at her mother, deep in conversation. "And give him this notebook? It's just some drawings. It's nothing, he'll probably think it's childish."

"I'm sure he'll appreciate it." I tucked it into my pocket.

Cards circulated, feasting on Cookie's goat cheese puffs. Apron on over her uniform, she served them herself. At least she was in the room with us. Progress.

"Young Jeanne seems happy," she noted. "During Mass, when she and Henri gawk at each other, they glow."

"They'll write themselves a happy ending," I replied.

At the hearth, Miss Morgan cleared her throat. "May we have your attention, please?"

She gestured for Marcelle to join her. With Madame Moreau looking on proudly, Miss Morgan presented Marcelle with a uniform and griffon brooch. "Congratulations to our newest '*chauffeuse*'!"

We raised our champagne glasses.

"*Mesdames,* a male driver is a 'chauffeur,'" Marcelle said. "It is a masculine noun. There is no feminine equivalent. A '*chauffeuse*,' is not a 'female driver.' Rather, it's a type of chair that one sits in while heating up—or '*chauffer*'—near the hearth."

"We'll continue to say *chauffeuse,*" Miss Morgan said in her matter-of-fact way.

"You would be mistaken," Marcelle insisted.

I admired her frankness.

Breckie's brows shot up. "I declare!"

"Gollywhoppers!" Lewis whispered. "Does she have a death wish?"

The two Annes were terrifyingly competent. They'd created teams of experts on skills varying from farming to child development. Under their leadership, CARD had received the Médaille du Mérite Agricole from the French government, yet this slip of a mademoiselle dared to correct them.

"Marcelle!" her mother admonished. "Respect your elders."

Placing her hand on Madame Moreau's arm to show that no harm was done, Miss Morgan said, "It's time the French language caught up with Frenchwomen."

The black-and-white definition of the *dictionnaire* would not sway us: Our motor service was made up of first-rate *chauffeuses.*

"You're right," Marcelle relented. "We women deserve a word of our own."

# CHAPTER 10

A t 6:00 a.m. on Sunday, my bedroom door creaked open. Who was awake at this hour? An icy draft entered with the intruder. I expected Max to snarl, but he merely licked their hand. The pigtailed grim reaper in a gray slicker whispered, "I need your help."

Next door, Breckie was still snoring. Lucky her.

I rubbed the sleep from my eyes. "It's still dark out."

"Precisely!" Marcelle shook the bed frame. "Hurry! Before Ma notices I'm gone."

At the thought of her mother bawling us out, I winced. "What kind of help?"

"Some of my friends are still in the Red Zone."

"The Red Zone was evacuated," I said.

Marcelle shot me a pitying look.

"Wasn't it?"

"To some people, it's home."

Marcelle's classmate Victorine and her little sister, Vivienne, had grown up in the Red Zone. Their father was killed at the front; their mother died when their village was bombarded. During the first evacuation, the schoolmaster had separated the girls. Victorine was sent to a refugee center in Brest. She escaped and tracked down Vivienne, who'd been sent to an orphanage in Nice. They now camped near their decimated home. To avoid separation, they no longer attended school and evaded adults.

"I thought I could talk them into coming to Blérancourt," Marcelle finished. "But they won't budge."

"You've been driving into the Red Zone on your own?" I shouted.

"Shh! How else are my friends supposed to get food? At the mercantile, I siphoned off goat milk, bread, cheese, and eggs. But my friends need more than food to survive. They need stories."

"Persuade them to come to here." I pulled the covers to my chin, wishing she'd take the hint.

"Don't you think I've tried?"

"What makes you think that I can convince them?"

"You're devious." From her tone, she meant it as a compliment. "You sneak in book learning. If Ma used your sly techniques with spinach, my brothers would eat it."

"Books aren't spinach!"

"I know. Books taste much better," Marcelle said with an impish grin. "But seriously, Kit, you can do anything."

Flattery was how I found myself in the passenger seat, lurching through the Red Zone. At dawn. On a bumpy corkscrew of a road. Twenty miles from the front. Passing through what had been a village, we could barely make out the foundations of homes. Marcelle's head jutted over the steering wheel, eyes peeled for debris and sections of cobblestone that had been blown away. The land was so empty, so unguarded that I felt vulnerable. There was no place to hide.

A few miles later, we traversed a forest whose carbonized, ebony trees pointed to the last of the morning stars. The bridge over the creek had been bombed. Marcelle eased Bessie down the sandy bank, over the trickle of water, and back up.

We parked in front of a lean-to made of a pine door propped over a thick log.

"It's me," Marcelle said softly.

The girls crawled out. They had the same sooty lashes; the same pink noses, from tears or the sniffles, I couldn't tell. Scowling at me suspiciously, little Vivienne clasped a plaid bunny. Victorine put her arm around her sister. To reassure them, I smiled my most welcoming library smile.

"Would you like a tour?" Victorine asked me.

She demonstrated how they laid a waxen tarp over the door of their old home to keep out the rain. "Ingenious," Marcelle murmured. The burrow was the kind of cozy, rainy-day hideaway that my sister used to fashion by hanging a sheet over our twin beds and padding the floor with quilts. But no child should have to live in the elements. I was about to say so when Marcelle stomped on my foot, effectively stamping out my lecture. The girls had been traumatized not only by the death of their parents and the loss of their home but also by having been separated. I needed to gain their trust. It took everything I had not to sternly order the girls into the Ford so we could leave. From the way they telegraphed messages (*Is it safe? Can we trust her? Should we run for it?*), I sensed they were spooked. If they took off, we'd never find them. So I ambled around their fire pit as if I were in Cookie's immaculate kitchen instead of this charred thicket of rusted shrapnel and burnt-out army trucks.

The earth was shrouded in soggy ash. In the wake of each step, there was a slurping sound as our boots sank into and pulled out of sludge. The air reeked of sulfur, or maybe ammonia. Were we breathing in poison? I wished we could convince the girls to leave. I wished they had deer or birds or hedgehogs to keep them company. Something other than the distant ricochet of machine guns.

Closer by, there were other noises—twigs breaking; leaves crunching underfoot; a cough, or was it just the wind? Strangely, I had the impression that we were being observed, more than just the sisters' suspicious glare. Even in the gentle morning light, I felt frightened.

"Do you girls ever get scared?"

Little Vivienne nodded, but her sister said briskly, "We're fine. This is home."

Seeing that her mind was made up, I asked if they'd like to hear a new song. In their rapid nods, I sensed they were starved for learning.

Victorine drew a sheepskin rug from the burrow. Marcelle and I taught them "Ring Around the Rosie," and when she and I plopped down, Victorine and Vivienne followed with a giggle and Bruno the plaid bunny in tow. From there, I read the first section of *Le Magicien d'Oz. The house whirled around two or three times and rose slowly through the air. Dorothy felt as if she were going up in a balloon.*

"*Oh là là,*" Victorine said.

*It was very dark, and the wind howled horribly around her . . . slowly Dorothy got over her fright; but she felt quite lonely.*

Little Vivienne chewed on the bunny's ear.

*She stopped worrying and resolved to wait calmly and see what the future would bring.*

When I closed the book, I asked the girls if they would return with us.

"No!" Vivienne hid behind her sister. "She'll split us up. Don't let her fool you!"

"Kit isn't like the others," Marcelle argued. "You can trust her."

"We'll be back," I promised. "To bring stories and supplies, not to force you out."

The sun had risen, inch by inch, melting the flecks of frost that had settled on the lean-to. I longed to linger with the sisters. Aware of the passing time, Marcelle hastened to the Ford, headfirst at a forward angle, as if her brain would not wait for her feet to catch up. I followed, once again in awe of this girl, who in addition to her own tragedies, bore the burden of care for her community.

On the drive, she was pensive. Once we left the pockmarked route of the Red Zone and were on the main dirt road, I thanked her for trusting me.

"I knew you'd want to go," she replied in a cheeky, know-it-all tone.

I tugged her pigtail. She stuck her tongue out at me. I crossed my eyes. She laughed a deep belly laugh, and I joined in. For a fleeting moment, we left behind the darkness.

We made it in time for church, Marcelle's mother blessedly none the wiser. From the vestibule, I couldn't help but notice Jeanne and Henri exchanging glances. After Mass, Madame Petit kept her daughter tethered to her side.

I asked if she'd enjoyed *A Room with a View.*

"I loved it," Jeanne gushed. "So romantic."

"Romance leads to trouble," Madame said.

"And to marriage," Jeanne added pertly. "Lucy Honeychurch is a heroine."

I reveled in Jeanne's confidence to speak her mind. Perhaps it was the example of Miss Honeychurch—through timidity and worrying overmuch, she nearly lost her true love.

Finding a break in the conversation, Henri approached with a fistful of violets for Jeanne.

"I can't help but think that nosegay resembles a bouquet," Cookie whispered to me.

"You're a romantic!" I replied.

"Marriage is for others," she corrected. "I'll take independence any day."

She invited Jeanne and Henri to the CARD party.

"I'm not sure that's a good idea," Madame Petit responded.

"I'm sure it is!" Jeanne said. "Thank you for the invitation. We'll see you there."

———

OUTSIDE LE CLUB-HOUSE, IN THE BRISK, ALMOST-BUT-NOT-QUITE-spring chill, I counted the seconds for our soldiers to arrive. Well, for Tom. Though we exchanged letters, it had been nearly a month since we'd last seen each other. Beside me, Lewis clenched a Gitane so tight that it broke in two.

"We never know who will be here and who's . . . gone west. At the CARD Christmas party, a pilot and I were dancing. The following week, he was shot down in a dogfight."

"I pray they'll all be here." Inside my pocket, my fingers tightened around my father's handkerchief, the same way I'd clung to his hand. When I was ten, I'd asked, "What did you want to be at my age?" He'd replied, "Oftentimes, what you do in life is not so much a choice as chance. Either something happens to someone close to you, or there's a reaction to events. More than anything, I want you and your sister to be able to decide your own futures." Snippets of our conversations came to me at the oddest times, as if he were saying, *I'm still here.* I wished I'd been wise enough to ask him more questions.

*Not so much a choice . . .* like the soldiers who'd been drafted for the war. *A reaction to events . . .* like the Cards who came to give aid. The army truck lumbered over the moat, and upon seeing Tom at the wheel, I loosened my grip on the handkerchief.

As the soldiers threw the canvas covering back and jumped from the bed of the truck, Lewis did roll call. "Carl, Tom, Alan, where's Jimmy?"

The last to exit, he did a little jig. "The gang's all here!"

Lewis handed him a nub of her broken cigarette, and they lit up together.

Tom greeted me with a peck on each cheek. "For once, I'm glad to be in France," he said. "I get to kiss you twice."

"Me, too." As his skin grazed mine, I reveled in his touch.

Jimmy set up the gramophone, and Marcelle gawked as couples danced the chicken flip. Tom and I moved to the quietest corner, our backs to the others. The voices, laughter, and even the war faded away.

"Why did you choose *The Count* for me?" he asked.

"I mainly brought children's books, and wasn't sure you'd enjoy *Anne of Green Gables.*"

"Why not? My sisters speak highly of Anne—seems like she'd be good company. Better than some of the self-absorbed officers I'm stuck with."

I appreciated that Tom spoke of characters as if they were people, too. And I understood it wasn't easy living in close quarters. As much as I adored the Cards, there were circumstances where I escaped to the library of my mind and lived in the books that I read.

"In a recent letter from home," he said, "my sister Catherine included a line from *Anne of Green Gables.* 'Isn't it nice to think that tomorrow is a new day with no mistakes in it yet?'"

I must have looked surprised.

He shrugged. "It's one of those thoughts that stays with you."

When I was in my twenties, I adored racy novels. I learned about everything—including passion—in books. I thought back to how I used to escape with a novel into a bubble bath. The balmy water, the cravings of the characters. As I read, I felt the same longings. In real life, desire was dangerous: if you married the wrong man, you lost your rights over your bank account and your body. With novels, the biggest risk was dropping the book in the tub.

Over the years, my penchants had evolved—mysteries, biographies, travelogues. These days, I found succor in the innocence of children's classics.

"What's your favorite passage of *Anne*?" he asked.

"'It's nicer to think dear, pretty thoughts and keep them in one's heart, like treasures. I don't like to have them laughed at or wondered over.'"

"It's lovely. Like you."

He caressed my cheek. His touch felt delicious. My pulse pounded, my body longed for more.

"Your skin is soft," he whispered.

Hearing Lewis shout, "Spin me faster, Jimmy!" reminded me that Tom and I weren't alone.

"Back to *The Count*. I knew you'd appreciate Edmond Dantès's courage."

"I loved how you underlined your favorite sentences and wrote in the margins."

I'd forgotten I'd done that, and felt strangely exposed, as if I'd bared a breast instead of my thoughts. "I can't read without a pen in my hand."

"It felt like we were reading together."

His earnest gaze drew me in, and I inched closer.

"I wanted to write you back, on the page," he continued, "but wasn't sure if you'd mind."

"I wouldn't have!"

"Which line spoke to you?"

The book had been my father's favorite; I'd turned to it in the days after his death. Now, I thumbed through the pages, rereading my notes in the margins. *I ask you—does time heal all wounds?* Beside this question, I'd underlined Alexandre Dumas's words: *For all evils there are two remedies: time and silence.*

I showed the line to Tom. "This one."

"'Time and silence,'" he read. "Both of which can be found in libraries. My favorite is 'All human wisdom is contained in these two words—wait and hope.' I also appreciated 'There are two ways of seeing: with the body and with the soul.'"

Body and soul. I wanted his.

He continued talking. Tom's lips looked soft, and I imagined that they tasted of apricot tart. I longed to kiss him. For the first time in my life, words were abstractions, distractions. My gaze lowered to his throat. I wanted to lick the salt from the skin. I wanted—

"Kit?" Tom said.

I blinked quickly. I didn't admit what I'd been thinking about. "On occasion, I travel . . . never on purpose. Usually to the library in my mind." There, that was mostly true.

"I bet it's cozy."

"It's even better here with you." Before he replied with a gallantry he might not feel, I added, "Would you like another book?"

"I was hoping you'd ask."

I drew *The Call of the Wild* from my purse. Tom tucked the slim tome in his breast pocket and asked about my week. I recounted my morning in the Red Zone with Marcelle. I pointed to her on the dance floor, where she was attempting the turkey trot with a mustachioed private. "She has such spirit."

"Wasn't the Red Zone evacuated?" Tom frowned.

"To some people, it's home."

"You shouldn't be going there, and you certainly shouldn't drag an apprentice into danger!"

*Shouldn't.* The word was like a bucket of cold water thrown in my face.

Mother had foisted suitor after suitor on me. *You shouldn't be working with children,* said one, *you should be starting a family.* Another said I shouldn't have stolen a job from a man. When a third suitor turned his nose up at my ink-stained fingers, because *a true lady has lily-white hands,* I ordered Mother to cease. Mabel insisted our mother merely wanted me to find the same wedded bliss she'd had with Father. Instead, the incessant matchmaking drove a wedge between us.

*He wants to protect you,* I could hear Mother say. *You shouldn't be so prickly.*

*He's domineering,* I shot back. *Just like the rest of them.*

"Imagine if I ordered you to stay away from danger," I told Tom.

"I don't have a choice. You do."

Wasn't this the crux? The man was the protector, the woman a damsel in distress. I longed for love, for passion, for companionship. But the price seemed to be submission. With most men, my instinct was to pull away and end discussions midconversation like a dull book snapped shut. Now, my intuition was telling me to go.

Just then, Jeanne walked in. At the rowdy spectacle of couples waltzing and partygoers shouting over the music, she retreated, backing into Henri. He steadied her with his good hand.

I turned to Tom with a tight smile, a type of armor, in place. "If you'll excuse me. Hostess duty calls."

"Kit . . ."

I ushered in the couple. "Welcome," I said brightly. "Would you care for a refreshment?"

"How about a dance first and punch later?" Henri asked Jeanne.

"I'm not sure I can." She gestured to her wooden leg.

"We'll just sway. Dancing is an excuse to hold you in my arms, well, arm."

Jeanne put her hand in Henri's. True to his word, they simply swayed. I returned to my usual spot: the refreshment table.

"You were right about *A Room with a View,*" Henri shouted over the music. "Wouldn't it be wonderful to go to Italy after the war?"

"Without a chaperone!" Jeanne replied.

"I loved your drawings and poems. You captured how being injured feels." He gestured to his empty sleeve. "I didn't think anyone could understand."

Tom sidled up to me. Together, we watched the couples dance. Exactly twelve inches separated Marcelle and a bashful lieutenant. Jeanne inched closer to Henri, while Lewis snuggled in Jimmy's arms.

"Should I call you Kit or Cupid?" Tom asked.

"Both."

"Sorry about what I said earlier."

"Thank you. I appreciate that."

"I couldn't bear it if something happened to you."

I cared for him, too, and wanted to think he was different than other men, but how to know for sure?

"I should be telling you how brave you are," he added. "You're right here with us. Thoughts of you and your books get me through. What are we fighting for, if it's not the people we love, the ideas we cherish, the stories we want to pass on? You're giving children the gift of a lifetime. I still remember the books I read as a kid, the characters I loved."

"Children's literature lives inside us," I agreed, taking the olive branch he was offering. In return, I poured him a glass of punch.

He poured me a glass. We touched rims. "To being able to talk things through."

"To talking things through," I echoed. "How was your week?"

Tom didn't answer right away, as if he was mulling over what to censor as he ran a thick black pen through his thoughts.

"I'm a librarian, remember? We deal in facts. No need to sugarcoat your story."

He downed his punch like it was whiskey. "My best friend, Ron, was killed at the front."

I took his hand. "I'm so sorry."

"I shouldn't have brought it up."

"Tell me about him."

He shook his head. "This is a party."

"Please."

"He wrote to his sweetheart every day. For luck, he carried a sheaf of wheat from his field. He was fearless in the cockpit. He could skunk anyone in cribbage. He hated chicory, drank hot water instead . . ." Tom stared out the window. This time it was he who pulled away. "This is a piss-poor eulogy."

"I disagree. Before bed, we'll each pour a cup of hot water and think of Ron. Little rituals will keep his memory alive."

"Tom, you're getting maudlin," Jimmy shouted from the dance floor as he twirled Lewis. "Quit jawing and dance."

Of course, he couldn't have known what Tom and I'd been discussing. We gazed at each other ruefully. Tom tendered his hand to me, and I moved into his arms. He smelled of woody tobacco and damp wool and sweet brioche. I touched the hollow of his throat. I wanted to memorize the feel of him.

Though I'd squeezed my eyes shut to stay with Tom in this moment, I still heard Dr. M.D. interrogate a colonel about the situation. He tried to put her off with niceties, but she persisted.

"We've observed enemy movement," he admitted. "They're closing in. When we give the signal, you must be ready to evacuate."

I felt Tom swallow. He held me too close. Or maybe I held him too close. Life was fragile. We only had this dance.

# CHAPTER 11

WENDY PETERSON
NEW YORK, JANUARY 1987

The worst hangovers are not a result of hard liquor, but of regret. I had made a mistake. Roberto is right, I never should have taken those documents. They could have been lost or destroyed—just like our friendship. He's angry with me, and rightly so. I'm angry with me, too. What was I thinking? *You never think* was my father's biggest criticism. *Think before you speak, think before you act, think before you breathe.* My head pounds. I down some ibuprofen and consider calling in sick, then consider my bank account. Besides, skipping work would just draw out the dread of facing Roberto. I need to apologize and make things right.

Today happens to be training day in Remembrance. Roberto is surrounded by a handful of adoring interns who gawk at him all googly-eyed. Who can blame them? I probably look at him that way, too. I try to make eye contact, but he steadily ignores me. Meanwhile, he shows the interns how to create a description of archive holdings ("That's Thadeus Billingsly III. His one true love was his abrasive African grey parrot, Melvin."), then explains NYPL workplace norms ("The way to make a name for yourself is to compose excellent bathroom graffiti. Among librarians, this is a point of pride. Nothing else matters."). The new arrivals to this staid land of annals find him hilarious. When I dare to chuckle at one of his quips, he scowls at me as if to say *My pearls are not for you, swine.*

The force of Roberto ignoring me feels like a malevolent presence. It upsets me so much that I step out. In the corridor, I wrap my arms around my torso. I can still hear his voice and can't take the tender way he addresses the interns. I leave the NYPL. The cool, smoggy air does me good. My mind doesn't know where to go, but my body does.

At the entrance of the Morgan Library & Museum, the guard directs me to the archives. I peer into the smallish reading room, at a dozen desks whose chairs are nearly filled. At one, a nun squints through neon pink reading glasses. At another, a man sporting a paisley bow tie chews on his pencil.

I tiptoe to the circulation desk, where a librarian with spiky red hair greets me.

"I'm interested in the Cards."

Her face lights up. "We have their diaries, photos, and correspondence."

My heart soars, and like a sprinter, I lean forward as if the circ desk is a finish line.

"Space is limited," she adds apologetically. "I'm afraid you must reserve in advance. We're full up in the coming weeks."

I feel like an idiot for not picking up the phone. The scholars hunched over the tables must be writing about Anne Morgan. Why else would they be here? Fear flows through me in a hot rush. I'm terrified that the real researchers have beat me, that they're penning the story I'm meant to tell. That I've fallen behind. This is another race I'm not going to win.

I've lost Roberto, and now this. "They're all researching the Cards?" I hate how whiny my voice sounds.

"Is this your first research project?"

Does she think I'm too young? That I don't look professional enough? I glance at my T-shirt. I should have worn my cardigan, or purchased a blazer like Professor Hill, a real writer.

"I only ask because you think everyone"—she gestures to the patrons—"is interested in the Cards. It's great to see your belief that people should be into them. I adore them, too."

She explains that the Morgan possesses an eclectic collection, from Anne Brontë's manuscripts to the original draft of *The Little Prince* by

Antoine de Saint-Exupéry. Her reassurance grounds me, and I ask to make a reservation. She hands me the dog-eared CARD finding guide, which outlines Anne Morgan's correspondence, a photo album, two diaries, and letters from volunteers as well as magazine and newspaper clippings.

The librarian consults the scheduling binder and informs me that there's been a last-minute cancellation. I want to give her a bear hug, but instead request every scrap of information. She shows me to the sink and explains that everyone must wash their hands before touching the documents. I put my belongings in a locker; scholars can keep only paper and pencils. Since I have only pens, she grabs a stubby pencil from her desk and ushers me to mine, where the files are spread before me. I feel giddy, like a kid at the church rummage sale, a five-dollar bill burning a hole in my pocket. So many treasures—a five-hundred-piece jigsaw puzzle of Dutch tulips, a Texas Instruments Speak & Spell, a game of Life—begging to be touched.

I debate what to dive into first—a crumbling photo album; newspaper clippings; a diary in faint, illegible handwriting; and copies of Anne Morgan's letters. I feel a surge of gratitude for Roberto. Without him, I never would have discovered Jessie Carson. I wish he were with me now, that I hadn't ruined things between us. Ruined things before they even had a chance to take off. Still, I can't help but wonder where he'd begin. At the end. He always reads the last page first. Sacrilege. I start chronologically.

Born in 1873, Anne Morgan was the youngest daughter of financier J. P. Morgan. I scrutinize a photograph of her as a debutante. It's the Gilded Age, when corseted ladies were all the rage, but young Anne does not follow the fashion—her dress is a straight cylinder. The hem forms a lace puddle on the marble floor. She appears to be shy, even hesitant, stiff like a department store mannequin. Her forearms are as white as her dress, her hands folded as if in prayer, *Dear Lord, let this photo session end.* There's no fire in her eyes, no protests on the tip of her tongue.

In another photo, a decade later, Anne and her father stand side by side, he in a three-piece suit, she, a white silk gown. In addition to his millions, she inherited his round face, dark brows, and blunt chin. She appears tense, a performer about to go onstage. Of course, I can't know what she's thinking, but her wary expression leads me to believe that young Anne understands there's no room for error. Her father is rich and powerful, and he has a temper. At his side, she's cautious, watchful. With him, as with newspapermen, she's never strident, and is careful never to openly praise the suffragettes. She aims to support working-class women, and she won't be in a position to help anyone if she gets herself disinherited.

Young Anne gets along well with her father's mistresses. She must. She even "chaperones" her father and his young lover on trips to Europe, providing the mismatched couple with a certain sheen of respectability. Until the age of twenty-eight, she lives with her mother, who, understandably, is deeply unhappy in her marriage. Anne is her confidante and crutch.

Hours pass as I study Anne Morgan's facets. From one angle, she's a devoted daughter, careful to present herself in a certain way. From another, she's the leader of the battalion of women in horizon blue.

I turn to the next folder and see that newspapers across the country run stories about her. MISS ANNE MORGAN DOES A SMOKING SOLO, screams a headline from a newspaper in Idaho. "At the Hotel Astor luncheon of 300 members of the National Civic Federation, Miss Anne Morgan couldn't find anyone to accept her proffer of a cigarette, so she smoked one alone." In the February 5, 1922, edition of the *Tulsa Daily World*, the syndicated article "Women Who Refuse to Wed Called Menace to the Race" cites Anne Morgan, "cultivated woman of the world and philanthropist," along with Queen Elizabeth I and Florence Nightingale as the ruin of society because "quality" women like these remain "willfully celibate." According to Harvard professor Dr. Sargent, "The ruin of any nation starts when its better-class women cease to become mothers. True she leaves a legacy of achievement in art, science, literature or in service to humanity, but along with this she might as well leave several children."

I chuckle at the absurdity, but slowly understand the sexism that the Cards faced. Next, I dive into a folder of correspondence. I'm grateful that Anne Morgan fell in love with the typewriter and that she kept carbon copies. In letters to her mother, she writes giddily about progress in the North. To Anne Murray Dike, it's mostly CARD business, but occasionally, there is a petulant line chiding the doctor for not responding quickly enough. And from Anne Murray Dike: "I am thrilled that you have bought the Blérancourt house. It gives me the most intense satisfaction. Cannot we arrange nice little graves for both of us, when we are ready?" Am I imagining it, or is the tone lover-like? Did Anne Morgan ever marry?

A canned loudspeaker announcement states that the library and gift shop will close in twenty minutes. I got through only a quarter of the files. Panicked at the thought of leaving, I skim a letter, then another. Thus far, there's no mention of Jessie Carson. I finish with a description from spring 1918. Anne Murray Dike wrote:

*Good Friday and Easter were ironic days—days of fighting, horror, and bitterness, of sad sights and questioning wonder, only to be relieved by the medical aid given to the sick, the physical aid given to the hungry and worn, and the moral encouragement to the hopeless. Though we had heard countless terrible tales of suffering, it was our first real experience of war.*

I couldn't even say when Easter was exactly. The end of March or the beginning of April? Why did it change every year? Were the Cards attacked? Were they able to evacuate? Like them, I do not know what day the offensive will strike. I only know that bombs will fall.

————

WORRIED ABOUT THE PAST, I FORGET ABOUT MY PRESENT. NOW I'M late. I grab my belongings from the locker and rush to my writing workshop. As I slink into the back of Professor Hill's class, he snatches the pages from a classmate's desk. Her name is Meredith, I think. He reads her story aloud. The main character is a shoplifter, and I'm riveted. When he finishes, there's a pause before his pronouncement. We wait. Maybe this will be the story he approves of.

"Trite," he declares. "I've read this kind of thing a hundred times before."

To my left, I hear a guy suck in his breath. I catch Meredith's eye and tilt my head in sympathy. She blinks back her tears.

*No story here. I've read this before. This is just notes.* And now, *Trite.* Familiar words. Maybe Roberto is right about trotting out the same comments.

"I'm preparing you for the writing life," Hill tells us. "Get used to criticism and pain. To being ignored and having your work judged."

The bell rings, but none of us moves.

"Editors love you until they drop you," he continues. "They celebrate your writing until they find the next new thing, a talent younger and shinier than you. Your agent won't return your calls. Your 'friends' won't have time to meet. You will be miserable. You'll learn that your heart is a clock. It will stop. Why bother to write? Why care? You'll never be reviewed in *The New York Times* again. Never forget, publishing is who you know."

Students glance at each other. Do we console Hill? Stop him? Hang on till the tirade ends?

"You'll die miserable and alone," he continues. "And by the way, rigor mortis is the third stage of death. The first is rejection. The second is becoming invisible to your peers. But enough of today's pep talk." He grabs his briefcase and flees the scene.

We students huddle in the hallway. We can't become like him. How do we not become like him?

"That was . . . intense," I say.

"Straight out of Dickens," Meredith responds. "The ghost of the future. Do you think that's what writing is?"

"It's his experience of publishing, but it's not writing," I respond. "We can't let Hill's angst and bitterness stop us."

"You're right."

Professor Hill insists that publishing is about who you know. I know no one, but I know how Jessie Carson felt. A lowly librarian among socialites. My undergrad classes consisted of wealthy blondes who toted Dooney & Bourke handbags and of clean-cut guys sporting shirts in J.Crew pastels. They went skiing in Gstaad at Christmas and to an island resort on spring break. As a scholarship student, I was paid to tutor—babysit—snide sorority sisters and swaggering frat bros. One turned up at my dorm room half-drunk. Ten minutes into the lesson, he jumped on me. I tried to shout, but his sweaty hand covered my mouth. He was pulling my jeans down when my roommate walked in. Her timing saved me.

The complaint I filed went nowhere. At university, I learned that no matter what those guys did, they'd be fine. Someone would sober them up. Bail them out. Hire a five-thousand-dollar-an-hour lawyer to make accusations disappear. I never let my guard down again. I continued to tutor, but only women, and only in public. I didn't date. I don't date.

That's why I write. I was silenced once, but never again.

I turn to Meredith. "I'm writing a book about Jessie Carson and the Cards." I'm stunned that I tell a near stranger something I had yet to admit to myself.

"Cool. Sounds like a band. You know, Joan Jett and the Blackhearts."

I grin. "They definitely rock."

Earlier, I was intimidated by the older, smarter, better scholars. But I can't worry about anyone else's credentials. I've got to go for it. I've got to write this story. I'll learn as I go, I can do the Cards justice. They're counting on me.

# CHAPTER 12

*D*ear Jessie,
 *Everyone in Allegheny has the sniffles. I had to take to bed. Thank the heavens for your sister, who's here to wait on me hand and foot. I pray you haven't contracted a cold while you're gallivanting around. But as I tell my prayer group, Jessie is doing the Lord's work, taking care of French widows and orphans. The neighbors go on about how courageous you are, but I can't help but think that we have needy folk in this country, too.*

*Your loving mother*

*~~Dear Mother,~~*
*~~The only thing I've caught is fleas. For the love of God, will you stop picking at me?~~*
*Dear Mother,*
*Everyone here wishes you a speedy recovery. Each day, our rolling story hour continues. For a few hours, the magic of books allows children—underweight and covered in chilblains—to dream. I still plan to rebuild the library. We are doing good work for the whole community. My best to your prayer group.*

*Your loving Jessie*

*Dear Mabel,*
*I miss you terribly and wish I could share all that I experience here. French-women are incredible, their will to work and start over leaves me in awe. Jeanne, whom certain villagers refer to as la mutilée because her foot was*

*severed when she was a prisoner of war, is the perfect example. Each week, when she checks out books, she says they give her courage. She's the one who gives me courage. She not only learned to walk with a prosthesis but chases after Madame Moreau's unruly boys when she babysits. She'd make the perfect children's librarian. If only there were female librarians in France. For now, I'm the only one.*

*I am grateful to you and for you. If you weren't looking after Mother, I couldn't "gallivant around" as she put it. With my work in the war zone, our friends believe I'm the brave one, but you and I both know that it takes courage and heart to stay home.*

*It's nearly midnight here, but I couldn't sleep before I told you how much I admire you.*

*All my love,*
*Jessie*

*DEAR JESSIE,*
*What a pleasure to receive your letter! No female librarians in France? You must do something about that.*

*There's no need to thank me. And how many times must I tell you—take things easy or take things hard, the choice is yours. You know perfectly well that I am a mule. Mother's words are drops of rain that flow down my pelt, onto the ground. I don't let them soak in. And neither should you.*

*Love,*
*Mabel*

*DEAREST KIT,*
*I'm sorry that I was overbearing. Are you still reaching out to the little girls in the Red Zone? I'm confident that you'll convince them to return to the village. How can they resist you?*

*The moments I've spent with you are the ones that I'm most grateful for. I carry your letters and the book you've given me. My favorite line of* Call of the Wild *is "But especially he loved to run in the dim twilight of the summer midnights, listening to the subdued and sleepy murmurs of the forest, reading signs and sounds as a man may read a book, and seeking for the mysterious something that called—called, waking or sleeping, at all times, for him to come."*

I'm reading this book set in nature, all the while pondering man's decision to destroy the land and each other. It makes me angry—for the men fighting, for the French who've lost everything, for you and the other Cards cleaning up the mess.

I pray that we survive this war. Thoughts of you get me through.

*Warmly,*

*Tom*

*Dearest Tom,*

It was wonderful to see you, to dance with you. Thank you for understanding that helping these sisters is something that I must do. Marcelle and I visit them each week. It's a joy to see her nurture these girls. I'm so very proud of her. Sadly, they are adamant about remaining in the Red Zone.

When will I see you next? I long for you to hold me close.

*Warmest wishes,*

*Kit*

*Darling Kit,*

I yearn to take you in my arms again. I long to kiss your cheeks, your hands, your lips, your throat. Do you want that, too? Memories of our conversations make the days less long. How I wish we were dancing and discussing novels back home instead of in the damn war zone.

I long to see you in a week's time. Save me a waltz. Save me all your waltzes.

*Love,*

*Tom*

At my desk, I held his letter to my heart, which thudded as if we were dancing again. The floating sensation took me back to discussions, to our love of books, and maybe of each other. I lit the lantern and penned pages of pent-up longing. *Dearest Tom, Yes, I want that, too. If only we could be alone this Sunday . . .*

"Burning the midnight oil?"

I jumped. Cookie had poked her head in.

"Just finishing a letter." I cleared my throat and gestured for her to enter, and she perched on the bed.

"To Tom?"

"How'd you guess?"

"I've seen how you look at each other."

There was something I needed to know. Something I didn't feel comfortable asking anyone else. "Cookie? Have you ever . . . been with a man?"

"I have."

"What's it like?"

"The first time, I was nervous. But with the right one, it's heavenly." She took my hands in hers. "May I ask what's held you back?"

I explained that in the communities where I lived, everyone seemed to know my business. If I was alone, if I had a suitor, if I arrived home late. At church socials, widowed fathers were pushed in my path, the whole congregation breathless. For one night, I longed be anonymous, to do what I wished, with no one to judge or comment or know. I wanted more than book learning about passion, I wanted my own experience.

———

ANOTHER DAWN, ANOTHER TRIP WITH MARCELLE TO THE RED ZONE to check on Vivienne and Victorine. It had rained the night before, and the potholes were filled with muddy water. Marcelle usually talked a kilometer a minute ("Can you believe that Ma doesn't want me to read immoral books? Those are the best kind!"), but now she gripped the steering wheel as she gnawed on her pigtail. The only sound was the hum of the motor. She slowed. What was a dip in the road, what was a deep crater? I prayed that we wouldn't get a punctured tire. I didn't want to be here any longer than necessary.

"Do you think we'll convince them?" Marcelle asked as we pulled to a stop.

"Each visit brings us closer to a yes."

This was what Breckie's nursing, Lewis's outreach through the mercantile, and rolling story hour were creating—trust. Trust took time.

Our boots sank into the soggy, sorry terrain. The charred trees cast sinister shadows. This was no place for children. Vivienne and Victorine crawled from their lean-to and threw their arms around my waist. I hugged them back with my whole heart. Unable to bear the thought of them being cold, I proffered a pile of blankets I'd purchased from the mercantile. Marcelle unloaded canned milk, cheese, bread, and books.

It was Victorine's turn to lead story hour. Her cheeks were bright as apples. She and Marcelle were only fifteen, yet so poised. This war made me despair, yet when I looked at these girls, I was sure that the future would be a marvelous place. We were in good hands.

Unsurprisingly, Victorine chose her sister's favorite, *The Railway Children* by Edith Nesbit, which featured three children who'd lost their home. "'She had the power of silent sympathy . . . . It just means that a person is able to know that you are unhappy, and to love you extra.'" As she read this section, Victorine glanced up from the text. She pointed at me then at her heart. I blew her a kiss. She finished with "'. . . everything has an end, and you get to it if you only keep all on.'"

When she finished, we clapped. "Encore, encore," lisped Vivienne.

"Girls," I said, "we want you to think about coming to Headquarters."

They exchanged glances. "We'll think about it."

Marcelle raised a brow. I, too, was surprised by the softening of their position.

"I saw a man." Vivienne clutched her plaid bunny to her chest.

"Just a boogeyman." Her sister dismissed the idea with a sweep of her hand.

"Boogeymen don't wear German military uniforms."

"A trick of the shadows," Victorine said. "No one else lives out here. We're staying put. We can't risk separation."

"Are you certain?" I asked.

Victorine nodded, but little Vivienne didn't seem so sure.

Discreetly, Marcelle lifted her father's watch from the pocket of her rain slicker. She couldn't risk being missed at Mass. Already it was a miracle that Madame Moreau had not caught on. I embraced the girls. It was getting harder and harder to leave them behind.

"Are you sure?" I asked one last time.

Victorine tensed and lifted her foot as if she was poised to run. I quickly stepped back and plopped onto the passenger seat to prove that I would not seize her. "No one will force you."

Back in Blérancourt, we greeted the other churchgoers. Marcelle took her place next to her mother and brothers in front. "Honestly!" Madame Moreau said. "I turn my back one minute, and you're tardy. And on Sunday, too! What would the Lord say?"

Through her lashes, Marcelle gave me an impish look. I could practically hear her cheeky response. *Surely He would thank me for doing His work.*

She bowed her head. "Sorry, Ma."

"That's more like it," Madame said. "A little humility wouldn't hurt you."

I stood in the vestibule, next to the other Cards. As usual, I hoped that Sidonie would join us; as usual, I was disappointed. When the pastor read the gospel, I prayed for the safety of Victorine and Vivienne, of the villagers, of the soldiers, of our families back home. I prayed to be more like my sister, prayed not to take things so hard. My thoughts turned to Tom. I couldn't help but remember Cookie's words. *When it's the right man, you know.* I wanted to be with him. We hadn't known each other long, but if this war had taught me anything, it was that tomorrow was not guaranteed.

After church, Jeanne limped over. "I'm engaged! Henri proposed."

"Congratulations!" I embraced her. "I'm thrilled for you."

"Thank you for your *special deliveries*. The books gave me resolve. And thank you for talking to Maman on my behalf. I understand why she's protective. We both miss my sister, and not knowing what happened to Suzanne is agonizing. Maybe it's selfish to go on, but I intend to live my life, to live with Henri. We set the date for the first day of spring."

I wasn't the only one unwilling to wait. "A good omen. Everything reborn and in bloom."

She frowned. "I would marry Henri tomorrow, but I'm afraid of leaving Maman. I don't want her to be alone with her thoughts."

I couldn't help but think of my mother, who'd also suffered the whiplash of widowhood. Learning to be on her own, to take the reins of the finances. This was why she wanted me to have a helpmate, she knew how hard it was to go it alone.

"Don't underestimate your mother."

"No one in this village would dare. Even the German general in charge here did not. But she's . . ."

"She wants you to be happy."

Jeanne's brow furrowed. "She wants me to be safe. It's not the same thing."

"It's good that you care about your mother, but you also have to consider your own future. You deserve to be fulfilled."

I asked if she wanted to share her good news. With a grin that took up the whole of her face, she nodded.

"Girls!" I said. "Jeanne has an announcement!"

Soon she was surrounded by a pack of Cards, each kissing her cheeks in congratulation, her face soon red from the lipstick.

"Smashing!" Lewis said. "Love is in the air!"

"Brilliant," Breckie added.

Jeanne's face radiated joy, and her joy delighted us.

In le club-house, as Cookie served the *soupe à l'oignon,* she waved her ladle like a baton. "Wonderful news! After the ceremony, let's offer champagne, canapés, and a wedding cake."

"Excellent idea," Miss Morgan said.

"What will Jeanne wear?" I'd only seen her in black.

"We'll procure her a gown," Miss Morgan said.

"That's rather costly," Dr. M.D. replied. "I can loan her one."

"I'll bear the expense," Miss Morgan said.

"But—" Dr. M.D. began.

"I feel strongly about this," Miss Morgan said, settling the argument.

After she finished the last drops of her onion soup, she rose and moved the chairs against the wall in preparation for the arrival of the soldiers. No task was too small for her. I suspected that this was why Cards were such hard workers. We strove to be as diligent and humble as she was.

At the rumble of the army truck, Lewis and I flew outside. Was Tom behind the wheel? Yes, I would know those hazel eyes anywhere. As the soldiers jumped from the rear, I rushed to Tom.

"I received your letter."

"I want to be with you."

Who said which words? We both felt them. I threw my arms around his neck and breathed in his salt-and-tobacco scent. He drew me close. I ran my hands through his bristly hair, along his nape, to the collar of his shirt. I kissed him, forgetting that we were in full view of the Cards.

He came to his senses before I did and stepped away, suddenly bashful. "Sorry. For weeks, I've been fantasizing about you . . ."

I felt my face flush with pleasure. "Let's go inside. We can dance."

"Anything to hold you close."

In le club-house, surrounded by other couples, we waltzed. But I couldn't bear to be surrounded by everyone else. I wanted more than a dance.

I tugged Tom's hand. "Let's go to my room."

He didn't budge. "What about your colleagues?"

"I'm not inviting them."

"Your reputation," Tom said. "We shouldn't."

"We definitely should."

In the bustling courtyard, Lewis and Jimmy played fetch with Lewis's dog, Tripod. Marcelle kept one eye on a bucktoothed lieutenant, the other on me. In the doorjamb of le club-house, Cookie wiped her brow with the back of her hand. Our gaze met. With a nod, she bundled the strays inside so that no one would see Tom and me slip away.

In my room, I slipped out of my jacket. Tom shrugged his off. He unbuttoned my blouse, I his shirt. We embraced, until our bodies locked together and the warmth of his skin engulfed me like fire. All I could think of was him. I wanted him. In his embrace, I forgot how to talk, how to write, how to read. All I could do was feel. Feel the up-and-down movement of his chest. Feel my hands on his ribs. Feel his mouth on mine. Mine. He was mine. I couldn't get enough of his skin. I couldn't get enough of him. We moved to the bed. I'd lived long enough worrying about what I shouldn't do. I was finally going to do what I wanted.

# CHAPTER 13

WENDY PETERSON
NEW YORK, FEBRUARY 1987

While the Cards endure the Great War, I withstand the Cold War with Roberto. He's entrenched on his side of Remembrance, I on mine. We haven't spoken for a week. An eternity. He is both a good friend and a wily adversary. With the shell game he plays with archive boxes, I expect him to trigger a landslide of life insurance contracts from 1926, but so far, the CARD boxes are still assigned to me. Today, I feel him sneaking looks at me, so I build a barricade of books on my desk. I remain undaunted. I will write Jessie Carson's story. I just have to find her.

Still, I miss Roberto. I miss our talks and even our games of *Jeopardy!* To fill the noon hour, and to understand more about CARD, I check out dusty tomes on World War I.

Back home, eating alone in a restaurant or going to a movie on your own is "weird." There, like on Noah's ark, people are supposed to be paired up. One of the reasons I love New York is that no one cares if you are a party of one or five hundred. Alone on a graffitied bench in Bryant Park, peanut butter sandwich in one hand, hardcover in the other, I learn.

In my undergrad European history class, we spent a grand total of four days on the Great War. With centuries of kings and queens to contend with, the professor didn't have time for in-depth explanations. He stated that the war began with "the shot heard around the world." In 1914, a teenager assassinated the heir to the Austro-Hungarian throne, Archduke Franz Ferdinand, and his wife, Sophie. But how did a double murder in Sarajevo lead to trench warfare in France?

Franz and Sophie were a love match. Despite the fact that she was a countess, his family considered her "common" and rejected her. The romantic in me appreciates that this middle-aged man fought his family and societal expectations to wed the thirty-something "old maid" he adored. Knowing they loved each other makes me feel closer to the couple—real people, not distant historical figures.

History is about perspective. Scholars have differing theories on the whys of the war, but they agree on the when—the assassination was the spark that lit a long and winding fuse of resentment, which wended through several European countries. After the slaying of its heir, Austria was determined to take action against Serbia, but how? And with what army? Most soldiers had been sent home to bring in the harvest. Expecting retaliation, Serbia reached out to Russia, its Slavic brother in arms, for support. Austria wrote to Germany and was gladdened when Kaiser Wilhelm replied, "Serbia must be disposed of, and right soon!" With this reassurance, Austria turned to Hungary. The prime minister preferred diplomacy, warning that a failure would lead to the "terrible calamity of a European war." The war minister retorted that "talk" would be interpreted as "weakness."

And where were England and France during these weeks of intense discussions? England occupied itself with a rebellion in Ireland. France was obsessed with a juicy political scandal involving infidelity, newspapermen, and an avenging murderess.

Meanwhile, Russia threatened to mobilize. One theory hypothesizes that combat began in part because of differing connotations of the term "mobilization." For the Russians, this undertaking meant a months-long process of gathering troops from as far away as Siberia. The Germans, who could mobilize in three weeks, considered this preparation an aggression. We speak the same words, but don't mean the same thing.

Reading about the balmy summer days before World War I is akin to observing a chess match in which at least two pieces are in motion at all times. It's not first a pawn, then a rook, but rather a swirl of knights seeking support. Half the board is hidden from view. Kings and bishops are on holiday as Europe lurches toward catastrophe.

Alliances formed with France, Great Britain, and Russia on one side; Germany, Austro-Hungary, and Turkey on the other. Pro-war politicians and military men believed the battle would last a few months at most.

Wishing to avoid a two-front war—fighting both France and Russia—Germany invaded Belgium in order to attack France. Belgium, a neutral country, had signed a treaty with Great Britain, which was honor-bound to defend Belgium. With the entry of England into war, Commonwealth countries such as Canada and Australia were drawn into the European conflict. These British subjects were forced to fight. Likewise, with colonies in Africa, France had an unlimited supply of soldiers.

According to the Robert Schuman Center, the number of military and civilian casualties in World War I was around 40 million. There were 21 million wounded and 20 million deaths, a number that includes 9.7 million military personnel and 10 million civilians. With so many deaths, I can't help but wonder if all of the Cards survived.

The number of lives lost is unfathomable, until I read up on the military leaders. On the French side, Général Joffre didn't believe in defense. He refused to let his men burrow in trenches "like worms." From the safety of his office, miles from battle, he gave the order to attack. From their trenches, the Germans mowed down French, Senegalese, and Algerian soldiers in hail after hail of machine gun fire. With this one decision, Joffre exterminated a million of his own men.

In the epilogue, there is photo of a grand bronze statue in Paris—Général Joffre astride a horse. His side won. He is a hero. Again, we come back to perspective.

Little seems to be written about Frenchwomen during the war. It's like they were not there. From the books I checked out, you might think that the French population was entirely made up of men. Yet while they were off fighting, wives, widows, mothers, and daughters held the country together. Genteel women who hadn't been allowed to work or study at university were now supposed to be nurses and doctors, teachers and farmers. Livestock and machinery had been commandeered for the war effort, so women tilled the fields like oxen. They worked to provide for families. Is anyone writing about them?

Back in Remembrance after lunch, I keep not glancing at the clock above the door, not wondering when Roberto will arrive. When he enters, my nape tingles. Somehow, I just know.

"Finding leads?" He peeks over my shoulder. He smells of café olé and newspaper ink. I've missed that scent.

I keep my head over the viewfinder. "You talking to me again?" My tone is just the right amount of snotty.

"About that. I'm sorry. In the moment, I was angry and disappointed, but I shouldn't have stalked off. And I shouldn't have let days go by without hashing it out."

I glance up at him. "Believe me, I understand it was a mistake to take those documents. It won't happen again."

"I know. Can you forgive me for being immature?"

I nudge his knee with my elbow. "Which time? You're often immature." There is a lightness in my chest. I can hear it in my voice, relief that we're patching things up.

"Only this week. I stand by the previous times," he replies in a teasing tone.

"I really am sorry for taking the documents."

"I know. I shouldn't have gotten so angry. I'm sorry, too." He holds out his hand.

When I shake it, I feel a spark. Did he miss me? I want to tell him that I missed him and his antics, the way he keeps a deerstalker hat in his desk, just in case he has a Sherlock moment. The way he helps out at story hour. Last week, when the children's librarian read a book about Versailles, Roberto donned a curly gray wig like the Sun King. The kids and staff loved it. Today, in 501s and an oxford, he is dropdead gorgeous.

"Have you found other mentions of Jessie Carson?" he asks, to put us on neutral territory, sweeping away the awkward remnants of our fight. For this, I'm grateful to him.

"I'm afraid she died in the war zone." I swallow. It hurts to even think it.

"Perhaps not. Death might not be the only impediment." He slaps on his Sherlock hat for effect. "Consider the case of the missing librarian. Occupied France, 1940. Jeanette Ettlinger, a Jewish librarian from Chicago, worked in Paris . . . until she vanished. After 1940, there isn't a single trace of her name in the archives. We feared she'd been killed by the Nazis."

"What happened?"

"She didn't die. She didn't even disappear. *She married.* Jeanette became Mrs. Herbert E. King. What we considered elementary was in fact matrimony."

I can't help but grin at his Sherlock posturing. Just like that, Roberto has me feeling better.

"Brides foolishly take their husband's name," he continues. "It's a researcher's nightmare. Women should keep their maiden names—it would make life easier for archivists."

Marriage. Maybe I'm looking under the wrong name and that's why I'm not finding her. On Sundays, the Cards entertained soldiers. Did Jessie Carson meet her soul mate? Could she have married some French guy? Or a soldier from the heartland? Did she make it out of France alive?

"How'd you find your librarian?" I ask.

"It took years. I found her on microfiche, in a diplomatic service magazine."

I nod. Preservation and diffusion of information are critical. Documents that molder in closed archives are no good to anyone.

"What are the chances of locating Jessie Carson if she married?"

"It wouldn't be easy. You'd have to find the date and place she married."

A wedding in New York or Allegheny? In Picardie or Paris? In

1918 or 1919 or 1920 or 1921? Maiden or married name? Roberto said it took years to find Jeanette. Years. And I'm only a civilian, not a librarian. I'm in over my head. The search feels impossible. Will I ever find her?

Roberto slips the deerstalker hat back in the drawer. He doesn't joke about the stars aligning or use Sherlock's "elementary" lingo. He cares for me. That's why he doesn't state that I may have lost Jessie Carson forever.

# CHAPTER 14

JESSIE "KIT" CARSON
BLÉRANCOURT, MARCH 1918

The following day marked the first day of spring, eleven weeks since I'd arrived. The morning mist settled over freshly plowed fields. The anemones that Madame Petit had planted in front of the infirmary brought a splash of pink and optimism. The master carpenter would soon begin reroofing the town hall. Perhaps the library would open in time for the first day of school in September. I'd ordered an arsenal of books; little by little, shipments arrived from Paris. Three carpenter Cards and the woodworking students were constructing shelves and furniture for the children's section. Homes were being renovated. Children were getting plumper. According to the schoolmistress, classes were going well. Most farms had been cleared of land mines. It had been a week since the last bursts of gunshot or snarl of a cannon. We wanted to believe that the war was receding. The two Annes were tight-lipped about confidential reports from a French general. In unguarded moments, the grim faces of the soldiers reminded us that the fighting was far from over.

Still, like the vanilla scent of Cookie's three-tiered cake, love was in the air. Today was a warm spring day, not a cloud in the sky—perfect for a wedding. On our way to Jeanne and Henri's nuptials, we Cards passed a field and admired the courage of the wheat, whose heads poked through the soil. As we entered the church, I recited a prayer for the villagers and their budding crops.

Unfortunately, during the night, another section of the roof had fallen in. Always ready to pitch in, Marcelle's mother swept the slate shingles toward the back corner. Bits of debris were caught in her bun, and her cheek was smudged with dirt. When we tried to help, she said, "*Mon Dieu*, there's no reason for you girls to get grimy, too." Luckily, the chandelier above the altar had not been damaged. For the ceremony, the nave was lit with taper candles, adding a touch of elegance. It was so beautiful, I wished that Sidonie would relent.

I recalled our last conversation, as we traipsed along the cobbles of the rue de Picardie. I shared the news of Jeanne and Henri's engagement. Sidonie told me that the expression for love at first sight was *coup de foudre,* or "thunderbolt." "It's nonsense." She gave a dismissive shrug. "An insipid fairy tale."

"I believe in fairy tales."

When the betrothed couple had met, I'd witnessed lightning strike. Their faces lit up when they saw each other. Both had gone through unspeakable pain and seen the worst man could do to man. The couple understood each other, the way one person could finish another's sentence.

"Jeanne and Henri invited the whole village. Will you attend?"

"I don't know. I'm not sure I believe."

"In God?"

"In God. In man."

We passed the bombed-out butcher shop, its display case now shards of glass that resembled a row of jagged bottom teeth. The cheesemonger, whose floor was covered with debris from the shell that had fallen through the roof. The public square with no flowers, only a defaced statue—now headless because German soldiers had used the marble as target practice. Who could blame Sidonie for her lack of faith?

"I wish I felt confident about the world, like I did before the war," she said.

"It's normal to doubt. Philosophers question everything, and we must, too. Are there people you believe in?"

"I believed in my husband. And in my baby girl."

"I wish she'd had the chance to know you, to love you."

"Me, too," she sighed.

We were quiet for a time. Finally, she asked, "What do you believe in?"

"I believe in books. In friendship. In potatoes smothered in butter and dill."

She nodded approvingly. "Elements that nourish us. I believe in crème Chantilly slathered on strawberries."

"And purple hydrangeas."

"Definitely purple hydrangeas."

"Little luxuries," I said. "Like apple pie still fresh from the oven."

"My husband loved apples."

I recalled that her knoll had been infused with the scent of simmering cider. I felt a fool for bringing up apples.

"I'll never bake another tart for my Gaston."

As Sidonie burrowed into her sorrow, we left the village, tramping along the road whose rocky rubble was strewn with shell casings. She moved ahead, and I let her lead. Silence was a part of the library, a part of life. We need silence to think. To feel. I knew about loss. Shoving my hands into my pockets, I felt around for my handkerchief. It was how I held tight to my father. During hard times, I'd dried my tears with the soft cotton, and it felt like he was comforting me.

She slowed to let me catch up. "Mourning is a winding path. Sometimes the walk is invigorating, and I feel fine. Then one word, one memory, and I trip and tumble to the ground. Pebbles of memory break through the skin of my palms. It hurts so much I can barely breathe."

"You don't have to explain."

She tucked her arm through mine. "Don't think you made me maudlin with your talk of apple tart. I was already blue. But I was happy once, too."

"Please attend the wedding," I urged, though we both knew that I was really asking her to come back to the community. "The priest who refused to share firewood is long gone. And if he dares to show his face, I'll punch him."

"You Wild Card!" A smile touched Sidonie's lips.

"I don't care. I'll do it. Please come."

"The scabby sheep spoils the flock."

Was Sidonie calling herself scabby? Was she comparing the parishioners to blind sheep? Another Northern expression with no easy translation? Sensing my confusion, she said, "I wouldn't want my long face to ruin Jeanne and Henri's special day."

"Promise that you'll consider attending." I nudged her hip with my own. "And when the time comes, promise you'll think about working with me in the library. You have much to give."

She nudged my hip in return. "Promise you'll be patient with me."

Now, the church was full, a chessboard of blue uniforms and the black of bereavement. For the occasion, the mother of the bride had cast off her mourning and wore emerald green. She started down what would have been the aisle, toward Henri and his father, both in military uniforms.

"How touching that the bride and groom chose their parents to be the matron of honor and best man," Breckie said.

In her gossamer veil and pastel pink dress, Jeanne looked regal. She strode toward the altar, faster than we'd ever seen her move, as if she couldn't wait to be Henri's wife.

"*Oh là là*," Marcelle said reverently.

Without rituals, there's no rhythm to our weeks, to our lives. Nothing to look forward to, nothing to hope for. Jeanne was more than a bride. In this bombarded church, on the scarred land, her wedding was a statement of optimism, a belief in the future. She positively glowed as she gazed at Henri, their love even more powerful in the midst of these ruins.

To my left, a villager clucked that "*mutilés*" shouldn't be rushing into marriage. Her neighbor asked how the bride could afford the dress, a frivolous extravagance. Petty, petty, petty. Sidonie had been right to stay home.

"'Do not let any unwholesome talk come out of your mouths, but only what is helpful for building others up.'" Madame Moreau aimed lines of scripture like a gun. Turning to me, she said, "Those biddies skipped over the 'Judge not, lest ye be judged' verse."

After that, the two parishioners held their tongues.

As the pastor blessed the union, a sunbeam streamed through the circle where the rose stained-glass window had been, bathing the bride and groom in light. I couldn't help but think of Tom. It had been two weeks since we'd been together, though we wrote to each other every evening. What would it be like to take our vows, then take a honeymoon in Paris? To spend Christmases with family, sleigh rides and caroling, snowy fields and covered bridges? To blow out birthday candles each year and hold hands on our anniversary? What a life it would be.

"Do you take this man to be your lawfully wedded husband?" the pastor asked. "In good times and bad, in sickness and in health?"

"*Oui*," Jeanne answered. I do.

On my right, the two Annes turned to each other. Dr. M.D. tucked a stray gray curl under Miss Morgan's hat. "A rebel to the tips of your hair."

"You wouldn't have me any other way." Her piercing black eyes softened as she took Dr. M.D.'s gloved hand in hers.

My great-aunt Sylvia, who Mother had tittered was "not the marrying kind," had lived with her dear companion, Deirdre, for over thirty years. In the two Annes, I recognized the same tenderness.

The pastor asked, "Do you take this woman to be your lawfully wedded wife?"

The answer was *I do*. Miss Morgan and Dr. M.D. fixed their attention on the ceremony, looking in the same direction, toward what they could accomplish together, toward their future. Congregants remained rapt by the bashful bliss of the bride and groom, yet I could not take my eyes from the Annes. I perceived their love, and understood that not all weddings were blessed by an officiant. Some marriages were lived between souls.

———

Outside the church, Cookie had organized a reception of champagne, canapés, and cake. Cards and villagers raised our glasses to the newlyweds.

"I love love," Lewis sighed as Jeanne and Henri fed each other bites of cake. "Doesn't she look smashing?"

"How he dotes on her!" Cookie said.

When the bridal party departed for the wedding feast at the Petits' farmhouse, we Cards wished them well and turned to washing champagne flutes and platters.

Back at Headquarters, we remained outside and sunned ourselves. I couldn't help but glance at my watch every few minutes. Tom and his unit would be here in an hour.

"I can't wait to tell Tom about the wedding," I said to Breckie.

"It might give him ideas," she teased.

I took in her words, took in the change in me. "I'm not sure I'd mind. He's different than any man I've met."

Beside us, Marcelle implored Lewis to borrow her lipstick. "I want to look grown-up."

"Nothing doing! Your mother made me swear you'd stay away from the stuff."

Marcelle pouted, peering through her lashes to see if Lewis would relent; however, she was as strict as a debutante's cranky chaperone.

An army truck barreled over the moat. Tom was at the wheel.

"They're early!" I couldn't help but grin.

No one else was in the cab. Odd. Were the men hiding under the canvas canopy? Was Jimmy playing a trick? I half-expected him to leap from the back, and yell, *Surprise!*, but when the truck screeched to a halt, we realized it was empty. Expecting the worst, my hand flew to my heart.

Tom's eyes searched our circle—the two Annes, Breckie, Marcelle, Cookie, Lewis—until his gaze met mine.

He approached. "The Germans have broken through. Thousands of them. We can't hold them back."

"What do you need us to do?" Miss Morgan demanded.

"Evacuate the civilians."

"Of course," she replied with a curt nod.

"And you yourselves must be ready to clear out," he added.

"We will be," Dr. M.D. said.

How had we gone from a wedding to war? From arguing about lipstick to having to vacate? None of us wanted to abandon Headquarters—le club-house, where we shared meals and experiences; the barracks, where we stayed up all night talking; story hour and the hope for a new library. What if we had to leave forever? What would happen to the villagers? Stunned by the news, no one spoke.

I walked Tom to the truck.

"Get those sisters to safety," he urged. "The enemy will plow through the Red Zone."

My God, the girls. I blinked dumbly.

He took me in his arms. "I wish . . ." he whispered into my hair.

"Me, too. Be careful."

"I don't know when I'll see you, if I'll see you."

I held him tighter. He kissed my temple. I wanted Tom to have something of me. In my pocket, my fingers closed around the dime novel that the girls had gotten me, *The Adventures of Kit Carson*, the frontiersman who'd inspired my nickname. I slid it into his breast pocket and kissed him with my whole heart. Our lips touched. Our souls touched.

"Let's not say goodbye," he said hoarsely.

He drove off, back to his unit, closer to combat. The truck barreled over the moat, leaving a wispy ribbon of exhaust that evaporated like joy. In an instant, my pleasure—at Jeanne and Henri's wedding, at the thought of the library opening soon—had vanished. The first day of spring represented renewal, all right. Renewal of combat. Another attack meant more destruction and death. In the distance, bombs hitting the earth crashed like lightning. A sound—and danger—that would soon envelop us.

"The Boches will take us prisoner like they did Jeanne and Suzanne," Marcelle whimpered.

Lewis wound her arms around the girl. Marcelle had always been outspoken—her way of being tough. Now I was reminded that she knew what we could not about war. Journalists had written about rape: *The Huns—lecherous beasts—ravish Frenchwomen, soiling their bodies and smearing their souls.*

Tears streamed down Marcelle's face. "Or they'll kill us."

"We'll do our best to evacuate everyone," Miss Morgan promised.

Marcelle dried her tears with the tip of her pigtail. It didn't quite do the job. I dabbed her cheeks with my father's handkerchief. It held so much heartache. Lost love, lost hope, and now fear of losing everything, all over again.

I waited for her to regain her composure. Only she knew the way to Victorine and Vivienne's campsite. But she was just fifteen. I shouldn't be asking for her help, I should be encouraging her to evacuate. I could find the girls on my own, probably. It might take me longer, but I would get there. I needed to move faster than the enemy.

# CHAPTER 15

WENDY PETERSON
NEW YORK, FEBRUARY 1987

f I can't locate Jessie Carson—for now—maybe I should research another Card. Side by side at my workstation, Roberto and I root around for signposts—names and organizations with connections to my elusive librarian. The Library War Service. The American Library Association. President Anne Murray Dike, whose nationality is listed as Scottish, Canadian, and American. Mary Breckinridge, "born into Southern aristocracy." Kate Lewis, a *"chauffeuse,"* who appears to be from a prominent Philadelphia family. When my arm brushes against Roberto's, I feel a spark. He leans over, to kiss me, I hope. My lips part, and I think *yes, now, please.* But he clears his throat and grabs a piece of scrap paper.

To shake off my disappointment and distraction, I take a ten-minute break and head to the reference room, where I look up the number for the Historical Society of Pennsylvania.

At closing time, Roberto and I linger at the revolving door. I open my mouth to invite him on a research road trip but lose courage. Saturday morning, I board the bus alone and watch the stretches of road fly past. Distance. Time. Miles. At least I was smart enough to call ahead to make an appointment. Over the phone, the archivist was frosty until I told her I work at the NYPL. Then she thawed because she believed we're kindred spirits. We are not. I'm nice to everyone, and I resent people who are stingy with basic kindness.

I arrive to a large box on the table before me. Most pages pertain to the Lewis menfolk, but at the bottom, I find a manila envelope. Inside is an eight-by-ten portrait of Kate Lewis in a snowy white gown. I imagine that the pearls around her neck are warmed by her skin, that this photo was taken in the minutes before she came out at a debutante ball. I visualize her contemplating her reflection in the full-length mirror, unable to see what is special inside her. She sticks more bobby pins into her bun. Each strand must stay in place. Kate tugs on satin gloves that seem to go on forever, past her elbows. Her mother ordered a size too small so they'd stay up; Kate doesn't complain that they cut off her circulation. Women must suffer for beauty. She learned that from the corset digging into her midriff, from the pins that poke into her scalp. Her head is a pincushion.

Kate dances the waltz. Kate talks to suitors. Kate wants more. But more what? She doesn't know. The way that corset binds her waist, her ambitions have been restricted by her parents, by society. I ponder the notion of "coming out," and how the meaning has changed through the decades, though even today there are debutantes whose families show off their purebred fillies. It makes me grateful to be from Saskatchewan, where virginity encapsulated in a white gown was never a thing.

The next picture is of Kate in France. Her hair has been bobbed, satin gloves swapped for leather ones. She's scrubbing a spark plug with her toothbrush. The next photo is her at the wheel of her truck, Bessie, along with three other Cards. They look like best friends. I wonder if one is Jessie Carson. In a third photo, she's at the cash register of the mercantile. She's grinning. She is radiant. She's done what she came to do. She set herself free.

I can't help but wonder what the before-and-after photos of my life will look like. Before I get my master's in creative writing and after? Before I publish and after? Before and after my first date with Roberto?

Next, I find Kate's engagement photo, dated 1927, with her future husband, Colonel Arthur Sidney Hay, a retired Indian Army officer, in England. Their only child, Charles Hay, was born on May 9, 1928. When the Second World War broke out, she joined the Women's Auxiliary Air Force. Incredible. She served in two wars. How many people can say that?

Maybe Kate Lewis is still alive. These days, people can live to be a hundred. It's a long shot, but it's all I've got. At the welcome desk, I scour the phone book. There are twenty Lewises and ten Hays. I dial the number for Edgar Lewis. In the scratchy pause before the first ring, I take a deep breath, trying to prepare myself to speak to an actual Card.

"Hello, I'm looking for a woman named Kate Lewis or Kate Hay. . . . She'd be around ninety-three years old. She's a war hero. . . . No? Maybe you're related to her son, Charles?" "Hello, I'm looking for Kate Lewis Hay. . . . I'm writing a book. . . . Have you heard of CARD? No, not card games, the American Committee for Devastated France. . . . Thanks, anyway."

Thirty calls later, and not a single lead.

As I board the bus, my mind is full of questions. Where do you look for a discreet librarian who did her job? How do you find someone who's disappeared from history? I stare out the window, seeing but not seeing. I'm happy that Kate Lewis survived the war and found happiness. I wish the same for Jessie Carson. The bus slows and enters the city. I'm grateful to the Cards, for proving that people from different backgrounds can become close. I think about how I've kept too much to myself.

———

MY WRITING WORKSHOP IS SOMETHING I USED TO LOOK FORWARD TO, but Professor Hill's insistence on the need for literary connections is demoralizing. I wish to believe that good writing is what matters, that a story to share, especially one like the Cards', is what counts. Hill is so negative that sometimes I consider dropping the class. But if I can't cope with his feedback, how will I handle comments from an editor?

On rare good days, he refers to our class as "hopefuls," since he doesn't consider us real writers. In less charitable moods, he calls us "hopeless." We write ourselves into a verbose lather to please him. When we hand in assignments, even the atheists pray that he won't hate them. We went from wanting to publish to being obsessed about getting an A.

Tonight, Professor Hill reads Meredith's story aloud. "Subpar world building," he concludes.

"It was brilliant," I say. "I was right there with the character."

Glaring at me, Professor Hill crows that in his twenty-year tenure, he hasn't uttered a compliment because he "refuses to coddle." He orders us to reread *The Scarlet Letter* by Nathaniel Hawthorne. The assignment is to write from Hester's point of view. The bell rings, he's the first to leave.

As usual, the other writers go for a bite. It's week six, and I still haven't joined them. Habit, I suppose. A bad habit.

In the bar, around a table, ten of us fill up on pretzels. They order beer; no one seems to care that I only got tap water.

"It was brave of you to speak out," Meredith tells me.

"Someone had to do it," I reply.

We discuss what we admire about her piece as well as a few things she could work on. Professor Hill has made us into a cohesive group. There's no competition, only compassion.

I schedule a coffee date with Meredith, whose writing and chutzpah I admire. She's put together, a real New Yorker. Her outfit—the tailored navy blazer, pristine white button-down shirt, jeans, and jodhpur boots—is tastefully expensive. Despite this, I have a good feeling about her. We meet at Roberto's favorite deli, and not because I hope to run into him, but because he's right that they have the strongest coffee. A whiff is enough to raise my heart rate.

Ensconced in a burnt-orange booth, Meredith insists that we were in a few undergrad English classes together, but I have no memory of her. After I was attacked in my dorm room, I kept my head down and did my homework.

"You used to quote *Slaves of New York* and demand we read more women authors," she says.

*I don't know what my greatest fear is; maybe just that I'll be caught and discovered, accused of being a child in an adult's body.*

"At the Strand, I was ten feet away from Tama Janowitz as she signed books," I said. "It was incredible to see an author our age. She made me believe I could do it, too."

"What are you reading these days?"

As I rack my brain for the title, I dump too much sugar into my coffee. Why am I nervous? Meredith and I should have a lot to discuss—the way we pursue the perfect sentence like an elusive white whale; how pedantic Professor Hill can be; our side gigs, mine at the NYPL, hers at an upscale Japanese restaurant—but our conversation is as stilted as a blind date. I'm used to staring at the page, thinking for hours in silence. But here, I have to articulate my thoughts, when in fact this is why I write, because I find talking so damn hard.

After an awkward pause that I'm sure Meredith felt as well, she says, "I'm getting a lot out of Professor Hill's class, what about you?"

He's condescending and bitter. I judge Meredith for her rotten taste in men. Trying to be open-minded, I ask what she likes about the class.

"He's honest about his experiences in publishing. He challenges us. He makes the classics accessible. In high school, I hated *The Scarlet Letter*. Writing from Hester's point of view is a revelation."

I find her take fascinating. Life really is perspective.

"Anyway, I hope he'll like my novella," she says.

We writers submit to teachers and editors, trying to appeal to someone, to get them to eat up our words. Submission—I wish there were another word for it.

"What's your writing process like?" I ask.

"It's mainly me complaining that I don't have time rather than actually sitting down to write."

"Do you use a notebook?"

She pats her backpack.

I hold up a green pad. "It's full of dates and details. Research lets me procrastinate on the actual writing."

"Same," she says with a rueful laugh.

"Do you underline phrases in books?"

"What's with the interrogation?" she jokes. At least, I hope she's joking. "This is starting to resemble a job interview."

That stings. I feel I've forgotten how to make friends. Maybe I never knew.

"A *literary* job interview," she rushes to add. "Like at a bookstore. I dream of opening my own someday, to be surrounded by my favorite stories."

"That's what I love about the library." I explain that I help document the collection.

"I'd love a behind-the-scenes tour."

"I could show you around." I wonder what Meredith would make of Roberto.

"And yes, I'm a hard-core underliner," she says. "When I love a phrase, I have to highlight it."

"Me, too." I explain that my mom reread books at various times throughout her life, underlining and writing in the margins in a different color each time. In perusing her favorites, I understand her thoughts from when she was twenty, thirty, forty years old.

She died when I was twelve. Until then, I'd been a pretty happy-go-lucky kid. Her death had been an earthquake that only my father and I felt—a tremor that changed everything. Classmates couldn't understand. Now, fourteen years later, there isn't a day that goes by that I don't think of her. The way she loved feeding our dog scraps from the table when she thought no one was looking, the way we blasted music on our three-mile walks around wheat fields, the way she listened to me. I still dream about her. When I awake, I'm happy for the seconds that it takes to remember she's gone. Pain washes over me anew, and I live the loss all over again. It hurts. Another thing that hurts is that folks back home never mention her. Maybe they don't want to remind me of my loss, maybe they've moved on. But remembering Mom and her stories keeps her alive. When she was in Catholic school, the nun who directed choir insisted that Mom was off-key and told her to mouth the words instead of singing them—though Mom recounted the story as a joke, I felt her hurt; the way she shot me a pointed look when another adult said something she and I knew to be ridiculous made me feel like we were on the same wavelength; the way she celebrated every single sunrise made me appreciative of them, too.

I don't tell Meredith that my mother's books are my greatest treasure. Maybe I will when, if, we get to know each other. We sip our coffee in silence, but not the uncomfortable, desperate kind. It is light, like the crisp, white margins in books. Necessary nothingness needed to make sense of words.

She pulls a notebook from her backpack and shows me a sketch of a town. I recognize the name of the grocery store and movie theater from her chapter. "You're really talented. Is this where your story's set?"

She nods. She explains that she's a visual learner and has to see the neighborhood to understand the rapport between the characters and place. "I'm all about place. Who we become is about where we're from."

Is this true? I recall the Cards' descriptions of the land and wonder if images would help me write the story.

———

THE FOLLOWING DAY, BEFORE MY SHIFT STARTS, I PAY A VISIT TO THE map division. According to NYPL lore, the librarian has the underbite of a bulldog and the brain of a supercomputer. Affectionately known as Map Man, he possesses an eidetic memory. Once he's seen a map, he can recall everything about it.

"Northern France in World War I?" he repeats, steepling his fingers as if I've given him a challenge. He dashes off. Ten minutes later, he reappears with a rolled-up map. When he spreads it out, I'm surprised to see swaths of green, yellow, and red. If pressed to describe the pattern, I would call it traffic-light camouflage.

I point to the biggest splotch; Map Man swats my finger before it can touch the canvas.

"That's the Red Zone," he explains. "It's full of unexploded shells."

"Unexploded shells?"

"Bombs and mustard gas, hand grenades and ammunition. Not to mention diseased animal cadavers."

I pause at that. "But the ladies I'm researching live near there. They drive through those areas."

"They probably didn't know about the arsenic, lead, and mercury contamination."

Of course, I knew that CARD worked in the war zone. I just didn't fathom the daily danger. I squint at the map and locate places I've read about, like Blérancourt and Soissons; however, other names don't appear.

"The map is missing several places."

He gets huffy. "Don't blame the map! Blame the German army. They annihilated entire towns."

"How old is this map?"

"Not that old. At the current rate of work, it'll take three hundred years to clean up the Red Zone. To put it bluntly: This is the Chernobyl of France."

"Chernobyl?" I side-eye him.

"Four hundred and sixty square miles, much of it ready to detonate."

# CHAPTER 16

JESSIE "KIT" CARSON
BLÉRANCOURT, MARCH 1918

B ombs whistled a shrill tune then crashed into nearby fields, throwing up dust and clumps of earth. They hurtled into buildings, destroying homes and setting fires. Smoke filled the air. Beneath our feet, the ground shuddered. For months, we Cards had lived with the threat of an enemy attack, but now that it was happening, we found ourselves stunned. Max swirled around my legs, perhaps fearing that he'd be left behind. I crouched down to comfort him. As I spoke, my teeth clattered. "I'm scared, too. But we'll get through. I don't know how, but we will."

First, we needed to evacuate families closest to the front, people like Victorine and Vivienne. *The enemy will plow through . . .* Tom had said. But thanks to house calls and story hour, we knew everyone in the four-county area. And they knew us. In building a network, we'd also built trust. Our fleet of Fords could take villagers to safety. But where was that exactly? What was the plan?

Twenty-five Cards awaited instructions. Miss Morgan proposed sending villagers to the train station ten kilometers away. Once there, they could continue on to Paris. Dr. M.D. argued that it was too close to the front. The roads and station would be targeted.

"Trains can evacuate the most people," Miss Morgan said.

"Are they even running?" Dr. M.D. snapped. There was no way to find out.

"If not, the *chauffeuses* can drive on to the capital," Miss Morgan reasoned.

"We don't have the luxury of sending vehicles away. We need them here. And what will become of villagers in Paris? We haven't had time—"

"There'll never be enough time." Miss Morgan raised her voice. "Our Paris depot has clothing, food, and a list of possible housing. We've prepared. We're prepared."

"Compiègne." Dr. M.D. pointed west. The town was twenty-five miles away. "The Huns never got that far."

"Which isn't to say they won't," Miss Morgan shot back. "Paris is safer. Villagers will find lodging and jobs there."

Southwest to Paris or west to Compiègne? *Would you tell me, please, which way I ought to go from here?* said Alice in Wonderland. All we could do was calculate, estimate, gauge, guess.

The Annes stood nose to nose, armed with strategies instead of boxing gloves. More than anything, this fight scared us. The two always spoke as one.

"Jobs?" Dr. M.D. said, her voice tight. "How long do you think this battle will last?"

Miss Morgan looked to the heavens, as if to appeal for patience. "The war's gone on for nearly four years, with no end in sight."

No end in sight. And no real decision. The argument ended in a stalemate.

Lewis cradled Marcelle in her arms. When Marcelle noticed me at her side, her head shot up.

I touched the small of her back. "You must evacuate. I will find my way to your friends—"

"*No.* I'm coming with you." She thanked Lewis for comforting her and disentangled herself.

Should I treat Marcelle like a young girl or like any other Card? Seeing her steel herself, I gave a single nod and tried to ignore the fear that gripped me.

Dr. M.D. turned to Lewis. "How many villagers can we fit into each Ford?"

"The better question is how much time do we have to evacuate the towns nearest the front?" she replied. "Civilians there are sitting ducks."

We could feel the bombs inch forward—the booming explosions louder and louder. An acrid odor filled my nostrils, making me sick to my stomach. The sky darkened. I told myself it was storm clouds, not the smoke from burning buildings.

Still in their nuptial finery, twenty villagers crossed the moat. The bride and groom held hands. With armfuls of belongings, the dazed bridal party trailed behind them. I didn't see Madame Petit.

"The bombs sound like they did in 'fourteen." Jeanne clutched her bouquet.

"We weren't sure what to do," Henri said. "My Jeanne insisted 'the ladies will know.'"

The bride and groom could have sought help from the mayor, the notary, or even the pastor; instead, they turned to CARD. Grasping my handkerchief, still damp with Marcelle's tears, my hand flew to my heart. How it swelled at their confidence in us. Even the two Annes were momentarily speechless: Dr. M.D.'s mouth formed an astonished O; Miss Morgan's eyes glinted with emotion.

"You did the right thing," she assured him.

"Lewis," Dr. M.D. said, "get them to the station and put them on the train."

Though she didn't say it, we heard the end of her sentence, *before the rails are bombed.*

"Jeanne, where's your mother?" I asked.

Her mouth trembled. "At home. I'm afraid she's holding out for my sister."

"Do you think she'll evacuate?"

"She won't give up hope that Suzanne will return. I can't leave without Maman."

"Give her time," Henri soothed. "Perhaps she'll come to her senses."

Dozens more villagers, including the pastor and Marcelle's mother and brothers, approached. Upon seeing her family, Marcelle embraced her mother. "I am going to help them."

"I won't leave without you, my girl."

"Please, Ma. I will find you. I'm needed here."

Madame Moreau wiped a tear and let her daughter go.

As Marcelle joined me, Dr. M.D. said, "You're too young."

"I know the roads better than anyone," Marcelle shot back.

She met my gaze. *We can do this,* she seemed to say. *Get in and out of the Red Zone before the enemy—or anyone else—is any the wiser.*

"I'll accompany her," I told Dr. M.D.

"Leave now," Miss Morgan ordered. "Save as many civilians as you can."

As Marcelle prepared the truck, her mother's chin rose a notch. "That's my girl."

"Ma, get in." Marcelle pointed to Lewis's Ford.

Madame didn't move, though the boys tugged on her arm.

"I said get in!" Marcelle ordered.

"The farther from here, the better," Madame Moreau replied as she and her sons climbed in the rear. The wedding party joined them.

"Breckie, load the medical supplies in the bed of a truck," Miss Morgan said. "I don't want a single vial lost. Cookie, box the food and merchandise in the mercantile. By God, the Boches won't get even one bar of soap from us."

A series of shells exploded, each one closer than the last. Black smoke enveloped us. I coughed and coughed.

"Change of plans," Miss Morgan shouted over the din. "Breckie and Cookie, we'll relocate our stock once we've evacuated everyone."

I climbed into the passenger seat. Marcelle's hands were steady on the wheel.

"Trust me," she said.

"I do."

In the Red Zone, my ears were attuned to the bombs. Did the blasts grow louder or fainter? Was that a truck backfiring or the blast of a rifle? A bomb landed just feet away, blowing rocks and clumps of dirt onto us, cracking the windshield and rattling my bones. The truck veered into the ditch. Marcelle brought us back to the road. When I could no longer hear the chug of the engine, I realized that the blast had deafened me.

"We're getting closer," Marcelle shouted.

Instinct told me to crouch down, but Marcelle had to keep watch, so I did, too. Almost there, almost there, I told myself as the Ford lurched down the bank, over the trickle of water, and back up. Would the girls know we were coming?

"What if they won't leave?" I asked.

"The danger of death outweighs their fear of being separated, I hope."

Were the girls in the same encampment? There was the lean-to covered with the tarp.

Marcelle slid from the cab and shouted, "Victorine! Vivienne!"

I lifted the tarp and peeked inside. Little black shoes; a copy of *Alice in Wonderland*; a pair of pink pajamas, neatly folded, Bruno the plaid bunny. Wouldn't Vivienne have taken him? Had someone abducted the girls?

"Girls!" Marcelle shouted again. I could hear tears in her voice.

"Maybe someone already picked them up?"

"Maybe the damn Boches. Are we too late?"

She fell to her hands and knees. I thought she was going to cry, but she spread her fingers like fans and felt around for tire indentations or footprints.

"It looks like they went that way."

We followed the tracks for about a mile, slowly, silently, winding our way through the forest of dead elms.

"Victorine! Vivienne!" I whisper-shouted, for we did not know who else might be in the area.

I couldn't help but remember my arrival in Picardie, when I'd ventured into a field full of land mines. And now here I was again, in the danger zone, this time with Marcelle in tow. Tom was right, it was reckless to risk her life. If she was injured—or killed—what would I say to her mother? The thought of it made me wobbly. To steady myself, I held tight to a blackened tree trunk. *Breathe.* When I let go, ash covered my hand. Ash, a symbol of grief and death.

"Kit," Marcelle whispered. "Are you all right?"

"Let's keep going."

Under the explosions of bombs, I thought I heard a rustle of dried leaves, the pounding of feet. Was it the wind or my imagination? Friend or foe? I charged in front of Marcelle to shield her in case we ran head-first into the enemy. Instead, two girls emerged from behind the trees.

"Victorine! Vivienne!" Marcelle whispered.

The sisters came running and embraced us.

"We thought you forgot us," Vivienne sobbed into my waist.

"Never," I said.

"This morning, we saw four German soldiers, so we ran," Victorine explained.

Hairs on my arm went up like antennae. The enemy had been nearby? Were the men doing reconnaissance work, or were they deserters? I asked Victorine if she'd seen any signs of troops—vehicles, cannons, munitions—in the area.

She shook her head. "Just those men."

Small mercies. Still, I didn't know if we should inch back to the Ford, slowly and quietly so as not to alert the enemy, or if we should just get the hell out. In the end, we ran, ducking under branches, tripping over logs, trying not to worry that the snap of twigs could disclose our location. We wanted to leave this place. Back at the encampment, we bundled the girls and their belongings into the Ford and set off.

Victorine glanced at the rear windshield, perhaps worried that we were being followed. "Can't we go any faster?" she asked.

"I wish we could," I responded, explaining that the jagged shrapnel on the road made the trip dangerous. A punctured tire would slow us down even more.

The deafening explosions of bombs grew closer. We left the charred forest and returned to a section of prairie, where vegetation and houses had been burned down, the devastation of entire towns so complete that we could barely make out the foundations of buildings. As creepy as the blackened trees had been, this barren, empty land frightened me even more.

"It's taking forever," Vivienne muttered with the tip of Bruno's ear in her mouth.

Five miles from Blérancourt, dozens of people from surrounding villages clogged the dirt road. Several carried bundles of belongings. A woman used a wheelbarrow to transport three small children. An old man had leashed his goat and was tugging her along. They all appeared to be heading in the same direction as we were, to CARD Headquarters. We loaded them in the bed of the Ford.

As we crossed the moat, I exhaled in relief. At tables in le clubhouse, women and children waited to be evacuated. Cookie proffered the treats that had been meant for the afternoon CARD party. While their children nibbled at cookies, mothers wrapped theirs in napkins for later. Victorine and Vivienne took seats next to little Benoit and Madame Hugo, who clucked over them. The girls wolfed down scones and punch. Marcelle said she wasn't hungry. I was shaking too hard to hold a glass.

Together, she and I leaned on the haunch of the Ford. Even now in the middle of this offensive, when I was scared and had trouble catching my breath, I looked at Marcelle and knew that the future was in good hands.

"My heart is still pounding," she admitted.

"You're amazing." I tugged on her pigtail. "Your sangfroid saved those girls."

"Couldn't have done it without you. But no one can know the risk we took. Ma would kill me. And she'd kill you."

This was not to be the only danger that Marcelle and I got ourselves into, nor the only secret we'd keep.

Dr. M.D. strode over. "Where have you two been? Break's over. Marcelle, load up the Ford and take people to the station. Carson, a handful of villagers refuse to budge. Encourage them to evacuate."

"Who won't go?" I asked, though I feared I knew the answer.

"Madame Petit and Sidonie Devereux."

I felt myself blanch. Both had been through so much. How could I hound them to leave if they preferred to remain?

"*Bon courage*," Marcelle said. "If anyone can persuade them, it's you."

# CHAPTER 17

JESSIE "KIT" CARSON
BLÉRANCOURT, MARCH 1918

The shelling grew louder and louder still as I ran down the road to the village, passing frightened folks attempting to make it to Headquarters. The air swirled with smoke and dust. An old man carried a mattress on his back; his wife clutched the family Bible to her chest. A pink-eared soldier hobbled on crutches. A mother walked with her four children clinging to her skirt. I headed in the opposite direction as if swimming upstream, knocking against shoulders and elbows.

Sidonie had said she had nothing to live for. Did she still feel that way? And would Madame Petit leave without word of her daughter Suzanne? Could I convince them to evacuate? Max and I sprinted down the turnoff to Madame Petit's farmhouse. With every bomb that fell, I ran faster. My heart thumped *move, move, move*. When I knocked, Madame opened the door immediately, as if she was expecting me. She still wore her wedding finery, and I thought again how wonderful it was that her daughter had chosen her to be her matron of honor. I peeked behind Madame, hoping to spy a packed bag.

"The buttons on your blazer are fastened wrong," she noted. "And your hair's a mess."

I didn't bother to fix my chignon. "The Boches, an offensive, started." I was so wiped out from the run that my voice was raspy, and my brain didn't put the French words in the right order.

"I'm not deaf."

"A bag—have you packed?"

"I'm not going anywhere." She plunked herself down on the stool at the butcher's block.

"Let's get out of here!"

"Who are you to tell me what to do? What do you know about war?"

She reminded me that she'd evacuated once. The road was rough. *Non, merci.*

"Please do what CARD and the army suggest."

She rubbed the ribbon that had belonged to Suzanne like a talisman. "I'm not evacuating. Better to die in the ruins of my own home, in my own bed, than retreat."

Time was not on our side. How long could I spend with Madame Petit, when others needed convincing? How could I give up on her?

"You have much to live for," I argued. "For Jeanne, and now Henri. The other villagers count on you. They love hearing your stories. So do the Cards. You must go."

"Go where?" She ran her hand over Max's brown coat.

"Paris. Miss Morgan knows a lady there. You can teach her how to make your delicious velouté."

"Tell her not to use turnips. Turns the soup bitter. There, now you know. I'm staying."

I knelt beside her. "I know you're remaining for Suzanne."

"She'll return home." Madame was oddly stoic, as if she'd foreseen the attack and had long since made up her mind to remain.

"If the bombs fall any closer, there might not be a home to come back to."

"I must be here for her. I wasn't before."

"And what about Jeanne?"

I thought of my own mother. She was stubborn, and that stubbornness had served her well. Luckily, the trait was hereditary.

"Madame, imagine how Jeanne would feel if anything happened to you. She loves you so much. Please think of her now."

I moved to the door, hoping Madame would follow. I didn't know if we had an hour or a day to evacuate. I didn't want to die on Madame Petit's stoop. More important, I didn't want to fail her, or the Cards.

"*S'il vous plaît*," I begged.

"*Non.*"

"Madame, I know something about leaving family behind. It was difficult for me to come to France without my mother and sister. There's not a day that I don't think about them and wish that we could be reunited. You have a chance to join Jeanne. She's not an ocean away, she's but a five-minute walk from you."

In psychological chess matches, my mother had perfected the game of guilt, move after move, pushing my sister and me toward her objective. I tried one of her tactics now.

"If something happened to you, Jeanne would be devastated."

"She has Henri now."

"What could possibly be stronger than a mother's love?"

Stalemate. I looked to Max. He took a fold of Madame's skirt in his mouth and tugged gently.

She snorted. "Even your dog is bossy!"

He tugged more forcefully. She patted his head, as if to concede that he had a point.

"You're right," she told us. "I do want to see Suzanne again, but Jeanne is here. She needs me."

He let go.

From the sideboard, Madame Petit fetched a cake mold. "A wedding gift from my parents, God rest their souls." She plucked her rosary from the bedside table and wrapped it in her husband's old shirt. She enveloped her three silver spoons, five porcelain plates, and her mother-in-law's earthenware pot in tea towels. She stuck them in a flour sack and tied the top with twine.

I was about to advise that she pack the minimum, but without a word, Madame strode out. I followed her to the stream behind her house.

"Let's go!" I said. "We don't have time."

She kicked off her shoes and hiked her skirt to her hips. Flour sack in hand, she waded in.

"What are you doing?" I cried, half worried that she was going to drown herself.

"The same thing I did before."

"Which is?"

"Securing this sack to a rock for safekeeping."

"What if the current carries your treasures away?"

"Better the river than the Boches!"

Back inside, she dabbed at her legs with a towel. After she packed, Madame stroked Suzanne's pink ribbon thoughtfully before tucking it in her pocket. Cane in hand, she looked around the farmhouse.

"You can't imagine how it feels to leave home."

"I know. It's unfair."

There was more I wanted to say. *I'm sorry. I wish you didn't have to go through this. I hope with my whole heart that we'll be back.*

On the road to Headquarters, Madame's bundle in my arms, I couldn't help but glance in the direction of Sidonie's sod house.

"Go on," Madame said. "She'll need convincing."

I wasn't so sure. These last weeks, Sidonie had opened up. Perhaps she was even en route to Headquarters. I decided it would be prudent to escort Madame the entire way, in case she changed her mind. Max hurried ahead and returned to us, hurried ahead and returned. Madame leaned on her cane, telling him, "I'm moving as fast as I can."

Headquarters swarmed with people. The mayor and the miller, the countess and the ragpicker, farmers and lame soldiers, widows and grandparents accompanying little ones. They came not only from Blérancourt but from surrounding towns. But where was Sidonie?

Clipboard in hand, Miss Morgan informed us that she hadn't seen her, but that the wedding party had been taken to the station. Madame would be reunited with them in Paris. I asked if Victorine and Vivienne had been evacuated. Miss Morgan said that Lewis put them on the train with Jeanne and Henri.

With so many counting on us, there was no room for error. Lives were at stake. What if we failed? What if I failed? I glanced at Madame Petit.

"See to Sidonie," she told me.

I wended through the throng of villagers eager to evacuate. On the road, lines of army vehicles barreled toward the front. The exhaust fumes drifted onto Frenchwomen, now refugees in their own country, as they maneuvered bundles filled with photos, pots, and clothing. I scanned every face, hoping to see Sidonie among them as they inched toward Headquarters. Fear pulsed through my veins at the realization that she hadn't evacuated. I understood that she was still grappling with sorrow, but I thought that she'd turned a corner in her grief.

At the prospect of arguing—maybe even fighting—with Sidonie, my jaw tensed. I needed to prevail, even if it meant losing her as a friend.

Upon arriving at her house, I threw open the door.

She was at the kitchen table, having a cup of tea. Much like the first day we met. *Cannons only kill people who have something to live for,* she'd said.

"What are you doing here? Why haven't you left?"

She shrugged. "If my time comes, it comes."

"We both know that it's more likely to come in the war zone than in Paris."

"What do you know about loss?"

"Back to that, are we?" I shouted. "Time is all we have. And you're wasting it. The longer it takes to convince you, the longer we remain in danger. I refuse to leave you here to die."

Both of us were taken aback. I didn't recognize my voice myself.

"I never asked you to come here," Sidonie said bitterly.

"You didn't have to. Now let's go!"

She didn't move.

I slammed my fist on the table. The teacup shook in its saucer. "I said now! Does our friendship mean nothing? Do you truly feel like you have nothing left to live for?" Tears were thick in my voice, and Sidonie looked away.

"My baby is buried in the church graveyard. I've never been more than two kilometers from her. How can I abandon my little girl?" Regret infused my being as Sidonie adjusted the pleats of her black dress, her mourning. How could I have been so callous? Finally, she said, "Do you think she would want me to stay or go?"

I took her hand, expecting her to push me away, but she didn't. "She'd want you to be safe."

Sidonie gave a single nod. "Help me pack." She pulled a carpetbag from beneath her bed and tucked her husband's *History of Picardie* inside before the two of us threw in her clothing.

Outside, smoke from the fires enveloped us. My eyes watered. I covered my nose with my handkerchief. My mouth felt as dry as a bowl of dust.

"It was like this the last time," Sidonie said.

I knew she'd stayed, and nearly starved, under the German occupation.

"I'm glad that you're here," she admitted. "Last time . . . last time was chaos. Villagers had no help."

I squeezed her hand. "There's no place I'd rather be than with you."

The château had become a transit center. Dr. M.D. was taking down names, so we could schedule departures and keep track of destinations. Beside her, Sidonie grabbed a clipboard and began writing names as well.

"Will wonders never cease?" Breckie said. "Sidonie has come back to life."

Miss Morgan directed people she appeared to have divided into two categories—the frail who needed to be transported and those who could walk if need be. Madame Hugo didn't want to leave without her husband, but Monsieur insisted that he and his father could walk. Three of our Fords had been dispatched. The one remaining was now filled to the brim with old folks and fretful mothers trying to calm their children. Miss Morgan offered the last seat to Madame Petit, who didn't budge. She simply regarded Madame Hugo, who clasped little Benoit and Sebastien to her breast.

"They should ride," Madame Petit insisted.

"We all should," Miss Morgan argued in flawless French, "but space is limited."

Around us, the boom of bombs exploding into the earth shook us. I coughed as clouds of smoke overcame us. I'd heard that the German cannon Big Bertha had a range of nearly eight miles. Or was it kilometers? Neither was reassuring. We needed to get away.

"We don't have time to argue," I shouted over the din. "Please take the seat next to the driver."

"*Non,*" Madame Petit said.

I appealed to Max, who lay on her dusty boots. I was outnumbered.

"Merci," Madame Hugo said.

The Ford roared to life and motored away. Madame Petit shifted from one foot to the other. Folks in the North were used to constant movement—weeding the garden, tending the chickens and rabbits, tilling the field. It was not in their nature to stand about.

"Would you feel better if we walked?" I asked Madame.

Monsieur Hugo and his father said they'd be joining us, too.

"I was right," Madame informed me. "Children first."

On our way out of Blérancourt, we passed a house where, two weeks ago, workers had patched the hole in the roof so skillfully that you could hardly tell a shell had hit it.

There was heartbreak in rebuilding, only to have the houses demolished. All that planning, effort, and hope gone. If I felt demoralized, how must Madame Petit and the Hugo family feel?

Madame Petit, Max, and I continued on the road along with Monsieur Hugo, his father, and a retired schoolmaster, joining handfuls of other refugees and wounded Allied soldiers separated from their units. No vehicles passed. Near and far, bombs continued to fall. The explosions spurred us on.

An hour before dusk, the sky turned black, and another cloud of black smoke rolled over the road and began to choke us. Our only hope was that the trains were still running. My pace quickened with each explosion. I rushed forward, then forced myself to pause for Madame Petit. Max matched his steps to hers, letting Madame find reassurance in petting him. She talked, and he listened.

Just as our group caught up to a solitary woman on the road, Lewis approached in the Ford on the way back from the station. She pulled to a stop. "Get in!"

During the last miles, I listened to the woman. Like Madame Petit, she had a burlap sack full of practical items (a shirt that she'd just pressed, an embroidery hoop from a childhood friend) and sentimental treasures (the New Testament from her godmother, an etching of her house by a traveling artist who she said had asked for only a franc for his work). To heat her feet, Madame Petit balanced her arches on the exhaust pipe. These women had been through evacuations before—during the Prussian War of 1870 and the evacuation in 1914—and could make small talk. My jaw was tight and my head ached. There was more dirt in my mouth than on the road. It felt like we could be hit by a bomb at any time.

When we arrived, I helped the villagers through the masses of panicked people to board the train. A soldier with a broken arm was hugging his wife and three children as they said goodbye. A woman showed a photograph to passersby. "This is my son. Have you seen my son?" The carriages were so packed that the conductor was unable to shut the doors.

Lewis and I returned to HQ, too drained to speak. I cast her what I hoped was a reassuring glance. Her mouth quivered. We crossed Marcelle on the road, her truck filled to the brim with families. I'm not sure she noticed us.

Ten more times, we shuttled villagers to the station, to safety. Until the road was deemed too dangerous because of the advance of the German army. Instead, we drove the Northerners to the west, to the town of Compiègne, where Cookie set up a canteen to feed refugees.

That night, the air raid lasted from 8:30 p.m. to 4:30 a.m. None of us got any sleep. In le club-house, a bleary-eyed Dr. Murray Dike read the general's telegram aloud. The Allies hadn't been able to stop the German onslaught. It would be a matter of hours before the enemy arrived.

We were given ten minutes to pack.

# CHAPTER 18

WENDY PETERSON
NEW YORK, MARCH 1987

Pale morning light. Around my apartment, shadows. Around me, stillness. Before me on the coffee table are history books and copies of documents. *On 21 March 1918, some 6,500 German guns and 3,500 heavy mortars opened up a terrifying five-hour barrage. . . . the British casualties on that day were enormous: 38,500 men, of whom 7,000 were killed and 21,000 captured.* A journalist wrote, *Over the hill, it appears the sleeping Hun has awoken. He begins not only to growl, but to paw the air with his shells. Word comes from the military that the Blérancourt base is no longer safe. Evacuation is necessary. Many assume that twenty ladies will throw a few treasured belongings into suitcases, bid a tearful farewell to their neighbors, and board the next train to Paris, abandoning their charges, their supplies, their post, and their million dollars' worth of restored fields and homes. Under such dangerous conditions, I should perhaps make a hurried departure, but the women of the American Committee for Devastated France were not of that kind. The women stayed and did their work.* According to a CARD report, *On March 23rd alone, CARD evacuated 1,600 refugees by train. By the 26th, working day and night, they evacuated almost the entire county, even villagers who initially refused to leave. They set up infirmaries and canteens, and found lodging and jobs for refugees.*

I'm in awe of the Cards and could read about them forever. But at some point, I must try to write. I balance my word processor on my lap and begin to type. *Destruction stretched to the horizon. There was not a single soul, nor a blade of grass, and the countryside blended with the gray clouds to form a colorless, hopeless terrain . . .*

An hour later, I finish the section and tuck the typed pages into my purse. Part of me fears they aren't good enough, fears I'm not good enough. Part of me wants to show Roberto. I enter the NYPL through the revolving door. Having the first chapter in the library feels good, and is a start to having my whole book here. I imagine Roberto congratulating me. I imagine hugging him. I imagine him kissing my cheek. I imagine his lips on mine.

When I walk into Remembrance, he isn't at his desk. Disappointment douses my excitement. I ask the Aardvark where Roberto went. Without looking up from his viewfinder, he replies, "The big boss summoned him to the reading room."

"For good?"

The Aardvark snorts. "Doubtful. Wasn't he pretty much banned from there?"

Curious, I wander upstairs to the reading room. And there he is, reigning from the circulation desk, a bibliophile surrounded by his first love—books. In a blue button-down shirt that defines his broad shoulders, Roberto is positively beaming. He looks so happy that it makes me happy for him. Beside him is a gray-haired patron. Who is she? Maybe one of his former habitués.

Of course, I wonder what he did to get banished, but don't dare broach the subject. For all of his extravagance and insistence on freedom of expression, he's close-lipped about the whole affair. In any case, being in the vast, airy reading room makes me content, and not simply because Roberto is here. I love seeing the bowed heads of readers lost in their research. I love the crinkle of the cellophane book jacket as Roberto opens to the library card, then the gentle thwack of the date stamp. I love the warmth of the sunbeams that wrap themselves around me. It makes me realize how depressing it is to work in a basement.

"You haven't been here in ages," the patron tells Roberto.

"I was . . . transferred to another department."

"One of the trustees tried to tell me you no longer worked here."

"I'd never leave without saying goodbye," he says so softly I barely hear.

I sense his devotion to the patrons. Observing him in his natural habitat, I now see how unhappy he's been.

"The head librarian said you were stuck in some back office." The patron scowled as she recalled the encounter. "I told him no one would stamp my books but you."

"Thank you. I miss you, miss being here."

"Old age is good for something—makes it harder for people to argue with me."

They laugh.

Remembrance isn't the right place for him. He's a people person and would rather work with patrons than paper. More than anything, I want him to be happy. He has encouraged me and been a sounding board. I need to find a way to help him, too.

―――――

WHEN HE RETURNS TO HIS DESK, I SHOW ROBERTO MY OPENING PAGES. At first, I'm nervous, but soon he is nodding in appreciation, then chuckling at something that Kate Lewis says.

"You have to keep going. I have to know what happens next."

I feel my cheeks flush at his praise. I tell him I could not have done it without him.

We stand there awkwardly, not wanting to end the conversation, not knowing what else to say.

"Do you want to grab a bite after work?" He speaks nonchalantly, but the invitation doesn't feel casual. We don't see each other or communicate outside of the NYPL. On my days off, I miss him. Monday through Friday, I'm dying to see him. Well, to see what he'll do or say. Roberto is everything I could ever want—smart, funny, caring, sexy, well read.

*Do you want to grab a bite?*

He regards me, eyes earnest. I take a step closer. The only sound is the buzz of fluorescent lights. I want to say yes. I haven't had a date in five years. This might not be a date, though it seems like he's opening the door for more. I'm scared. But I want more.

"That would be great," I say, striving for the same nonchalance.

———

AT THE DELITRON, AFTER THE WAITRESS SERVES US COFFEE AND CREAM, Roberto hands me a box wrapped in silver paper.

"What's this?" I balance the present on my palm. It's the weight of a book.

"Something to celebrate your two-year anniversary at the NYPL."

"How do you remember? Even I don't."

"The first day of spring. You wore a striped cardigan, and had a copy of *The Color Purple* tucked under your arm. I said to myself, *She's definitely a main character*."

*The more I wonder, the more I love.* My heart flitters like a firefly. *I love his dear eyes in which the vulnerability and beauty of his soul can be plainly read.*

"You're my favorite leading man," I admit. "Unlike the Aardvark."

"He's an extra, at best."

"Who gets killed off in the first fifty pages."

I remembered seeing Roberto on my first day. In the staff room, he was hunched over my third-favorite novel. I hadn't been sure about taking the job, but when I saw the corner of his mouth upturned as he read *Bones of the Moon,* I took it as a sign. *If you are very lucky, you're allowed to be in certain places during just the right season of your life: by the sea for the summer when you're seven or eight and full of the absolute need to swim until dark and exhaustion close their hands together, cupping you in between.*

"Is this the right season of your life?" I asked back then.

"It is now," he replied. "'People are always waiting to be discovered.'"

"Open the gift," he tells me now.

Knowing that I will treasure everything he ever gives me, I gently tear the paper at the seam. Inside is *Wide Neighborhoods*, Mary Breckinridge's autobiography. It's a first edition published by Harper in 1952. How long did it take him to track this down? And how much did it cost? I tell him I love it and reach across the table and hug him.

He looks pleased by my pleasure.

"Pick a random section and read us a paragraph," he says.

I mock frown. "Sacrilege! You know I'm a begin-on-the-first-page reader."

He doesn't tell me to loosen up or to quit being so uptight. "Pick any paragraph you like."

To change things up, I open to page 78. "*Tartier was a village of 365 inhabitants before the war. Now it has four men and three women—no children—who have returned . . . we drove up through that country on a road broken with shell holes, past fields with barbed wire, and seamed with trenches and dugouts, past roadside graves of soldiers . . . the earth was torn apart, broken into ghastly crevices, seamed with jagged openings, thrown over and over, and furrowed with large craters. Nothing recognizable was left . . . not a weed, not even ruins for long distance. . . . A farmer sticks a spade in the ground and is likely to strike a hand grenade. Our casualties in the past week were three men and two women, of whom only two men survived, one with the loss of both hands.*"

When I finish the page, we don't speak. It's a shock to go from a date to war. He gulps down his coffee. The waitress comes over for a refill and takes our order. We choose the same thing—matzo ball soup.

Roberto says that the Cards are amazing and that he didn't realize how much danger they faced.

I trace the fragile dust jacket with my fingertips, wondering what the gift means. "I can't believe you found this for me."

He shrugs. "You must finish writing the Cards' story. You know that, don't you?"

"I do." Instinctively, I touch my purse, where the pages are nestled. The book will help with that. I tell him that it's the most thoughtful gift I've ever received.

He raises a brow. "How can that be?"

I explain that my mom was a reader, but she died when I was young. My dad never really knew what to do with a daughter. For birthdays and Christmas, he got me baby dolls when I was little, and perfume now that I'm older. He has never understood the magic of books, and has never understood me. Roberto asks about friends.

I swallow. "Mostly, I feel a distance from people, like we're in a subway station, and they're on a different platform. I can't cross the tracks to join them, and the noise from the trains is so loud I can barely make out what they're saying."

He frowns, like what I've confided pains him. "We're friends, aren't we?"

"You get me." It feels good to talk to him.

"I'm lucky. I'm pretty outgoing. Everyone likes me, but the big boss."

"That's a pretty big 'but.'"

I admit that I went looking for him and noticed how happy he was in the reading room.

"I don't mind Remembrance," he replied.

"Maybe it's time to move on. You deserve a job where you're a main character, not just a bit player."

"I love working with you."

"I love working with you, too. And I would never want to hold you back."

"Today made me realize that I miss working with patrons," he admits.

"And how much they miss you."

We slurp down our soup as we discuss favorite lines of Faulkner. Mine is *It's not when you realize that nothing can help you—religion, pride, anything—it's when you realize that you don't need any aid.* Roberto's is *They all talked at once, their voices insistent and contradictory and impatient, making of unreality a possibility, then a probability, then an incontrovertible fact, as people will when their desires become words.*

The hours slip by unnoticed, until we look up and it's dark outside. In the station on the way home, we pass a photo booth. I pull him in and close the curtain behind us. I kiss his cheek. The touch is a spark that sends electricity through my body. I kiss his lips. Again. Again. They taste of coffee. I want more. I want him. He pulls me close. I wrap my arms around his shoulders and kiss him again. It feels divine.

The patter of high heels brings me back to myself.

Roberto and I stare at each other. For once, he doesn't have a glib comment.

"I'm glad I finally kissed you."

"I'm glad, too."

He kisses me again and again. Wrapped in his arms, I don't want to leave. From the moment I saw him, from our first conversation, I have wanted this. I have spent two years scared to reach out, but I'm not scared now. The Cards' courage has rubbed off on me.

# CHAPTER 19

It had been two months since we Cards had evacuated. I was assigned to a makeshift army hospital, where the injured were cared for in a large surgical tent. My job was keeping track of arrivals, mainly British and American soldiers. Those first days, each time an ambulance screeched to a stop, I searched for Tom. At best, he could have been the driver; at worst, unconscious in the back. As stretcher-bearers unloaded the wounded, my heart bounced in my chest, my regard drawn to any black-haired soldier. After weeks of wishing yet fearing that he would appear, of not sleeping through the night—worried about Breckie and Lewis and Marcelle and Sidonie and the Annes and Tom—my tired brain settled into a routine. At a desk in a small hut, furnished with a hot plate and a lantern, I filled ledgers with information about the wounded.

Each time an ambulance backed up to the entrance of the triage tent, I rushed to help the patients however I could—offering reassurance, removing mud-caked uniforms, fetching a doctor for a more complex case. Max knew he couldn't follow me inside, so he sat patiently near the flap.

Fortunately, I wasn't the only Card stationed here. Cookie prepared meals such as bone broth. We saw more of each other here than we had at Headquarters. Though she and I didn't always have time to talk, in exchanging glances, we said more than words. I was grateful that someone from home bore witness to all that we experienced, grateful that we shared this connection.

We were cut off from the other Cards or our French friends. Likewise, I hadn't heard from Tom and didn't know where his unit was fighting. All I could do was pray. There was barely time for correspondence home—I jotted one-line missives to my sister and mother.

On the battlefield, there was a first triage—only the injured with a chance of survival were loaded in an ambulance. A second triage happened at a clearinghouse just miles from the front. Now with us, a third, in which stretcher-bearers—who suffered from clubfoot, palsy, or polio, otherwise they'd have been at the front, too—set the wounded gently on the earthen floor of the tent. Mary Sun, a nurse nicknamed for her sunny disposition, examined the tag that medics had fastened to the button of each man's uniform, detailing the injury. Critical cases were taken into surgery. For the rest, Cookie ladled broth while I moved among the men, ledger in hand. Crouching beside them, I took down each soldier's name and regiment, as well as his birthplace, date of arrival, and particulars about his injuries. Then I asked for the name of a loved one and an address back home, just in case.

Some soldiers reached for my pen and wrote their names in a shaky scrawl. At first, I thought that maybe they didn't trust me to spell their names correctly. I soon learned that it was because they'd lost the ability to speak. Others spoke in grave, hoarse tones as if already in a tomb. Mustard gas had blistered their throats and lungs, and even caused burns on their bodies. Unlike when they were hit with a hailstorm of bullets, soldiers didn't sense the gas attack until it was too late.

Mary Sun, Cookie, and I stripped the men of their mud-soaked, bloodstained shirts and trousers in case the cloth was contaminated with gas. Before their uniforms were delivered to the fumigator, soldiers emptied their pockets, veritable treasure troves. Everything from a grandfather's pocket watch to a family photo to a letter from a fiancée. I made a show of stowing the keepsakes in a locked box, which I'd scoured a nearby town for on my first and only day off.

"Thank you, sister," they said, the relief written on their faces as clear as type in a book.

The first time one called me "sister," I didn't know whether to laugh or correct him—I was no nun. Cookie and I wore our uniforms, but instead of our hats, we donned blue cloths, which covered our hair and framed our faces. Perhaps the men had distant memories of holy sisters singing at Midnight Mass. Mary Sun said it was a term of affection and respect.

Our patients had been hit by bullets or shrapnel or gas. They'd been prodded by the medics, loaded in ambulances, and jostled for miles before coming to us—in great pain, caked in blood, starving, and miserable. Still, many insisted that they were "lucky" because they'd "only" had an arm blown off or a bullet in their thigh. Sometimes as I took down information, a soldier gripped my hand. His eyes closed, and I wondered who he was imagining me to be—his dear mama, a high school sweetheart? I stroked his arm and let him dream that he was home.

If the men were not too tired, we gave them a sponge bath. If they were exhausted, a stretcher-bearer transferred them to the hospital tent, which was enveloped in the stench of pus, formaldehyde, sickeningly sweet ether, and sometimes even death. Inside, it was quite an intricate dance—there was little room to maneuver because the beds were packed together. Some soldiers had been up for forty-eight hours straight and were more in need of rest than of medical care. They immediately fell asleep—perhaps intuiting that they were finally safe.

In between ambulances, I responded to frantic letters from mothers and wives trying to locate their men. A mum from Brighton even arrived at my doorstep, or tent flap as it were, and I escorted her to her son, a sergeant convalescing from a gun wound.

In the evening, by the light of a gas lantern, I typed reports that could never convey the crowded conditions, the suffering, the lack of sleep and supplies, the bravery of the wounded, the devotion of the medical staff. The reports could not show what the wounded felt, what they endured. We treated so many that I wondered who was left to fight at the front. When my head ached from the paperwork, I moved to the hospital tent, where I made beds, served meals, or got a soldier a gulp of water. For the first time in my life, I was so busy that I had no time to doubt, only to do. One corner of the main tent was reserved for soldiers who'd been gassed. A dozen men curled up in agony, unable to cough that poison out, their eyes swollen and bloodshot. They could barely swallow because their throats were in agony. One soldier was racked with a hacking cough and got no relief in four long days. Cookie and I fashioned a small tent around him and boiled water inside to create a moist vapor. Either she or I stayed with him. The longest he went without coughing was a minute and a half. Gassed patients couldn't eat, so they couldn't heal. Medicine couldn't help them, not even the best medicine of all—time.

Doctors did rounds, peeling back a bandage to evaluate a wound, bringing bad news that another surgery needed to be performed or, worse, that the soldier was well enough to return to active duty. Some wept at the news that they would have to go back to the trenches.

When the soldiers' suffering got to be too much, when I became overwhelmed at the number of wounded—proof of what man was willing to do to fellow man—I sought solace in the library of my mind, in the comfort of leather-bound books. Meandering along the shelves, I sought dear friends such as *My Ántonia, Emma,* and *Madame Bovary,* and marveled that the spines of books seemed sturdier than those of men. On a particularly tough day, I took refuge in the stacks. *Touch the gold lettering you loved as a child,* I told myself. *It's like the tinsel that glints on the Christmas tree. List the books that you loved best, like Madame Petit recites prayers on her rosary.*

Books my sister, Mabel, swore by: *Sister Carrie, Lord Jim.*

My eternal to-read list: *Moby-Dick, The Scarlet Letter, Les Misérables.*

Childhood favorites: *The Secret Garden, Anne of Green Gables, The Wizard of Oz.*

Being among books raised my spirits. As long as I could return to the library in my mind, I felt I could face whatever came.

———

At night, I ached for Tom and longed to lace my fingers in his, longed to feel the warmth of his body next to mine as we drifted off to sleep. I liked to think of him reading *The Adventures of Kit Carson*, and dreaming of me, his Kit Carson. I missed the villagers, too, and recalled sipping tea at Madame Petit's butcher's block as she recounted how she and her husband used rusty scythes to harvest the wheat, and how she wished she could use one to lop off the fat heads of the Boches. Were Jeanne and Henri able to have any kind of honeymoon, or even one special night? I wondered about the Hugos, where they were, and if they'd be able to return to their wheat fields in time for harvest. I yearned for walks with Sidonie, to tromp over the hill as she explained that of course we were surrounded by wheat fields in Blérancourt, wasn't wheat, or *blé*, the very first syllable of the town's name? I hated that we'd lost touch, that the German attack had sent us careening like marbles on the playground.

One morning, it was a shock to hear my name announced during mail call. From the faraway city of Orléans, Sidonie must have tracked down the address of the Paris CARD depot, and someone there forwarded it on to me. She was resourceful, a born librarian. I prayed I would have the chance to tell her that.

*Ma chère Kit, I am writing you in French so that you will practice. I do not want you to forget the elegant language of Molière. English is all good and well, but no one has ever mistaken it for the language of love.*

*I am doing quite well as a seamstress. My first days in the Loire Valley were a shock. Imagine seeing houses still standing. A thriving farmers' market where milk is plentiful. A library complete with a bald bureaucrat, zealously guarding the books, which are locked in the closet behind his desk. In the street, I listen to passersby discuss things other than graves, barbed wire, and land mines. Here they speak of flowers.*

*I forgot that people could live normally. I'm tempted to remain, to begin my life again. To pretend that the first twenty-nine years did not happen. And yet I long to have news of our friends and neighbors. How*

*are you and Breckie and Lewis and Marcelle? Has anyone heard from dear*
*Madame Petit?*

*Affectionately,*
*Sidonie*

I drank in her decisive cursive. The letter filled me with happiness
and wonder, the same wonder I felt upon seeing winter's first snow-
flake. It was a reminder that this war couldn't last forever.

———

THE TART COLD OF SPRING TURNED TO SUMMER. ON A BLESSEDLY SERENE
Sunday morning—no ambulances in sight, Cookie and I took tea. At my
desk, I pushed the thick ledgers to the side to make room for the ceramic
pot and cups. Idle instants were rare, and we intended to savor this one.
Cookie removed the cloth covering her hair. Curls cascaded down her back.

"At Headquarters, why didn't you join us at mealtime?" I asked.

Cookie huffed out a laugh. "Do you know why I'm such a good
cook? My mam taught me how to make do. I'm able to bake bread and
prepare recipes—even missing key ingredients. Most meals I cooked
were without meat. That's why my cauliflower tastes as hearty as a
ham."

"But why didn't you eat with us?" I persisted.

"Because I have more in common with the village charwoman."

I harked back to the few interactions we'd had. Why hadn't I been
friendlier, like Breckie had been to me? "Had the Cards been rude?"
I asked, but what I really wanted to know was *Had I been dismissive?*

"Not really. Staying in the kitchen is my habit. My mam lectured
about the importance of respecting the 'natural order.'"

"I can relate. My mother has old-fashioned ideas about me and
matrimony. But times are changing."

Cookie snorted. "Nothing changes. Miss Morgan is a millionaire,
I'm the cook. I would no more join my employer for dinner than I
would roast a cat for Thanksgiving."

"Well, promise when we get back to HQ . . . if we get back, that you'll sit by me."

"I promise to think about it. Enough about me. How are you getting on? The surgical tent is a far cry from the library."

"But it doesn't have to be." I wished to create a cozy place like the library of my mind, a rest tent where the wounded could take a break from the ward, where they would forget their worries. We drew up a list of materials that we could procure from the army, such as a canvas tent, as well as from town, such as donated tables, chairs, and a bookcase. Could we order newspapers? Absolutely, but which should we subscribe to? What books would appeal to the wounded? Maybe some westerns. Could we create a coffee and hot chocolate station? The men would love it. Should we order cigarettes? Personally, I hated the damn things, but they did bring respite.

The following Sunday, Cookie and I pitched the rest tent. I wished erecting a library were as simple. Inside, she set up the refreshment station, and I loaded a wobbly bookcase with a special delivery from Paris—novels and newspapers in English. Stretcher-bearers lifted the soldiers into wheelchairs and delivered them to our tent. Other patients walked slowly, so that they could soak in the sun. The flap was kept open for fresh air, which lessened the stench of sick. With a hodgepodge of chairs and tables, we had enough room for ten patients and Max, who sniffed every proffered hand.

John, a soldier from Cornwall who'd had an arm amputated, was the first to try our hot chocolate. There was a glimmer in his eye as he and Cookie bantered about who could whistle the best.

Beside them was Bill, a strapping Kansan who barely fit in the wheelchair. "I'm too big for this contraption," he bemoaned.

As they often did, the men recounted how they got hurt. Bill had gone into no-man's-land to track the enemy. "Good thing was, I got him! Bad thing was, a shell exploded into my thigh." He'd passed out from the pain, and three of his men dragged him through the mud and barbed wire to safety. "Thorn, Lybbert, and Ober." He recited the names as reverently as the pastor did *Jesus, Mary, and Joseph.*

What surprised me most was the tenderness the soldiers showed each other, sharing a cigarette, having a laugh. John from Cornwall held a Gitane to the mouth of Elliot from Kent, a mustachioed private with no arms.

We had three categories of wounded: up-and-abouts, who had the use of their arms and legs; sitters, who were able to sit up on their own; and the bedridden, who were unable to move. Our up-and-about patients spoiled the others. They were seriously injured as well, or they'd have been shipped back to the front or to a convalescent camp. They wrote letters home for and read to the gravely injured. How inspiring to see men who struggled themselves find the will to help those who suffered even more.

Inside the rest tent, there was no talk of ailments. The men had a tea or cocoa, just like they would at a hometown café. Wisecracking with the customers, Cookie made a good waitress. Max made the rounds, and some men spoke to him more than they did to humans.

Each afternoon, we held news hour, where a soldier read articles aloud, sometimes in a hoarse baritone, other times a timid tenor, depending on their exposure to gas. Mail was distributed, and Cookie and I helped the wounded respond. She and I would forever remember those tender words to folks back home, the way soldiers shielded their loved ones. As Cookie delivered the mailbag to town, I read aloud to patients who were too ill or tired to read on their own. Today's novel was *Light of Western Stars* by Zane Grey.

*When Madeline Hammond stepped from the train at El Cajon, New Mexico, it was nearly midnight, and her first impression was of a huge dark space of cool, windy emptiness, strange and silent, stretching away under great blinking white stars.*

*"Miss, there's no one to meet you," said the conductor.*

Bill was so engrossed that he forgot the cigarette in his mouth. The embers burned his lips, and he yelped. The other men, anxious to learn Madeline's fate, merely shushed him. What would she do? Who would help, or hurt, her? On a dark stretch of road, she happened upon a cowboy.

I continued to the end of chapter one. *The night seemed dark, yet there was a pale, luminous light—a light from the stars—and she fancied it would always haunt her.*

*"Where are you taking me?"*

I closed the book.

"Where's he taking her?" Bill demanded.

"Will she be safe?" asked Elliot.

"We'll find out tomorrow," I said.

Then I received the best compliment in the realm of books: "Please, sister," Elliot said. "Just one more chapter."

I shook my head. "Tomorrow."

"I've been to New Mexico," Bill told the men. "It's the prettiest place you've ever seen. After Kansas, of course."

John from Cornwall lobbed a newspaper at Bill's face, and the men laughed.

While they enjoyed a smoke, I tidied the magazines on the bookshelf. The tent flap rustled, and a soldier with his arm in a splint entered. He cursed his gun, the war, his sergeant, and the doctor who'd informed him that he was returning to the front. When he noticed me, the swearing stopped.

"Sorry, sister." He blushed.

I liked being called "sister"—it was like having a thousand brothers whom I cared for, the sweetest, bravest boys.

"As a New Yorker, I've heard much worse," I replied.

"You've crossed the ocean to tend to us," Bill said, glaring at the soldier. "The least we can do is take care with you."

"It ain't right to cuss in front of a lady," Elliot the private added.

"What lady?" I heard a familiar voice ask from behind me. "All I see is a tough-as-nails librarian."

I turned to the tent flap to find Lewis standing there, horizon-blue sky breaking through the clouds.

"Sweet splatter dashers!" I threw my arms about her waist and swung her around. "How?" I asked as I set her down.

How she'd changed. Bags under her eyes, faint lines across her forehead. Instead of a cheeky grin, her expression was grim. Like Cookie and me, she'd seen the wounded, the scared, the exhausted, the dead. According to the newspaper, at her canteen near Château Thierry, workers fed as many as seven thousand soldiers per day.

"Tell me everything," I said.

She glanced at the men, as if to say, *That's too dark a tale*. "I'm on *permission*. After working three months straight, with only a half-day off here and there, the matron gave me four days off."

"And you came here?"

"It was that or le Ritz."

"You could have had a hot bath! And a meal in a real restaurant with waitstaff to coddle you."

She shrugged. "I preferred to see how you and Cookie were getting on."

I hugged her again.

"Meet Lewis," I told the men. "She saved my life when I walked into a field of land mines. Her bravery has made me braver. You'll get along great. She smokes like a chimney, just like you all."

The men stared at Lewis, a brunette vision. Used to the staff, old enough to be their mothers, they teased and spoke freely, but with someone their own age, the soldiers were suddenly shy.

"And speaking of smokes . . ." Lewis rooted out a tin from her pocket and proffered a cigarette to each man. She didn't act surprised when she saw Elliot, the English amputee. She merely lit the cigarette and placed it in the teen's mouth, as reverently as a priest proffering a host.

"A smoke always makes me feel better," she told him as they puffed away.

"Open the flap even wider," I bellowed, and the men guffawed.

Despite the tobacco fumes, Lewis was a breath of fresh air. She shared the news she'd gleaned from other Cards. In Versailles, Madame Petit had reunited with Jeanne and Henri, who were taking care of Victorine and Vivienne. The Hugos roomed at a boardinghouse near Notre Dame and worked at a bookshop nearby. The Moreau family lodged near the Eiffel Tower. While the boys attended school, Madame worked as a seamstress and Marcelle "chauffed." Apparently, a young American soldier followed her home, begging her to accept a date. She said *non*, but he returned the next day and the next, calling her his favorite Card, his queen of hearts. Her mother threatened to whack him with a spade.

"Poor Madame!" I said. "Her children are a handful."

"Listen, Kit." Lewis took a drag on her cigarette and blew out the smoke slowly. "I'm being a coward."

She asked if there was a private place to talk. We went to my tent, and she sat me down.

"The truth is, I came because I have news."

And I knew. Tom.

My mouth went dry. For the longest time, Lewis and I stared at each other dumbly, she not wanting to say the words, I not wanting to hear them. Finally, I asked.

"How?"

"At the end of May, our fellows were caught in an ambush. Most of them didn't make it. Jimmy was laid up in the hospital for over a month. He came to me as soon as he could. He said Tom's last words were about you. Most of his words were about you. He asked Jimmy to give you this."

She handed me a mud-splattered copy of *My Brilliant Career* by Miles Franklin. I flipped through the pages, where Tom had written in the margins. "What do you think of this?" "What a brave woman— like you." A passage was underlined: "Our greatest heart-treasure is a knowledge that there is in creation an individual to whom our existence is necessary." And beside it was written, "This is how I feel about you, dear Kit."

"I'm so sorry." Lewis embraced me.

I could only cradle the book to my chest; grief had lodged in my throat and I had trouble breathing. My head rested in the crook of her shoulder. As Lewis stroked my hair, I found myself yearning for my mother, who was always able to make childhood hurts go away.

Over the coming days, I mourned Tom, the loss of our future. A modest home in rural Pennsylvania with a view of a covered bridge. A hearth with a real poker instead of a bayonet. A velvet love seat, where we could discuss books or read quietly. Old age spent together in a small town, where the biggest news would be not war but rather a stubborn filly who refused to leave the meadow in a downpour. Though the owner tugged on her bridle, the horse resisted because she instinctively understood the restorative power of rain.

This is what death does. It steals what is ours. It takes what could be, what should be. Memories are all I have, and too few at that. Never enough, never enough. A year, a decade, a lifetime would not have sufficed.

At night, alone in bed, I waited for the tears to flow, but I could only stare at the ceiling of my tent. As I drifted off to sleep, I relived our conversations, reveling in the wonder in his voice as he said, *Isn't it funny that we traveled all the way to France to meet?* At dawn, I awoke with an empty ache. But the wounded needed me, so I soldiered on. Over breakfast, I met Cookie's concerned looks with a tired shrug. In the rest tent, I forgot my own sorrows as I recommended books or read aloud to the patients.

In late July, the summer evening was tranquil. It was nearly nine and the sun was painting the sky brilliant shades of orange and pink. There was no longer the rush of arriving ambulances like there had been in the spring. Now, I watched what I hoped was the last one of the day putter along the pockmarked road and screech to a halt. As Milton, the Canadian stretcher-bearer, began to transfer the wounded to the triage tent, I noticed that one of the soldiers gripped a mud-smeared book.

"It's nice to see you reading," I told him.

"I had four westerns in the trench. Kept them dry in my helmet. That's how I got this head wound." He pointed to his bandaged temple. "Should have listened when my captain ordered me to keep my gear on. For a while, I was in the Wild West, and forgot there was even a war on."

"Books make you forget bullets?"

"I was in the desert, next to a cactus as tall as me. I could smell the sand . . ."

I glimpsed the title and felt a jolt of recognition. *The Adventures of Kit Carson,* the dime novel I'd given Tom. For one wild moment, hope flared in my chest. It seemed too much of a coincidence. I asked if I could see the book and flipped through the pages, wanting one last message, one last word from Tom. The margins were empty, and that's when it hit me that he was really gone.

I felt the soldier's callused hand on mine, and realized my tears had finally begun to fall. "Are you okay, sister?"

His gentle voice was too much to bear. He was just a boy. I wiped my face and took a shaky breath. "I gave a copy to someone I cared about, very much. It was the last time I saw him."

"He went west?"

I nodded. "My mother would call this book a 'heavenly hello.' A greeting from the beyond. I used to think that was ridiculous. That she was ridiculous."

"And now?"

"And now I want her to be right." Fresh tears streamed down my face.

"You can keep the book," he said.

I placed it in his hands. He needed it more than I. Blood was seeping through his bandage at the temple. I'd tarried long enough.

"Let's get you taken care of." I gestured to a nurse. "Tomorrow, I'll show you the little library."

Though a part of me would always love Tom and mourn his loss, I understood that my work in France was far from finished.

# CHAPTER 20

WENDY PETERSON
NEW YORK, MARCH 1987

On Saturday evening, when Roberto comes to pick me up for our date, I open the door and hug him. "Thanks to Mary Breckinridge's autobiography, I found a mention of Jessie Carson! Page eighty-seven, 'This library, set up by Jessie Carson, whose Card name was Kit, was as frequented as my clinic by a literate and book-starved people.'"

"I'm happy for you. Your research is paying off."

"You're the one who got me *Wide Neighborhoods*."

"You're the one who tracked down Mary Breckinridge."

"I love that Jessie has a cool nickname. I guess she didn't get married like we thought."

"She survived the war though, right?"

"The autobiography is pretty dense reading. I'm only up to page one hundred."

Roberto is dapper in his gray suit. I want to tell him that he doesn't have to change for me. I appreciate his offbeat style. My favorite was his short-lived eau de mustard cologne, when he smelled as delish as a corndog at the state fair.

We go downstairs to the Ramen Place. In my neighborhood, it's well known that within a matter of minutes, the broth can cure the common cold. Plus, the owner's son gives me the senior citizen discount. It started as a joke when I was a senior in college. Three years on, he plays along with a sly wink. It's an example of the unexpected kindness and connection with New Yorkers that make me appreciate the city.

At the table, Roberto slides a paper over to me and asks if I saw that the position of program manager has opened up. I read the job description. Outreach to authors, inviting them to speak at the NYPL, coordinating with bookstores to sell their books. I have to admit that it sounds interesting.

"You'd book speakers—writers, historians, journalists, and artists," he says. "Plus, you'll make all sorts of contacts for when your novel comes out."

"Leave Remembrance?" As awesome as the job sounds, I'd miss Roberto. And if I hadn't worked there, I never would have discovered the Cards.

"You're too talented to languish there."

"Actually, I intended to say the same thing to you."

"With so many treasures to preserve, there's job security," he argues.

"But no advancement. A third of your life is spent at work. Don't you want a job that utilizes your knowledge?"

I dig in my purse and hand him applications from the Morgan, the New York Society Library, and the Conjuring Arts Research Center. He leafs through them.

"You don't want to work with me any longer?" he asks.

"We'll see each other outside of work."

He takes my hand. My whole body comes alive. God, I want him.

"Are you hungry?" he asks.

"What?" I demand, scared he could read my thoughts.

He points to the menu. "Dinner?"

"Do you want to go to my place?"

We order to go.

In my studio, we're intent on each other. I don't feel self-conscious and double-check that I did the dishes. He doesn't examine the packed bookcase and half-dead fern for clues to my personality. Roberto knows me. He closes the distance between us. I run my fingers through his hair. He kisses me, and I pull him close. I trust him. We move to the daybed, where he lies down and eases me on top of him. Our tongues become entangled. It feels like I can't get close enough, and I push my chest to his and straddle him. In response, his hips rise to meet mine. I groan. It feels so damn good. I tug at the buttons of his shirt, wanting his skin on mine. A little voice in my head says, *This is happening too fast. Slow down.* Like a seasoned librarian, I tell it, *Shhhh,* and let myself revel in the heat of Roberto's hands as they explore my back.

He turns, and we find ourselves lying on our sides, torsos together, his thigh nestled on mine. My leg is trapped. I can't move it. I go from in the moment to snagged in a memory that hits me like a slap. I relive the last time I was alone with a man, that study session in my dorm room, when the frat guy pinned me to the bed, his hand covering my mouth, his beer breath as he muttered, *Just shut up.*

Panic bites into my brain, and I freeze.

Roberto immediately shifts to the edge of the bed. "What happened?"

I inch away, telling myself, *I'm safe. Everything's okay.*

"It's nothing."

"When we were kissing, I felt you leave. We were together in the moment, then you were gone."

"What?" I sit up. My breath is ragged.

"Where did you go?"

"The past. I'm stuck in the past." My voice is small.

"Do you want to talk about it?"

I stare at a spiderweb in the corner. "Not now."

Roberto extends his hand, letting me take the lead. I enlace my fingers with his.

"We can take it slow," he says. "There's no hurry. Can I hug you?"

I nod.

We sit, hip to hip, knee to knee. His arm around my shoulders feels warm and safe, like a cocoon.

"Thank you," I whisper.

"Let's have dinner." He heats the soup on my hot plate.

The scent of chicken broth makes my stomach growl. As we dig into the ramen, bits of noodle hit us on the chin, and we giggle. Being with him feels like home, like nothing bad can happen, like he will always be here for me.

He does the dishes, then moves to leave. I tell him I don't want him to go.

On the daybed, I spread my star quilt over us. We burrow underneath. The earlier electricity of desire transforms into a desire to know everything about each other. How old is he? Twenty-six. How long has he been a librarian? Since he was a page in high school. The last time he'd been in love? He and his ex broke up two years ago.

It's his turn to ask questions. "Do you plan on staying in New York?"

"I figured I'd be here forever. When I first got here, I was too busy to think of home, of family, to be homesick."

"And now?"

"The city is expensive. And loud. I'm starting to miss the quiet of Saskatchewan." I swallow. "I never thought I'd say that."

"Are you thinking of leaving?"

"No. I want to finish writing my book."

"Good," he says, "I need to see how the story ends."

I know he means my novel and our relationship.

"Do you think the Cards made it back to Blérancourt?" I ask.

"I like to think so."

It's nearly 5:00 a.m. We don't want to say goodbye. I yawn. He yawns.

In his arms, I sleep.

———

I AWAKE AT DAWN. I GAZE AT ROBERTO, HAPPIER THAN I'VE BEEN IN A long time. Since he's fast asleep, I crack the blind and continue Mary Breckinridge's autobiography, in hopes of finding another mention of Jessie Carson. When I turn the page, a fragment of paper flutters to the floor.

**NEWS FROM DEVASTATED FRANCE**
October 20,1918
CARD President Anne Murray Dike and
Vice President Anne Morgan announce
the tragic death of

# CHAPTER 21

D*ear Jessie,*

*Mabel and I were sorry to hear about the passing of your beloved Tom. Cherish his memory and remember that sometimes hours can be more powerful than years. We purchased a copy of* My Brilliant Career *and donated it to the library in his name. I read an interview with the author and was stunned to learn that Miles Franklin is a woman. She said, "Someone to tell it to is one of the fundamental needs of human beings." Getting your feelings down on paper might help. You can always write to us. We wish we could do something to ease your ache.*

*Mabel and I love receiving your letters and can see how indispensable you are and how fulfilling the work is. You have always been one to finish what you start. I'm proud of you, and I know that your father would be, too.*

*Your loving mother*

As the humid summer days ticked away, Cookie and I found solace in story hour, the soldiers' attention rapt as I took them to places far beyond the absurd, broken one we found ourselves in. Novels were more than escapes to us all—they were lifelines.

At the end of August, five months since we'd been assigned to the military hospital, Cookie and I received orders from Miss Morgan at her office in Paris. It was time to return.

Days later, I found myself bumping down the dirt road I'd traversed a mere nine months ago, on my first trip to Blérancourt. Back in January, I'd been eager to save the world, or at least this corner of France. Each time we'd hit a bump, Lewis's auburn curls had bounced gaily. *Cacklefarts! We're kept on the jump, delivering supplies to a hundred villages*, she'd explained. *The ruts are so awful that the poor little Ford nearly gets shaked to bits.*

Now, as she, Cookie, and I drove through the familiar ruins, Lewis didn't say much. Her bob had grown out and was tied in a low pony-tail. She must have worked on the engine recently; her nails were black from the grease. Somewhere along the war, she'd lost her driving gloves. Sandwiched between Cookie and me, Max remained watchful. Like us, he peered through the cracked windshield. Could more bombs fall? Would we evacuate again?

Ten miles from Headquarters, Bessie was barely advancing. Was Lewis stalling? Perhaps she, too, dreaded what we'd find, if we found anything at all. I longed to see our homey barracks. Not to mention Sidonie's sod house and Madame Petit's crumbling farmhouse. It struck me that this might have been another reason Madame had initially re-fused to leave—because she was afraid to return to nothing.

Our satchels were crammed between our legs because the bed of the truck was laden with supplies: vegetables grown by CARD farmer-ettes in Versailles, sacks of flour, four cages of chickens, buckets of feed, cans of condensed milk, clothing, and household linens. With these necessities, CARD could welcome back the villagers.

Five miles from Headquarters, wheat fields eagerly anticipated har-vest. What a relief to see that Monsieur Hugo's seeding had paid off. It seemed a good omen, though looks could deceive. How could we know if the fields were studded with mines? I didn't realize that I was clutching Max—bracing myself for the worst—until Lewis quipped, "My driving's not that bad."

"Not at all," Cookie soothed, "especially compared to some of the am-bulance drivers—the poor soldiers, jostled within an inch of their lives!"

She and I exchanged glances. Though we were anxious to return to Blérancourt, it had been hard to say goodbye to our patients. At the thought of them, my heart swelled with pride, love, and cigarette smoke. The closing of the military hospital was a good thing—perhaps fewer casualties meant the end of the war.

My favorite word was "finifugal," sorrow at the end of something, whether it was the end of summer, the end of a book, or spending time with soldiers who'd become dear friends. As with the best books, endings are also beginnings. But what would we encounter at Headquarters?

"What if the Boches stole Madame Petit's treasures?" I asked. "What if they burned down our barracks?"

"Then we'll find our courage," Cookie said, "just like the French."

We motored up rue de Picardie. Blérancourt was a ghost town. No villagers discussed the weather in front of the church, no women gathered at the *lavoir* to wash their linens. The town hall was still standing, the oiled tarp in place. It appeared that my library hadn't incurred further damage. We crossed over the moat to Headquarters, where the shuttered barracks and château were intact. I loosened my grip on Max, who barked once, as if in encouragement.

Lewis backed the Ford up to the mercantile and unlocked its door. There was nothing but silence. No pupils reciting lessons, no Madame Moreau chastising her children, no patients chitchatting in front of the infirmary. While Cookie and I stretched, Max scampered from barrack to barrack, sniffing each doorjamb. Everything looked the same. But how could we be certain that the Boches hadn't laid traps?

"Is it safe?" I asked.

"As safe as a war zone can be," Cookie replied.

Empty shelves soon brimmed with linens, sacks of flour, and canned goods. In their wire cages, the chickens clucked nervously. We set them behind the counter for safekeeping.

"Will our friends return?" I asked.

"Many shall, I reckon," Cookie said. "Families have been farming this land for generations."

"Miss Morgan advised that villagers have train tickets for the coming days," Lewis replied. "Work at the Paris depot is overflowing. The two Annes plan to arrive within two weeks."

"It's suppertime," Cookie said. "Shall I toss a dandelion salad?"

"Could we do one thing first?" I asked, and explained how Madame Petit had hidden her belongings by putting them in a burlap sack and tying it to a tree root in the river. "I'd like to place everything on her butcher's block as a surprise."

"Oh, Kit," Cookie said. "Surely, the current washed the sack away."

*Better the river than the Boches,* Madame had said.

"And there's no guarantee that she'll return," Lewis said gently. "These last months, so much has happened—to us and to the villagers. She might not come back. At her age, she might not be able to start over again."

What had kept me going at the military hospital was the thought of Headquarters, everything just as before. How naïve to assume that we could just pick up where we left off.

"We don't want you to get your hopes up," Cookie finished.

"My hopes are all I have."

I whistled for Max, who stayed by my side as we strode to Madame's farmhouse. Cookie and Lewis followed us to the stretch of the stream where the roots of the hollowed-out tree reached into the water. I couldn't see the sack. I wished I could swim, so I could dive in. Kneeling on the damp, sandy bank, I pushed up the sleeves of my blazer and stuck my hands into the icy cold. Not finding the sack, I inched forward, until my skirt was soaked. Lewis grasped my arm, so I could wade in deeper. Feeling around, I found nothing but water.

"You were right," I told Cookie, who watched with worried eyes. "It's gone."

Gone was the earthenware teapot that had been a gift from Madame Petit's in-laws. Gone was the silver spoon used to stir honey in her tea. Gone was the hope of seeing Madame with her toothy grin, gratified at having outsmarted the Boches.

"Not so fast." Lewis was in up to her ankles. "Step a little to the left."

I reached as far as I could, until my chin bobbed in the waves. My fingertips touched something soft. I yanked, freeing it from the tangle of roots. It was the burlap sack.

Lewis righted me. Water dripped from my uniform as I dragged the sodden sack onto the sandy shore. We three knelt around it. Inside was the teapot, the spoons, the plates. Other than books, I'd never been so happy to see inanimate objects. I needed this to be a sign that Madame would return. That the Hugo family would harvest their wheat. That Victorine and Vivienne would continue their love of literature. That Miss Morgan would write fundraising missives on her typewriter, and Dr. M.D. would pen exacting CARD reports that gauged progress the way Breckie measured children's growth. That Marcelle and Sidonie would assist me in the library.

Gingerly, I rinsed the sand from the teapot's belly. Cradling the items in our skirts, we made our way to the farmhouse. Lewis jimmied the door, and we let ourselves inside. The woodburning stove was still there. Hard to believe that Madame Petit wasn't.

Cookie buffed the butcher's block with her sleeve. I laid out the belongings as if I were setting the table, convinced, then unsure, then convinced again, that Madame and her family would return.

———

THE NEXT MORNING, LEWIS MOTORED TO THE STATION TO COLLECT villagers. Would Sidonie be among them? Would Marcelle? I couldn't stop pacing. After an hour of feeling useless, I decided to examine the library's roof. Cookie and I hauled the ladder to the town hall. She steadied it as I climbed. I got distracted by the view—blue sky with nary a cloud, the dreamy kind described in the very best books.

"Kit!" I heard from below. "You're supposed to be inspecting, not noodling!"

Cookie sounded like a cranky librarian chastising a child who'd scaled the bookshelves to fetch a book at the very top.

"Well?" she asked. "How does it look?"

"There's been no further damage."

"Small mercies."

As I replaced the tarp, I spied the Ford lumbering over the moat, with the Hugos in the cab, Benoit perched on Monsieur's lap.

"Usually, you're ordering me off the ladder," Monsieur Hugo called up at me from the passenger seat, and I chuckled. With all that had happened, I couldn't remember the last time I had laughed.

Before Bessie could come to a complete stop, Marcelle leapt from the back, and I hurried down the rungs to greet her. She hugged Cookie and me—jumping, jumping, jumping—as she held us tight. "*Oui! Oui! Oui! Mes amies!*" The youngest Card still had bright pink cheeks, though her pigtails were now knotted atop her head.

"You're a sight for sore eyes," I told her. "And all grown up."

She preened before us, holding the skirt of her uniform out as she curtsied.

Madame Moreau alighted from the truck bed, followed by her sons. "Marcelle! Next time, allow the vehicle to come to a complete stop. When will you learn to be ladylike? A frisking nanny goat will never be a bride!" Madame turned to her sons, who ran along the contours of the dried-up moat. After their having been cooped up, no one could blame them. Well, one person could. "You boys! Am I a mother or a goat herder?"

"How was Paris?" I asked Marcelle.

"Marvelous! I'm definitely a city person. *Parisiennes* loved Ma. She's so handy with a Singer that fine ladies lined up at our door."

The Hugos joined us. "*Dieu merci, Dieu merci,*" Madame murmured as she took in the waiting wheat fields, and the Cards who longed to embrace her. I couldn't believe how much her son had grown. Still shy, Benoit contemplated me from the safety of his mother's skirt. I wondered if he remembered story hour with us. Cookie swooped up Sebastien from Madame's arms and cooed over him.

"We weren't sure we'd ever be back." Monsieur Hugo reached down and patted the ground the same way I did Max.

"We're here. That's what matters," Madame Hugo said. "I missed you girls. Parisians are a distinctive breed."

"Distinctive how?" I asked.

Marcelle's mother joined us. "They weren't as bad as I thought."

From dour Madame Moreau, this was sparkling acclaim. She

glanced around before whispering, "I don't want to get Marcelle's hopes up, but if a position pans out, we might move. After the war, of course."

Her praise for Paris reminded me of Sidonie's letter about leaving her life in Blérancourt behind. Perhaps she was content to remain in faraway Orléans.

"Has Sidonie arrived yet?" Marcelle asked, as if she could read my mind.

I shook my head, worry etching a line between my brows. Marcelle took my hand.

"*True friends are always together in spirit*," she said.

My hand tightened on hers. "That's one of my favorite lines from *Anne of Green Gables*."

"I know. I've been working on my own library of the mind. What else was I to do while we were apart?"

Pride swelled in my chest as I took in the glowing young woman before me. Together, we watched her brothers and little Benoit play in the moat. Other children would be returning, too.

"I think it's time we restart the story hour," I said. "Don't you?"

Marcelle's grin was a beautiful sight to behold.

———

EACH DAY, LEWIS MET THE 10:30 TRAIN TO FETCH VILLAGERS. YESTER-day had brought the mayor and the Countess d'Evry. The day before, the town crier and his aunt. The week passed, and there was still no word from Sidonie or Madame Petit. The pastor hadn't returned, so no Mass. Today, Cookie and I couldn't help but glance at the time. It was nearly noon; Lewis should have been back by now.

Upon hearing the Ford rumble through the village, Cookie and I ran to meet it. Jeanne and Henri each took one of Madame Petit's hands to help her alight from the cab. Victorine and Vivienne hugged me before forming a whispering huddle with Marcelle.

"Wasn't sure you girls would be back," Madame told Cookie and me. "Wouldn't have blamed you, either."

Cookie winked at me. We didn't admit that we had shared the same concern about her.

"Kit fished your belongings out of the river," Cookie said.

"You mean the Boches didn't get them?" Madame replied with a wily smirk.

In the back of the Ford, I spied a slim, dark-haired figure, who grinned when she saw me. Sidonie.

It was my turn to jump like a schoolgirl. "You came back." I threw my arms around her and pulled her from the bed of the truck.

She'd cast off her mourning for a pale yellow dress. No longer washed out, she glowed like Botticelli's Venus, albeit with a chignon. Perhaps her serenity was due to the fact that she'd left this place of tragedy. Was she merely here to collect her sparse belongings before returning to Orléans for good?

"I thought you might have preferred the city," I said, torn between wanting her to stay and wanting the best for her—a new start. How could I ask her to remain, when one day I would leave for New York?

She tucked her arm through mine. "Growing up in bustling Lille, I thought of myself as a city dweller. In Orléans, I realized I've become a country bumpkin."

"Never a bumpkin. You're as elegant as always. Are you certain about returning?"

"But of course. I'm ready to be a librarian."

I felt a quiet thrill. I could catalog titles but was often unable to find the right words to express my feelings. Thank heavens for books. *It's so hard to get up again—although of course the harder it is the more satisfaction you have when you do get up. . . .* Another thing Anne of Green Gables was right about.

"Believe it or not," Sidonie continued, "I missed my sod house and the earthy scent of peat."

"If you're fond of mossy odors, you're in luck. Classic novels have that smell."

"Then I shall be right at home."

———

To celebrate the arrival of Breckie and the two Annes, Cookie served a Northern *plat de résistance*—endives wrapped in thin slices of ham, baked in béchamel, and topped with bubbling Maroilles cheese. My mouth watered before the Recipe Card brought the platter through the swinging door.

"Cookie, do join us." I pulled up a chair.

"Too much to do," she replied.

"For the love of God," Miss Morgan grumbled as Cookie retreated to the kitchen.

A moment later, she returned with a plate and silverware and sat beside me. I dished up her plate, Lewis filled her water glass, and Breckie spread her napkin over her lap. "Forget rebuilding this section of France, our biggest accomplishment is persuading Cookie to join us," Miss Morgan crowed. Cookie met my gaze. We belonged. No matter our perceived station, we'd earned our place at the table.

———

In September, life resumed. Children returned to school. Farmers harvested. And we Cards were back to rebuilding homes and lives, one brick, one shingle, one scone, one conversation at a time. We didn't think much of it when a villager came down with a sore throat. In Picardie, even in summer, there were downpours, and the drizzle made its way into our lungs. Many Cards and villagers had damp shoes and cases of the sniffles. Then at Mass, little Benoit's cough echoed through the church. He seemed to have trouble catching his breath. *Croup,* we said. *It's just croup.*

Before the pastor raised his arms in welcome, Madame Petit said, "I hope the rain will cease, so that the farmers can finish bringing in the wheat."

What could we do, but gauge storm clouds in the distance? What could we do, but pray?

The following day, we learned that Madame Hugo had become feverish, so Breckie checked her in to the infirmary. There was nothing worrying about this. Nothing at all. It was a precaution. We knew that women tend to family members and forget to take care of themselves.

Over lunch, Breckie told us that Madame Petit could not keep food down, not even her favorite pumpkin soup. Since Madame lived aways from town, she would rest at the infirmary. But surely she would be fine. She'd lived through the Prussian invasion of 1870 and now this endless war. The woman could survive on willpower alone.

Over dinner, we learned that Jeanne's husband, Henri, wheezed and wheezed. But he'd survived combat—a little wheezing wouldn't slow him down.

"Each patient has different symptoms," Breckie muttered to herself, since we weren't listening.

Over slices of jiggly flan, we chatted about the first week of school—would the new schoolmarm tame the feisty Moreau brothers? Were the woodworking apprentices good builders?

The farmerettes recounted that one of their billy goats kept escaping. He jumped the fence like an Olympic gold medalist. They kept raising the bar, and the goat kept surpassing his record.

But then we learned that the schoolmarm had taken ill, as had three farmerettes. Benoit hacked and hacked. He ended up in the infirmary, in the cot next to his mother.

At dinner, Breckie muttered, "What is this perplexing illness?" This time, we listened.

From *The Herald,* we learned that the German army continued to retreat, but in Blérancourt, the good news barely registered—for years, folks here had endured advances and retreats. Our attention turned to the patients in the infirmary. Wanting to be useful, Cookie and I prepared chamomile tea for them.

Each morning, Monsieur Hugo checked on his family before he headed out to harvest. He took his wife's hand. "I wish I could stay. You're more important than any crop."

"Don't worry about me," she rasped. "It's merely a cold."

He looked at her askance.

"How can this be happening?" Henri asked from his cot. "One day we're fine, the next I can barely lift my head from the pillow."

"I might know what it is," Breckie murmured.

"What?"

"Influenza," she said firmly. "Visitors must leave."

When we hesitated, Madame Hugo gave her husband a nudge. "A few more days and we'll be celebrating a bountiful harvest."

"Go," Madame Petit seconded from her cot.

On the stoop, Breckie rubbed her forehead. She blinked slowly and gathered her words. In a worried whisper, she informed us that the virus was contagious. Beginning in the spring, it had ravaged America, Europe, and possibly Asia. Yesterday she'd received a letter from a former classmate. At Camp Devens, an army base near Boston, more than 14,000 cases were reported—one-quarter of the total population, resulting in 757 deaths.

"If it's influenza," Breckie finished, "this is just the beginning."

———

At lunch, we noticed that Cookie's cheeks had turned scarlet red. Though she was burning up with fever, we had to drag her to the infirmary.

"I'm fine," she insisted as Breckie slid the thermometer into her mouth.

While waiting for the reading, she shoved us outside.

At the military hospital, nurses had worked in shifts. Here, Breckie was alone. The infirmary's ten cots were all filled. I jumped in Lewis's Ford and drove straight to the Scottish Women's Hospital. The last vehicle I'd manned was my uncle's tractor, so the trip to enlist reinforcements was a bumpy ride, but at least I was doing something.

Back in Blérancourt, the doctoress concurred: no visitors for our patients.

At the mercantile, villagers and Cards chatted. *We survived a*

*German offensive. How bad can this influenza be?* We were confident that all would be well.

"If it really is influenza," Marcelle's mother said, "I doubt that it would travel from Paris—where it killed a famous poet—to a village that isn't even a dot on the map."

In Picardie, we were used to straightforward attacks by bombs, but this sickness attacked by stealth. Day and night, Breckie and the doctoress kept a vigil of sponge baths to soothe fevers and mustard plasters to ease coughing. Breckie didn't return to the barracks. We left changes of clothes for her and the doctoress. Wishing to check on Cookie, we delivered meals but were not allowed in.

"It's dangerous," Breckie told us. "You need to take the situation seriously."

Lewis peeked through the window. "But they look fine."

"How they look is not how they feel," Breckie replied. "We must stop the flu from spreading. You should close the mercantile."

"Nonsense," Lewis said. "People need provisions."

Two days later, she developed a cough and staggered to the infirmary. The two Annes not only closed the mercantile but canceled school and our Sunday gatherings. In the church, the pastor said Mass alone.

We congregated on the steps of the infirmary. Breckie wore a handkerchief over her mouth and nose. She said that the situation was grave and that we should remain in our barracks.

"It doesn't seem that dangerous to me," a Card said. "Lewis seemed fine, just a little under the weather."

"Quarantined because of a cough!" added another. "Nothing a bowl of soup won't fix."

"Daddy says the key to any infection is the dewormer he uses on his hunting dogs," a third insisted.

"Quit speaking nonsense," Breckie said.

We prayed that the fever would break, that patients would stop coughing up blood. As a prisoner of war, Jeanne had suffered, but she'd put painful memories behind her. How could God take her mother or her husband? Madame Hugo had a family. Would God leave two more little boys motherless? Lewis was the most popular Card for a reason—she was generous, quick to diffuse awkward situations, and lovely to everyone. Cookie nourished us with meals and wise words. What would we do without our friends?

A few Cards prayed the rosary. Some couldn't eat a bite, while others downed all the cake they could. Miss Morgan chain-smoked, raising her ashen face to the sky, blowing out reams like a factory pipe. Some of us wrote home. *I'm scared. Which of us will be next? If I die, how will I get home?* We ripped the letters into tiny pieces.

———

HENRI WAS RETURNED TO JEANNE. THE NOT-SO-NEWLYWEDS KISSED tenderly before she tucked her arm around his waist to shore him up on the walk to the farmhouse. Madame Petit soon joined them. Confined to our barracks, we Cards waited for news of Lewis and Cookie. Lewis was released three days later. In her bedroom, so many of us gathered around her that she shooed us out. Only Marcelle remained. She slugged Lewis. "Never scare me like that again!"

A week later, Breckie emerged from the clinic, appearing as wrung out as the wrinkled flour sack that Cookie used to wipe down the wood-burning stove. In her sad moue, we read the news of death. Cookie had died holding Breckie's hand, and we were grateful that she did not pass alone.

We did not get to thank our dear friend for her three meals a day, every single day. Why hadn't we told her how much we loved her buckwheat crêpes? Why hadn't we insisted that she dine with us from the beginning? The worst was that we did not get to say goodbye.

Who were her loved ones back home? What would we tell them? Life was fragile, a bright flame that could be extinguished, an empty train that leaves the station for good, a good book closed half-read.

At mealtimes, with every creak of the swinging door, we half hoped Cookie would come bursting through with a piping hot gratin or news from the village. It was painful to go on without her.

Madame Moreau took over kitchen duty, and though she prepared delicious omelets and buttermilk biscuits, we ate little and spoke in hushed tones. We read that the 1918 flu pandemic virus killed an estimated 195,000 Americans in one month alone. In Philadelphia, more than 500 corpses awaited burial, some for more than a week. Cold-storage plants were used as morgues. A manufacturer of trolley cars donated some 200 packing crates to use as coffins. We said prayers, we disinfected everything twice, we tried to comprehend how invisible influenza could be as deadly as a war. All this was hard for us to understand. We didn't think it could happen, until it happened to us.

# CHAPTER 22

WENDY PETERSON
NEW YORK, MARCH 1987

In the early morning, sunlight reaches into my studio. Instead of turning on the lamp, I read before the window, so that I don't wake Roberto. I stare at the snippet of the announcement I found between the pages of Mary Breckinridge's autobiography:

> **NEWS FROM DEVASTATED FRANCE**
> November 9, 1918
> CARD President Anne Murray Dike and
> Vice President Anne Morgan
> announce the death of

Desperate to know what happened, I leaf through *Wide Neighborhoods* to find the other piece, and learn that a Card named Marie "Cookie" Jones passed away from influenza. Though I'm not religious, I send up a prayer for her, a prayer that her spirit made it home and that she's with loved ones now. It pains me to think that she died in a foreign country, never to see family again. The pang makes me vow to phone my dad tonight. We aren't close, but I could make more of an effort.

I tape the announcement back together, wishing it was this easy to piece together information, and to repair relationships.

Roberto stirs, and we kiss hello. I run my fingers through his hair. He's even more handsome with bedhead.

"You're finally awake," I tease.

He blushes. "I'm sorry. Have you been up long?"

"A whole ten minutes."

He grins. I make us some café olé and recount what I've learned. He raises his mug to Cookie. We sip our coffee and contemplate the sacrifice of the Cards. Breakfast turns to lunch. We end up talking the rest of the weekend, everything from our favorite books, to our families (he has a big family, his favorite is his little sister Carmen), to our wish lists of places we want to visit (him, Biblioteca di Brera in Milan; me, the Franco-American museum in Blérancourt).

Monday morning, we hold hands the whole way to work. Once we enter the revolving door of the NYPL, I worry what coworkers will say. When the Archivist, the biggest stickler, sees us, she says, "Finally! You two are perfect for each other."

In Remembrance, I'm up to year 1922 of the *Under Two Flags* bulletin, and I have nearly finished documenting the fourth and final CARD box. The timing seems apropos to apply for the program manager position. I've learned all I can here and am ready for a new challenge. Still, moving on makes me nervous. In this basement bunker, I feel safe. We work with paper, not the public.

I'm also jittery about tonight's writing class, where I'll submit a CARD chapter for the first time. This past year, I spent weekends crafting short stories about failed relationships. Stories that Professor Hill annihilates: "Too sentimental." "Maudlin." "One-sided."

"Write what you know, that's what Professor Hill says," I explain to Roberto.

"I guess that's why his novels are about aging, alcoholic misogynists."

I can't help it, I laugh. And just like that Roberto has me feeling better about everything—our budding relationship, my workshop, and the possibility of a new job.

The Aardvark shushes us.

"Pretty soon you'll publish your book," Roberto adds. "You'll show him."

I shake my head. That's not why I write. Nonetheless, his faith in me is a balm.

"You're making progress, right? As in actual writing of the CARD story, not as in skulking in the archive boxes? In other words: procrastination."

He knows me too well. It's equal parts reassuring and annoying.

I glance at my submission for tonight's workshop. Did I successfully re-create Jessie Carson's voice? *In CARD, we called each other by our surnames. Lewis was Kate Lewis, a sunny brunette Vassar girl; I, Carson, originally from Pennsylvania. We were both in uniform, a horizon-blue jacket and skirt—the exact same color of the French military uniform.* Not bad, but for now, I must finish photographing the bulletins. The Cards' memories must be preserved.

I find where I left off and continue reading, flipping the pages faster and faster (but also slowly and gently because they're fragile). *Chauffeuse* Marcelle Moreau, the first CARD scholarship recipient, will study librarianship at the New York Public Library.

There's a black-and-while photo of a teen in pigtails next to a prehistoric car (maybe a Model T?). She's sporting a slicker over her dress and appears to be cleaning a spare part with . . . I squint . . . a toothbrush? Her expression, straight and undaunted, is almost insolent. She'd be a handful, I can tell. Wow. Another Card at the NYPL. Unbelievable. Chills. I have chills. She walked these same halls, perhaps studied in the same room I'm sitting in now? Wow, wow, wow. The ups and downs of the trail. Yesterday, I awoke to the heartbreaking death of a Card, and now I find that I'm walking in the footsteps of another. Research: there is no better high.

I'm dying to tell Roberto but see that he is filling out a job application. I slip out of the room and head to the Archivist. "Please, please, please, look up any information you have about the students in the NYPL library program in 1923. I'm interested in a French student named Marcelle Moreau."

She promises that she will see what she can find.

Still buoyed, I return to the bulletins. Six months later, in the very last one: Marcelle Moreau, our youngest Card, accepts a teaching position at the prestigious Alliance Française in Manhattan. Her contract is for two years.

I'm not sure what this school was, or if it still exists. If it does, I'll find it. How long did Marcelle Moreau stay in New York? Did she know my elusive librarian? Is the Frenchwoman still alive? I do the math: if she was eighteen in 1918, that would make her eighty-seven. Did she return to France? Oh my God, what if she survived World War I only to die in World War II? Or maybe she was like me, in love with New York, and determined to stay.

Learning that yet another Card walked the hallowed NYPL halls inspires me to write in my notebook. *We entered the war-torn village of Blérancourt at dusk. The fading light did not cloak the ruins of a stone cottage. Under what was left of the roof, a pug-nosed teen with pigtails perched on a pile of rubble, hunched over a book. She was so taken by the story that the beams of our headlamps did not register.*

Before I leave for the day, I return to the Archivist, who's found a list of the ten students in Marcelle Moreau's class and their grades. Definitive proof that she was here. Unsurprisingly, she got A's in every subject.

I'm so jazzed for workshop that I arrive early. Meredith will appreciate my chapter, but who knows what Professor Hill will say? In the classroom, I fiddle with my folder. I tell myself that even if my writing isn't the greatest, the real-life Card characters will compensate. Who wouldn't fall in love with these women dedicated to helping civilians?

Meredith slides into the seat behind me. "Ready for your turn in the torture chamber?"

"I'm a little nervous."

"Hopefully he won't hate it."

This is the best we can hope for. I consider leaving before Professor Hill arrives to insult the Cards. It's not too late to protect them.

He sails in and plops his beat-up briefcase on the desk. "No time like the present. Who's up?"

I hand him my text. Professor Hill reads in a deep baritone. He could have a career reading Books on Tape. My heart soars at hearing the Cards come to life. As the bombs fall, classmates gasp. Their interest makes me feel like I've done something right.

"Enthralling," Professor Hill says.

I glance around the room, wondering if I was the only one who heard his praise. Maybe I'm having a psychotic episode?

"A charming fairy tale," he continues. "No one helps others like this, giving years of their lives for no reason. And where are the men? How can you have a war without men?"

I remember Roberto's words, something like: *Could your professor be so obsessed with his own experience that he isn't able to help others?*

That could be. Was I seeking approval from the wrong person?

"I liked it," Meredith mouths.

Afterward at the bar, classmates say nice things—they learned about France during the war, the characters were interesting. They also point out that the Cards get along a little too well and that I should find the points of tension.

"Better play your Cards right," one says.

"Sounds like your Jessie Carson is the trump card," another adds.

"You can do it," Meredith finishes. "You have talent in spades."

We laugh, and for once, I feel a part of the group, not outside it. An unexpected gift from the Cards.

On our way out the door, I ask Meredith if she knows what the Alliance Française is.

"Of course," she responds. "I'm a member. Aren't you?"

I shake my head.

"It's the best! There are chapters all over the U.S. and all five continents. They show French movies, offer wine tastings, teach cooking classes for croissants and coq au vin—my mouth waters just thinking about it. My favorite is their conversation classes. You meet great people." She regards me quizzically. "If you're not a member, how do you keep your French up?"

"Could you give me the address?"

"It's in the most beautiful Beaux-Arts building, reminiscent of Paris's Haussmannian architecture, at twenty-two East Sixtieth Street. You simply must go."

I memorize the address, my whole body buzzing with excitement at the idea of what—or who—I might find.

# CHAPTER 23

**D**ear Mother and Mabel,

I'm sorry to hear that you, too, have lost friends to influenza. Our hearts are broken with the death of our beloved Cookie. Since my first day, I've been surrounded by death—from black-clad widows to the shallow graves of soldiers—but losing one of our own is more than painful.

And yet . . . the growing season is a reminder that life goes on—from seedlings to budding, then flowering and ripening. Without machinery to harvest, Monsieur Hugo scythed the wheat stalks and Madame Hugo stacked them, like all farm families in the area.

Yesterday, we were stunned to see a tractor putting up the road, smoke rising from its upright exhaust pipe. Monsieur Hugo caressed the gleaming fender. Lewis was eager to drive it. Dr. M.D. informed us that Miss Morgan had convinced Mr. Ford to donate tractors. She's too modest to mention her accomplishments, so Dr. M.D. shines a light on her.

Have you received my letters? It has been ages since I've heard from you. I pray it's because of the unreliable post, and not because you are unwell. Please write. I do worry.

Love,

Kit

For the communal harvest dinner, we decorated a long table with braided wheat centerpieces. At the head, Sidonie and I conversed with Lewis and Breckie. At the foot, Marcelle was sandwiched between her brothers and glanced longingly at us.

"I'm bored," she whined to her mother.

When I was twelve, I'd uttered that fateful phrase to my mother. Once. *Bored?* she snarled. *I'll give you something to do.* She thrust a rag and beeswax into my hands. *Polish the china cabinet until it shines like the sun.*

Unlike Marcelle, who bickered like she breathed, I didn't dare argue. Mother was to be obeyed, Or Else. I buffed the mahogany until I could see the reflection of her frown as she supervised over my shoulder. When I finished, she announced, *Only boring people get bored.* She paused to let her pronouncement sink into the soil of my mind.

*Are you a boring person?* she demanded.

Like each of us, I chose to believe that I was unique, with something to say, someone with a rich inner life.

*Are you?*

*No, I'm not,* I responded.

*Let's find something to occupy your mind.*

She took my hand, and we strode to the library. My father brought me to the NYPL shortly after that, and I was never bored again. And I would ensure that girls like Marcelle were never bored, either. Of course, I acknowledged ruefully that one was never bored with Marcelle.

A chef and two helpers placed the platters before us—wild boar from Brittany, potatoes from Burgundy, and bread baked with wheat from local fields.

The pastor rose and began his blessing. "Praise God."

"Praise CARD," Sidonie whispered to me.

I elbowed her in the ribs.

"I'm no longer a nonbeliever," she told me. "I believe in you."

"Believe in *us*. You've come a long way."

Everyone tucked in; hungry, I sawed at the meat like a lumberjack. Sidonie cut hers with the precision of a surgeon, Breckie nibbled daintily, like royalty at Versailles.

A French military messenger entered and scanned the room.

Sidonie grabbed my arm. "I learned of my husband's death by telegram."

Monsieur Hugo groaned. "Has another enemy offensive begun?"

"What if it's bad news from home?" Lewis asked.

Miss Morgan rose. "Whatever information you have, you may bring it to me."

As she read the telegram, her hand went to her mouth.

"You won't believe it," she told us. "It's from . . . The war . . ."

Dr. M.D. scanned the telegram. "It's from the general," she announced. "The war is over."

The proclamation rang in my ears but couldn't quite make it to my brain. The room was steeped in stunned silence for the time it took to veer from fear to incredulity and finally to relief that the fighting was truly at an end.

Sidonie trembled, and I wrapped my arm around her waist. I wondered if she was remembering her husband and their life before the war.

"It's over," she said in disbelief.

We watched as Marcelle and her brothers linked arms and pranced, shouting, "*C'est fini, c'est fini.*" On his mother's lap, Benoit clapped. Copying the big kids, he shouted, "*Fini.*" Tears of joy streamed down Madame Hugo's face. Lewis and Breckie sang, "Oh, happy day." Henri put his good hand on Jeanne's belly. Madame Petit hugged Victorine and Vivienne. I said a silent prayer for the soldiers I'd met and grown fond of, thankful that they were now safe, then let out a whoop as emotions I'd kept in check—fear, hope, dread, longing—spilled out. The two Annes faced each other. Hands clasped, Miss Morgan mouthed, "My love. Thank the heavens."

"Our prayers have been answered," Dr. M.D. replied.

Miss Morgan turned to us. "We must discuss what comes next."

"You'll go back to America," Sidonie told me in the prickly tone she'd used during my first visit to her home.

She'd lost her husband and daughter, and she expected to lose us Cards, too. I longed to go home and hug my mother and sister. I was wanted there, but *needed* here.

"I signed a two-year contract and intend to stay," I said forcefully.

Sidonie half smiled, and it was enough.

The sun was setting now, the row of mud-spattered Fords lit by the golden embers of twilight. Books and imagination and rolling story hour. I had a wild idea. Now that the war was over, we could convert ambulances into bookmobiles. In place of gurneys, shelves. In place of patients, books. In place of injury and fear, comfort and safety. Sidonie, Marcelle, and I would roam the roads, sharing a love of reading with the villagers.

"In fact," I added. "I have big plans for us."

———

TWO DAYS LATER, OVER LUNCH AT THE HEAD TABLE, I UNROLLED MY blueprint of a bookmobile with shelves installed in the back and a system of fasteners to hold the books in place.

"It won't be cheap," I warned. "With the cost of the vehicles, not to mention gasoline and spare parts."

Dr. M.D. kept track of money down to the last centime—there was no waste or extravagance on her watch.

"A brilliant idea," Lewis said. "The only downside is that those ambulances have no springs!"

"Put a pillow on the seat," Breckie said with a chuckle. "I don't worry about an aching bum because I have plenty of 'cushion.'"

"A superb way to use vehicles that would otherwise languish in a junkyard," Dr. M.D. said.

"You're onto something," Miss Morgan told me. "From the ashes of war, the headlights of the bookmobile."

———

BLÉRANCOURT WAS SOON A BOOMTOWN. FROM FARAWAY BRITTANY AND Burgundy, families returned to their land. From the United States and Canada, more Card volunteers arrived to expand our network. The American army offered supplies such as barracks to use as makeshift schools and clinics. French soldiers helped rebuild homes and demined fields. Under guard, ten German soldiers—now prisoners of war—had been assigned to reroof and replaster the town hall.

Arms crossed, Madame Petit passed the construction site without acknowledging the enemy. Madame Moreau scowled and hurled foul words at them. The POWs fell into categories. The first group were defeated, we sensed it in the way they refused to meet our eyes. The second must have felt remorse, because they worked hard to repair the damage they'd caused. The last frightened me. I felt anger radiating from their pores and hated the way they leered at Marcelle. One sneered as he looked her up and down. He shouted something in German. The guttural words were menacing, like a threat, and somehow, not knowing what he had said made it worse. She raised her chin slightly and kept walking.

"That one's not right in the head," Sidonie told me.

"Don't pay attention to that *Schwein*," Marcelle told us loud enough for him to hear. Then quieter, "I can't wait to get out of here. When can we get the bookmobile on the road?"

CARD had purchased three dilapidated ambulances and some surplus blue paint. Parked before the château, the vehicles appeared to stand at attention. Examining each motor, Lewis took inventory of damaged or missing parts while I disinfected. The Moreau family came to view our latest acquisitions. Marcelle donned her slicker and began to paint the hood.

"You missed a spot," Madame pointed out.

Marcelle was used to her mother's criticism; still, I tried to deflect Madame's attention by explaining that soon the ambulance would be a *bibliobus*.

"You missed a spot! You missed a spot!" the boys shouted as they ran circles around their big sister.

Marcelle paused, lips scrunched together, her inner struggle out there for us to see. On the one hand, she longed to prove she was a grown-up; on the other, she craved revenge. With a flick of the brush, drops of paint splattered near her brothers. They yelped, and a diabolical grin lit her face.

When Madame Hugo and her son approached, Madame Moreau smacked her boys on the head. "Stop that horseplay! Don't give little Benoit any ideas!"

Meanwhile, Benoit dipped his hand into the bucket of paint, and before his mother could catch him, he slapped the back fender. Madame Hugo rubbed his blue palm with the hem of her skirt and didn't stop apologizing until I assured her that the finishing touch of a child's handprint made the *bibliobus* more approachable.

In the back, three woodworking apprentices outfitted shelves that tilted slightly in order to keep the books in place.

Sidonie walked slowly around the bookmobiles. "Beautiful. Absolutely beautiful."

I had to agree. I was enchanted. Now, each village would have a weekly bookmobile visit. Already, Victorine and Vivienne and Madame Petit had gathered to inspect our armada. I was relieved to see that the girls had settled in so well with the Petit clan. As they checked out books, Madame said, "A town needs a library in the same way that a home needs a hearth."

———

ON THE FIRST BOOKMOBILE ADVENTURE, MARCELLE DROVE SIDONIE and me through the charred forest in the Red Zone. We were nearing Le Bacq. One of the towns closest to the front, it had suffered the greatest destruction.

"This area gives me the chills," Sidonie admitted. "I know it's silly, but it feels like someone is watching us."

We parked near the communal *lavoir,* where children played hide-and-seek among the drying bedsheets, while women helped each other scrub and wring out laundry, come rain or frost.

Despite the fact that it was so cold we could see our breath, I was heartened to see a dozen children and their mothers lined up to greet us. Marcelle and Sidonie set four short bookcases on the ground while I set up the makeshift desk and two chairs, one for the librarian, the other for the patron checking out books. Two children, a gaunt boy and a girl wearing a back brace, asked if I was going to read to them.

"Of course!" I replied in French. "But first you get to pick out your own stories."

A young mother approached. "Thank you for coming. I'm Laure, and this is my daughter, Juliette, and my son, Matthieu."

"We really get to choose our books?" Juliette asked.

I pointed to the shelves. "Really."

Slowly, other children approached, their mien solemn.

"Are these for us?" a little boy asked Sidonie.

"You may check out a book for two weeks, and when you return it, you may select others," she explained as she readied the inkwell and pen.

"You'll sign your name here." Marcelle opened the book to show the card peeking out of its pocket.

As the children browsed, which was not easy, given it was hard to turn pages while wearing mittens, the mothers chatted with us.

"Because of the war, my daughter has never seen so many books in one place," Laure said.

"My son's books and toys were destroyed when the Boches set our house on fire," another woman added. "We didn't have the francs to replace them. The funds we have must go toward food."

"What a luxury to have stories again," said a third. "My Marguerite's spirits have already been raised."

I exchanged glances with Sidonie and Marcelle. Our spirits were raised, too. Sharing our love of stories, seeing children happy—this was what made our profession a joy.

"Of course, we have books for adults," Sidonie was quick to add, and soon the women were checking out novels of their own.

On the way back, Marcelle chatted animatedly about Christmas. *We could decorate doors with holly. Let's find some mistletoe for Jeanne and Henri. I penned three westerns, one for each of my brothers.*

At Headquarters, our chipper mood changed quickly when we learned that a villager had been attacked. At the town hall, Monsieur

Hugo had been inspecting the drying plaster, which had been completed by the prisoners of war. When he briefly turned his back, the bigmouthed German grabbed him by the shoulders. Because of his war injuries, Monsieur was overpowered quickly. The prisoner threw him to the ground and struck his face and chest. It took three guards to pull him off. They tried to handcuff him, but he took off at a run.

I looked in on Monsieur in the infirmary, where Breckie was bandaging his broken nose. I must have blanched because he said, "It looks worse than it feels."

I told him that as much as I wanted the library rebuilt, it shouldn't come at the expense of his safety.

"No one wants this library more than my wife and me," he said. "Some fellows from my old unit volunteered to finish the renovation. The Germans will work in another sector."

I recalled how the prisoner had eyed Marcelle and didn't like to think of him on the loose. "Did they catch him?"

"He's probably long gone."

# CHAPTER 24

JESSIE "KIT" CARSON
BLÉRANCOURT, DECEMBER 1918

In le club-house, as Sidonie and I decorated a small fir tree, a messenger in a gray uniform entered. "Telegram for Mademoiselle Carson," he said.

"That's me." My stomach plummeted.

He placed the envelope on the table and tipped his hat in farewell. "Holiday tidings from family?" Sidonie asked.

I swallowed. Bad news was delivered immediately, no expense spared. Good news could wait. It was sent in a letter that spent leisurely weeks on a ship sailing across the ocean. No, the telegram heralded bad news. The only question was—how bad? Gingerly, I opened the envelope.

> I am sorry to inform you that Mother has died. Pneumonia. She did not suffer. There is nothing to be done. Do not return home. Think of the children. Continue your mission in France.

I shook my head, trying to unsee the words.

When I'd left Allegheny, Mother was fine. In her letters to me, she'd seemed fine. She'd always seemed fine. Mother was a bedrock, a cornerstone. Life chipped away at her, but like a weathered pillar, she found a way to remain upright. She'd kept the family—and our finances—together after Father died. Oh, Mother. . . . I missed her already. I'd missed her and Mabel since I'd arrived in France, and now I would miss her always.

"What is it?" Sidonie asked.

"My mother."

I put my sister's words back in the envelope. I imagined her at the telegraph office, deciding which words to use. Each hard to tell me, each so expensive. Each word cost her, each painful to utter.

I felt Sidonie's hand on my cheek. *What a shock,* she said. *You've had a shock. I'm so, so sorry.* Words she must have heard herself many times.

Father and now Mother. My parents were everything. Because everything I was—or wasn't—was thanks to them. They were the books that I loved, the food I ate, the dreams I dreamed. Now both those beautiful, ephemeral plants had passed on, uprooting me, leaving no ties to the past.

But what was my loss compared to Sidonie's? She mourned a husband and a baby. Compared to Madame Moreau's loss of her husband, leaving her to raise four children alone? Or Madame Petit, in the agony of limbo, she might never learn what happened to her missing daughter Suzanne? Every single villager mourned someone.

Sidonie would say it's not a competition.

"I'll escort you to your room," she said. "We'll sit there."

"If you don't mind, I'd like to be alone." I yearned to be with my family, if only in my mind.

"Of course, dear Kit."

I was relieved that she understood my desire for solitude. In my room, I sank into the rocking chair and pulled books onto my lap, hugging them to my chest. Their sharp edges dug into my belly, and I was glad for the pain. What I endured on the outside matched the hurt inside.

My mother had been the window to my world. Through her, I first experienced the wonder of bedtime stories. As children, at 8:00 p.m. on the dot, Mabel and I knelt at the foot of our beds, staring out the window at the solemn moon as we recited our prayers. While Mother closed the curtains, Mabel and I scampered under the covers, and Mother read to us. In the morning, when she threw open the curtains, Mabel and I squinted in the sunlight. When we protested, Mother

pointed out the geraniums in the planter, the bumblebees in our garden. And yet, like a windowpane, my mother had been invisible to me.
There to keep in the warmth, there to let in the light. And now, it was
as if oilcloth had been fitted to my window frame. My world was dim.
I couldn't see out. Everything was dull. The light. The perspective. The
people passing by mere shadows.

For years I'd been resentful, viewing her as hard-hearted when she
sold our home after Father died. Now, I could see that she didn't have
the luxury of being sentimental. She could not dwell in the past, could
not remain in the stupor of mourning. Mother, who'd never worked
outside the home or balanced a budget, had taken over the reins,
our futures spurring her into action. Too late, I understood. I never
thanked her.

Rereading her letters, I couldn't help but note her concern. I'd
waved it off, a pesky fly buzzing around my head. Why had I not
shown more interest in her? Why hadn't I asked more questions about
her life, about her own family? She'd named me Jessie after her own
mother, who was from Canada. Though I'd never met my grand-
mother, the name tied us together. What else did we have in common?
Now I'd never know.

———

THE NEXT MORNING, MISS MORGAN KNOCKED ON MY DOOR. "WHAT A
loss, Carson. What a loss. I'm forty-five years old, and don't know what
I'd do without my mother. If you choose to take a leave of absence, we
certainly understand."

I couldn't afford the trip home.

"Of course, CARD will pay for your passage. And your return trip,
should you decide to come back," she said.

"That's generous of you."

"It's normal, given the circumstances."

I sighed. What was normal?

"Losing a loved one is a risk that we don't know we're taking when we travel," she continued. "We assume everyone at home will remain in hale health."

What did she know about loss? Miss Millionaire crossed the ocean with the same frequency that New Yorkers crossed Central Park.

Now, I was being cross. She was trying to be kind.

"I'll think about it," I told her.

"That's all I ask."

After she left, my mind raced. Like a metronome, it went back and forth. Here, there. Stay, go. Yes, no. I could remain here. My sister would bear the expense of the funeral and of settling the estate (what little of it there was), write the eulogy, pay the pastor, purchase the headstone.

I ached to be with Mabel. I'd be there too late for Mother's passing, but I could be with my sister now. Mabel had told me not to return. But she'd be relieved to see me, grateful for the support. I sighed. First my father, then Tom, and Cookie, and now Mother. How much loss could one heart take?

Cards and villagers came to my bedroom to pay their condolences. Madame Moreau's melancholy expression told me she understood.

"I'm here, sweet girl," Breckie said. "If you want to talk, if you don't want to talk."

"If you need a good cry, come over, I'll put on a pot of chamomile tea," Madame Petit said.

"Work is a salve and a salvation," Dr. M.D. said.

"You mustn't work too hard," Miss Morgan countered.

Their sympathy overwhelmed me. Perhaps sensing that I was about to break down, Miss Morgan gestured for me to follow her. At the château, she let five dogs, including Max, inside. She opened a lacquer box full of bone-shaped biscuits. She snapped one in two and gave me half. As we fed them, the dogs wagged their tails.

"Tending to others—whether man or beast—allows us to concentrate on something other than our own grief."

I considered the ways she'd tended to others and wondered at her grief.

———

FOR THREE DAYS, I RARELY LEFT MY ROOM. MAX KINDLY KEPT ME COMpany. Marcelle set a tray of tepid tea and toast on my nightstand. Braids tied atop her head, she resembled a demure novice entering a convent. Looks could deceive.

"If you want a hot breakfast, you'll have to go to le club-house like everyone else," she said. "That's what my mother would tell you."

I smiled at the mention of Madame Moreau, a scrawny saint run ragged by her children. Then I teared up at the thought of my own mother, whose last days I had missed. Had she lost consciousness or stayed lucid? Had she eaten as usual or become bony? Mother had seen me into this world, and more than anything, I wished that I could have seen her to the next—to have heard her last words, her last breath. I wasn't there for her. I wasn't there.

Observing Marcelle, who pampered me by stirring a spoonful of sugar into my tea, I felt ashamed of my self-pity. Her father had been killed in combat.

"I'm sorry that you lost your mother," she said. "I suppose that the best ones are like mine. Somewhat annoying, forever pushing you to do what you don't want to do. But gentle, too, like a pillow that softens a thousand blows from this hard life."

Again, I was struck by Marcelle's wisdom. She was young, and yet because of war and her own losses, she'd matured quickly. Too quickly.

"Do you think that you'll go back to America?" She seemed to hold her breath.

I shrugged. "My sister insists that there's no need."

"Do you believe her?"

"I do."

"There is need, and there is want," Marcelle said.

I tugged at my handkerchief, angry with myself because when I packed for my voyage, I'd chosen nothing that belonged to Mother. Even one of her tea towels would have brought me solace. Poor mother. A line from *Little Women,* one of her favorite books, came to me. *There are many Beths in the world, shy and quiet, sitting in corners till needed, and living for others so cheerfully that no one sees the sacrifices . . .*

"I read something nice about you." Marcelle grinned slyly.

"Have you been snooping?"

"Of course!"

"Marcelle," I scolded in my sternest voice, not that it did any good.

"It's not snooping if the paper is on Miss Morgan's desk, there for anyone to see."

"Why were you in her office? Presumably when she wasn't there?"

"That's precisely when you glean things you didn't even know that you wanted to find out!"

I grinned, even as tears rolled down my cheeks. Far-fetched excuses, outrageous rationalizations, and general cheekiness. "Oh, Marcelle, you're the best." I dabbed at my face with my handkerchief.

"You probably think that you can't complain to us French because we've lost so much."

She wasn't wrong.

"But it's good to talk to us. You can be *certaine* that we comprehend."

I recalled my first days at Headquarters, how I'd chuckled when she informed her mother that the war had aged her, turning her into a twenty-five-year-old. Now, I saw that she'd been correct. She was a compassionate young woman with a beautiful heart and a good head on her shoulders. Truly, she could be CARD's queen of hearts.

"Want to know what I read?" she asked impishly.

"I know that you're dying to tell me." Truth be told, I was curious. Miss Morgan's opinion mattered.

"I went to request an afternoon off. The two Annes were not in. The paper—still curled in Miss Morgan's typing machine—stated, 'I don't know what change the death of Miss Carson's mother will make to her plans, but it would be a distinct loss if she should leave us.' They need you! You're indispensable. Ma says that this is the best possible thing a person can be."

Immediately, I felt guilty for even considering going home and composed the letter in my head: *After much reflection, dear Mabel, I see that you are right. It is best for me to remain. But I miss you so.* I sighed.

"Oh, no." Marcelle's bottom lip trembled. "I wanted to make you happy, or at least content that your work is vital. I thought the knowledge would bring you pleasure." She reverted to a young girl in need of comforting.

"It does bring me pleasure. It does!"

"It doesn't." She sniffled.

I handed her Father's handkerchief. She blew her nose. Marcelle reminded me of myself—a bookish woman with a strict mother who would need to make her own way in the world.

"Keep the handkerchief."

"*Mais non,* you need it. You're sad."

"But I'm happy, too. Truly."

"*Merci.*" She tucked it into the pocket of her uniform.

Once CARD finished rebuilding, we'd sail home. And what would become of Marcelle and girls like her?

With war expenditures, the finances of the French government had been stretched to the limit. Women's education would not be prioritized. I'd promised myself that Marcelle would have a happy ever after. I needed to ensure her future.

# CHAPTER 25

The two-story town hall had been rebuilt. Its slate roof gleamed. Inside, the parquet had been varnished. Upstairs, the library was ready to be furnished. The woodworking apprentices installed shelves. Monsieur and Madame Hugo carried crates of books, while Benoit and Vivienne played with Bruno the bunny under a table. Marcelle hung posters featuring French book covers such as *Around the World in Eighty Days* on the wall. Sidonie helped me organize the furniture for children—five small tables and twenty chairs—on one side of the room, furniture for adults on the other. Possibilities and the scent of new books infused the space.

By dinnertime, Sidonie and I were the last ones left. I ran my hand over the circulation desk. She grasped a hammer to reinforce a wonky shelf. I couldn't help but think that the last time she'd held one, it had been to nail shut her baby's casket.

Noticing my concern, she said, "*Oui, mais non.*" Yes, but no. "My heart is broken, and part of it always will be. But much of it has been repaired. By time. By books. By you. The best way to honor my daughter and husband is to make life easier for others."

"After the losses you've experienced, you have the right to feel sad."

"Sadness, yes. But not self-pity."

Once again, hammer or no, Sidonie had hit the nail on the head.

I studied the disposition of the room. It was symmetrical—children's furniture on the left, adults' on the right—and even elegant, with lace curtains framing the windows. Yet something was off. I reflected on how I wanted the children to *feel*. Welcome, of course. But more than that—comforted and even cradled in a warm, cozy nook.

Sidonie looked at me askance. "I know that expression. You intend to shift the children's tables and chairs to the right, the adults' to the left."

I laughed. "Not quite."

We rearranged the furniture, then set a vase of snowdrops on each table.

She pointed to the boxes of books. "Will you show me how to organize them on the shelves?"

"Class starts here on Monday morning."

I explained that we would create a full house of Library Cards. I'd prepared a curriculum, and we'd be joined by Jeanne, Victorine, and Marcelle.

———

RATHER THAN ME STANDING AT THE FRONT OF THE ROOM, LECTURING the students, we sat together at the table, where I presented the tome that many librarians considered to be the Bible: *Decimal Classification and Relative Index for arranging, cataloging, and indexing public and private libraries and for pamflets, clippings, notes, scrap books, index rerums, etc.* The epigraph read, "To Learn to Classify is in itself an Education."—Alex Baim.

I spelled out the principle of the Dewey Decimal system—that each book had its own special place on the shelf and that any reader could find any book in the library.

"Numbers to classify words," Jeanne murmured. "What would my number be?"

I suggested we look at the categories.

"Well, 440 is the French language," Marcelle said.

"Henri's number would be 630, agriculture," Jeanne decided.

"What's your number?" I asked Victorine.

"I'd love to own some 636.1."

"It's solving a mystery." Sidonie searched for the magic number. "Ah! Horses."

"What number would Breckie be?" I asked.

They scrutinized each page before flipping, flipping to the next.

"I've got it!" Marcelle said. "She's 610—medicine and health."

"What about you, Jeanne?"

She blushed. "Someday, I want to be 649."

The other students scanned the entries to find "child rearing."

"You'll make a wonderful mother," Marcelle said.

I cast a glance at Sidonie, hoping the allusion wasn't painful. With a nearly imperceptible shake of the head, she let me know she was enjoying the girls' high spirits.

"This isn't like the classroom I remember," Sidonie remarked. "The schoolmaster lectured from a raised platform. He insisted that it was so that we could see him better, but we students felt he looked down on us."

Victorine fiddled nervously with her pencil. "Will we be quizzed on these numbers?"

"School should be a pleasure, not a burden," I replied. "Hands-on work makes more of an impression than memorizing. You'll learn by doing." I demonstrated how to catalog our collection, a mixture of my favorites from the States and new arrivals from Paris.

When Marcelle lifted each book from the box, she said, "Hello, friend. Welcome to Picardie."

As we were finishing shelving the books, class was interrupted by Lewis, Breckie, and the two Annes, who entered for "a peek," and ended up staying an hour.

"Well done, Kit!" Lewis said.

"The library is heaven," Breckie added.

"You've done a wonderful job," Miss Morgan said.

At the NYPL, compliments had been rare. I let myself savor their words.

"Where's the children's section?" Dr. M.D. demanded. "Shouldn't it be front and center?"

I could practically hear my former boss scoff, *This is why you were hired, and you couldn't even do it properly.*

"After all the children have been through," I explained, "we want them to feel sheltered, so we put their section in the back corner, nestled near the hearth."

Dr. M.D. said it made sense. Miss Morgan suggested a formal grand opening for villagers and beneficial attendees from Paris.

"Beneficial attendees?" Marcelle asked.

"Wealthy donors," Breckie whispered. "Politicians to help grease the wheels of bureaucracy. Journalists to promote our work."

Sidonie shook her head. "City officials will never appreciate a country library."

"We shall see," Dr M.D. said breezily.

"Blérancourt is hours from Paris," Victorine pointed out. "Will they come?"

Miss Morgan permitted herself a satisfied smile. When politicians and businessmen heard the Morgan name, they bent over backward—or in this case, traveled to the backwaters—to meet her. She was our Drawing Card.

———

ON THE DAY OF THE *CÉRÉMONIE D'OUVERTURE,* SIDONIE SET DAFFODILS in matching vases (empty bombshells). Marcelle's brothers roughhoused their way through the door, but when they saw the low bookcases that featured bright book covers, they stood still.

"*Le Magicien d'Oz,*" one read aloud.

"*Jo et sa tribu,*" another said. Jo and her tribe, in English. *Jo's Boys* by Louisa May Alcott.

The Hugos arrived next. At the sight of the roomful of shelves, Monsieur stared, mouth agape.

"The books aren't under lock and key?" Madame asked.

"Absolutely not," I replied.

"What about theft?" A villager glared at Marcelle's brothers. "Anyone could take the books."

"We won't have to worry about that," I replied firmly.

"Would you believe that the former librarian kept most books in a closet, arranged according to height?" M. Hugo said.

"No." I looked at him askance, certain that he was teasing.

"Even a novelist couldn't make that up."

All at once, the air changed, charged with a sudden silence. At the circulation desk, Sidonie sat straighter. I looked to see what had made the difference. The two Annes entered with a dozen men—the politicians, journalists, and librarians. I wondered if these Parisians would denigrate our women's work.

Like the Moreau brothers, once our guests spied the shelves, their eyes lit up at the open-stack system.

"Greetings, gentlemen. I'm Mademoiselle Carson, the librarian. Welcome. Children's libraries are needed all over France, but especially in the devastated regions, where families don't have the funds to purchase books. A little later, we'll present story hour. But until then, please enjoy browsing."

The politicians—one with a monocle, another with a carnation in his buttonhole, and a third with a cane—cornered Miss Morgan. I wondered what that was like, to have people press themselves upon you, always wanting something. I decided that being a nobody wasn't a bad thing.

A journalist scribbled at a table, stroking his chin as he considered the books. Another interviewed Sidonie. A handful of librarians gathered around me.

"We read an article about *le bibliobus* and were most eager to visit," one said.

Even in faraway Paris, they'd heard of our fleet of bookmobiles? His name was Eugène Morel, the first librarian to have implemented the Dewey Decimal system in France.

"Look at what you ladies have erected in the midst of ruins." He stroked his goatee. "Perfection, from the scale of the chairs and shelves to the inviting atmosphere."

"This is just the beginning. We have many plans."

When it was time for story hour, Sidonie set the chairs in a semi-circle and gathered the little ones. Jeanne held up *The Ransom of Red Chief* by O. Henry. "Mischievous children are fun to read about," she said to the crowd.

"Maybe when they aren't your own," Madame Moreau noted dryly.

Jeanne gripped the novella like a life buoy. I sympathized. Sometimes I, too, felt that books were the only things that kept me from drowning. But I'd reminded her from the beginning that being a librarian was more than cataloging information, it was interacting with people.

"'*It looked like a good thing: but wait till I tell you,*'" Jeanne began.

When she finished, children and adults applauded. I was proud of her for overcoming her shyness.

Everyone seemed to appreciate story hour. However, one librarian's attention was taken by the mayor and Monsieur Hugo, who chatted quietly while they perused the stacks. The mayor had worked in an office and was pale and wiry, while anyone could tell by M. Hugo's ruddy complexion that he'd toiled outdoors.

"In England," said Vincent Charon, the director of a prestigious academic library, "people from all walks of life associate without embarrassment. Libraries bring together the wretched, the skilled workers, the bourgeois. I can hardly see this situation prevailing in France. We require different books for the distinct classes, as well as separate premises."

"Why divide readers into categories?" I retorted. "Who are you to decide which books people should enjoy?"

Pointing to the open stacks with his pipe, he said, "We must preserve morals. We should be the ones to decide what the public reads."

"The library should be thought of as a river," I argued, "where knowledge flows. It's not a reservoir, where ideas stagnate."

He snickered. "When I heard there was a lady librarian, I thought it a good thing."

I was surprised by his admission.

"After all," he continued, "bookshelves require dusting."

I frowned. "The only things that need dusting are your antiquated ideas."

My entire career, I'd dealt with people like him. They did not question themselves or consult others. M. Charon was certain he knew what was best. He'd never experienced a different system and was incapable of seeing through the eyes of others.

Many people did not examine their beliefs. I recalled my uncle and his cronies who partook of brandy and cigars in the study, opining loudly on politics, the stock exchange, and all that was wrong with other folks. They refused to explore the other sides of issues, other possibilities. For them, there was only one way—their way.

I used to admire people like my former boss, who knew their own minds. I'd thought of myself as weak for questioning, for being uncertain. After observing the two Annes, who investigated and explored, who interviewed experts and researchers, who scrutinized newspapers and communiqués, I saw curiosity as a strength.

Confidence is necessary in life—to leave your parents' home, to begin a new job, to travel. But too much confidence leads to complacency, and to believing that *my* way is *the* only way, that *my* worldview is *the* view. Everyone should ask: Why do I think this? What is a strong counterargument? How did growing up the way I did inform what I believe now? Why does this book or belief make me uncomfortable?

The fact that I questioned things, that I questioned myself, was not a weakness. It was a strength.

"Well," M. Charon said, "the least I can do is draw up a list of suitable books for good country folk."

"That won't be necessary," Marcelle replied. "This is the town library, and we like its eclectic collection just fine."

M. Morel took me aside. "If it were up to Charon, only noblemen and scholars would have access to books. Mademoiselle Carson, in fifteen months—during a war—you've accomplished what I've attempted to do my entire career. Unfortunately, French administration is made of men like him."

"That may change," I said. "These politicians can see that people from all walks of life enjoy the library."

"Alas, if only we could take your library to Paris. You said you have big plans. Would you consider coming to the capital to create a model library? It could convince stodgy bureaucrats. We could find the land, build from the ground up. Your design."

It was an incredible opportunity. A tempting offer. I would relish a return to city life, to an apartment with running water. But I would miss the Cards. My attention turned to Sidonie. At the circulation desk, she listened to Marcelle's brothers. "Why does the moon light up at night? Who's your favorite author? Do you know how to draw a bear?"

"Thank you for your faith in me, M. Morel. I'm honored by your proposition."

"We invited you to admire our work, not to poach our workers," Miss Morgan told him.

"You can't blame a fellow librarian for trying," he said to me before rejoining the others.

"Bravo on speaking up to that pompous Charon," Miss Morgan told me. "You've come a long way."

Back at the NYPL, I'd become used to living in the shadow of my boss. She made the decisions—what books to stock, how the shelves should be laid out, which books were suitable for story hour. Here, I'd come into my own. Her criticism no longer paralyzed me. I'd finally managed to leave her in New York. It took a war, but I was finally my own person again.

Miss Morgan and I turned to watch a little girl check out the book *Pollyanna*. I remembered the lines about living life to the fullest. *Oh, of course I'd be BREATHING all the time I was doing those things, Aunt Polly, but I wouldn't be living. You breathe all the time you're asleep, but you aren't living. I mean living—doing the things you want to do: playing outdoors, reading (to myself, of course), climbing hills . . . and finding out all about the houses and the people and everything everywhere . . . That's what I call living, Aunt Polly. Just breathing isn't living!*

Here in Picardie, I had finally started living.

———

AFTER THE SUCCESS OF THE GRAND OPENING, I FLOATED FOR WEEKS, until it came.

A telegram from New York.

Sent by my former boss.

"I became a member of CARD, too. STOP I read an article in *The Times* about you and your little library. STOP Clearly you require my help. STOP I have booked a ticket to France and am on my way. STOP."

Stop!

# CHAPTER 26

WENDY PETERSON
NEW YORK, MARCH 1987

**M**eredith is right about the lavish Alliance Française headquarters. The secretary is pretty ornate, too, with a platinum pageboy and a zippy silk scarf. She doesn't know what to do with me. No, I didn't sign up to attend the discussion of Godard's influence on modern cinema; no, I don't speak French (yet); no, I'm not interested in putting my name on the mailing list.

"I'm here to inquire about a teacher or librarian named Marcelle Moreau."

"What year was she employed?"

"She started in 1925."

The secretary guffaws. "Sorry, but you're asking for a miracle."

"Can we consult employment records?"

She shakes her head apologetically. "They go back to the early 1970s."

A man in a pin-striped suit glides by with a cordial "Bonjour."

"Is there anything we can do to find her?" I plead.

"Find who?" he asks from the doorjamb of his office.

"She's looking for a former employee, *Monsieur le directeur*."

"Marcelle Moreau," I say.

"What do you want with Mademoiselle Moreau?" he demands.

After I explain my interest in interviewing Marcelle Moreau, the director softens. A retired teacher and librarian, she remains their longest-running donor. In his own words, "I remember the names of people who write the checks." He phones her to ask if she'd consent to speak to me. He hands me the receiver. She informs me that she rarely goes out but would be delighted to "receive" me at her apartment on Saturday.

Excited about our meeting, I sing Elton John's anthem all week. "Saturday. Saturday. Saturday." At the NYPL, I glide through the revolving door and nod to the security guard, feeling like a detective, a literary detective with a real live clue. My fingertips trace a path along the wall. It makes me happy to think that Jessie Carson and Marcelle Moreau may have touched them, too.

I'm ten minutes early. So is Roberto. Alone in Remembrance, I perch beside him at his desk. My arm is an inch, then a centimeter from his. A magnet shimmers between us, drawing us closer. I don't resist. We kiss.

He tells me he has a job interview at the Morgan Library tomorrow.

I kiss him again. "Good luck. Not that you need it." He makes an excellent first, second, and third impression.

I tell him about my upcoming interview with Marcelle Moreau.

"I'm dying to read the next chapter."

As much progress as I've made in my novel, I'm still glum.

"What is it?" Roberto asks.

"Jessie Carson worked in this building," I tell him. "She talked to patrons, laughed with coworkers. There must be some molecules of her oxygen, of her. Yet she seems to have disappeared into thin air."

"Not into thin air. Into a forgotten file. We can figure it out. Tell me again what you know about her. What section did she work in?"

"The children's department."

"Hold on. You never said she was a children's librarian."

"I didn't?"

"This changes everything."

"It does?"

"*Les enfants, mais bien sûr!*" French is his language of discovery. "*Voilà!* I have it!"

"Have what?"

"Carson's boss was Winnifred Smythe. Everyone who ever attended library school has learned about her. She's a pioneer, a legend. Let me set the stage. We're in Maine. The year is 1871." He contemplates the twittering fluorescent lights as if he can see history itself. "A pink wee babe named Winnie was born to a homemaker and a lawyer. With seven older brothers, who called her 'Shrimpie,' you can imagine that she developed a certain mental toughness. Books became her refuge. As a teen, Winnie planned to follow in her father's footsteps, but with the death of both parents, her dream died. Instead, she attended a one-year library course. At the NYPL, her programs became so popular that patrons waited in line to enter her cozy reading room."

"She sounds amazing."

"And yet there was a darker side." Roberto scowls. "With her years of seniority, she became New York's most influential bookwoman. A book review from her could make or break an author. She used a bright red stamp that read 'not suitable for publication.' When it came time for her to retire—well, she refused. Though the NYPL hired a new director of the children's section, Winnie attended meetings. When her replacement chose secret off-site locations, Winnie showed up."

I see what Jessie Carson was up against, and why she'd rather be in a war zone than here.

"To find your Jessie, we must peruse Winnifred Smythe's papers."

Jessie Carson wasn't her own entity but a stray in her boss's collection? On a literary mission, Roberto strides from Remembrance. I scramble to follow, wondering what, if anything, we'll find.

We pass rumpled students who reek of clove cigarettes, tourists gaping at the photo exhibition of the Stonewall riots on the walls, and the Bookniks reading club huddled on the steps (this month's pick is *Beloved*). In the hallowed reading room, we make a beeline to the circ desk. Roberto compliments the librarian on her vintage military jacket and nods sympathetically as she recounts her travails. "Christ on toast, this morning alone, old Mr. Jacobs—remember him?—returned a waterlogged *War and Peace*. He dropped it in the tub during his weekly bath. And you know Clarice Duval. Nothing's changed. The richest woman in New York, and instead of checking out our books, she shoves them down her pants to sneak them out. The brass won't let me confront her. God forbid she change her will and leave everything to her cat. And don't get me started on Mike Henderson, who cornered yet another baby-faced freshman in the stacks."

"If anyone deserves a lifetime ban . . . ," Roberto says.

"It's him," they finish together.

"What brings you to these shores?" she asks.

"You're the resident expert on Winnifred Smythe," Roberto replies. "We're looking for Jessie Carson, one of her employees—"

"Colleagues," I correct.

"Who worked here from . . ." He glances at me.

"From 1914 to 1917. Can you help us?"

"Never heard of a Jessie Carson."

I feel despondent. Like it's only the rich and famous whose lives are documented and valued. Like you can make this amazing contribution to a country, to kids' lives, and no one will ever know.

"That doesn't mean anything," she reassures me. "I'm writing a biography of Winnifred Smythe, and I've researched hundreds of people in her sphere. Roberto listened to me natter on about her for years, well, until he . . ."

Perhaps realizing she was about to say too much, she finishes by telling Roberto, "We miss you here."

"I miss being here."

She digs in the drawer and whips out a copy of the Winnifred Smythe finding guide. It looks to be thirty pages, front and back. We three confer about which boxes might hold information about Jessie Carson—correspondence, the Goodwill Tour, reports on the children's section—and she requests the files.

Upstairs in the archive room, two cardboard boxes await. We carry them to a nearby table. Mine is heavy, a career devoted to children and literacy. I have no idea of what we'll find. A handwritten memo by Jessie Carson? A library report she penned? Perhaps a photo? Please, archive gods, produce a photo.

We each open a box. Writing is solitary. Research is solitary. Life is solitary. Having Roberto at my side feels good. Intent on our piles, he and I sift through pebbles, looking for gold. He skims newspapers of the day, while I dig through documents dealing with the children's section, which turn out to be mainly book reviews by Winnifred Smythe. "I may as well confess that I find E. B. White's *Charlotte's Web* hard to take . . . *Stuart Little* disappointed me . . ." She didn't like E. B. White? Of course, not every reader loves every story, but man, I reread *Charlotte's Web* every year and still bawl at the end.

"Morgan is a trailblazer." Roberto points to a half-page article in the *Tribune* touting Anne Morgan for raising millions to help French civilians, from selling raffle tickets, to organizing a championship match between top boxers, to creating the Goodwill Delegation, of which Winnifred Smythe was a member. Anne Morgan was also one of the first people to use film and photography in fundraising. "Why not focus on her?"

She's more well known, for sure. In 1915, she penned a book called *The American Girl: Her Education, Her Responsibility, Her Recreation, Her Future.* Photos of her were splashed over newspapers on two continents. But with the gift of literacy, Jessie Carson provided a safe haven for children, whether they were going through tough times in America or through a war in France.

"She worked here like us," I tell Roberto. "Compared to the other Cards—mostly wealthy socialites—Jessie Carson was an outsider. She's proof that more than connections or an Ivy League diploma determination gets you somewhere."

"I like to think that dedication can get you somewhere, too. And I know how maddening it is when rich people behave like the rest of us don't matter. We do the work, they get the credit. The archives are a testament to that."

I find an envelope of newspaper clippings. "Something should be said of the CARD library work. In the North, French peasants, who had very few books, now have reading material. Consider the story told by Miss Jessie Carson, director of the library department. Monsieur

Hugo was reading aloud by lamp in his partially rebuilt home. While she knitted, his wife became so engrossed in the story that without being seen, she stopped the clock. The man looked up from time to time only to ensure that it was not becoming too late. And so, he kept reading until the end. Madame Hugo confessed what she'd done, and he replied, 'All the better—I wanted to see how the story ended, too.'"

"Here she is!" I whisper-shout, my heart full.

"Your persistence has paid off." Roberto kisses my temple.

A few minutes later, he finds an article written by Winnifred Smythe about the Goodwill Delegation, a CARD fundraiser in fifty-six American cities. Each voter paid ten cents to the committee to elect a representative who would tour the battlefields and ruined châteaux of France. These women—telephone operators and debutantes, teachers and housewives—became ambassadors of solidarity toward the French people.

"Can you imagine finding a job across the ocean only to have the big boss show up at your new place of work?" I shudder.

"It's bad enough that he shows up in Remembrance."

At least my interview with him went well. I feel cautiously optimistic about the program manager role.

Though we leaf through the children's section files from 1920 to 1922, we don't find a mention of Jessie Carson. "You said she was on loan to CARD for two years, right?" he says. "So she should reappear in 1920."

We surmise that she did not return after the war. I will ask Mademoiselle Moreau.

———

ON SATURDAY, I GO TO THE ADDRESS ON THE UPPER WEST SIDE. MARcelle Moreau greets me at the door. She's affixed two white pigtails atop her head. So kicky! A brooch sets off her red cashmere cardigan. The silver figure appears to be a griffon, the CARD insignia. That can't be a coincidence.

"Are you the *chauffeuse*?" I ask.

"Why, yes. How . . . ?"

I found a Card. We gape at each other.

"No one has called me that in a very long time," she whispers. "A very long time."

Which of us is more stunned? I can hardly believe I'm in the presence of a Card and wish I could hug her. Settling for a handshake, I gently pump her hand up and down for the excuse to touch her. With her firm grip, it's easy to imagine her at the wheel of an unruly Ford.

"What an honor to meet you!" I say.

I haven't let go of her hand. I finally relate to the narrator in *Bright Lights, Big City*, and the high he feels from drugs. But who needs cocaine when you have research?

I have a million more questions, but before I can formulate one, she asks, "How do you know about CARD?"

No surprise that Marcelle beat me to the punch. I explain that the bulletins are stored at the NYPL and that I pieced the story together from reports, letters, and newspaper clippings.

Growing up, I'd longed to see my name in lights, the author of a novel. Now all I wanted was to make Marcelle and the other Cards famous, to share their story of courage and dedication.

She beams. "I didn't think anyone today had heard of us. But we Cards were near the front doing our part."

"I know."

"History books don't tell the half of it."

"Especially where women are concerned."

On the dining room table are a tea set, a plate of scones, and a photo album.

"We Cards started every gathering with pastries," Marcelle explains. "Miss Morgan said it put attendees in a good mood."

"A wise woman." I take a bite. "Is this Cookie's recipe?"

"How did you know?"

I tell her that I feel as if I know the Cards. Anne Morgan's letters to her mother are so evocative that I ache for the villagers, while Anne

Murray Dike's statistics help me visualize the role of each Card. Newspaper clippings present a time line and even a few anecdotes. I want to know more about Kit.

"I can help with that," Marcelle says.

When she opens the album, the worn leather binding creaks. Inside, the first photo is of Marcelle in uniform. Her cheeky grin is as wide as Fifth Avenue. I'd have known her anywhere.

I ask how she ended up in New York. She explains that her mother got a job as a seamstress in a grand Parisian fashion house, and married one of the managers. Knowing her mother and brothers were taken care of made it easier for Marcelle to follow the other Cards to America.

I'm in awe of how she left behind her family and her country.

"When you're young, you don't think of it that way," she explains. "It was an adventure—every day in Manhattan was exciting. People here were so optimistic. In Blérancourt, there was much death and destruction. It made my brothers and me realize that if we wanted to do something, we should. We never knew what the future might bring. We grew up not knowing if we'd have a second chance. I did what I thought best. Much later, I realized how much I gave up—time with family, living close by to lend a hand. Instead, I inspired teens to dream about France. But you didn't come here to hear about how we conjugated verbs." She points to the photos on the next page. Lewis frolicking with her dog, Tripod; Lewis cleaning spark plugs with a brush.

"She was so bouncy and full of fun. I thought my heart would break when she died."

We pause at that, the way we see someone every day, and then they're gone and nothing can bring them back. All we can do is continue without them.

"And here's Breckie," Marcelle continues.

With doe eyes and a melancholy twist of her lips, she's exactly as I'd pictured. Marcelle says that when Breckie returned to her native Kentucky, she founded the Frontier Nursing Service and worked among rural women, specializing in care of mothers and babies. In the craggy mountains, some families could be reached only on horseback. Several Cards helped raise funds and awareness for her organization across the United States.

Marcelle says that they saw each other regularly because Breckie traveled to New York for fundraising. "*Quelle femme d'action!*" What a go-getter! Did you ever see photos of her on her horse? She fashioned cradles to carry an infant on horseback. They resembled feedbags. Back then, some mothers used a drawer as a crib. Nowadays in Manhattan, if you don't have the in-style, brand-name gear for a baby, you're practically accused of child abuse."

On the next page, Marcelle points to a black-and-white portrait. "Here is Kit. She taught my incorrigible brothers to sit still and read. She was their favorite teacher."

I feel such tenderness for her. It's as if I am seeing an old friend. I trace my finger along the lapel of her jacket. Her light hair is braided in a crown. Worry lines are etched between her brows. Her complexion is pale. No rouged cheeks or lipstick for her. Intelligent eyes illuminate her face. Though Kit's gaze is direct, I can imagine her expression turning dreamy when she escaped into a book.

Words are unable to convey the emotion of seeing photos of the Cards as I eat the scones they'd raved about, and listen to stories from an actual Card.

"I haven't discussed my friends in decades. Over the years, we stayed in touch—New Year's greetings in January, a French tradition that the girls continued even in America; funny valentines sent with love; birthday wishes that teased about getting another year older; Veterans' Day cards, when we recalled the Armistice; and Thanksgiving phone calls reminding each other to count our blessings. And then, one by one, I received cards from their relatives, informing me of their deaths. Now, I only get bills and ads in the mail. I'm the last Card, and it's lonely."

I take her hand, wishing I could do more to ease the pain of loss. I recall how sharing stories about my mother resuscitated her for me. Maybe, in a similar way, I can help bring back the other Cards for Marcelle.

"I can't tell you how moving it is to hear you say my friends' names," she says.

"What more can you tell me about Jessie Carson? Did she return to the NYPL?"

Marcelle frowns. "That boss of hers. Mon Dieu!"

# CHAPTER 27

The feminine invasion was three days away. To impress the fifty members of the Goodwill Delegation, our uniforms were being ironed with an extra dose of starch. In front of the newly built school, the gym teacher coached her pupils to perform calisthenics in perfect synchronization. "Touch your right toe with your left hand, now reach for the sky with your fingertips, stretch those spines!" Monsieur Hugo tilled his fields with the straightest lines you've ever seen. Madame Hugo directed the town choir to sing "La Marseillaise." Madame Petit shouted the lyrics "To arms, citizens,/ Form your battalions,/ Let's march, let's march!" with off-key gusto.

Out of the wind, nestled between two barracks, Breckie and I crouched on hands and knees before a long strip of canvas, readying the Welcome, Goodwill Delegation banner. She slapped her paintbrush onto the canvas with the enthusiasm of a child; I dipped mine in the black ink like a cagey calligrapher. For a moment I was unable to remember the next letter, and my brush remained poised over the canvas.

"G," Breckie said.

I forged on.

"Don't dwell on your boss," she told me. "Consider the new friends you'll make."

She was right. Instead of ruminating, I needed to appreciate the thousands of volunteers from all over the United States and Canada who'd contributed to CARD's wartime efforts, whether by raising funds, distributing our *Under Two Flags* bulletin, or digging gardens where children grew sunflowers so we could use the seeds as chicken feed. Miss Morgan wanted a portion of these fervent supporters to see the difference that their contributions had made. Of course, the two Annes were counting on the Goodwill Delegation to spread the seeds of our labor in local newspapers and church newsletters.

Winnifred Smythe, along with two donors, was arriving ahead of the delegation. Like Marcelle's youngest brother, Maurice, I gnawed on my thumbnail. Of course, I wanted my boss to see CARD's accomplishments. I just didn't want to see her.

———

LEWIS AND MARCELLE FETCHED THE THREE EARLY BIRDS IN PARIS. When the passenger door opened, I steeled myself for criticism. Miss Smythe had a habit of marching in and setting my mistakes right. She alighted on wobbly legs. She held the door handle with one hand and straightened the brim of her hat with the other. She was rattled, not only by the bumps in the road but by what she'd seen along the way. Perhaps for the first time, my former boss was dumbstruck.

With her wool coat unbuttoned, I could see the Battenberg lace of her blouse, the one feminine touch she permitted herself. With her benign eyes and round cheeks, she resembled someone's unassuming aunt, but a withering comment was just a word away.

I was ready for her, or thought I was, until she fixed her regard on me. I fidgeted like a five-year-old.

"Miss Carson! At long last!" The pitch of her voice was higher than I remembered. She latched onto my arm the way she had the door handle. Certainly, I was a familiar fish in this sea of destruction.

I was unsure how to greet her. Or perhaps in her presence, I'd simply become unsure.

Too shaken to stand, the other ladies pulled their fur coats closer and leaned against the mud-spattered Ford. As Marcelle unloaded their trunks, she caught my attention and crossed her eyes to let me know what she thought of our guests. I stifled a laugh.

"That one is most impertinent." Miss Smythe glared at Marcelle. "Her parents would do well to nip such insolence in the bud."

"My father died in the war," Marcelle shot back.

For all of thirty seconds, Miss Smythe was unnerved by the rebuke. She then thrust out her bosom like a general on the warpath and pointed to Lewis. "The driver hit every rock on the road. Inexcusable!"

This was the voice in my head, insisting nothing I did was right. It now occurred to me that she criticized everyone.

"Lewis is our best driver," I said firmly. Strange that I could defend her but not myself.

"Thank you," Lewis whispered.

"We were shaken half to death." My former boss continued to complain.

"Bombs obliterated the roads," I replied.

"Where's Miss Morgan?" Miss Smythe demanded, clearly expecting to confer with a woman she considered of her station.

"As I mentioned earlier,"—Lewis shot me a look that said *She's a piece of work*— "Miss Morgan and Dr. Murray Dike express their regrets at not being here to greet you. They're speaking at a conference."

"What truck!" my boss said. "How impolite not to welcome guests."

"In their defense," Lewis said with clenched teeth and a mutinous smile, "you arrived three days early."

"We're not expected?" one of the donors asked.

"The way to get a true picture is the element of surprise," my boss informed her. "It unmasks unruly children and scheming adults."

The donors clearly did not know of the plan to catch us unawares and stammered an apology.

"It's quite all right," Breckie said, rushing to greet the new arrivals. "We're delighted you're here."

"The trip is tiring. Would you like to rest?" I gestured to the barracks. "Or would you care for a tour?"

The two donors inched toward the barracks.

Miss Smythe let go of my arm. "A tour of the library, of course!"

As Lewis escorted the donors, she told me, "*Bon courage.*"

I led the way. Breckie and Marcelle trailed so close that they felt like wings, like guardian angels. The day before, I'd polished a few books until they shone, then asked myself why I was making more effort for my former boss than for the children and stopped. I imagined her scowling at the covers and saying "What truck!" as she did when she didn't approve of a book. I imagined her regarding me and saying, "What truck!" My stomach tightened with the thought of having to work for her again.

At the circulation desk, Sidonie greeted us with a chipper bonjour.

Miss Smythe entered the children's section. Her lips narrowed until they were as straight as a line in a book. "It's terribly small."

"Compared to the NYPL, most things are," I said.

She plucked a book from the shelves. "*Le magician d'Oz?*" She raised a brow. "You know how I feel about such nonsense."

In the past, I'd accepted her criticism without response. But this library was the labor of love of an entire community and deserved to be defended.

"I worked for you, but am not you. Please respect the thought I've put into the collection."

*Gardyloo! You told her,* Lewis said.

*Bravo, Kit,* the two Annes added in sync.

*Well done you,* I heard Cookie say.

*You're a brave woman,* Tom said.

*I'm proud of you,* my mother said.

These would be the voices I would keep not only in my mind but close to my heart. Theirs, along with my own, were the only opinions that mattered.

"Miss Carson!" Miss Smythe said. "I'm surprised by you. Such insubordination!"

"What's insubordination?" Marcelle asked Breckie. "It sounds wonderful!"

"In this instance," she replied, "it means following your own path, no matter what others think."

"Well, Miss Carson, what do you have to say for yourself?" my former boss demanded.

"I no longer answer to you."

She continued her inspection. "You've had to refurbish the entire building, I take it? You've managed quite a lot with very little. You've done the NYPL proud."

I was more unnerved by her praise than by her criticism. Wasn't her approval what I'd coveted? Not always. In the beginning, I wanted to help children. Somewhere along the way, her esteem became more important. That needed to change.

"In this village, you help hundreds of people," she continued. "At the NYPL, you influence millions."

Eventually, my CARD contract would end. I'd planned—and even relished the chance—to return to my colleagues and patrons at the NYPL. Now I knew that wasn't possible. Miss Smythe would always view me as an assistant. I would be stuck under her callous thumb. How could I work for someone who censored the collection and invalidated my decisions? What to do when home is no longer home?

"It's time to return to the fold," she added.

The fold: an enclosure for livestock, especially sheep.

"That's not for you to decide," I said.

"The boondocks or the summit. The choice is easy to make."

"Indeed it is." I took a deep breath. "I won't be going back to New York. I quit."

From now on, I would make my thoughts known. I would defend my ideas. I would no longer retreat to the library of my mind. I would remain in the real world, among disagreements and uncomfortable moments. I would have my say. I'd changed. I would not let anyone chip away at my self-worth. I wouldn't accept being treated as less than. There were other jobs in other libraries—in Paris, for example. Here in France, I'd become independent, a dauntless explorer, an outspoken librarian, a Card.

# CHAPTER 28

WENDY PETERSON
NEW YORK, APRIL 1987

I begin to write—not in the hope of becoming famous or receiving Professor Hill's seal of dour approval—but to shine a light on the Cards' accomplishments. In reading about them, what strikes me is their devotion to the French and their dedication to each other. Kit was friends with Breckie, Lewis, Marcelle, and Sidonie. The Cards shared their affection among dozens of people, while I've been a loner. That's got to change. I reach out to coworkers and classmates. Instead of spending my free time alone, I meet with Meredith to write in the park. On sunny days, we find a bench and scribble away. It feels good.

Each week, I help Marcelle by delivering her groceries. She insists I stay for dinner. Tonight, her kitchen smells of sizzling bacon and bubbling Gruyère. My mouth waters in anticipation. The wall is decorated with a neat row of framed class pictures. I admire a rosy-cheeked Marcelle with a group of fifth graders.

"Did you ever want kids of your own?" I ask.

"I love children and practically raised my brothers. Did you ever read Willa Cather? She was Kit's favorite author. In *My Ántonia*, I found so many passages that described my youth, even though I was born on a different continent. 'She couldn't remember a time when she was so little that she wasn't lugging a heavy baby about, helping to wash for babies, trying to keep their little chapped hands and faces clean.' My mother leaned on me a lot. But enough of that."

She takes the quiche from the oven and cuts us each a slice.

"Bon appétit," we say at the same time.

The crust is so buttery that I groan in pleasure. I eat too fast, but it's so delicious, I can't slow down. We both take seconds.

After we finish, I share the news that I got the program manager job.

"Congratulations!" She takes a bottle of champagne from the fridge, and we toast my good fortune.

"You keep champagne in the fridge?"

"If you have it on hand, there'll always be something to celebrate."

I vow to buy a bottle, just in case.

"Life is hard," she says. "You must mark the victories. In CARD, Breckie measured every gram that spindly babies gained, Kit noted every book my rowdy brothers checked out. When you look for the positive, you find it. Sometimes, when I can't quite believe all that we accomplished, I read one of Anne Murray Dike's reports. It shores me up. Tell me more about your new job."

At my interview, I proposed a "Living Legends" series. Now, each Wednesday evening, a fascinating New Yorker will recount their life.

"Will you be my inaugural speaker? I'm dying for everyone to learn about the Cards."

"I'd be honored." Tears well, but before they fall, Marcelle dabs at them with a monogrammed handkerchief.

———

I WANT TO BE CLOSER TO ROBERTO, TOO. CURLED UP ON MY DAYBED, we talk about our defining moments, those right and wrong seasons of our lives. I outline the interrupted assault in my dorm room, how thinking about it still makes me freeze, how it stopped me from trusting and making friends. I only now realize the effect it had on me, how it stopped me from connecting with everyone, including fellow writers like Meredith. Spending time with the Cards has made me understand the importance of friendship. They, along with Roberto, have restored my belief in people's goodness.

"How'd you end up in Remembrance?" I ask.

"I suppose you heard the rumors about children's scissors and a trustee's fur coat?"

I visualized him clutching the coat in the crook of his arm, scissors in hand, threatening, *Back off or the mink gets it.*

"I don't believe a word of it." I'm certain he made up the story when nosy coworkers pestered him about what happened—he's every bit the fiction aficionado that I am. I ask what really happened.

He sighs. "Four years ago, the big boss viewed me as a protégé and promoted me to management. Fundraising, that sort of thing. But I declined because I preferred the reading room. He got offended and demoted me."

It's an abuse of power. "I want to kill him."

"I wanted to kill him, too. Now I'm grateful." He kisses me. "Thanks to him, you and I met."

"He's punishing you for your refusal?"

"He assumed I'd come around to his way of thinking. He underestimated my stubbornness. And I underestimated his. Neither of us has backed down. You were right when you said it's time to move on."

He says his job interviews went well, but that submitting his resignation will be bittersweet. He's always considered the NYPL home, especially since his family is in Honduras. He can only afford to fly there every other year.

Remembrance is for part-timers with no background in library science. Roberto needs to work in his field, something that won't happen as long as the big boss holds a grudge. I remind him that the NYPL will be there for him—he can always return as a patron.

We kiss, and this time, nothing holds me back. To show him that I'm ready, I bring his hand to my lips and kiss his fingers and palm. Still a little nervous, I inhale deeply and am calmed by his bergamot-and-citrus scent, the smell of trust and friendship and patience and love. Yes, love. Our gazes meet.

"I love you," he says.

"I love you, too."

Tenderly, he runs his fingers through my hair, then cradles my head in his hands. I wrap my hands around his waist. Part of me wishes we could remain entwined like this forever. But I want more, I want all of him. I unbutton his oxford and slide my hands from his shoulders to his slim hips. He gently takes off my T-shirt and bra. He caresses my back and breasts. *You're so beautiful,* he whispers before sprinkling my belly with kisses. He lays me back and tugs off the rest of my clothes. He undresses. *You're the beautiful one,* I say. He sprawls beside me and pulls me onto him. The heat of his skin makes me melt. He strokes my bottom. *Yes,* I tell him, *yes.* I graze his cheek, his neck, his chest with my lips. *Feels so good,* he says. I move my hips over his. He groans, or I groan. We move together, softly, softly, then harder, then more, more, more. *Yes,* he says. Or maybe I say it. In this moment, I can no longer distinguish between my desire and his, his belly and mine, my lips and his, his body and mine.

# CHAPTER 29

WENDY PETERSON
NEW YORK, MAY 1987

Marcelle is right about keeping an eye out for occasions to cele-brate. On the last day of the semester, I take a bottle of bubbly to writing class to commemorate our stories and budding friendships. Classmates exchange news—who submitted a short story, who received a rejection, who got a fellowship. As I pour Prosecco into paper cups, I invite everyone to Marcelle's presentation, and they seem jazzed about attending. It feels good to share.

When Professor Hill arrives, I submit the penultimate CARD chapter. I haven't written the ending yet because I'm not sure what happened. I keep asking Marcelle, but she sticks to facts I already know—CARD left France in 1924, making certain that the services that they had created would remain. I asked if Kit and Miss Morgan remained on friendly terms, but Marcelle didn't answer.

Hill reads everyone's work aloud, neither giving praise nor saying anything rude. It feels like a victory. Mine is the last. When he finishes, he throws the pages onto his lectern.

"Unbelievable! Where's the betrayal? Where's the backstabbing?"

"Are you asking that because they're women?" I demand.

He rolls his eyes at my accusation. "Charitable organizations are hotbeds of outsize personalities and do-gooder syndrome."

"Jessie Carson's bookmobile visited a hundred and sixty villages. She's the patron saint of readers. Cards were on call twenty-four hours a day. They worked seven days a week. They really were that giving."

"I can see the temptation to portray them that way."

I expect him to sneer. *You're young, wait until you see what people are really like.*

"Each of us is flawed," he continues. "If you present the Cards as perfect, your readers won't trust your narration. If you share the Cards' negative traits or bad decisions, readers will relate to them and see them as real people."

"But this is how I see them."

"Look again. 'Good causes' are the worst. Where is the dysfunction? The burnout? The resentment? Do you think J. P. Morgan got his money by being nice? Do you think his daughter held on to her inheritance by giving it away? I'm sure she was generous—with money that others donated to the cause. Was CARD able to donate millions of dollars' worth of goods to French civilians by hiring employees and paying a decent wage?" Professor Hill scans the class. "How many of you have volunteered? How many of you have been run ragged at work, used up and thrown away when you had nothing left to give?"

And suddenly, I understand that Professor Hill is disillusioned. Meredith was right—he's trying to impart his experience, to warn us. I take his critique to heart.

Weekends are spent contemplating the fault lines in the Cards' relationships. At the Morgan, I review the correspondence. Last time, I read to understand the time line. Now, I establish nuance in my understanding of the relationships. Despite her limousine and couture clothing, Anne Murray Dike complained about the cost of everything from bolts of fabric to bales of hay. You'd think the money came from her own silk purse. How might this penny-pinching have affected her dealings? Anne Morgan was constantly solicited. Would that have made her suspicious of others? More generous or less? *Where's the betrayal? Where's the backstabbing?* In the previous draft, I captured the triumphs, the times everyone got along. Now, I map the disappointment, the frustration. *Lewis and Breckie gush about jaunts to see a cousin or a school chum who was passing through Paris. No one I know can afford to travel to Europe. I'm alone and never have firsthand news from friends.*

Only one person can tell me if I nailed the tone. At eight in the morning, I show up on Marcelle's doorstep. She takes one look at me and asks, "Were you up all night?"

More like all weekend. In her entryway mirror, I catch my reflection. My hair is greasy, and mascara is smeared on my cheeks. I can't remember the last time I washed my face.

"Will you read my work in progress?" I hold up my offering, a messy manuscript held together with twine.

She doesn't respond.

"I know it's a big ask," I babble. "You probably don't have time. You might not like it. My professor said it reads like a fairy tale, and that in real life no one helps anyone."

"Maybe he said that because *he* never helps anyone," she replies tartly.

"I was inspired by Jessie Carson, by all of you. I'm a nobody, and it probably won't be published. But I'd love to know if I got the characters right."

She pulls a handkerchief from the sleeve of her blouse and dabs at her eyes. I hug her.

"I'm fine," she insists. "They're good tears. It's just . . . I never thought people would learn CARD's story. After so many decades, I assumed we'd remain forgotten. It would be a privilege to read your work."

After I hand her the pile of pages, I feel some qualms. The print is too small. This is too much to ask of a new acquaintance. She's just being polite. I tug on the manuscript, ready to tell her I've changed my mind, but she won't let go. Surprisingly, her grip is stronger than mine.

"Years of tug-of-war with my brothers finally pays off," she says. "What's the title?"

"I'm not sure. Maybe *Wild Cards? A Deck of Cards? Miss Morgan's Brigade? The Library Card?*"

"There's still time," she responds, which lets me know I haven't found the right one.

Late for work, I rush to the library. It's Roberto's last day. The staff room is packed with coworkers. He throws one hell of a going away party, serving laughs along with café olé and a coconut dessert called *conservas de coco*. When Map Man and the Archivist get glum, Roberto reminds everyone that he'll be only four blocks away at the Morgan.

I ask Roberto how he's doing. It's emotional, leaving after several years. He's made a lot of friends and many memories. He says he's nervous and excited. I am, too.

He walks me to my new office. It's the size of a closet, but it's *my* closet.

On the way, I say, "Famous quotes for two hundred points. Who wrote, 'Those who dream by day are cognizant of many things which escape those who dream only by night'?"

"Only two hundred points?" Roberto demands. "Seems like it's worth four hundred."

I elbow him. "No back talk from candidates."

"Edgar Allan Poe?"

"Correct. Foreign words for one thousand points. What is the definition of 'kilig'?"

"The groggy, happy feeling after a large meal?"

In lieu of a buzzer, I blow a raspberry. "Incorrect. Tagalog in origin and associated with romance, it describes the feeling of butterflies in your stomach."

"So basically, how I feel when you're near."

"No buttering up the host."

"I'll take Bookish People for two hundred points."

I could banter with him for the rest of my life. "Who would like to have dinner with you after work?"

He kisses me. I kiss him back.

———

THE FOLLOWING MORNING, MARCELLE APPEARS AT MY OFFICE. HER braids are askew. There is sleep in her eyes. She's wearing the same blouse and skirt as yesterday, only now they're rumpled. She sets the manuscript before me.

"Is everything okay?" I ask.

She yawns. Does that mean she found the story boring?

"I didn't expect to see you so soon," I add.

"I devoured the whole thing in one sitting. All four hundred pages!"

"What did you think?"

"I just told you! 'Unput-downable!' How's that for a blurb?"

My hand covers my mouth. I never expected such praise.

"There were a few errors," she says. "One heading was dated March 20, when clearly it should be March 21. We didn't call them 'the two Annes,' we called them *les patronnes,* lady bosses. I'm not sure that you quite captured Anne Murray Dike—she was a hard woman."

Trust Marcelle to be blunt.

"Since your professor called it a fairy tale, why not utilize extracts from CARD reports to underline the facts?"

"I could."

"He isn't wrong about frustrations. There was a time that *les patronnes* got it wrong." Marcelle says that one day, she sneaked into the château. When the two Annes arrived, Marcelle hid behind the curtain. They argued about Kit.

"Kit saved me, and I saved her." Marcelle twists her handkerchief. Eyes wide, she stares at me, distraught. "She deserved so much more."

Does she mean figuratively that books had saved her? Or did Kit somehow rescue her during the war? Marcelle is a little old lady, and I upset her. I hesitate to press for answers.

"And one more thing," she adds.

I expect more corrections, but she says, "Thank you for bringing my friends back to life. Reading about them was poignant. I love the book. Which, by the way, is missing a few chapters."

As she recounts the story, I write as quickly as I can.

# CHAPTER 30

The French government decided to seal off the Red Zone for good. Little by little, they evacuated decimated villages and erected barbed-wire fences. Marcelle and I were both relieved that this would be our last bookmobile visit to Le Bacq. Skirting the debris—charred branches, discarded mess kits, a tailpipe, broken glass—she drove fast. Fine by me. I wanted to be done, too.

We rounded the bend. Too late, we saw a felled tree blocking the way. Marcelle swerved. The brakes squealed as the bookmobile skidded off the road, over uneven ground. Bump, bump, bump. Headed for a ravine, we braced ourselves for the crash, through a blackened hedge and down the gulley. We were goners. The newspaper headline: SKELE-TONS OF TWO CARDS FOUND, TWENTY YEARS AFTER CRASH.

The Ford jerked to a stop at the cliff. Dazed, Marcelle and I stared at each other.

"That was close," she said.

I stood on quivering legs. As always, I was struck by the silence of the Zone. No birdsong, no crickets. Even the wind avoided this lifeless patch of earth. The lone sound was our labored gulps as we caught our breath. We checked the truck for damage. The front tires were lodged in a bed of gnarled roots, but the motor didn't appear to be damaged. On my side, the rear tire was punctured. Of all the rotten luck.

*You shouldn't be going there, and you certainly shouldn't drag an apprentice into danger!* I tried to brush aside Tom's warning.

Marcelle opened the toolbox. Together, we jacked up the book-mobile. As nimbly as her mother threaded a needle, Marcelle picked out the piece of glass and patched the tire. We lowered the vehicle. As we knelt to pick up the bolts, we heard the quiet snap of a twig.

We turned. Fifty feet away was a German soldier. The drab gray uniform gave him away. Probably one of the prisoners of war. His face was gaunt. He was so thin that he swam in his trousers, which were torn at the knees. How long had he been hiding in these scorched woods? He squinted at us. Marcelle and I wore our horizon-blue uniforms, the same color as those of the French army. Our hair was covered by our hats. Kneeling as we were, he couldn't see that we wore skirts, not trousers. Perhaps he assumed that we were a search party, come to re-capture him. Perhaps he recognized us. Or perhaps he wanted to steal our vehicle and escape to Germany. He inched closer.

Was he alone? Could Marcelle get the bookmobile going?

He didn't have a weapon. Or did he?

The war was over. Its destruction, its loss would continue for de-cades. The dead would stay dead. Some soldiers and civilians would never recover. France was blocking off the Red Zone rather than re-pairing the damage—an admission that some things couldn't be fixed. He inched closer, and under the grime on his face and uniform, I recognized him. It was the prisoner of war who'd harassed Marcelle. At the time, Sidonie had said he wasn't right in the head. Why was he here now? Did he know our route? Was it chance? Or had he been waiting?

"Leave us alone," I shouted in French.

A raged-filled howl tore from his chest. He rushed toward us, fists raised. I shifted to shield Marcelle. "Run!" I told her.

He grabbed my neck and shook me. Choking, I pulled at his grip but could not get his hands to budge. I tried to talk, to reason with him, but the words were trapped, a gurgle in my throat. I couldn't breathe. Beside me, Marcelle let out a cry. *Run,* I tried to say again. Dots—like at the optometrist's, a line of letters that I couldn't read—crept into my vision.

Dimly, I saw Marcelle appear behind the German. She swung the jack, pounding him on the head. He hit the ground with a thump.

I gasped for breath and rubbed my throbbing throat. Coughs racked my body.

Marcelle threw the jack to the side. We stared at the man. His skull had cracked open, his blood seeped into the soil. There was no doubt that he was dead.

"You saved us," I rasped. It felt like a miracle that I was still alive.

"But I killed him."

"You had no choice."

In silence, we replaced the bolts on the tire and put the wrench in the toolbox. Eventually, in a small voice, she said, "I thought I'd be happy to kill the enemy. That I'd laugh and spit on his corpse."

"Marcelle." I put my arm around her. She was trembling.

"But I feel sick to my stomach."

"That's normal."

"Should I recite a prayer? Say I'm sorry?" She joined her hands together.

"It's your choice. Do what you think is right."

"Must we bury him?"

I shook my head. "From Headquarters, I'll inform the military authorities. They'll arrange for burial."

Near Blérancourt, a cemetery for fallen German soldiers had been designated. But for now, I got a slicker from the cab and hunched down to cover the man. When Marcelle helped spread the material, a few drops of his blood seeped into her cuff. I'd take care of that at Headquarters, too. As shaken as she was, I prayed she wouldn't notice.

Marcelle leaned against the bookmobile and covered her face with her hands. I didn't want to hurry her, but I didn't want to stick around.

"We have to get going," I said. "They're waiting for us."

"How can we go back to Blérancourt as if nothing happened?"

"We can't go home just yet. Folks in Le Bacq are counting on us."

"Of course. Story hour." She stared at the bookmobile like she'd never seen one in her life.

"I'll drive."

She got in the passenger side. I picked up the jack. The tip was smeared red. I wished we could have left it—proof of what we'd done—behind. But with equipment scarce, every tool counted. I dragged it in the dirt to remove, or at least cover, the blood.

In the cab, Marcelle huddled next to me. At story time, the children—giddy at seeing the bookmobile—didn't question our drawn faces. I don't recall which story I read, only that I turned to Marcelle midway through to carry out the rest of the hour when my voice gave out.

———

THE FOLLOWING WEEK, I HAD TROUBLE SLEEPING. JUST AS I DRIFTED off, I heard the sound of the jack hitting bone. Marcelle was not her sassy self. Perhaps she was not getting any rest, either. I could only imagine the toll it had taken on her. I tried to get her to talk, knowing all too well that if she did not deal with what had happened now, the trauma would revisit at odd times and deal with her later. She insisted she was fine, she'd seen worse.

At a CARD party, a handful of American soldiers who'd stayed on took turns twirling their partners around le club-house. Marcelle leaned against the wall. A soldier invited her to dance; she declined with a distressed moue. She was withdrawn, as if she thought she didn't deserve to have fun.

"It's downright suspicious," Madame Moreau said. "She used to beg me to attend. Beg! Now she won't dance, and hardly says a word." Madame turned her eagle eye on me. "What do you think about all this?"

"We had a scare," I confessed as I fingered the scarf that hid my bruises. My voice was mostly back to normal, though some wounds would take longer to heal.

Marcelle gave a shake of the head.

"A punctured tire," I continued. "It shook us both."

Marcelle slipped away. I followed, but by the time I made it out the door, she was no longer in view. Just then, the two Annes, deep in conversation, were entering the château. Perhaps they'd seen her? I knocked and entered, as per their open-door policy. From the foyer, I spied them on either side of the gilded desk.

"Why are you being stingy?" Miss Morgan brandished her cigarette like a pointer.

Dr. M.D.'s arms were akimbo. "Are we here to help an American woman or destitute French civilians? Where do you propose our money go?"

To give them privacy, I retreated, but stopped short when I heard my name. I assumed they'd noticed me and turned to respond.

"Carson doesn't come from money," Miss Morgan said. "She more than fulfilled her contract. I'd like to give her a bonus of two thousand dollars."

"That's exceedingly generous," Dr. M.D. replied in a stilted tone.

"She's worked tirelessly. She could have left after the death of her mother. In her position, I don't know that I would have remained. Yet she stayed on because she knew we'd be lost without her expertise. For her dedication, she deserves to be rewarded."

I felt myself standing straighter, as if a medal was about to be pinned to my chest. Heat flooded my cheeks, happiness my heart. With the money, I would invite my sister to France. I'd never dared to dream that Mabel would bear witness to CARD's work. What a gift this was—to be reunited with family.

I would show Mabel the library here, then take her to Paris. Arm in arm, we would enter the shop of a real Parisian modiste, where we'd be fitted for dresses of the finest silk. Mine would be a calm periwinkle to match my eyes, hers a forest green. We would then feast in a real French restaurant—*bouillabaisse, mousse au chocolat,* and champagne—before attending the ballet. We'd tour the Louvre, we'd stroll the leafy boulevards until our feet ached. Then we'd find a sidewalk café and watch Parisians saunter by. It would be heaven, absolute heaven. I would finally, finally have experiences that Breckie, Lewis, and Miss Morgan took for granted.

It would be a dream come true to pamper my sister after the tragedy of Mother's death, when Mabel had to remain in the same house, each day a reminder of her loss. The change of scenery would do her good. And of course, the bonus was a testimony of CARD's appreciation. I was about to say thank you when Dr. M.D. replied.

"Her salary is sufficient. She gets as much from her work in France as she has given to it. What experiences we've given her!"

"Anne, dearest," Miss Morgan murmured.

I waited for her to argue on my behalf.

"I have too much respect for the money that donors have sent," Dr. Murray Dike continued. "They expect every dollar to aid French civilians. I feel strongly about this."

From her tone, I could tell that it would do no good to insist. I imagined my sister floating away, across the ocean. Mabel would not see firsthand the progress that the Cards and Northerners had made. I missed Mother every day, and now I was missing out on seeing Mabel. Something that would have meant everything to me signified nothing to the two Annes.

I rubbed at my throat. It was time to move on—I was ready for a change.

# CHAPTER 31

JESSIE "KIT" CARSON

**D**ear Mabel,

Yesterday was Mother's birthday. I've been missing her, and I know that you are, too. I've been feeling sorry for myself, for us. There are days that I wish I hadn't come to France. A chasm I thought had closed has been ripped open like a wound whose stitches have been torn out.

When Miss Morgan and Dr. Murray Dike denied me a bonus, I felt hard done by. How I wish I hadn't overheard that unfortunate conversation.

"After all I've done!" I told Max, before explaining how the class system that many pretend doesn't exist keeps the rich rich and the poor dependent upon them. He wagged his tail through my tale of woe.

Then, today at dawn, Mother came to me. Was it a dream, or my own longing? Neither asleep nor awake, I heard her voice as clearly as if she were with us at our table in Allegheny, reciting grace. It felt like the most natural thing in the world. Hearing her made me happier than I've been in ages.

"I know you're disheartened," she said. "But don't become bitter because of one heedless decision. It's true, folks will disappoint. Sometimes, those closest to you disappear in an hour of need, while strangers surge to attend to you. Or the people closest to you don't understand, while others give more grace than you deserve. And let's be honest, growing up, you weren't exactly easygoing."

(I know I was difficult with her.)

"There will be people," she continued, "who don't recognize your contributions, while others give you your due. Yes, one Anne disappointed you, but remember, that French archivist sang your praises and invited you to work in Paris."

*(This is true. The grand opening ceremony was lovely.)*

*"Life is long and terrible, but death is not much better."*

*(Of course, I chuckled at this. Are you thinking what I'm thinking? That it's no surprise that Mother isn't happy in heaven—there's nothing to complain about!)*

*"So enjoy life while you have it. Appreciate what you've accomplished. The houses and the lives that you've rebuilt. The smiles you've brought about. Consider the people like Marcelle and Sidonie and Breckie, who have seen you and understand your value. They know, and you know—you gave it your all. You can be proud. Appreciate everything now, because soon enough, you will be gone."*

*That's Mother, equal parts wisdom and doom and gloom. She disappeared before I could ask if she meant gone from France, or gone from this good earth. Either way, she is right. And her wise words told me what I must do next.*

*All my love,*
*Kit*

*Dear Kit,*

*I understand those pinches of jealousy at the sight of new frocks and furs, at realizing that many opportunities are afforded to a select few. It seems to me that today, people have never been so divided—those with automobiles, those with horse and carriage, those with none. We live in separate spheres, the ties that once connected us severed. As I amble along the muddy road on my way to work, old man Jeffers motors by, his tires thoughtlessly spitting muck at me. Somehow, it feels personal, though I know it's not. He splatters everyone he crosses. The wealthy give no thought to the harm they do.*

*Yet, as Mother said, any day aboveground is a blessing. You and I have our health and have made the choice to be happy and productive (if not reproductive). Most importantly, we have each other, which means our lives are rich, even if we are not. Be proud of what you have accomplished. You've made a difference.*

*Love,*
*Mabel*

After what happened in the Red Zone, I was still shaken, and imagined that Marcelle was, too. I couldn't tell if she was avoiding me, or avoiding everyone. I cornered her in the library. She wouldn't meet my eye.

"Please let it out," I said. "You'll feel better. I'll feel better."

Marcelle let out a shaky breath. "I've lost my father and most of my school friends. Our home was bombarded. In the quarry, I have to pretend to be cheerful for my brothers. I can't let them see me cry. If I'm babysitting them, I feel resentful that I'm missing out with you and Lewis. If I'm with the Cards, I feel guilty for neglecting them. Just when things were looking up, that man attacked us. And I had to . . ."

"I wish I could carry the burden for you. There was no choice. He would have killed both of us."

"I know. We were both brave. I don't like keeping big secrets from Ma, but if I tell, she'll never let me leave the quarry. She's lost so much, too."

"She loves you. She's worried about you."

"I worry about both of you. And I have something to confess. The day of the Card party, I overheard something the two Annes said. I shouldn't have sneaked into the château. I just wanted one second of peace—I didn't mean to eavesdrop, I promise. When they came in, I hid behind the curtains. These past two years, I've watched you work miracles, and then *the good doctor* said you don't deserve that money. Ma's right. Life is impossible and then you die."

"Listen." I took her cheeks in my hands. "In life, you have to look for the good. It won't always find you on its own. Yes, I was disappointed—not for me, but for my sister. You know what? That letdown was a kick in the bottom, urging me to move on. I'm ready for a change."

"I knew you were going to leave!" she wailed.

"I am. I was invited to build a library in Paris. And I require your help."

"Truly?"

"I'm leaving, but I'm not leaving you behind."

Here in the North, the library adventure would continue. CARD had purchased four large prefabricated barracks. The walls would snap together like puzzle pieces. My French apprentices were versed in everything from ordering books and organizing them on the shelves to welcoming patrons of all ages and backgrounds. They would partner with CARD's latest library recruits from America.

In Paris, I would design the library and oversee the builders. It was an opportunity to change the reading landscape of the City of Light.

———

I FELT FORTUNATE THAT BRECKIE HAD ALSO DECIDED TO REMAIN IN France. The moon shone through my bedroom window. In our nightgowns and robes, she held two flutes at the ready while I popped open the champagne. The bubbles represented celebration and happiness, friendship and milestones.

"Well," Breckie said as the rims of our glasses touched. "Here's to two more years."

"I don't think I'd remain here without you."

"Same, sweet girl. Same."

"To staying the course."

"To staying, of course."

"To more clinics and libraries!" I toasted.

We did not acknowledge the painful task that lay ahead—informing loved ones that we would not be returning home as planned. Tonight was for celebrating all that we had and would accomplish.

———

OUR GOING AWAY PARTY WAS AS FESTIVE AS A CARNIVAL. CHILDREN bobbed for apples. Cards and villagers drank cider. An accordionist played jolly tunes. In the library, a parade of friends passed before me. The Hugo family brought a beautiful English edition of *The Three Musketeers* wrapped in a red bow. I kissed Madame and Monsieur on each cheek. "You must have gone all the way to Lille for this!" I said.

"Lille," Sebastian repeated.

Little Benoit, who was not so little anymore, but a brawny boy, handed me a nosegay. "Merci, mademoiselle," he whispered.

Sidonie proffered *Les Misérables*. "It's because I'm miserable at the thought of you leaving."

"Paris is not so far away."

The Moreau family approached, lined up according to height.

"We prepared a musical surprise for you," said the oldest of the three brothers.

"Shh! You weren't supposed to tell." The youngest kicked him in the leg.

"So much for them being on best behavior." Marcelle rolled her eyes good-naturedly.

More and more families entered. Two dozen children squeezed together. Madame Petit led them in a rousing round of "Frère Jacques." From Benoit's squeaky voice to Vivienne's sweet stutter, it was sheer perfection. Beholding the library filled to the brim, I felt such satisfaction at what we'd accomplished together.

When the children finished, the audience clapped.

"I've never seen a more heartfelt serenade," Miss Morgan said.

Soon I was hugging everyone—Lewis, Jeanne and Henri, Victorine and Vivienne, the two Annes.

That evening, after I packed the last of my parting gifts—a book of regional songs from Madame Petit and a stack of drawings from children—I tried to close the lid of my trunk. It sprang open like a jack-in-the-box. Marcelle entered and gauged the situation. Delicately, she sat on the trunk so I could fasten the straps.

"You've grown so much. I'm proud of you."

Once I found my bearings, I would send for her.

———

Sidonie insisted on accompanying me to Paris. Outside the train station, we saw more people in five minutes than we did in a week in Blérancourt. Horses and automobiles jostled for room on the cobblestone streets. The golden limestone buildings gleamed in the sunlight. Balconies—wrought iron with curlicue flourishes—resembled black lace.

On the sidewalk, men wore dark suits, women brightly colored dresses. The bodices were tighter, the skirts shorter than in Picardie. Some Parisians hurried along so quickly it was like they were on a conveyor belt. Others lingered in cafés.

"I won't rest until you have a suitable apartment," Sidonie said.

"I managed on my own in New York."

"New York is not Paris. French is not your native tongue."

"Monsieur Morel promised to help."

"Who?"

"The archivist who'd traveled to Blérancourt for the grand opening of our library."

"As if a gentleman who spends days in dusty archives understands a woman's needs."

I could have settled in on my own; however, I was comforted to have Sidonie at my side. Ten apartment viewings later, we found the perfect two-bedroom place, at a decent price, with running water.

———

On the way to the meeting with Monsieur Morel at the parcel of land in eastern Paris, we strolled through the lively quartier called Belleville, or "beautiful city." Sidonie and I walked up the steep pavement of narrow streets. Here, there were no trees. Once again, I found myself gawking—at the butcher shop with skinned rabbits stretched in the window, the flower girl on the corner selling nosegays for a few centimes, the line at the bakery as people grumbled about waiting for their daily baguette. Oh, the heavenly scent of bread. My mouth watered as I breathed in.

Monsieur had referred to this part of the city as "*populaire.*"

"Does that mean it's a popular place to live?" I asked Sidonie.

"'Populaire' often means 'working-class.' It's also a euphemism for 'uneducated' or 'poor.'"

"He said that we would be building *une bibliothèque populaire.*"

"He meant a library for the working class."

I recalled the snobby librarian who believed that various classes of people—castes, he meant—should not read the same books. I would make it my mission to prove him wrong. The Belleville library would be for everyone. By the time I finished, it would be the most visited, the most modern, and the most popular in all of Paris.

Sidonie grinned. "Ah, my friend, I can see that you are planning another French revolution."

"Yes. A quiet one, since it will happen inside the library."

With his black goatee, I recognized Monsieur Morel immediately. We stood on Rue Fessart, on the empty lot that the city of Paris had donated. We could have grown fruit and vegetables, but decided instead to cultivate knowledge.

"*Bonjour, mes amies,*" he said, his arms opened wide. "We have much to do. It is exciting!"

We spoke of the ideal number of windows for good lighting, a welcoming paint color for the walls, the ideal location of the hearth, the type of parquet, and comfortable furniture for adults and children—elements that, if a library is designed in the right way, patrons don't even notice.

It wasn't fair to compare wartime Blérancourt with après-guerre Paris, but I will say that in a few short months, we were ready to inaugurate the Belleville library.

Breckie invited me to parties hosted by her classmates from her Swiss boarding school, Southern belles from her debutante days, and politicians and ambassadors from her father's embassy work, not to mention aristocrats like the Countess Clara de Chambrun, who happened to be a trustee of a newly founded library for English speakers. The Countess agreed that The Paris Library was the perfect place to house the library school for Frenchwomen.

At a gilded embassy reception, I shared my latest news with Breckie.

"The curriculum is decided, the students selected, including our own Marcelle. She'll be here for the library inauguration."

"Congratulations, sweet girl!"

"Of course, the French library establishment doesn't approve."

"You'll win them over, like you've won over everyone else."

I glanced around at the other guests, men in tuxedos, women in long strands of pearls. "I hope you don't feel obliged to introduce me to your fancy friends."

"You're my fanciest friend! They're the ones who are lucky to meet *you*."

———

THE NEXT MORNING, SHE AND I MET MARCELLE ON THE TRAIN PLAT-form. Marcelle lifted me up and spun me around. "How I've missed you!"

Once outside the station, she cried, "Hello, Paris! I'm back!" Like Lewis, she spoke in exclamations. And like Lewis, she barely noticed that young men tried to get her attention with appreciative glances.

"Merciiiii for rescuing me—briefly—from my mother!" she said with a devilish grin.

My face must have fallen. Sadness at losing my mother seeped into my skin at the strangest times. One instant, I was fine, the next inconsolable.

She threaded her arm through mine. "And thank you for reminding me how lucky I am to have my dear ma!"

Marcelle could read the situation as well as any book.

To my relief, it was clear that Marcelle's vivid spirit had returned as the time had passed since our run-in with the German prisoner of war. Perhaps the magic of Paris helped heal us further. We allowed ourselves to gawk at the sights. In the Louvre, we admired the Winged Victory of Samothrace, spreading out our arms as if we, too, had wings. We climbed the steps of the Eiffel Tower, in awe of the view spread before us like a picnic blanket. Our feet were so sore that Breckie proposed a rest. Over coffee at an outdoor café, we watched passersby file in front of us—plump children in navy school uniforms, a businessman checking his pocket watch, a flirty Parisienne who twirled a parasol as she strolled.

"Paris has recovered from the war," Marcelle noted.

"Blérancourt will, too," Breckie told her. "Miss Morgan intends to create a Franco-American Museum."

"Then it's as good as done," Marcelle said.

"The Belleville grand opening is this evening," I said. "The champagne is chilling."

"I do so love celebrations," Marcelle said. "I can't wait to see the library!"

And off we went.

# EPILOGUE

WENDY PETERSON
NEW YORK, MAY 1987

On Wednesday evening in the NYPL reading room, I tap on the microphone and patrons take their seats for our inaugural Living History lecture series. It's standing room only. I'm excited to see my whole writing class, including Professor Hill. He appears interested despite himself. Meredith and I exchange a glance that says, "Miracles do happen."

Roberto gives an encouraging nod, and I introduce Marcelle. At the podium, she is radiant in her CARD uniform, the griffon brooch shined for the occasion. When she speaks of the devastation and heartbreak of losing her father, the audience is transported back to the Great War. We feel the shudder of the land as the bombs exploded, taste the dust in our mouths as soil and debris rain down. After she recounts the perilous evacuation of villagers, Marcelle says, "Their faith in us, in CARD, remains the greatest honor of my lifetime."

I cue up a silent film that Anne Morgan commissioned, and we attendees view demolished towns and roads. There isn't a sound as we take in the quarries where villagers lived. A second sequence shows young women in front of a bookmobile. I can't help but wonder if they were Kit's apprentices.

After the film, Marcelle describes how Kit worked in Paris to lay the foundation for a library school to train female librarians.

Her expression becomes serious once again. "With her model library in the north, Jessie 'Kit' Carson changed the course of French libraries. By introducing children's sections, she improved the lives and education of French kids. She not only brought them stories but created a haven where they knew they'd be welcome, at a time when people believed that children should be neither seen nor heard. She feminized the profession of librarian, hitherto only for men. Of course, the French establishment did not approve. They called her classes 'the Wild West Library School.'"

The audience chuckled at the moniker.

"The libraries that she created in France still exist. Kit changed lives. She changed my life. Without her, I wouldn't be here, wouldn't be who I am today. Thank you for your attention."

My classmates, and even Professor Hill, give Marcelle a standing ovation. Soon, the whole audience is on their feet. "Brava!" Roberto cries.

Marcelle nods. "Thank you again."

I wonder what Kit would think of us here, where she used to work, acknowledging her incredible contribution.

As if reading my mind, Marcelle says, "If she saw us praising her, she'd blush. Though she worked tirelessly, she never took credit for herself. Kit was quick to celebrate the community of helpers."

"Great presentation!" Roberto says to Marcelle before turning to me. "I'm proud of you. The CARD story will make an incredible book. You're going to make a name for yourself."

What I really want is to make a name for the Cards. They deserve to have their names not only in lights but in history books.

"Thank you, Wendy," Marcelle says. "You brought my friends back to life in your book and now this evening. I've been lonely without them. You made me remember stories I'd forgotten and reminded me how brave we were."

"How brave you still are. You crossed an ocean and started over again."

She shrugs off her accomplishments with a wave of her hand. "More than anything, I'm glad that you shared Kit's story and showed her contribution to French letters. Her name wasn't known. Now it will be." She pulls something from her pocket. "I want you to have this."

The handkerchief smells of lavender.

"It belonged to Kit, and her father before that."

I unfold the cotton and trace the "C" monogram. Carson. Holding something that Kit treasured almost seventy years ago feels like a miracle, like love. I hug Marcelle, who feels slight in my arms. She hugs me fiercely and I feel her force.

"I've carried it everywhere," she says. "To library school in Paris. On the ship to America. To my job at the Alliance Française. On nights when I missed my mother. To Kit's funeral. As I read your manuscript. And others are going to read your book. It will be published. I just know it."

The handkerchief weighs as much as a piece of paper, but I grasp the weight of history. I will carry it with me, always.

# AUTHOR'S NOTE

**J**essie "Kit" Carson (1876–1959) revolutionized French libraries. She overcame the stagnant French bureaucracy, that refused to fund, or even acknowledge, the importance of libraries for children and the working class. The libraries she founded featured children's sections and open-stack systems—both unheard of in France at the time.

Carson worked as children's librarian in Pittsburgh, Tacoma, and New York. She joined the war effort in 1917, when she became the chair of the businesswomen's unit of the National League for Woman's Service. She was then recruited by Anne Morgan, the vice president of the American Committee for Devastated France. (In French, the organization is called *Le Comité américain pour les régions dévastées*, or CARD. Members called themselves Cards.) Though she signed up for two years, Carson ultimately stayed from 1918 to 1924. While she was working as the director of CARD's library department in France, her mother died. In correspondence, Anne Morgan acknowledges that the CARD library services would collapse without Jessie Carson.

With Carson at the helm, CARD founded five libraries and created fifty circulating libraries in the North. It financed the development of Frenchwomen in library science by sending students to school in the United States. In Paris, Jessie Carson created a library in Belleville, a working-class neighborhood. That library celebrated its centennial in 2022.

To better appreciate the change she brought to French letters, I quote André Chevrillon, an author and member of the Académie Française, who describes French libraries as "forlorn storage places for books." At the inauguration of the Belleville Library, he explained:

> *One must not think the American Committee introduced public libraries in France. There are some in large towns and small villages. But these libraries . . . do not meet the needs of the community; they are incomplete and badly organized; most of them are in small rooms, badly kept, poorly lit, with crowded shelves up to the ceiling. The public can only make the choice of a book by consulting a poor, dirty, torn, often incomplete catalogue which is on a wooden stand at the entrance of the room and which must be hastily perused. The entrance to the library is formally prohibited to the reader, who is invited to wait patiently behind a railing for the book that he has asked for. The readers are obliged to stand in line in a narrow hall and are forbidden free access to the shelves. The librarians are generally schoolmasters or city clerks who have had no professional training and are so overworked and taken up by their own calling that they can bring to the service of the library but little vitality and interest.*

In his homage to Carson, French librarian Ernest Coyeque wrote: "On Easter Day 1921, the Committee solemnly inaugurated the [CARD] library. Kindly invited to the ceremony, Eugène Morel and I were amazed; for eight long years, I had tried to make Parisian municipal authorities understand the need for better organization through reports, brochures, and articles. With her library, Jessie Carson made the point."

Before returning to the States in 1924, she laid the groundwork for a library school for women. Jessie Carson forever changed the cultural landscape of France.

I first learned of her in 2010, while researching the library director Dorothy Reeder for my novel *The Paris Library*. Intrigued by the incredible women of CARD, who worked forty miles from the front during World War I, I researched online, tracking down as much information as I could.

When my editor, Trish Todd, acquired *The Paris Library* manuscript, the advance allowed me to travel for research. I visited the New York Public Library as well as the Morgan Library & Museum in order to access the CARD archives, which included the correspondence between Anne Morgan and CARD president, Anne Murray Dike, a couple ahead of their time, devoted to each other and to their activism.

In 1917, a French general recommended Blérancourt as CARD Headquarters. Located eighty miles north of Paris, it is in an agricultural region that the Allies had recently liberated after three years of German occupation. During this time, schools were closed. French women and children were enslaved and forced to toil in the fields. The women of CARD worked tirelessly to help malnourished children. Many of the children had never known their fathers, who were soldiers killed in combat. CARD hired teachers and reopened schools. Families who had fled to other regions of France were able to return, thanks to the food, clothing, household goods, medical care, and jobs that CARD provided. From July 1917 to March 1918, the Cards assisted more than eight hundred families—including five hundred children—in returning to their land.

When the German offensive began in the spring of 1918, the French army requested CARD to evacuate civilians. Despite the danger, some families were reluctant to leave their homes and had to be persuaded to go. Others entrusted their children to CARD. Evacuating civilians from the Red Zone, just miles from the front, was dangerous. The French awarded several Cards with the Croix de Guerre, or War Cross, for their courage under fire.

In the autumn, when it was safe, CARD once again helped villagers return home. From 1917 to 1924, 350 Cards worked hand in hand with the French to rebuild. Fundraising was crucial to CARD's success. Anne Morgan hired filmmakers and photographers to show the plight of the French. Thousands of women—in the United States and Canada—answered the call; 373 CARD chapters were created. Members raised $5 million, as well as printed and distrubuted *Under Two Flags,* the weekly bulletin. Several key Cards, including Jessie Carson's former boss at the NYPL, visited Northern France as a part of the Goodwill Delegation.

One of my goals in writing this book was to show the courage of the Cards and how they remained until the people in the region were again self-sufficient. With American, British, Canadian, and French volunteers, there was an incredible exchange of knowledge. Thanks to their curiosity, generosity, and open-mindedness, Cards accomplished great things during and after World War I, in France and at home.

**Mary Breckinridge** (1881–1965) was a driving force for healthcare in rural America as well as a leader in nurse-midwifery. According to Marc A. Shampo, PhD, and Robert A. Kyle, MD, "The most important contribution Mary Breckinridge made to nursing was her work as a pioneer in nurse-midwifery and in the development of modern nursing services in rural communities. She introduced the first modern comprehensive health care system in the United States and provided professional services for primary nursing care and midwifery."

Inspired by her work with European nurses and midwives in CARD, Breckinridge founded the Frontier Nursing Service in her native Kentucky. In rural areas, nurses rode on horseback to tend families who lived in remote areas, covering seven hundred square miles of rough terrain. By 1930, thanks to the Frontier Nursing Service, childbirth was safer in rural Kentucky than in most of North America.

Jessie Carson and Mary Breckinridge remained lifelong friends. Carson and other Cards were a great help to Mary Breckinridge as she created the Frontier Nursing Service, which she directed for thirty-seven years. In 1998, she was honored on a stamp issued by the United States.

A LA MÉMOIRE
D'ANNE MORGAN
1873    1952
CITOYENNE AMÉRICAINE
COMMANDEUR DE LA LÉGION D'HONNEUR
CROIX DE GUERRE 14-18 ET 39-45
INTRÉPIDE ET GÉNÉREUSE AMIE DE LA FRANCE
SECOURABLE AUX BLESSÉS AUX RÉFUGIÉS AUX PRISONNIERS
INSIGNE BIENFAITRICE DES POPULATIONS ÉPROUVÉES
ET DES RÉGIONS DÉVASTÉES PAR DEUX GUERRES
FONDATRICE DU MUSÉE FRANCO-AMÉRICAIN DE BLÉRANCOURT

A plaque in Anne Morgan's honor at
the Hôtel des Invalides in Paris

**Anne Morgan** (1873–1952) was the daughter of financier J. P. Morgan and his second wife, Fanny. She lived at home until the age of twenty-eight.

One of the wealthiest people in the world, Anne Morgan was a tireless campaigner for women's rights, from better pay to paid vacation. Aware of the power of images and publicity, she and her society friends picketed with female factory workers in New York to bring awareness to their plight. Morgan knew that by attending strikes she could afford protection to vulnerable women, who were often beaten by police and factory owners' thugs. Journalists often sneered at and diminished her efforts, referring to Morgan and her friends as the "Mink Brigade." She continued to use imagery as a way to raise awareness for the plight of people in Northern France.

As a couple, Morgan and Anne Murray Dike kept work and their private life separate. In letters about CARD business, both alluded to personal letters they'd written, but this private correspondence is not among the collection at the Morgan Library. An archivist told me that it is not clear if these letters were destroyed by Anne Morgan or her secretary.

Morgan came to France's aid during both world wars. At the be-

ginning of World War I, she opened her home in Versailles to convalescing soldiers. In World War II, she once again helped the people
of the North by founding the *Comité Américain de Secours aux Civils*
(American Committee for Civilian Relief) to evacuate civilians to the
Free Zone and to help the French throughout the war. She was forced
to return to the United States because of pressure from the Nazis.

She received the Croix de Guerre medal in both world wars. In
1932, she became the first American woman appointed a commander
of the French Legion of Honor. In the Court of Honor at the Hôtel des
Invalides in Paris, where Napoleon is buried, a commemorative marble plaque states that Morgan is "an intrepid and generous friend of
France."

Anne Morgan (left) and Anne Murray Dike

In their tribute to her, *Life* magazine wrote, "World War II saw Anne Morgan back in France, where she went through bombings as head of her relief committee, and stayed on to make sure its work would go on during the Nazi occupation. Until 1948 she kept going back in the interest of what had become her life work—tidying up the devastation of war."

Anne Morgan (left) and Anne Murray Dike
in their CARD uniforms

**Anne Murray Dike** (1878–1929) was born in Scotland and trained as a physician. She married a Bostonian professor, whom she later divorced. She kept impeccable records for CARD. Her reports, now available online, are a fascinating account of the organization's challenges and progress. In addition to receiving the Croix de Guerre for her courage under fire and to becoming an officer of the French Legion of Honor, Anne Murray Dike had the distinction of becoming the first woman elected to the French Academy of Agriculture.

After the war, the couple lived together in Paris until 1929, when Anne Murray Dike died of cancer at the age of fifty-one. Upon her death, a *New York Times* headline proclaimed, "MRS. ANNE M. DIKE

DEAD; FRIEND OF FRANCE." The article states, "A death which was deplored by all France and the entire American colony was that which occurred here today of Mrs. Anne Murray Dike, who, since 1917, had been one of the greatest forces in rebuilding the regions in France devastated by the war. Mrs. Dike, who was a staunch personal friend of Miss Anne Morgan, consecrated her entire energies to the work of the American Committee for Devastated France . . . Voicing the sentiment expressed by the entire French press the *Journal des Debats* says tonight: 'The work accomplished upon ravaged battlefields by this woman of ready sympathy and keen intelligence, who was an impassioned friend of France, will remain in the memory of all who knew her as a magnificent example of friendship and devotion.'" She is buried in the churchyard of Blérancourt.

———

Two Cards inspired my character Kate Lewis. **Marian Bartol** and **Kate Lewis** (1892–1969) traveled together from the United States to France and formed a friendship. Marion Bartol was from Philadelphia, where her father was president of the stock exchange. A fervent believer in the war, he put a stand on the floor of the stock exchange to encourage men to enlist. He didn't want his daughter to volunteer, but when he died in 1917, she felt able to join CARD. A volunteer from 1920 to 1921, she wrote nearly four hundred pages of letters home.

Kate Lewis was originally from Illinois and graduated from Vassar. During World War I, she worked in Naval Intelligence in Washington, DC. In France, she worked as a "*chauffeuse*" and a nurse. She was poisoned by mustard gas and had trouble with her throat for the rest of her life.

Several French Cards worked as nurses, librarians, and drivers. The character of Marcelle Moreau is inspired by **Marcelle Monod**, who later became a nurse.

The character of Sidonie Devereux is inspired by the work of **Victorine Verine**, who was trained by CARD and became one of the first French female librarians.

Other notable Cards include English volunteer **Phyllis Puckle** who worked as an ambulance driver on the battlefields of Flanders for the First Aid Nursing Yeomanry (FANY) before joining CARD after the war. **Lucile Atcherson Curtis** became the first woman in the U.S. Foreign Service.

There is still work to do in France. Over one hundred years after World War I ended, the Red Zone still exists. This area was defined just after the war as "Completely devastated. Damage to properties: 100%. Damage to agriculture: 100%. Impossible to clean. Human life impossible." Covering more than 460 square miles, it is still deemed too physically and environmentally damaged for human habitation, and restrictions to enter still exist. The French government has allowed the land to return to nature. Authorities estimate that if they continue cleanup at the current rate, it will take three hundred years to complete.

In the novel, I have modified some elements. Initially, Anne Morgan began her aid work with the American Fund for French Wounded (AFFW). Founded in 1915, it had as its goal to aid wounded soldiers. Morgan wanted to help civilians and created the American Committee for Devastated France in order to give them direct aid. Although she first arrived in the North of France under the auspices of the AFFW, I have named only CARD.

In addition to Headquarters in Blérancourt, CARD created centers in Soissons, Vic-sur-Aisne, Anizy-le-Château, and Coucy-le-Château. Each served twenty-five outlying villages. I placed the Cards and villagers at Headquarters and tightened the time line. Jessie Carson did not arrive in France until the spring of 1918.

In her autobiography, *Wide Neighborhoods,* Mary Breckinridge wrote, "Northern France was a part of the world where I felt I could be of use to children. . . . Meanwhile, a ruling was passed by the State Department that no woman with a brother in the military services could be sent to the war areas." Thus, in 1918, Breckinridge treated patients with the Spanish flu in a Washington, DC, hospital. Kate Lewis was also affected by the "Brother's Ruling." Both Breckinridge and Lewis arrived in France in 1919.

———

This novel has taken ten years to research. Early on, when I read about how the Cards dealt with the Spanish flu, I didn't pay much attention. When I reviewed the texts in 2020, the 1918 pandemic took on greater significance. It strikes me how timing plays a crucial role in what we retain and value.

My latest book is a story of women bringing about change. Thank goodness for the strong, brave people who have come before us, who have tried to lighten our load. I draw my inspiration from the heroines I read about in books but also from the ones I know in real life. I think for me the lesson is that we can't know what impact we will have on others, but by sharing stories, reaching out, and creating community, we can make life easier for others and for ourselves. We can help and inspire the next generation.

I have now written two novels about real-life librarians fighting to get books into the hands of readers. In *The Paris Library*, during World War II, Dorothy Reeder dealt with the censorship and racism of the Nazis, while in this book Jessie Carson delivered books in a war zone and later fought stagnant bureaucracy and sexist, elitist bureaucrats.

In 2023, as I write this, librarians in America are on the front lines of the culture war. Censorship is at an all-time high. According to the American Library Association's Office for Intellectual Freedom, "a record 2,571 unique titles were targeted for censorship in 2022, a 38% increase from the 1,858 unique titles targeted for censorship in 2021." This is the highest number of attempted book bans since ALA began compiling data about censorship in libraries more than twenty years ago.

Libraries are the foundation of democracy. They are among the few places where people may enter for free and enjoy culture, whether through books, author readings, games, classes, computers, films, or music. Today's lending libraries have it all, from books to tools to toys to neckties to classes on adulting, thanks to librarians who have adapted to the needs of their communities. I urge you to support your local library and librarians by raising your voice about the importance of reading and accessibility to books and culture.

———

A FEW FILMS AND WEBSITES ABOUT CARD MEMBERS:

Short film about Mary Breckinridge:
https://vimeo.com/149551126

Website featuring Mary Breckinridge's letters home:
http://www.uky.edu/HON301/

*Letters from Devastation: Mary Breckinridge in the Aisne, 1919* is a digital scholarly edition of selected correspondence from the University of Kentucky Libraries Special Collections Research Center's Frontier Nursing Service records, 1789–1985.

WEBSITES FEATURING ANNE MORGAN AND HER WORK WITH CARD:

https://www.themorgan.org/exhibitions/anne-morgans-war

https://www.americanfriendsofblerancourt.org/anne-morgan

http://us.media.france.fr/en/node/3384

A few books have been written about Anne Morgan in French. Here are a few recent graphic books: www.association-amivat.com/boutique.

# ACKNOWLEDGMENTS

I am in awe of the book lovers who come together and work so hard to get stories into the hands of readers. A huge thank-you to agent extraordinaire Heather Jackson and to her subsidiary rights co-agent Linda Kaplan and her assistant Abigail Snyder. Many thanks to everyone at Atria: Peter Borland, Sean deLone, Libby McGuire, Lindsay Sagnette, Suzanne Donahue, Mark LaFlaur, Lexy East, Lisa Sciambra, Wendy Sheanin, Dana Trocker, Gena Lanzi, Dayna Johnson, Karlyn Hixson, Gary Urda, Nicole Bond, James Iacobelli, Tom Spain, Tiffany Frarey, Hana Matsudaira, and Erin Larson; and at Simon & Schuster Canada: Sarah St. Pierre, Jasmine Elliott, Rita Silva, and Mackenzie Croft. Thank you to Trish Todd and Natalie Hallak, who were each a part of this journey. I am also grateful to Susan M. S. Brown, Lisa Nicholas, and Barbara Greenberg for their attention to my words. *Un grand merci* to Veronique Cardi, Amelie Bouton, and Constance Trapenard of JC Lattès, Elisabetta Migliavada of Garzanti, Hedda Sangers of Luitingh-Sijthoff, and Suvi Clarke of Bazar for signing on for another adventure! In the UK, my thanks to Sherise Hobbs and the team at Headline.

I'm grateful to the people who helped with research or gave me permission to use their photography and artwork. Cara Setsu Bertram; Julia Breckinridge Davis; Bobbi Silver of Frontier Nursing University; the artist Claude Jumelet and La Poste; Valérie Lagier, director of the Franco-American Museum in Blérancourt; Fatima Louli of La Réunion des Musées Nationaux; and Loren M. Clark at the United States Postal

Service. At the Morgan Library, my thanks to Maria Isabel Molestina, as well as to Christine Nelson, who is now at the Library Company of Philadelphia.

My gratitude to friends and colleagues who have read drafts and supported me: Amanda Bestor-Siegal, Craig Carlson, Sue Dumond, Penelope Fletcher, Rachel Kesselman, Kaaren Kitchell, Pauline Lemasson, Anne Marsella, Alannah Moore, Anca Metiu, Jade Maître, Emily Monaco, Anna Polonyi, Mary Sun de Nerciat, Diane Vadino, Yara Zgheib, and Laurel Zuckerman.

I'm grateful for the support of my husband, father, sister, and nieces. While I was writing this book, my family lost my mother to cancer. We remain grateful to hospice and Wendy Peterson.

Books have been a solace in these turbulent times. I'm grateful to booksellers and librarians who have recommended my books to readers, who invited me to Zoom, and who posted about my work. I am grateful to the readers who took the time to post about the book or to write to tell me how much they enjoyed my work. These messages and kindnesses keep me writing.

# ILLUSTRATION CREDITS

# ABOUT THE AUTHOR

Janet Skeslien Charles is the *New York Times* and internationally bestselling author of *The Paris Library*. Her work has been translated into thirty-eight languages. She has spent a decade researching Jessie Carson at the Morgan Library, the New York Public Library, and archives across France. Her shorter work has appeared in the *Chicago Tribune*, the *Sydney Morning Herald*, *Literary Hub*, and the anthology *Montana Noir*. She loves to connect with readers. Visit her website JSkeslienCharles.com, @JSkeslienCharles on Instagram, or @SkeslienCharles on Twitter.